S0-ADB-186

"THE FUTURE IS A WATERSLIDE
THAT LASTS FOREVER."

-INSPIROBOT

IMAGE COMICS, INC. • **Robert Kirkman:** Chief Operating Officer • **Erik Larsen:** Chief Financial Officer • **Todd McFarlane:** President • **Mar** **Silvestri:** Chief Executive Officer • **Jim Valentino:** Vice President • **Eric Stephenson:** Publisher / Chief Creative Officer • **Jeff Boison:** Director of Publishing Planning & Book Trade Sales • **Chris Ross:** Director of Digital Services • **Jeff Stang:** Director of Direct Market Sales • **Kat Salaza** Director of PR & Marketing • **Drew Gill:** Cover Editor • **Heather Doornink:** Production Director • **Nicole Lapalme:** Controller • IMAGECOMICS.CO

• **Deanna Phelps:** Production Artist for CROWDED •

CROWDED, VOL. 2. First printing. June 2020. Published by Image Comics, Inc. Office of publication: 2701 NW Vaughn St., Suite 780, Portland, OR 97210. Copyrigh © 2020 Christopher Sebela, Ro Stein, Ted Brandt, Triona Farrell, Cardinal Rae & Juliette Capra. All rights reserved. Contains material originally published in singl magazine form as CROWDED #7-12. "Crowded," its logos, and the likenesses of all characters herein are trademarks of Christopher Sebela, Ro Stein, Ted Brandt, Trion Farrell, Cardinal Rae & Juliette Capra, unless otherwise noted. "Image" and the Image Comics logos are registered trademarks of Image Comics, Inc. No part of thi publication may be reproduced or transmitted, in any form or by any means (except for short excerpts for journalistic or review purposes), without the express writte permission of Christopher Sebela, Ro Stein, Ted Brandt, Triona Farrell, Cardinal Rae & Juliette Capra, or Image Comics, Inc. All names, characters, events, and locale in this publication are entirely fictional. Any resemblance to actual persons (living or dead), events, or places, without satirical intent, is coincidental. Printed in the USA For international rights, contact: foreignlicensing@imagecomics.com • ISBN: 978-1-5343-1375-0.

VOLUME TWO
GLITTER DYSTOPIA

CHRISTOPHER SEBELA
::.SCRIPT + DESIGN..::

RO STEIN + TED BRANDT
::.LINE ART.::

TRIONA FARRELL
::.COLORS.::

CARDINAL RAE
::.LETTERS.::

JULIETTE CAPRA
::.EDITS.::

DYLAN TODD
::.LOGO.::

YESFLATS
HOLLEY MCKEND
RICHEL TAGYAMON
::.COLOR FLATTING.::

::.CREATED BY SEBELA, STEIN, BRANDT, FARRELL, RAE & CAPRA.::

CHAPTER SEVEN

TIME TO PRETEND

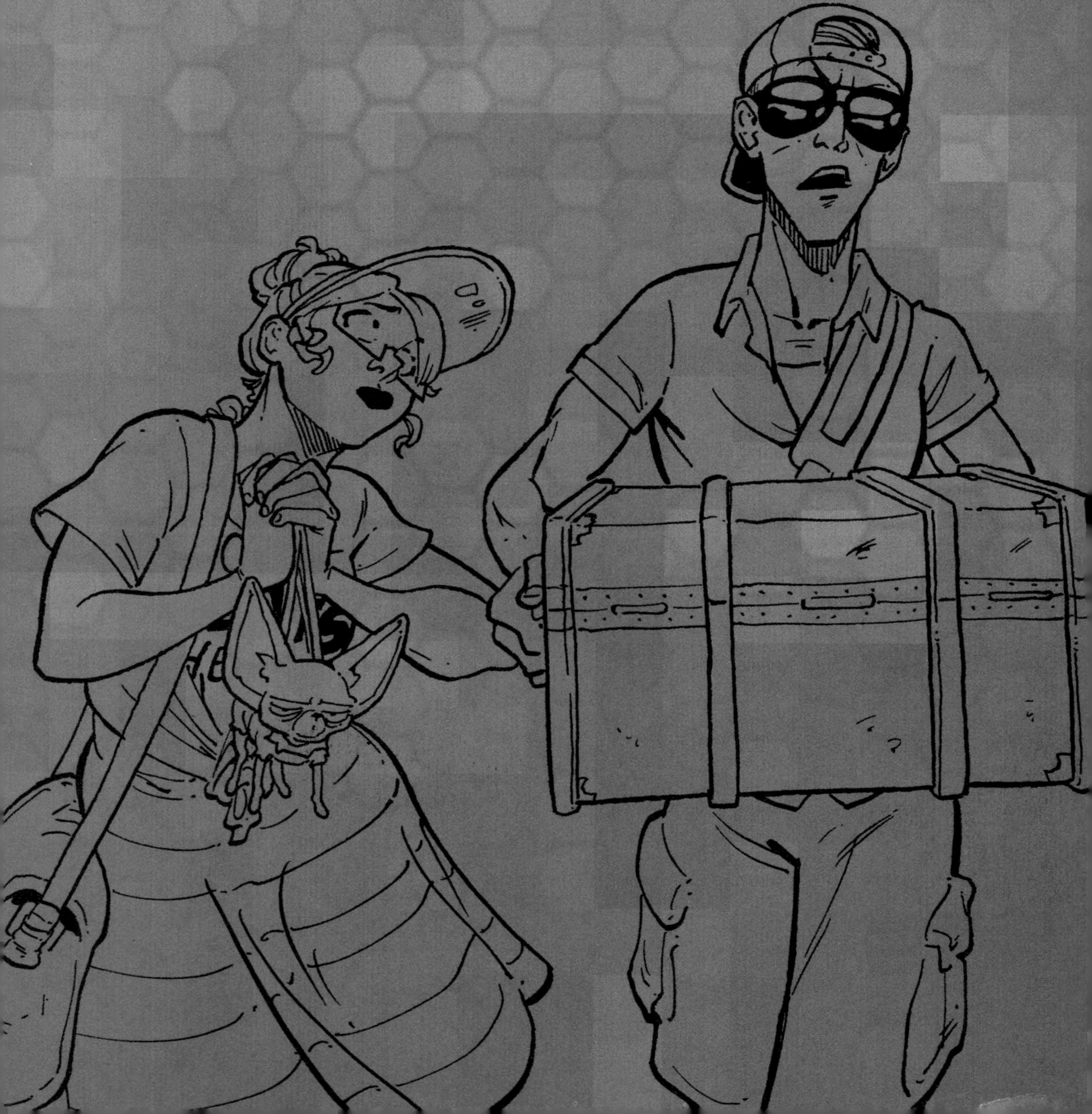

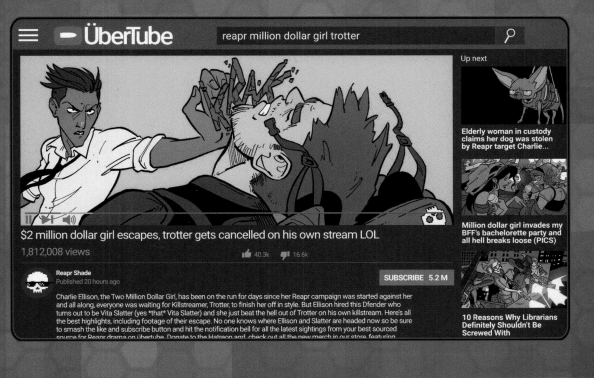

reapr million dollar girl trotter

$2 million dollar girl escapes, trotter gets cancelled on his own stream LOL

1,812,008 views

40.3k   16.6k

Reapr Shade
Published 20 hours ago

SUBSCRIBE 5.2 M

Charlie Ellison, the Two Million Dollar Girl, has been on the run for days since her Reapr campaign was started against her and all along, everyone was waiting for Killstreamer, Trotter, to finish her off in style. But Ellison hired this Dfender who turns out to be Vita Slatter (yes *that* Vita Slatter) and she just beat the hell out of Trotter on his own killstream. Here's all the best highlights, including footage of their escape. No one knows where Ellison and Slatter are headed now so be sure to smash the like and subscribe button and hit the notification bell for all the latest sightings from your best sourced source for Reapr drama on übertube. Donate to the Hatreon and check out all the new merch in our store, featuring

Up next

Elderly woman in custody claims her dog was stolen by Reapr target Charlie...

Million dollar girl invades my BFF's bachelorette party and all hell breaks loose (PICS)

10 Reasons Why Librarians Definitely Shouldn't Be Screwed With

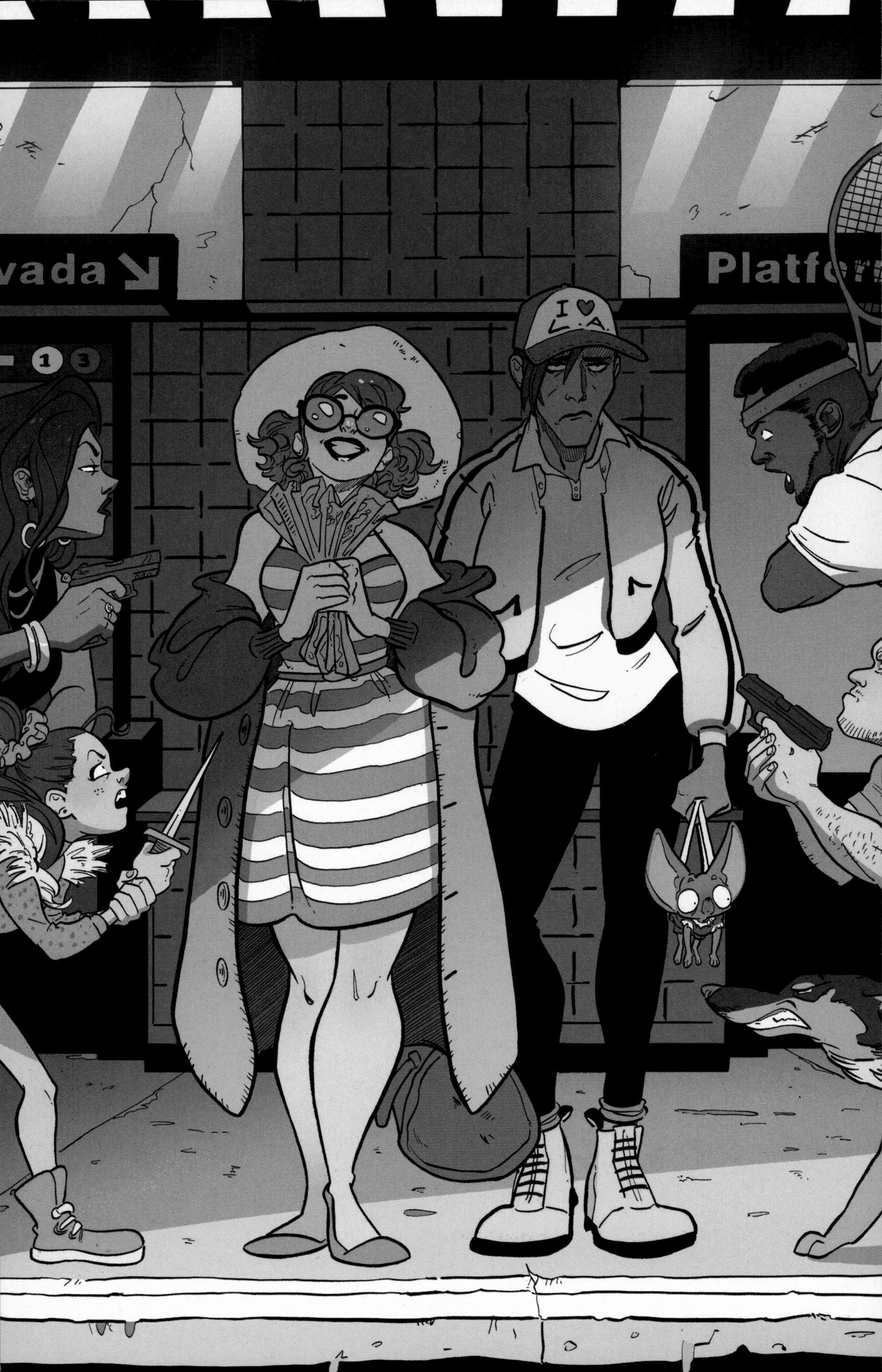
vada
Platfo
1 3
I ♥ L.A.

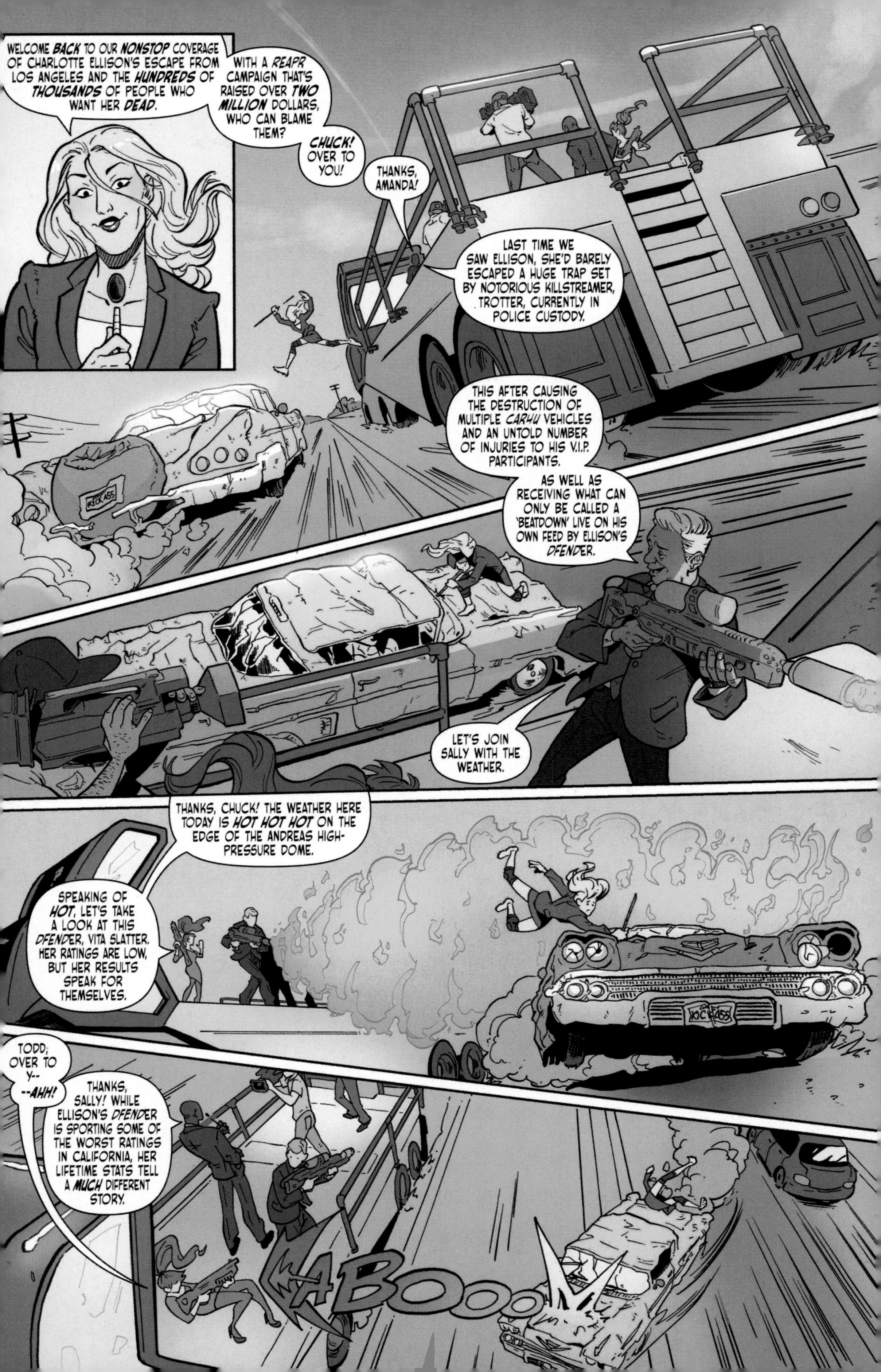
WELCOME BACK TO OUR NONSTOP COVERAGE OF CHARLOTTE ELLISON'S ESCAPE FROM LOS ANGELES AND THE HUNDREDS OF THOUSANDS OF PEOPLE WHO WANT HER DEAD.
WITH A REAPR CAMPAIGN THAT'S RAISED OVER TWO MILLION DOLLARS, WHO CAN BLAME THEM?
CHUCK! OVER TO YOU!
THANKS, AMANDA!
LAST TIME WE SAW ELLISON, SHE'D BARELY ESCAPED A HUGE TRAP SET BY NOTORIOUS KILLSTREAMER, TROTTER, CURRENTLY IN POLICE CUSTODY.
THIS AFTER CAUSING THE DESTRUCTION OF MULTIPLE CAR4U VEHICLES AND AN UNTOLD NUMBER OF INJURIES TO HIS V.I.P. PARTICIPANTS.
AS WELL AS RECEIVING WHAT CAN ONLY BE CALLED A 'BEATDOWN' LIVE ON HIS OWN FEED BY ELLISON'S DFENDER.
LET'S JOIN SALLY WITH THE WEATHER.
THANKS, CHUCK! THE WEATHER HERE TODAY IS HOT HOT HOT ON THE EDGE OF THE ANDREAS HIGH-PRESSURE DOME.
SPEAKING OF HOT, LET'S TAKE A LOOK AT THIS DFENDER, VITA SLATTER. HER RATINGS ARE LOW, BUT HER RESULTS SPEAK FOR THEMSELVES.
TODD; OVER TO Y--
--AHH!
THANKS, SALLY! WHILE ELLISON'S DFENDER IS SPORTING SOME OF THE WORST RATINGS IN CALIFORNIA, HER LIFETIME STATS TELL A MUCH DIFFERENT STORY.
KABOOOM

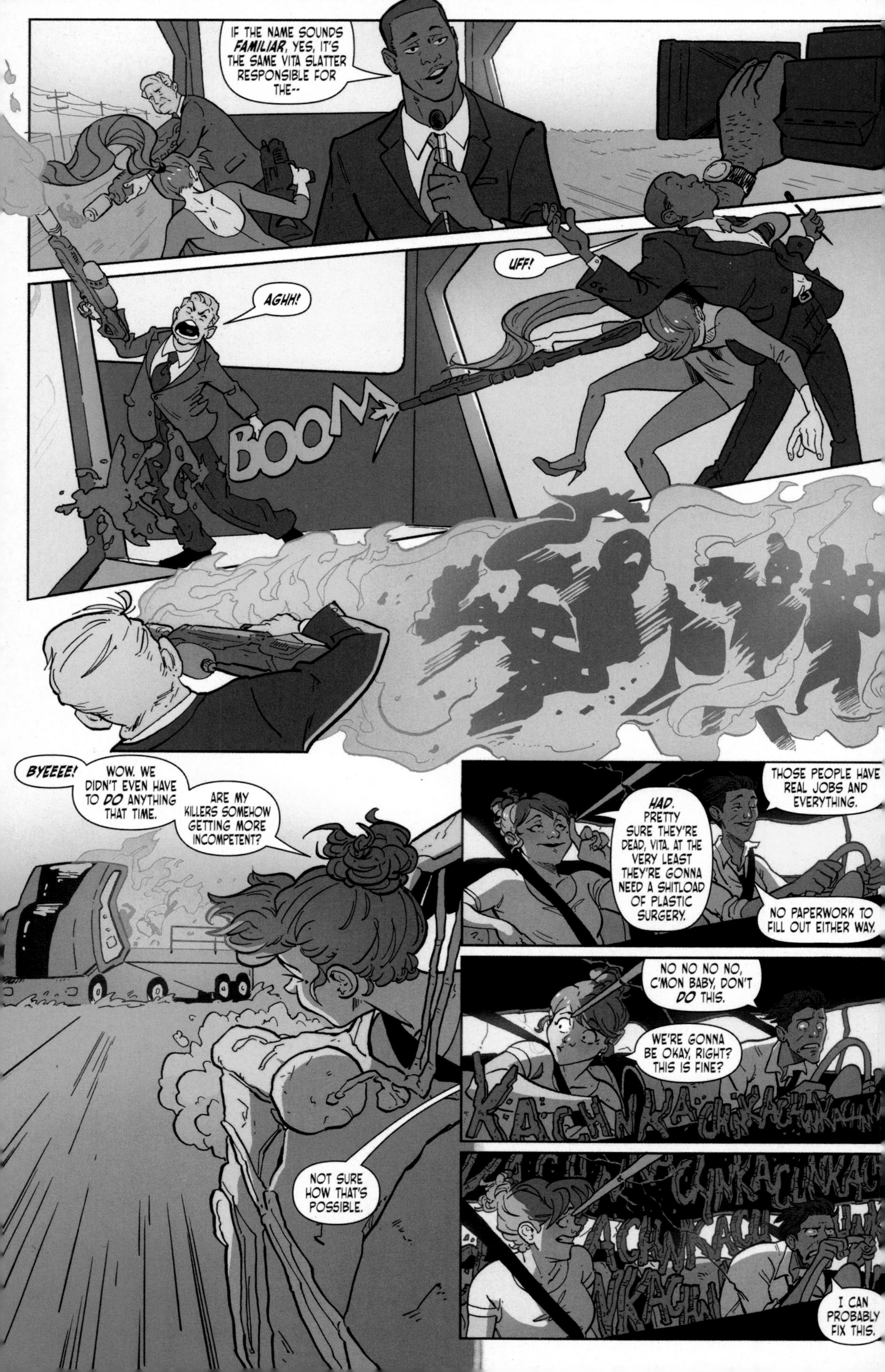
IF THE NAME SOUNDS FAMILIAR, YES, IT'S THE SAME VITA SLATTER RESPONSIBLE FOR THE--
UFF!
AGHH!
BOOM
BYEEEE!
WOW. WE DIDN'T EVEN HAVE TO DO ANYTHING THAT TIME.
ARE MY KILLERS SOMEHOW GETTING MORE INCOMPETENT?
NOT SURE HOW THAT'S POSSIBLE.
THOSE PEOPLE HAVE REAL JOBS AND EVERYTHING.
HAD. PRETTY SURE THEY'RE DEAD, VITA. AT THE VERY LEAST THEY'RE GONNA NEED A SHITLOAD OF PLASTIC SURGERY.
NO PAPERWORK TO FILL OUT EITHER WAY.
NO NO NO NO, C'MON BABY, DON'T DO THIS.
WE'RE GONNA BE OKAY, RIGHT? THIS IS FINE?
KACHNKA
I CAN PROBABLY FIX THIS.

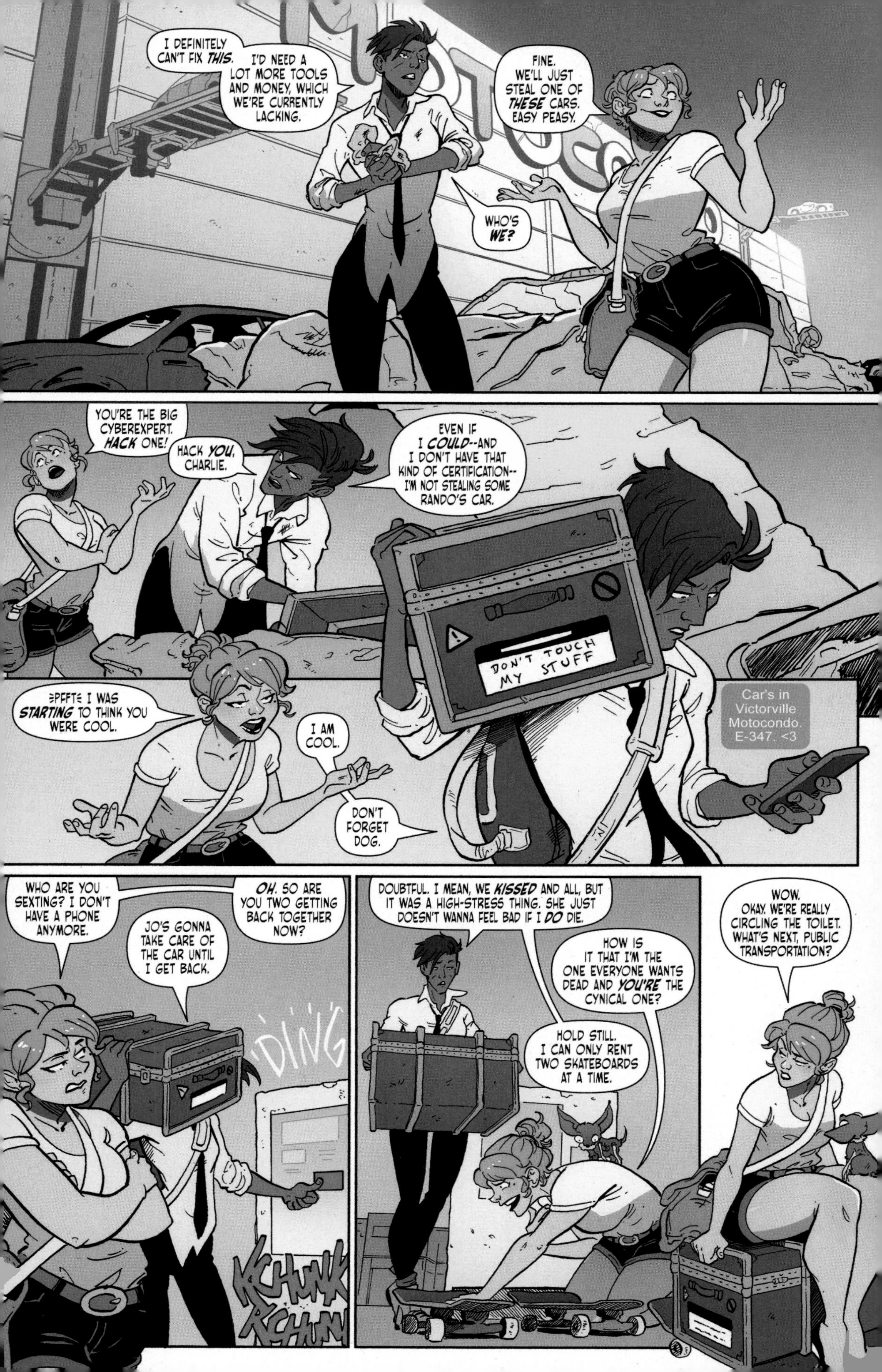
I DEFINITELY CAN'T FIX *THIS*.
I'D NEED A LOT MORE TOOLS AND MONEY, WHICH WE'RE CURRENTLY LACKING.
FINE. WE'LL JUST STEAL ONE OF *THESE* CARS. EASY PEASY.
WHO'S *WE?*
YOU'RE THE BIG CYBEREXPERT. *HACK* ONE!
HACK *YOU*, CHARLIE.
EVEN IF I *COULD*--AND I DON'T HAVE THAT KIND OF CERTIFICATION--I'M NOT STEALING SOME RANDO'S CAR.
DON'T TOUCH MY STUFF
PFFT I WAS *STARTING* TO THINK YOU WERE COOL.
I AM COOL.
DON'T FORGET DOG.
Car's in Victorville Motocondo. E-347. <3
WHO ARE YOU SEXTING? I DON'T HAVE A PHONE ANYMORE.
JO'S GONNA TAKE CARE OF THE CAR UNTIL I GET BACK.
OH. SO ARE YOU TWO GETTING BACK TOGETHER NOW?
DING
KCHUNK
KCHUN
DOUBTFUL. I MEAN, WE *KISSED* AND ALL, BUT IT WAS A HIGH-STRESS THING. SHE JUST DOESN'T WANNA FEEL BAD IF I *DO* DIE.
HOW IS IT THAT I'M THE ONE EVERYONE WANTS DEAD AND *YOU'RE* THE CYNICAL ONE?
HOLD STILL. I CAN ONLY RENT TWO SKATEBOARDS AT A TIME.
WOW. OKAY. WE'RE REALLY CIRCLING THE TOILET. WHAT'S NEXT, PUBLIC TRANSPORTATION?

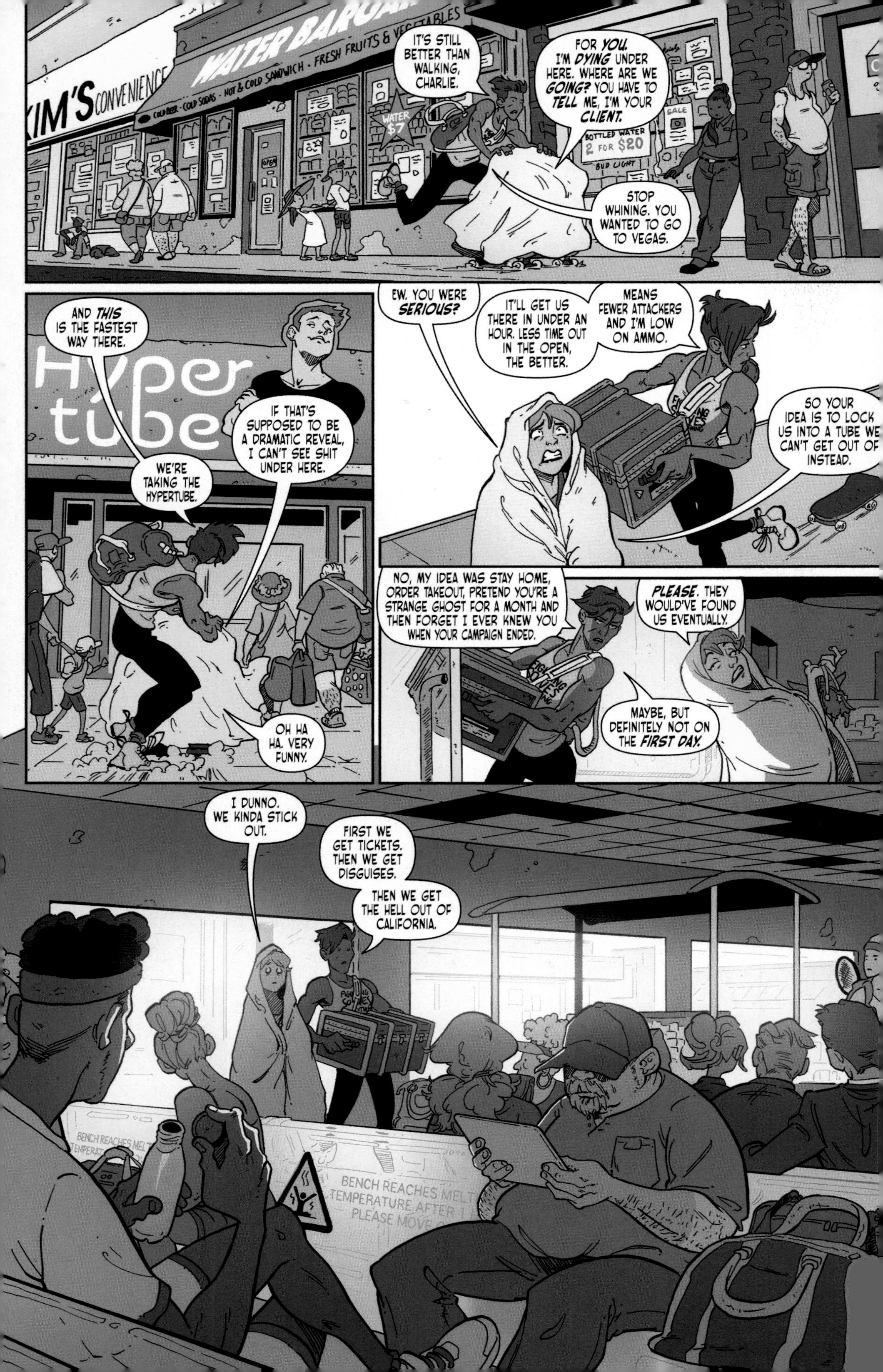
KIM'S CONVENIENCE
WATER BARGAIN
FRESH FRUITS & VEGETABLES
HOT & COLD SANDWICH
COLD BEER · COLD SODAS · HOT & COLD SODAS
WATER $7
OPEN
BOTTLED WATER 2 FOR $20
BUD LIGHT
SALE
IT'S STILL BETTER THAN WALKING, CHARLIE.
FOR YOU. I'M DYING UNDER HERE. WHERE ARE WE GOING? YOU HAVE TO TELL ME, I'M YOUR CLIENT.
STOP WHINING. YOU WANTED TO GO TO VEGAS.
AND THIS IS THE FASTEST WAY THERE.
Hypertube
WE'RE TAKING THE HYPERTUBE.
IF THAT'S SUPPOSED TO BE A DRAMATIC REVEAL, I CAN'T SEE SHIT UNDER HERE.
OH HA HA. VERY FUNNY.
EW. YOU WERE SERIOUS?
IT'LL GET US THERE IN UNDER AN HOUR. LESS TIME OUT IN THE OPEN, THE BETTER.
MEANS FEWER ATTACKERS AND I'M LOW ON AMMO.
SO YOUR IDEA IS TO LOCK US INTO A TUBE WE CAN'T GET OUT OF INSTEAD.
NO, MY IDEA WAS STAY HOME, ORDER TAKEOUT, PRETEND YOU'RE A STRANGE GHOST FOR A MONTH AND THEN FORGET I EVER KNEW YOU WHEN YOUR CAMPAIGN ENDED.
PLEASE. THEY WOULD'VE FOUND US EVENTUALLY.
MAYBE, BUT DEFINITELY NOT ON THE FIRST DAY.
I DUNNO. WE KINDA STICK OUT.
FIRST WE GET TICKETS. THEN WE GET DISGUISES.
THEN WE GET THE HELL OUT OF CALIFORNIA.
BENCH REACHES MELT
TEMPERATURE AFTER 1
PLEASE MOVE

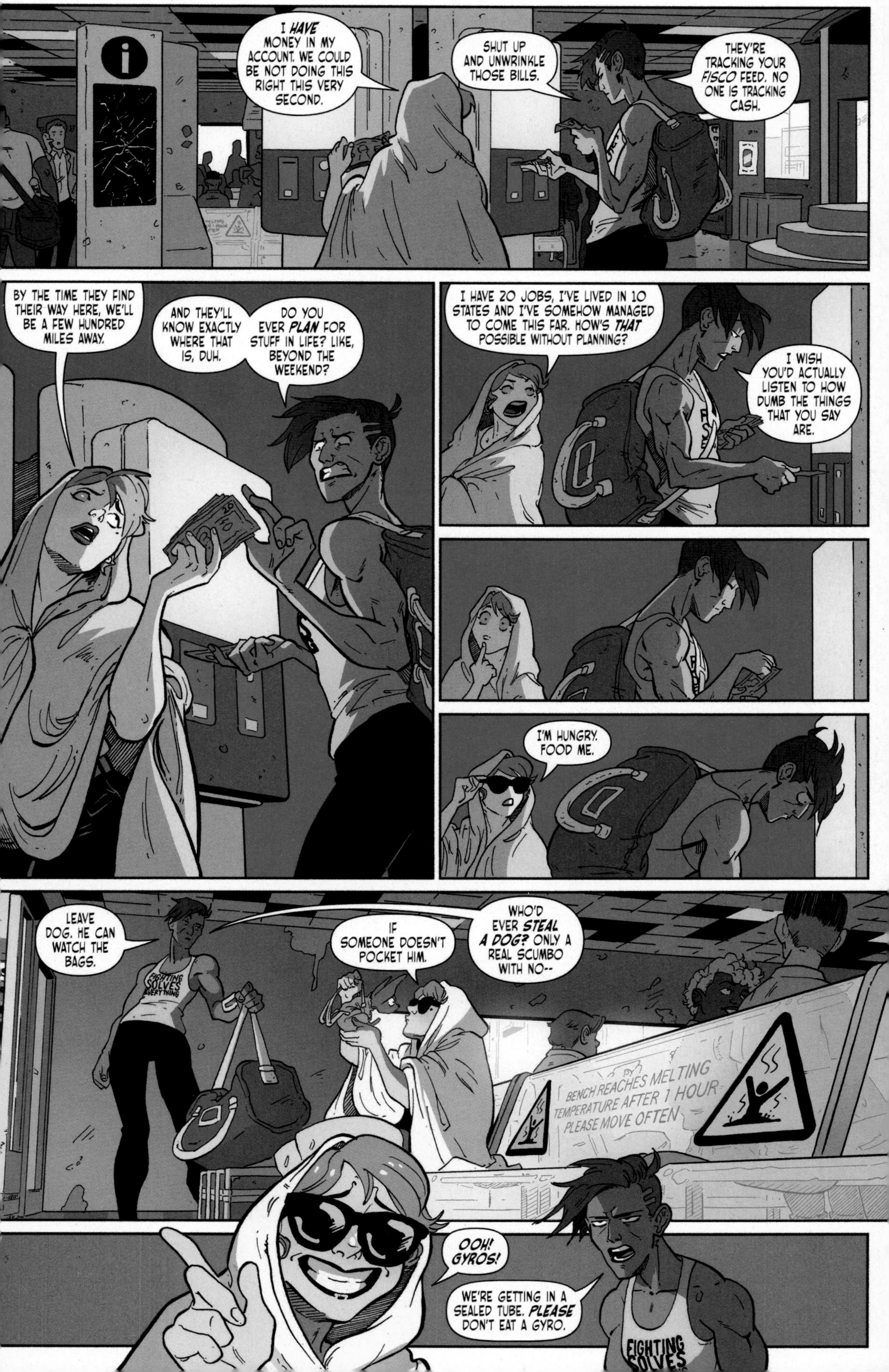
I HAVE MONEY IN MY ACCOUNT. WE COULD BE NOT DOING THIS RIGHT THIS VERY SECOND.
SHUT UP AND UNWRINKLE THOSE BILLS.
THEY'RE TRACKING YOUR FISCO FEED. NO ONE IS TRACKING CASH.
BY THE TIME THEY FIND THEIR WAY HERE, WE'LL BE A FEW HUNDRED MILES AWAY.
AND THEY'LL KNOW EXACTLY WHERE THAT IS, DUH.
DO YOU EVER PLAN FOR STUFF IN LIFE? LIKE, BEYOND THE WEEKEND?
I HAVE 20 JOBS, I'VE LIVED IN 10 STATES AND I'VE SOMEHOW MANAGED TO COME THIS FAR. HOW'S THAT POSSIBLE WITHOUT PLANNING?
I WISH YOU'D ACTUALLY LISTEN TO HOW DUMB THE THINGS THAT YOU SAY ARE.
I'M HUNGRY. FOOD ME.
LEAVE DOG. HE CAN WATCH THE BAGS.
IF SOMEONE DOESN'T POCKET HIM.
WHO'D EVER STEAL A DOG? ONLY A REAL SCUMBO WITH NO--
FIGHTING SOLVES EVERYTHING
BENCH REACHES MELTING TEMPERATURE AFTER 1 HOUR PLEASE MOVE OFTEN
OOH! GYROS!
WE'RE GETTING IN A SEALED TUBE. PLEASE DON'T EAT A GYRO.
FIGHTING SOLVES

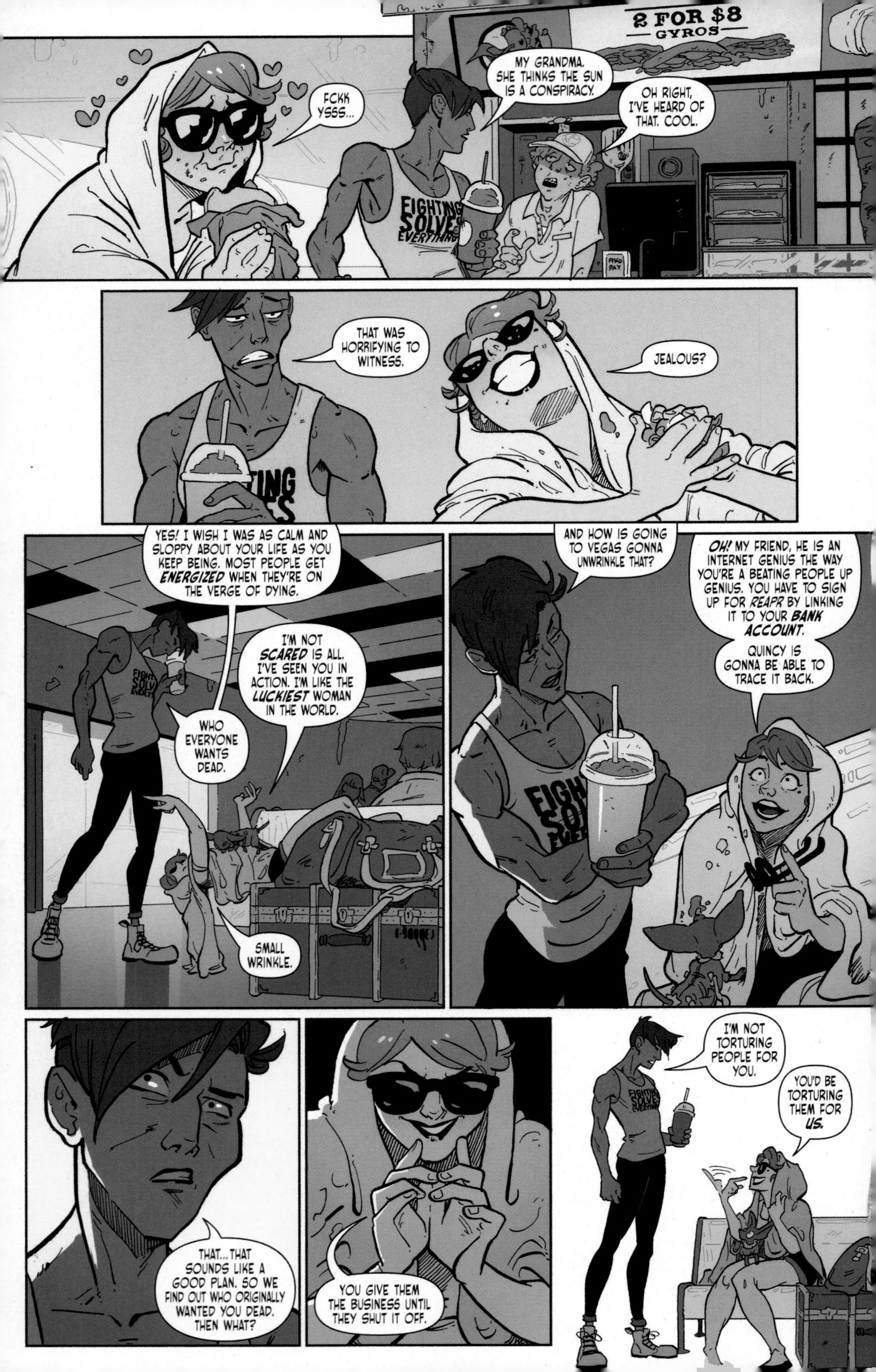
2 FOR $8
GYROS
FCKK YSSS...
MY GRANDMA. SHE THINKS THE SUN IS A CONSPIRACY.
OH RIGHT, I'VE HEARD OF THAT. COOL.
FIGHTING SOLVES EVERYTHING
THAT WAS HORRIFYING TO WITNESS.
JEALOUS?
YES! I WISH I WAS AS CALM AND SLOPPY ABOUT YOUR LIFE AS YOU KEEP BEING. MOST PEOPLE GET ENERGIZED WHEN THEY'RE ON THE VERGE OF DYING.
WHO EVERYONE WANTS DEAD.
I'M NOT SCARED IS ALL. I'VE SEEN YOU IN ACTION. I'M LIKE THE LUCKIEST WOMAN IN THE WORLD.
SMALL WRINKLE.
AND HOW IS GOING TO VEGAS GONNA UNWRINKLE THAT?
OH! MY FRIEND, HE IS AN INTERNET GENIUS THE WAY YOU'RE A BEATING PEOPLE UP GENIUS. YOU HAVE TO SIGN UP FOR REAPR BY LINKING IT TO YOUR BANK ACCOUNT.
QUINCY IS GONNA BE ABLE TO TRACE IT BACK.
THAT...THAT SOUNDS LIKE A GOOD PLAN. SO WE FIND OUT WHO ORIGINALLY WANTED YOU DEAD. THEN WHAT?
YOU GIVE THEM THE BUSINESS UNTIL THEY SHUT IT OFF.
I'M NOT TORTURING PEOPLE FOR YOU.
YOU'D BE TORTURING THEM FOR US.

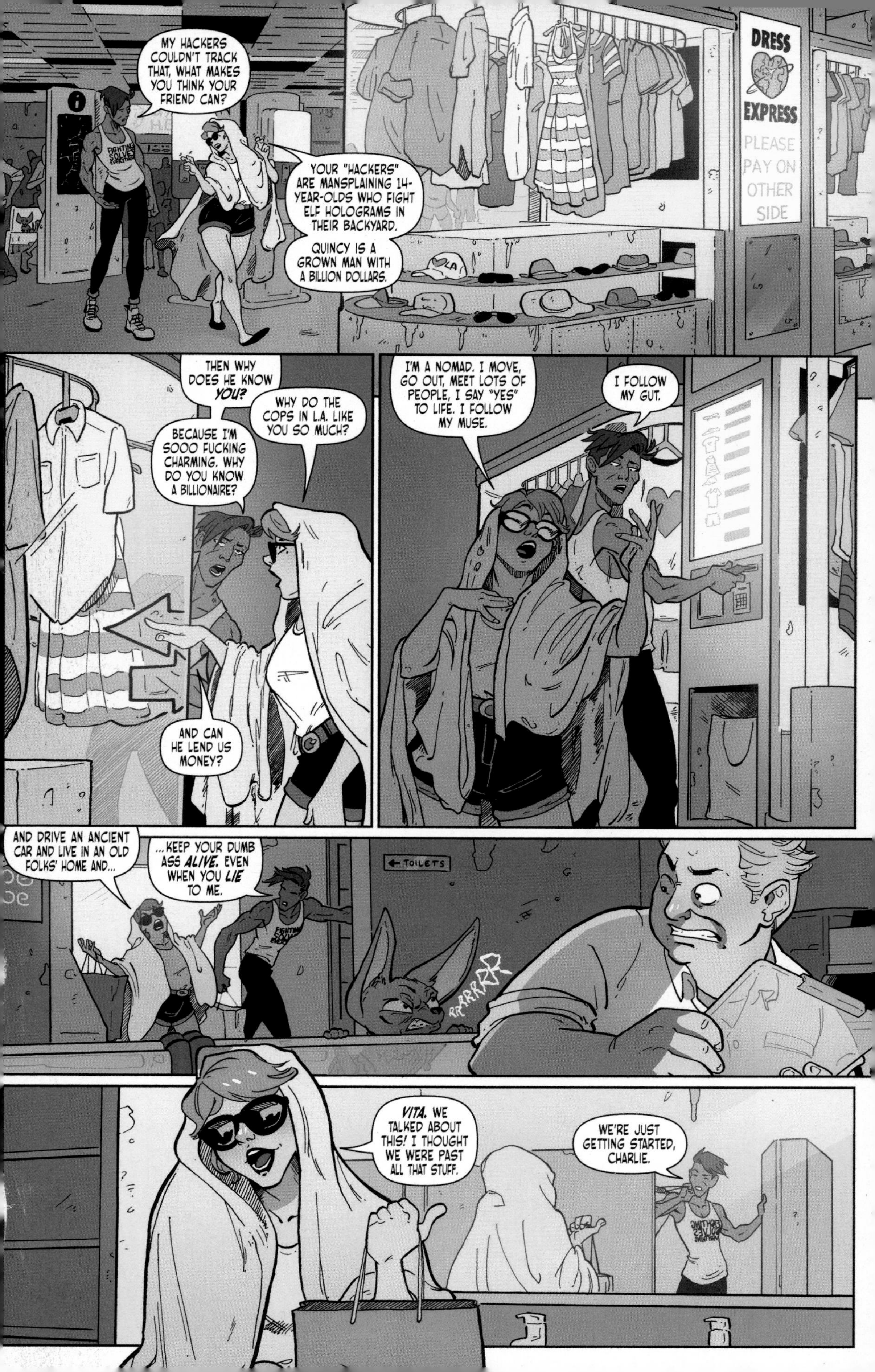

MY HACKERS COULDN'T TRACK THAT, WHAT MAKES YOU THINK YOUR FRIEND CAN?
DRESS EXPRESS
PLEASE PAY ON OTHER SIDE
YOUR "HACKERS" ARE MANSPLAINING 14-YEAR-OLDS WHO FIGHT ELF HOLOGRAMS IN THEIR BACKYARD.
QUINCY IS A GROWN MAN WITH A BILLION DOLLARS.
THEN WHY DOES HE KNOW *YOU?*
WHY DO THE COPS IN L.A. LIKE YOU SO MUCH?
BECAUSE I'M SOOO FUCKING CHARMING. WHY DO YOU KNOW A BILLIONAIRE?
AND CAN HE LEND US MONEY?
I'M A NOMAD. I MOVE, GO OUT, MEET LOTS OF PEOPLE, I SAY "YES" TO LIFE. I FOLLOW MY MUSE.
I FOLLOW MY GUT.
AND DRIVE AN ANCIENT CAR AND LIVE IN AN OLD FOLKS' HOME AND...
...KEEP YOUR DUMB ASS *ALIVE.* EVEN WHEN YOU *LIE* TO ME.
TOILETS
RRRRRRR
VITA. WE TALKED ABOUT THIS! I THOUGHT WE WERE PAST ALL THAT STUFF.
WE'RE JUST GETTING STARTED, CHARLIE.

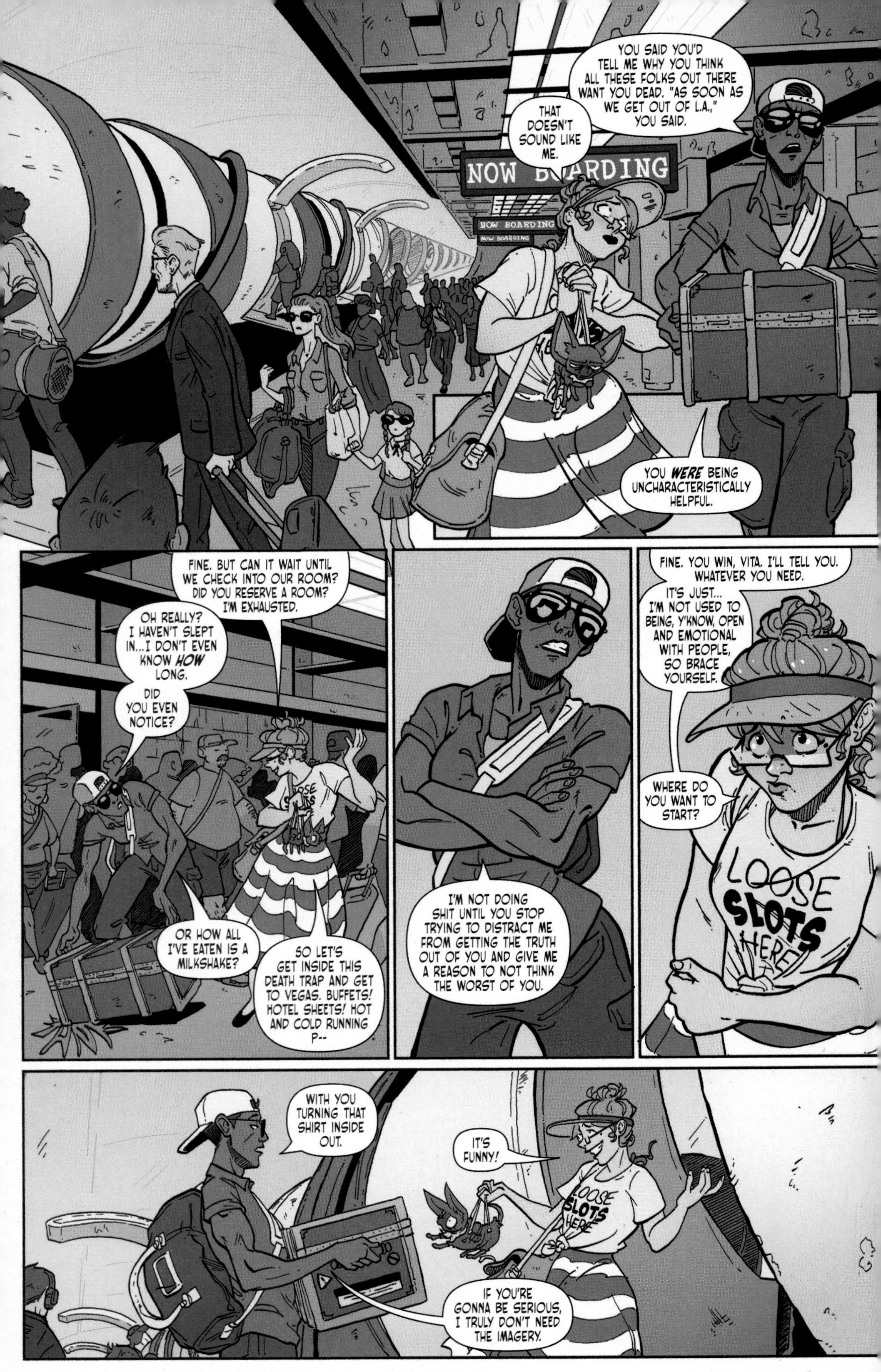
NOW BOARDING
NOW BOARDING
NOW BOARDING
YOU SAID YOU'D TELL ME WHY YOU THINK ALL THESE FOLKS OUT THERE WANT YOU DEAD. "AS SOON AS WE GET OUT OF L.A.," YOU SAID.
THAT DOESN'T SOUND LIKE ME.
YOU *WERE* BEING UNCHARACTERISTICALLY HELPFUL.
FINE. BUT CAN IT WAIT UNTIL WE CHECK INTO OUR ROOM? DID YOU RESERVE A ROOM? I'M EXHAUSTED.
OH REALLY? I HAVEN'T SLEPT IN...I DON'T EVEN KNOW *HOW* LONG.
DID YOU EVEN NOTICE?
OR HOW ALL I'VE EATEN IS A MILKSHAKE?
SO LET'S GET INSIDE THIS DEATH TRAP AND GET TO VEGAS. BUFFETS! HOTEL SHEETS! HOT AND COLD RUNNING P--
I'M NOT DOING SHIT UNTIL YOU STOP TRYING TO DISTRACT ME FROM GETTING THE TRUTH OUT OF YOU AND GIVE ME A REASON TO NOT THINK THE WORST OF YOU.
FINE. YOU WIN, VITA. I'LL TELL YOU. WHATEVER YOU NEED.
IT'S JUST... I'M NOT USED TO BEING, Y'KNOW, OPEN AND EMOTIONAL WITH PEOPLE, SO BRACE YOURSELF.
WHERE DO YOU WANT TO START?
LOOSE SLOTS HERE
WITH YOU TURNING THAT SHIRT INSIDE OUT.
IT'S FUNNY!
LOOSE SLOTS HERE
IF YOU'RE GONNA BE SERIOUS, I TRULY DON'T NEED THE IMAGERY.

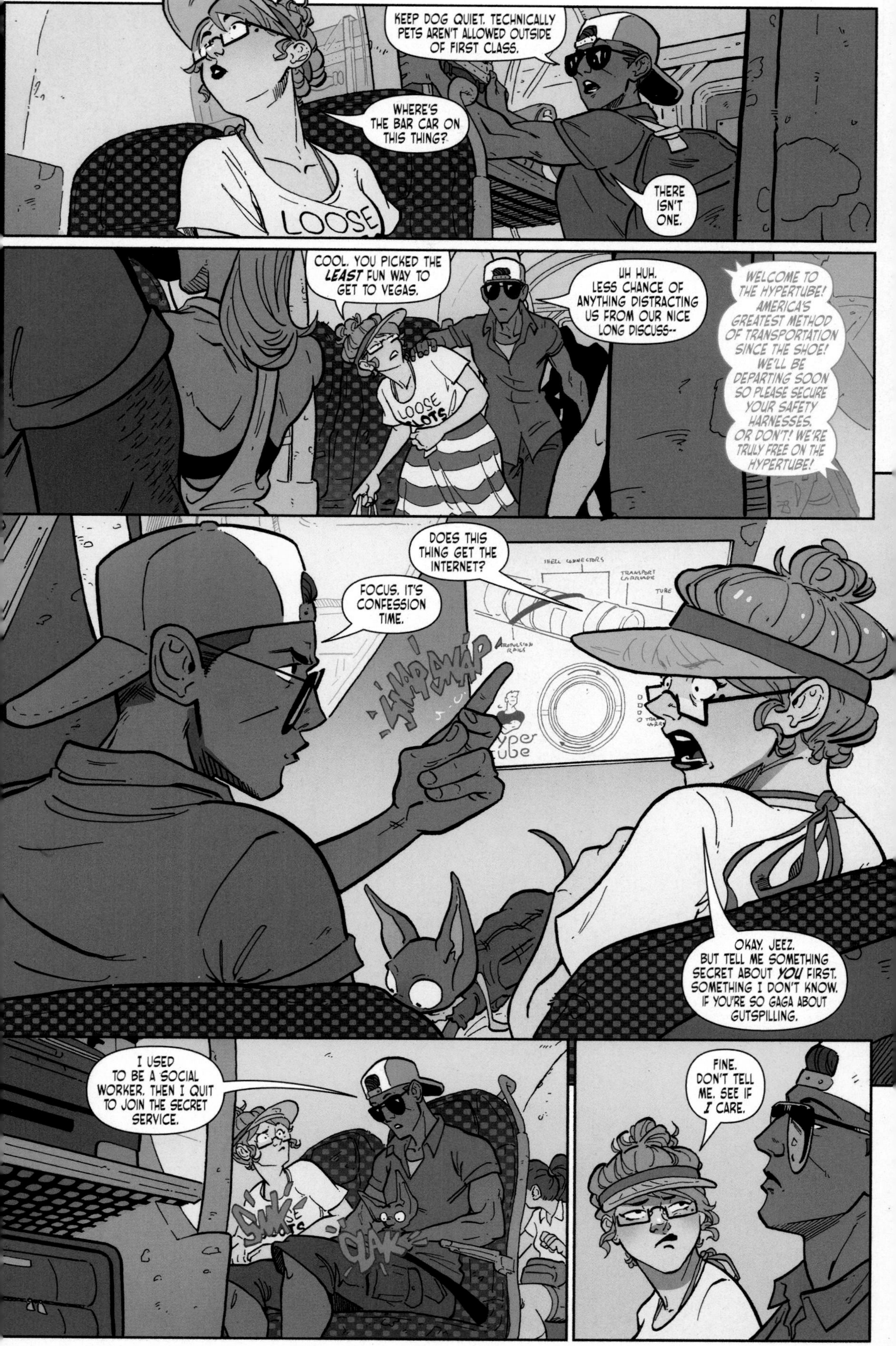
KEEP DOG QUIET. TECHNICALLY PETS AREN'T ALLOWED OUTSIDE OF FIRST CLASS.
WHERE'S THE BAR CAR ON THIS THING?
THERE ISN'T ONE.
LOOSE
COOL. YOU PICKED THE LEAST FUN WAY TO GET TO VEGAS.
UH HUH. LESS CHANCE OF ANYTHING DISTRACTING US FROM OUR NICE LONG DISCUSS--
WELCOME TO THE HYPERTUBE! AMERICA'S GREATEST METHOD OF TRANSPORTATION SINCE THE SHOE! WE'LL BE DEPARTING SOON SO PLEASE SECURE YOUR SAFETY HARNESSES. OR DON'T! WE'RE TRULY FREE ON THE HYPERTUBE!
LOOSE SLOTS
DOES THIS THING GET THE INTERNET?
FOCUS. IT'S CONFESSION TIME.
SNAP SNAP
SHELL CONNECTORS
TRANSPORT CARRIAGE
TUBE
PROPULSION RAILS
OKAY. JEEZ. BUT TELL ME SOMETHING SECRET ABOUT YOU FIRST. SOMETHING I DON'T KNOW. IF YOU'RE SO GAGA ABOUT GUTSPILLING.
I USED TO BE A SOCIAL WORKER. THEN I QUIT TO JOIN THE SECRET SERVICE.
CLAK
FINE. DON'T TELL ME. SEE IF I CARE.

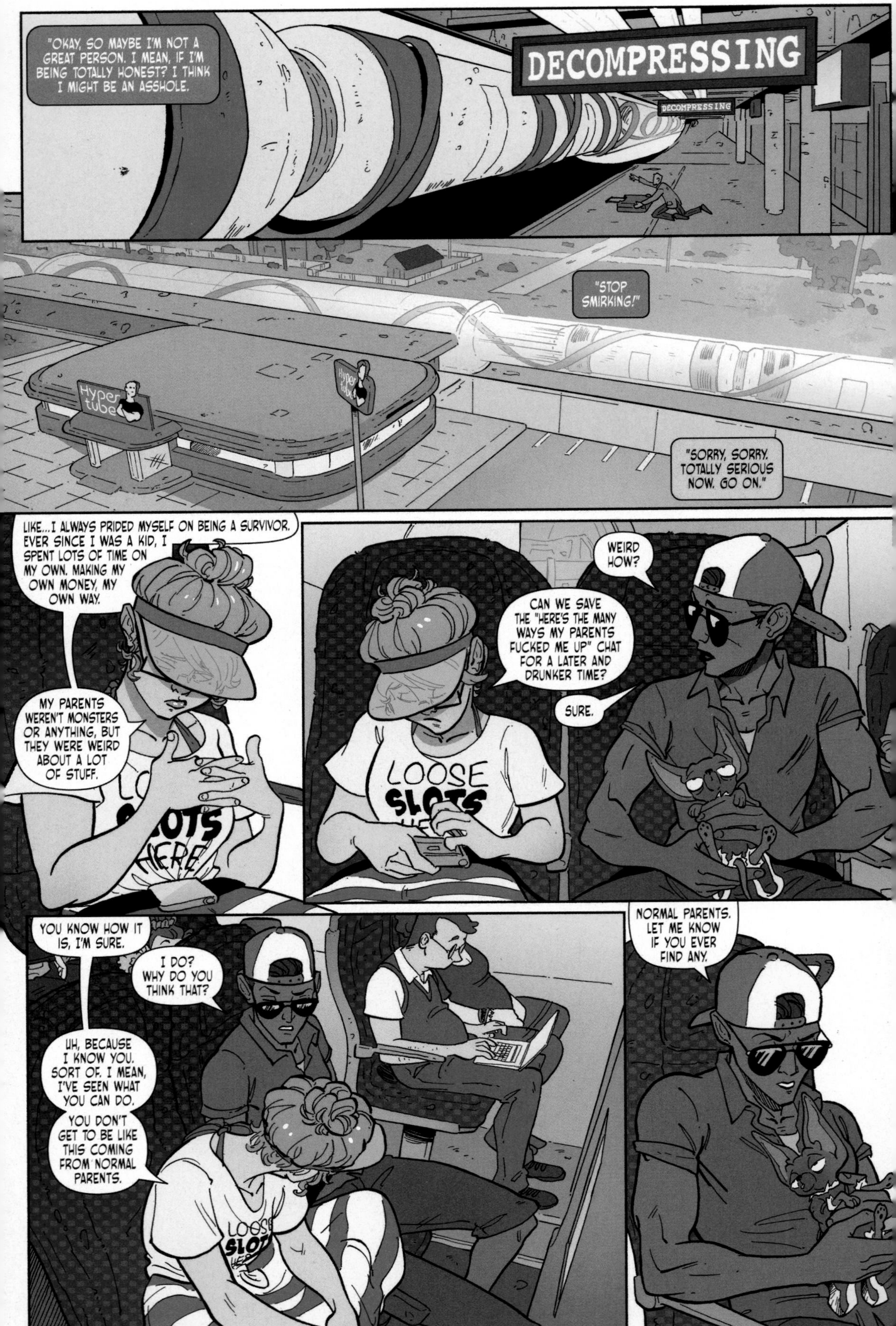
"OKAY, SO MAYBE I'M NOT A GREAT PERSON. I MEAN, IF I'M BEING TOTALLY HONEST? I THINK I MIGHT BE AN ASSHOLE.
DECOMPRESSING
DECOMPRESSING
"STOP SMIRKING!"
Hyper tube
Hyper tube
"SORRY, SORRY. TOTALLY SERIOUS NOW. GO ON."
LIKE...I ALWAYS PRIDED MYSELF ON BEING A SURVIVOR. EVER SINCE I WAS A KID, I SPENT LOTS OF TIME ON MY OWN. MAKING MY OWN MONEY, MY OWN WAY.
MY PARENTS WEREN'T MONSTERS OR ANYTHING, BUT THEY WERE WEIRD ABOUT A LOT OF STUFF.
WEIRD HOW?
CAN WE SAVE THE "HERE'S THE MANY WAYS MY PARENTS FUCKED ME UP" CHAT FOR A LATER AND DRUNKER TIME?
SURE.
LOOSE SLOTS
YOU KNOW HOW IT IS, I'M SURE.
I DO? WHY DO YOU THINK THAT?
UH, BECAUSE I KNOW YOU. SORT OF. I MEAN, I'VE SEEN WHAT YOU CAN DO.
YOU DON'T GET TO BE LIKE THIS COMING FROM NORMAL PARENTS.
NORMAL PARENTS. LET ME KNOW IF YOU EVER FIND ANY.

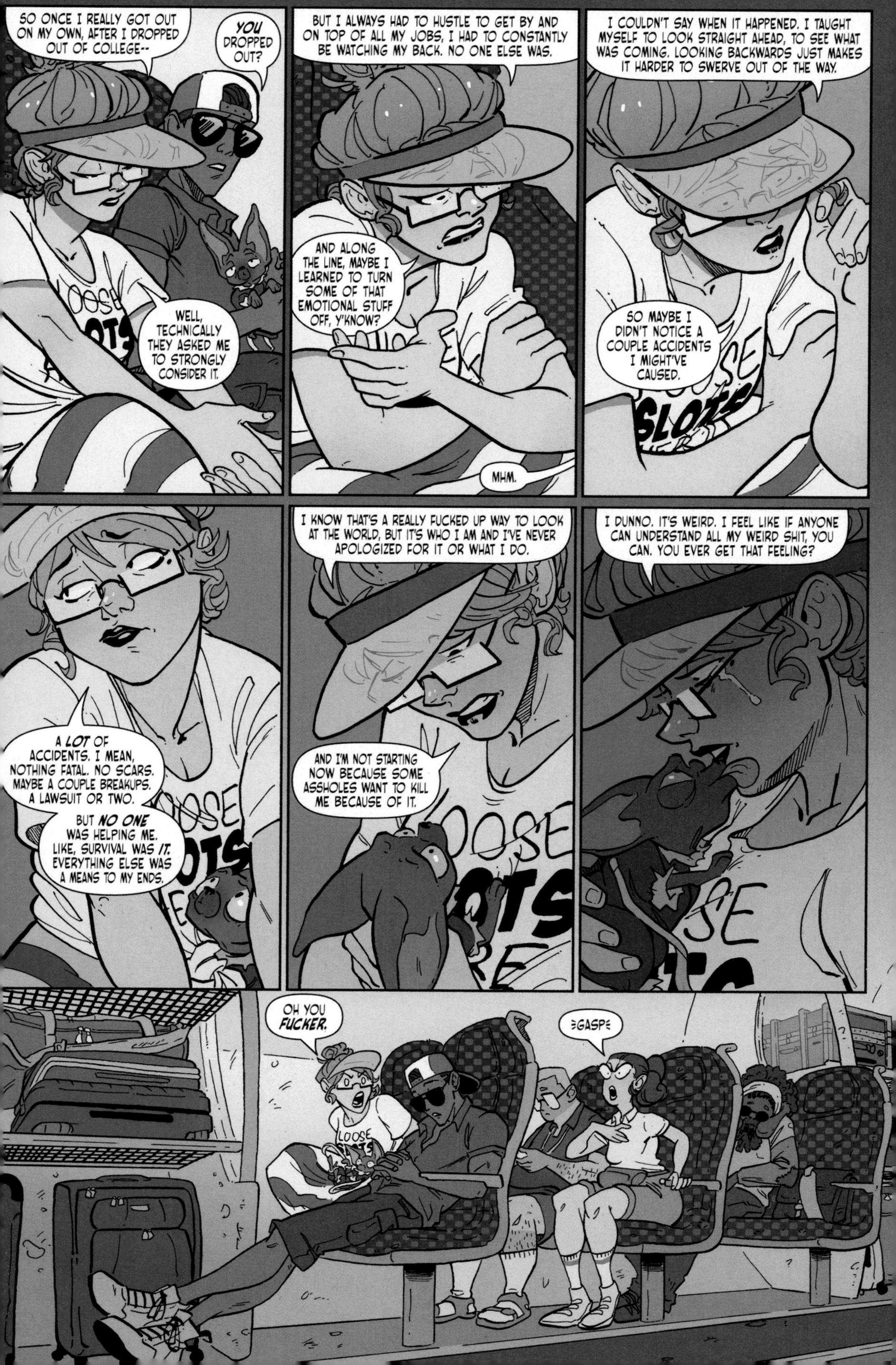
SO ONCE I REALLY GOT OUT ON MY OWN, AFTER I DROPPED OUT OF COLLEGE--
YOU DROPPED OUT?
WELL, TECHNICALLY THEY ASKED ME TO STRONGLY CONSIDER IT.
BUT I ALWAYS HAD TO HUSTLE TO GET BY AND ON TOP OF ALL MY JOBS, I HAD TO CONSTANTLY BE WATCHING MY BACK. NO ONE ELSE WAS.
AND ALONG THE LINE, MAYBE I LEARNED TO TURN SOME OF THAT EMOTIONAL STUFF OFF, Y'KNOW?
MHM.
I COULDN'T SAY WHEN IT HAPPENED. I TAUGHT MYSELF TO LOOK STRAIGHT AHEAD, TO SEE WHAT WAS COMING. LOOKING BACKWARDS JUST MAKES IT HARDER TO SWERVE OUT OF THE WAY.
SO MAYBE I DIDN'T NOTICE A COUPLE ACCIDENTS I MIGHT'VE CAUSED.
A *LOT* OF ACCIDENTS. I MEAN, NOTHING FATAL. NO SCARS. MAYBE A COUPLE BREAKUPS. A LAWSUIT OR TWO.
BUT *NO ONE* WAS HELPING ME. LIKE, SURVIVAL WAS *IT.* EVERYTHING ELSE WAS A MEANS TO MY ENDS.
I KNOW THAT'S A REALLY FUCKED UP WAY TO LOOK AT THE WORLD, BUT IT'S WHO I AM AND I'VE NEVER APOLOGIZED FOR IT OR WHAT I DO.
AND I'M NOT STARTING NOW BECAUSE SOME ASSHOLES WANT TO KILL ME BECAUSE OF IT.
I DUNNO. IT'S WEIRD. I FEEL LIKE IF ANYONE CAN UNDERSTAND ALL MY WEIRD SHIT, YOU CAN. YOU EVER GET THAT FEELING?
OH YOU *FUCKER.*
GASP

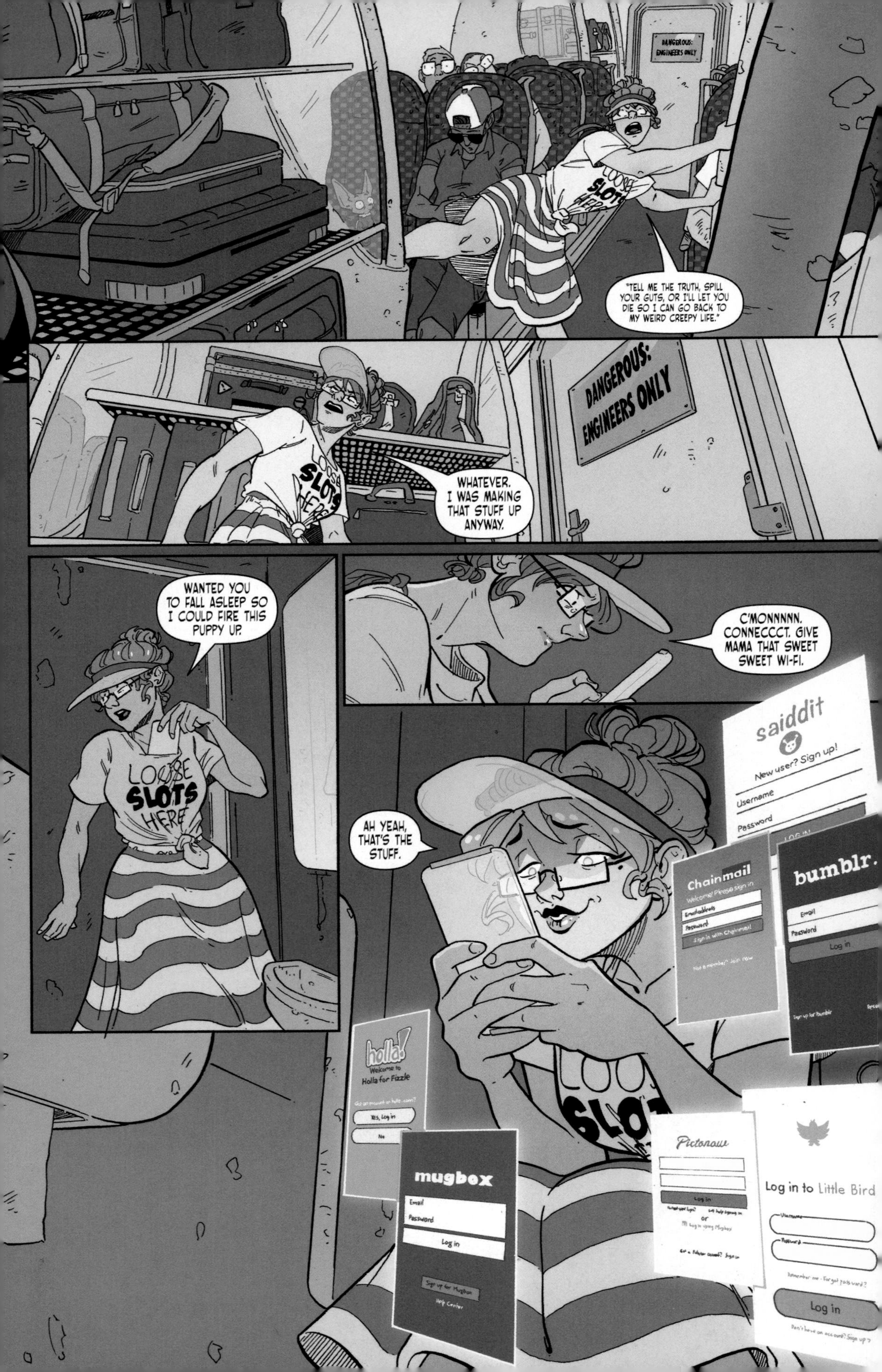
DANGEROUS: ENGINEERS ONLY
LOOSE SLOTS HERE
"TELL ME THE TRUTH, SPILL YOUR GUTS, OR I'LL LET YOU DIE SO I CAN GO BACK TO MY WEIRD CREEPY LIFE."
DANGEROUS: ENGINEERS ONLY
WHATEVER. I WAS MAKING THAT STUFF UP ANYWAY.
WANTED YOU TO FALL ASLEEP SO I COULD FIRE THIS PUPPY UP.
C'MONNNNN. CONNECCCT. GIVE MAMA THAT SWEET SWEET WI-FI.
AH YEAH, THAT'S THE STUFF.
saiddit
New user? Sign up!
Username
Password
Chainmail
Welcome! Please sign in
Password
Sign in with Chainmail
bumblr.
Email
Password
Log in
holla!
Welcome to Holla for Fizzle
Yes, Log in
No
mugbox
Email
Password
Log in
Sign up for Mugbox
Help Center
Pictonow
Log in
or
Log in to Little Bird
Username
Password
Remember me · Forgot password?
Log in
Don't have an account? Sign up

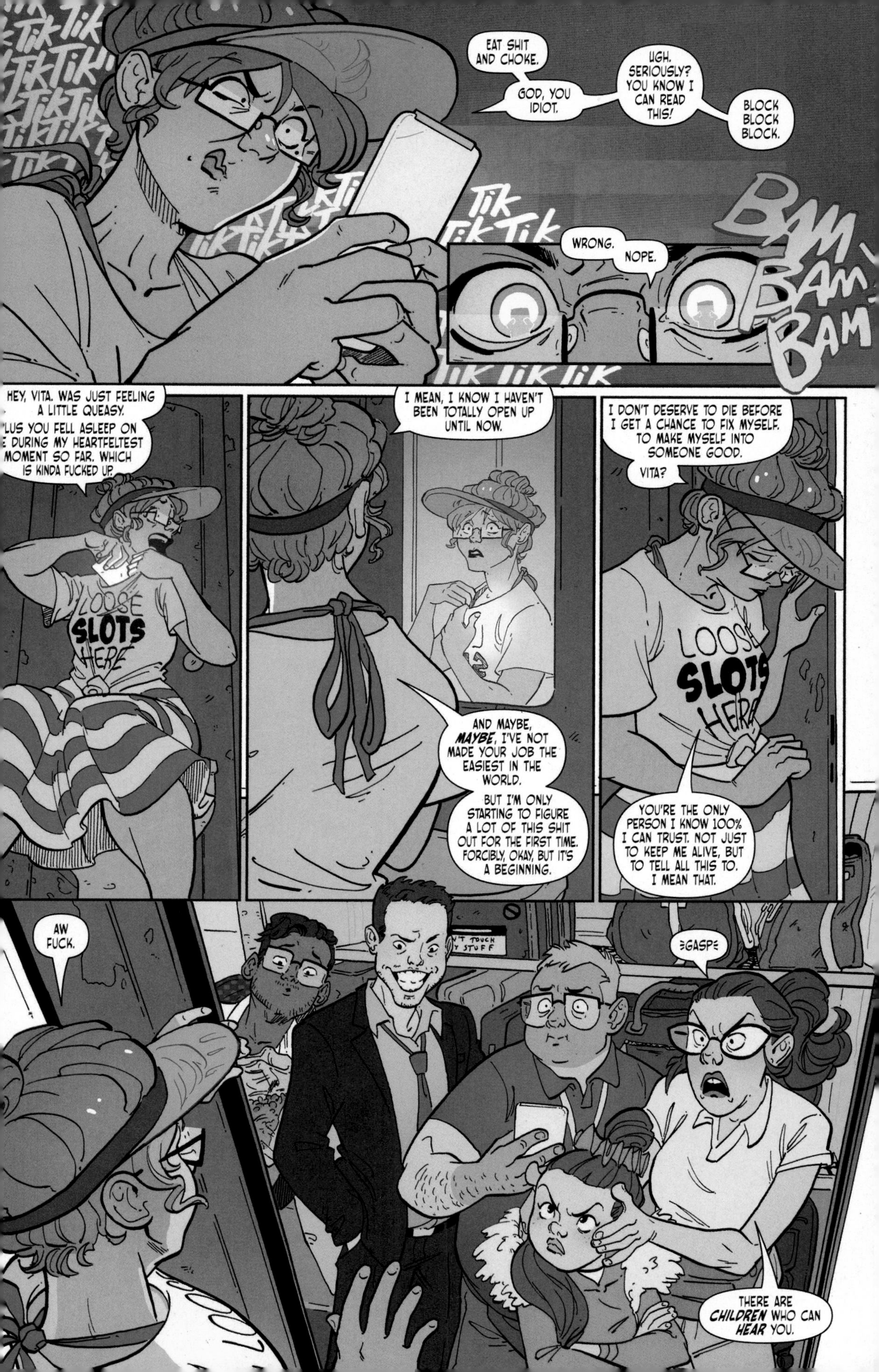

TIK TIK TIK TIK
EAT SHIT AND CHOKE.
GOD, YOU IDIOT.
UGH. SERIOUSLY? YOU KNOW I CAN READ THIS!
BLOCK BLOCK BLOCK.
TIK TIK TIK
WRONG.
NOPE.
BAM BAM BAM
TIK TIK TIK
HEY, VITA. WAS JUST FEELING A LITTLE QUEASY.
LUS YOU FELL ASLEEP ON E DURING MY HEARTFELTEST MOMENT SO FAR. WHICH IS KINDA FUCKED UP.
LOOSE SLOTS HERE
I MEAN, I KNOW I HAVEN'T BEEN TOTALLY OPEN UP UNTIL NOW.
AND MAYBE, MAYBE, I'VE NOT MADE YOUR JOB THE EASIEST IN THE WORLD.
BUT I'M ONLY STARTING TO FIGURE A LOT OF THIS SHIT OUT FOR THE FIRST TIME. FORCIBLY, OKAY, BUT IT'S A BEGINNING.
I DON'T DESERVE TO DIE BEFORE I GET A CHANCE TO FIX MYSELF. TO MAKE MYSELF INTO SOMEONE GOOD.
VITA?
LOOSE SLOTS HERE
YOU'RE THE ONLY PERSON I KNOW 100% I CAN TRUST. NOT JUST TO KEEP ME ALIVE, BUT TO TELL ALL THIS TO. I MEAN THAT.
AW FUCK.
N'T TOUCH Y STUFF
GASP
THERE ARE CHILDREN WHO CAN HEAR YOU.

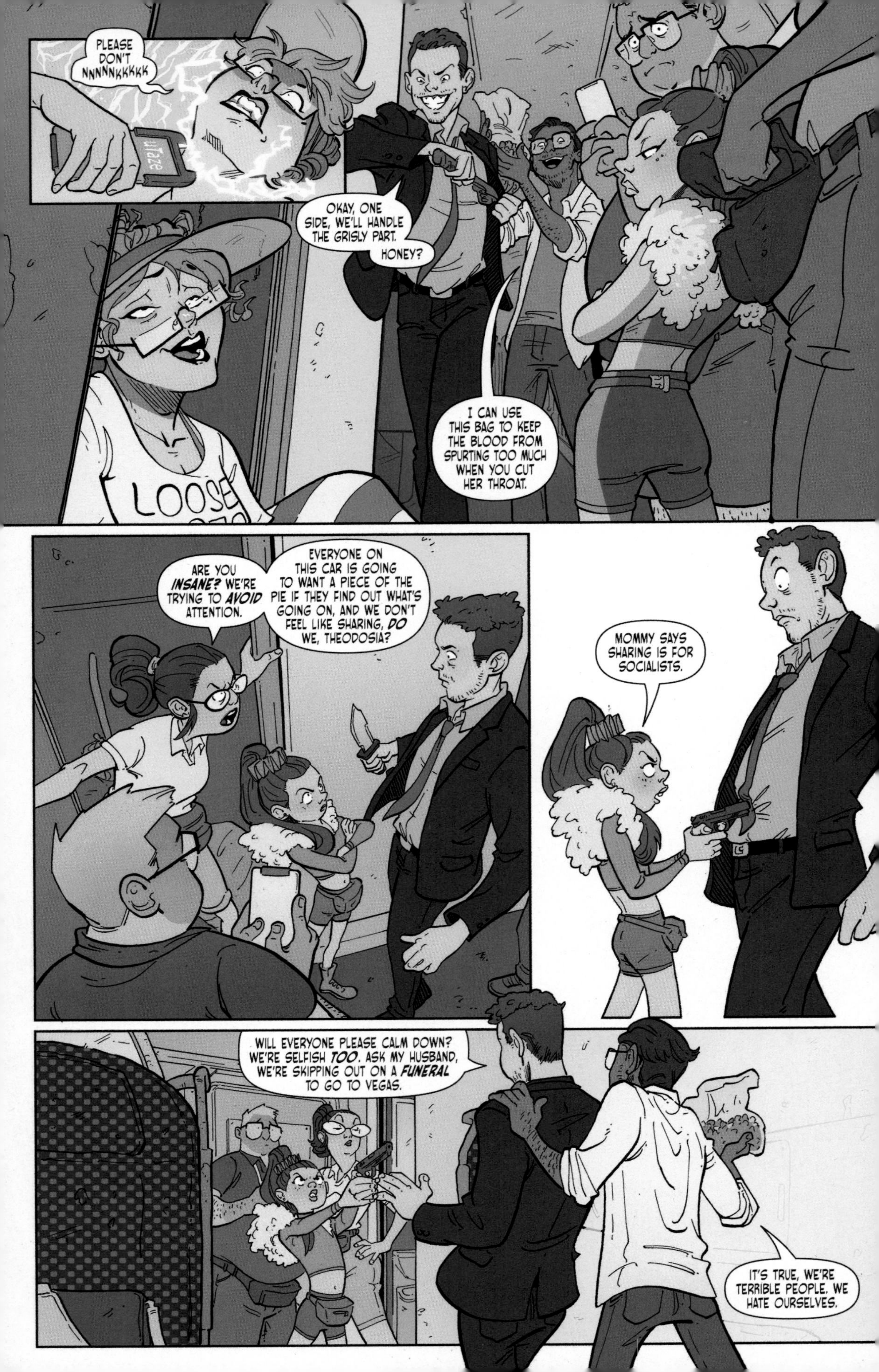
PLEASE DON'T NNNNNKKKKK
uTaze
OKAY, ONE SIDE, WE'LL HANDLE THE GRISLY PART.
HONEY?
I CAN USE THIS BAG TO KEEP THE BLOOD FROM SPURTING TOO MUCH WHEN YOU CUT HER THROAT.
LOOSE
ARE YOU INSANE? WE'RE TRYING TO AVOID ATTENTION.
EVERYONE ON THIS CAR IS GOING TO WANT A PIECE OF THE PIE IF THEY FIND OUT WHAT'S GOING ON, AND WE DON'T FEEL LIKE SHARING, DO WE, THEODOSIA?
MOMMY SAYS SHARING IS FOR SOCIALISTS.
WILL EVERYONE PLEASE CALM DOWN? WE'RE SELFISH TOO. ASK MY HUSBAND, WE'RE SKIPPING OUT ON A FUNERAL TO GO TO VEGAS.
IT'S TRUE, WE'RE TERRIBLE PEOPLE. WE HATE OURSELVES.

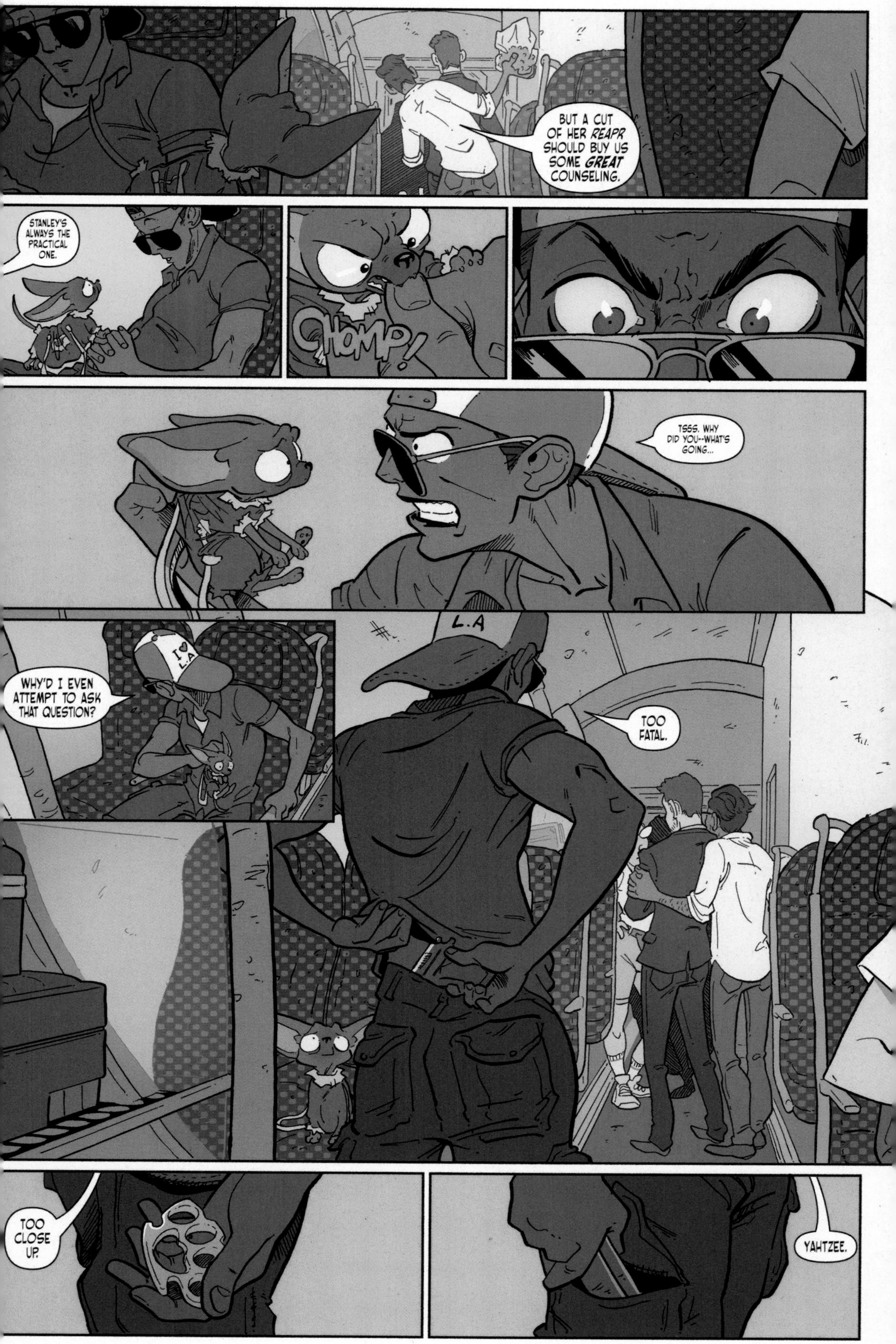

BUT A CUT OF HER REAPR SHOULD BUY US SOME GREAT COUNSELING.
STANLEY'S ALWAYS THE PRACTICAL ONE.
CHOMP!
TSSS. WHY DID YOU--WHAT'S GOING...
WHY'D I EVEN ATTEMPT TO ASK THAT QUESTION?
I ♥ L.A
L.A
TOO FATAL.
TOO CLOSE UP.
YAHTZEE.

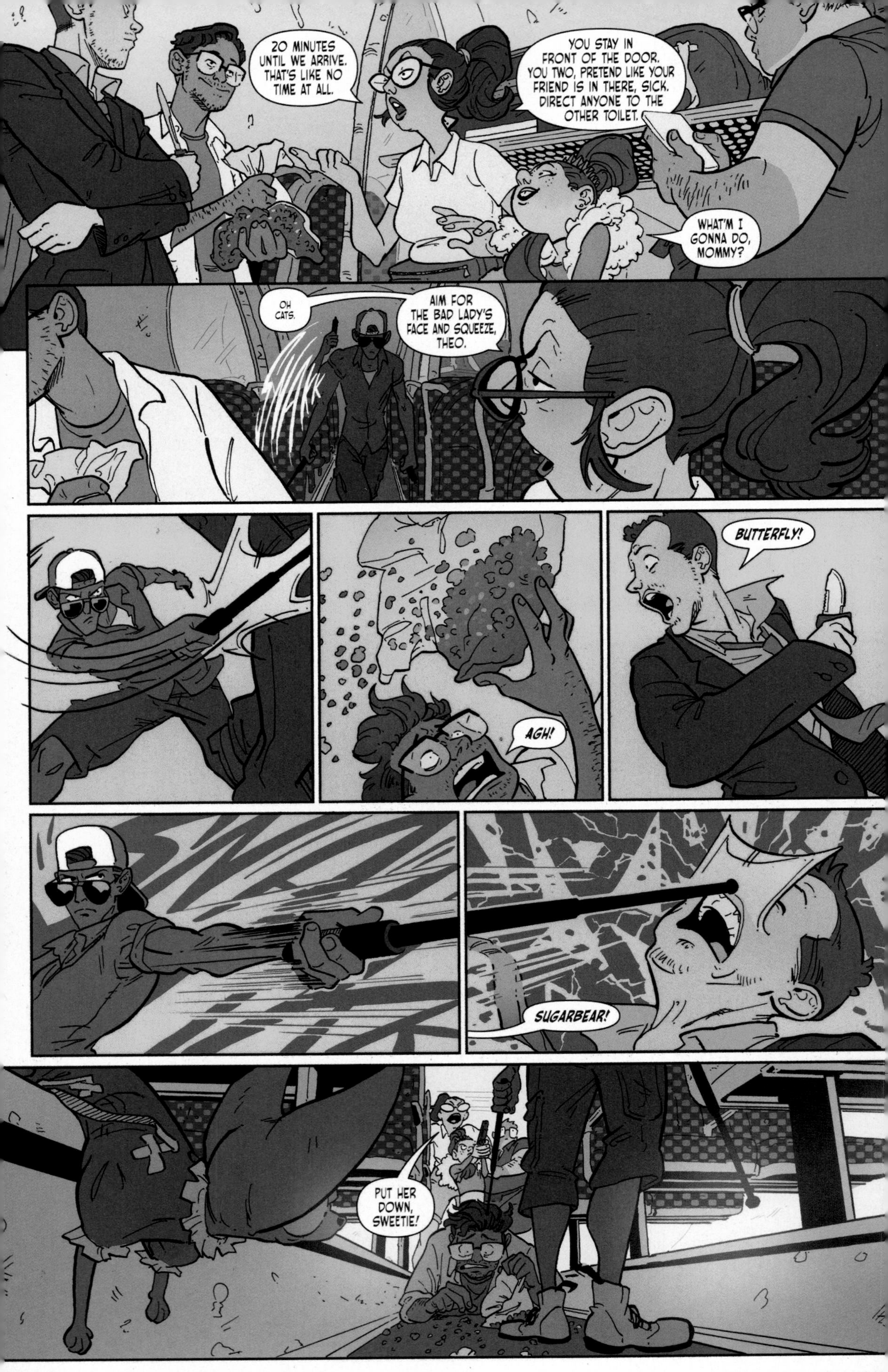
20 MINUTES UNTIL WE ARRIVE. THAT'S LIKE NO TIME AT ALL.
YOU STAY IN FRONT OF THE DOOR. YOU TWO, PRETEND LIKE YOUR FRIEND IS IN THERE, SICK. DIRECT ANYONE TO THE OTHER TOILET.
WHAT'M I GONNA DO, MOMMY?
OH CATS.
AIM FOR THE BAD LADY'S FACE AND SQUEEZE, THEO.
SHAKK
AGH!
BUTTERFLY!
SUGARBEAR!
PUT HER DOWN, SWEETIE!

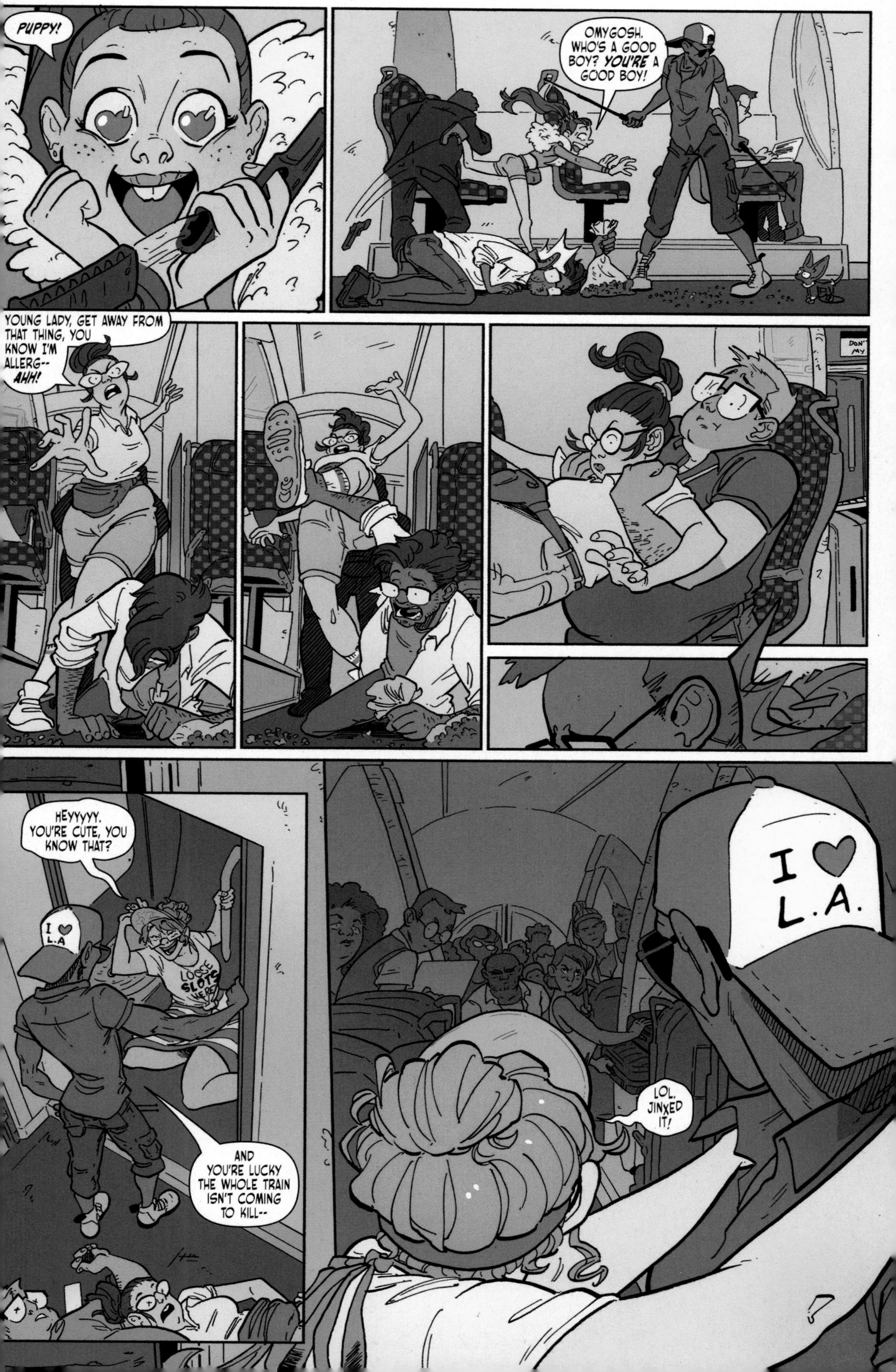
PUPPY!
OMYGOSH. WHO'S A GOOD BOY? YOU'RE A GOOD BOY!
YOUNG LADY, GET AWAY FROM THAT THING, YOU KNOW I'M ALLERG-- AHH!
DON'T MY
HEYYYYY. YOU'RE CUTE, YOU KNOW THAT?
I ♥ L.A.
LOOSE SLOTS HERE
AND YOU'RE LUCKY THE WHOLE TRAIN ISN'T COMING TO KILL--
LOL. JINXED IT!
I ♥ L.A.

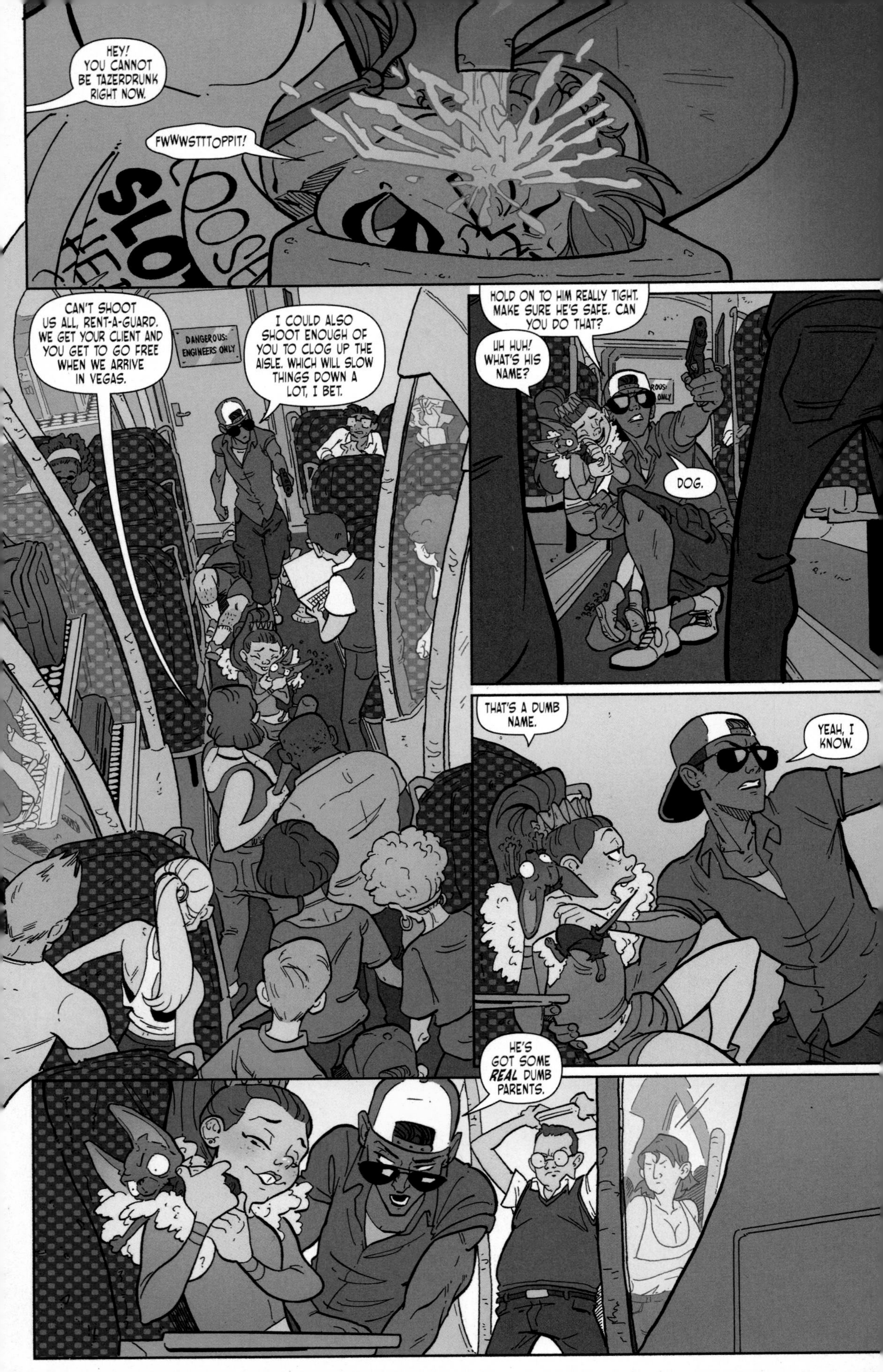
HEY! YOU CANNOT BE TAZERDRUNK RIGHT NOW.
FWWWSTTTOPPIT!
CAN'T SHOOT US ALL, RENT-A-GUARD. WE GET YOUR CLIENT AND YOU GET TO GO FREE WHEN WE ARRIVE IN VEGAS.
DANGEROUS: ENGINEERS ONLY
I COULD ALSO SHOOT ENOUGH OF YOU TO CLOG UP THE AISLE. WHICH WILL SLOW THINGS DOWN A LOT, I BET.
HOLD ON TO HIM REALLY TIGHT. MAKE SURE HE'S SAFE. CAN YOU DO THAT?
UH HUH! WHAT'S HIS NAME?
DOG.
THAT'S A DUMB NAME.
YEAH, I KNOW.
HE'S GOT SOME REAL DUMB PARENTS.

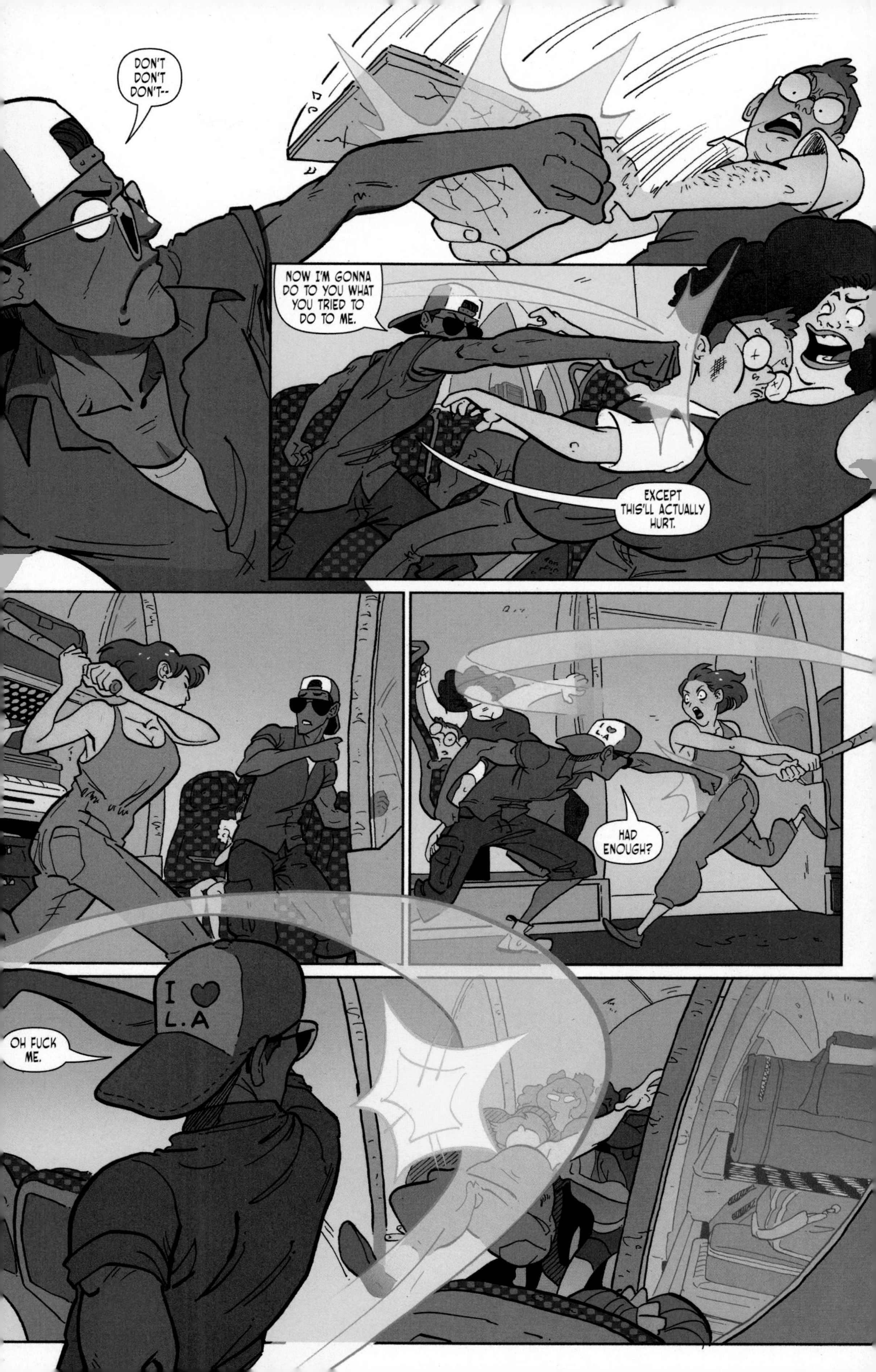
DON'T DON'T DON'T--
NOW I'M GONNA DO TO YOU WHAT YOU TRIED TO DO TO ME.
EXCEPT THIS'LL ACTUALLY HURT.
HAD ENOUGH?
I ♥ L.A
OH FUCK ME.

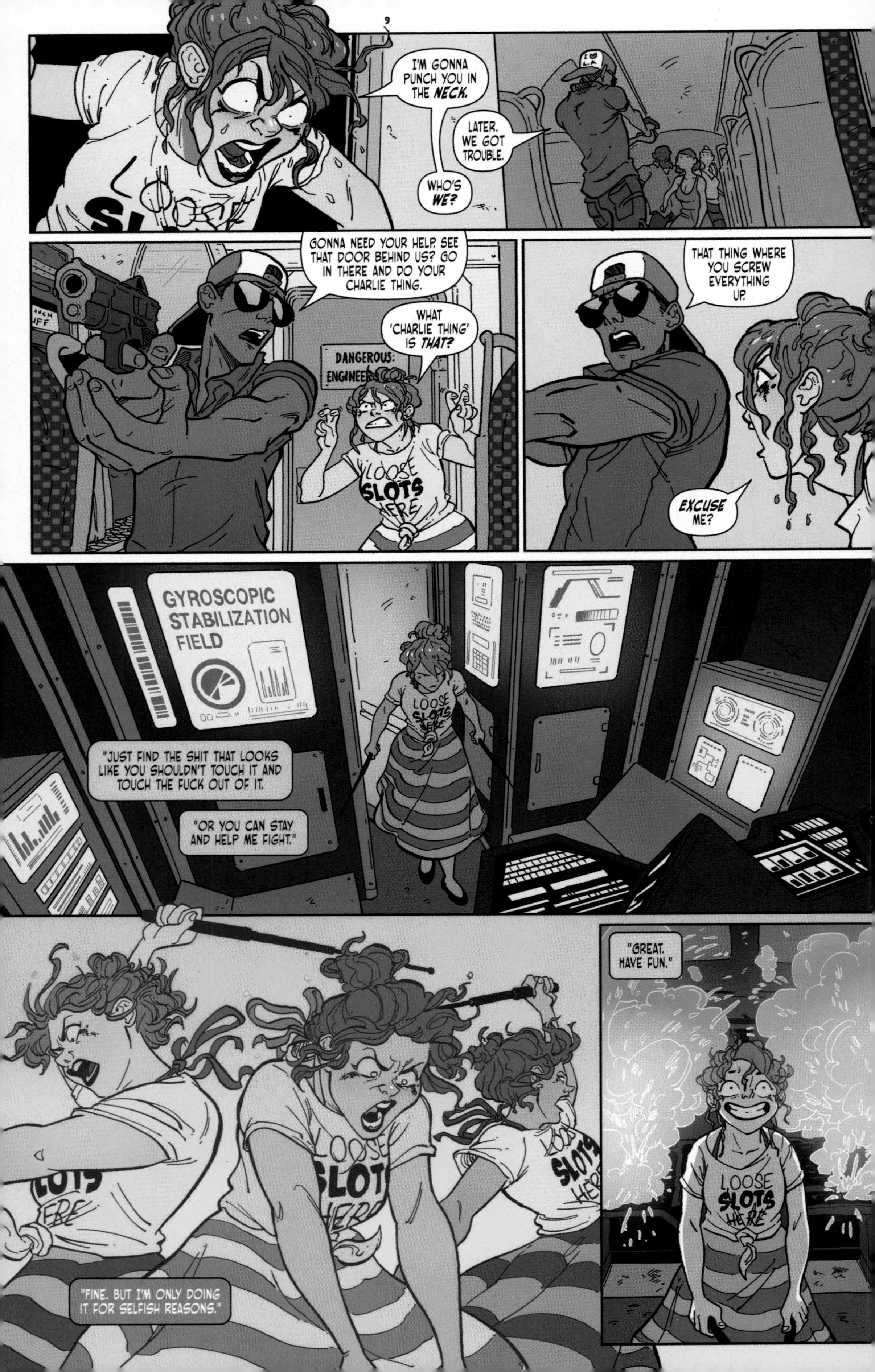
9
I'M GONNA PUNCH YOU IN THE NECK.
LATER. WE GOT TROUBLE.
WHO'S WE?
GONNA NEED YOUR HELP. SEE THAT DOOR BEHIND US? GO IN THERE AND DO YOUR CHARLIE THING.
WHAT 'CHARLIE THING' IS THAT?
DANGEROUS: ENGINEE
LOOSE SLOTS HERE
THAT THING WHERE YOU SCREW EVERYTHING UP.
EXCUSE ME?
GYROSCOPIC STABILIZATION FIELD
"JUST FIND THE SHIT THAT LOOKS LIKE YOU SHOULDN'T TOUCH IT AND TOUCH THE FUCK OUT OF IT.
"OR YOU CAN STAY AND HELP ME FIGHT."
"FINE. BUT I'M ONLY DOING IT FOR SELFISH REASONS."
"GREAT. HAVE FUN."
LOOSE SLOTS HERE

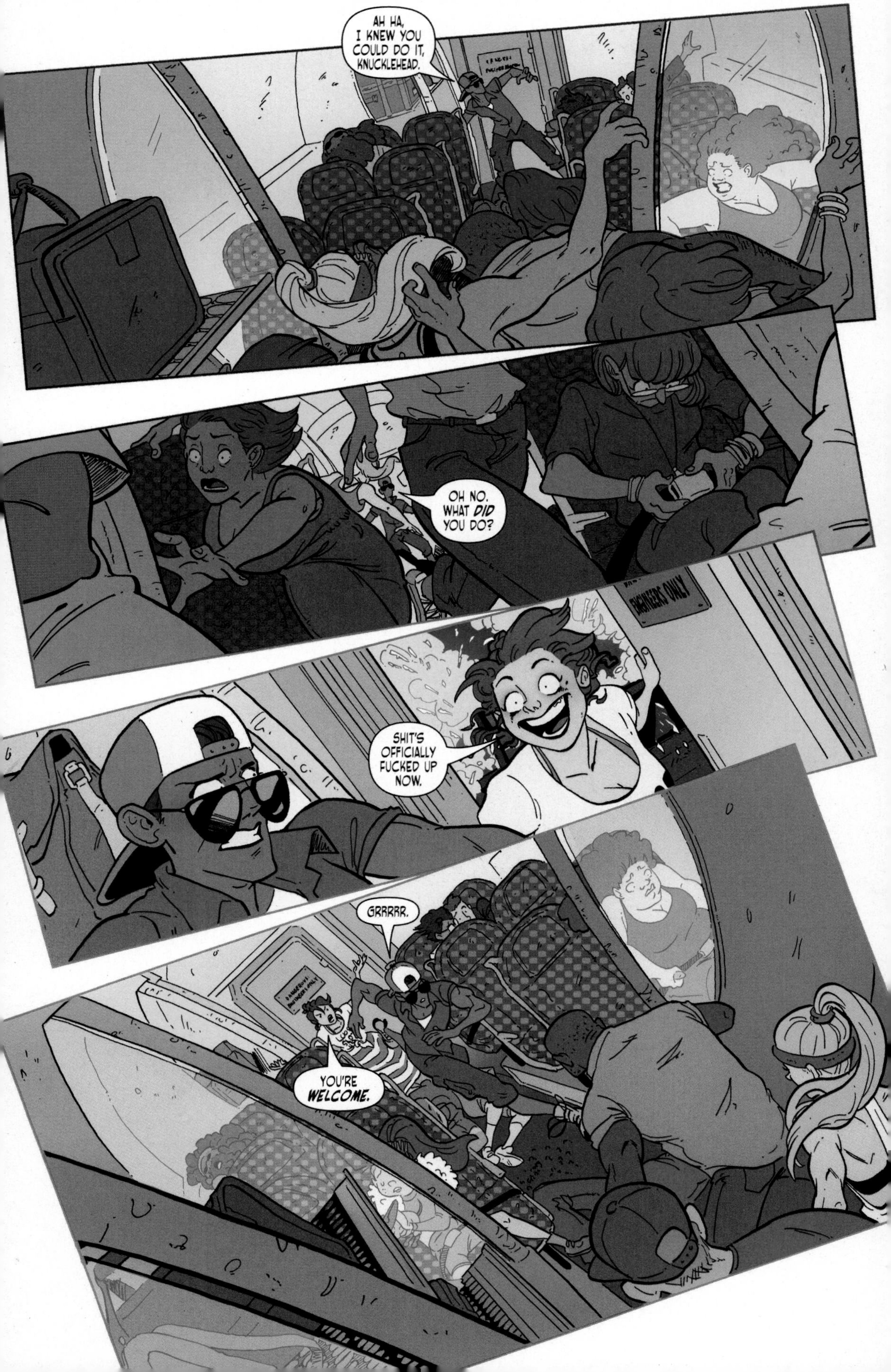
AH HA, I KNEW YOU COULD DO IT, KNUCKLEHEAD.
OH NO. WHAT *DID* YOU DO?
ENGINEERS ONLY
SHIT'S OFFICIALLY FUCKED UP NOW.
GRRRRR.
YOU'RE ***WELCOME.***

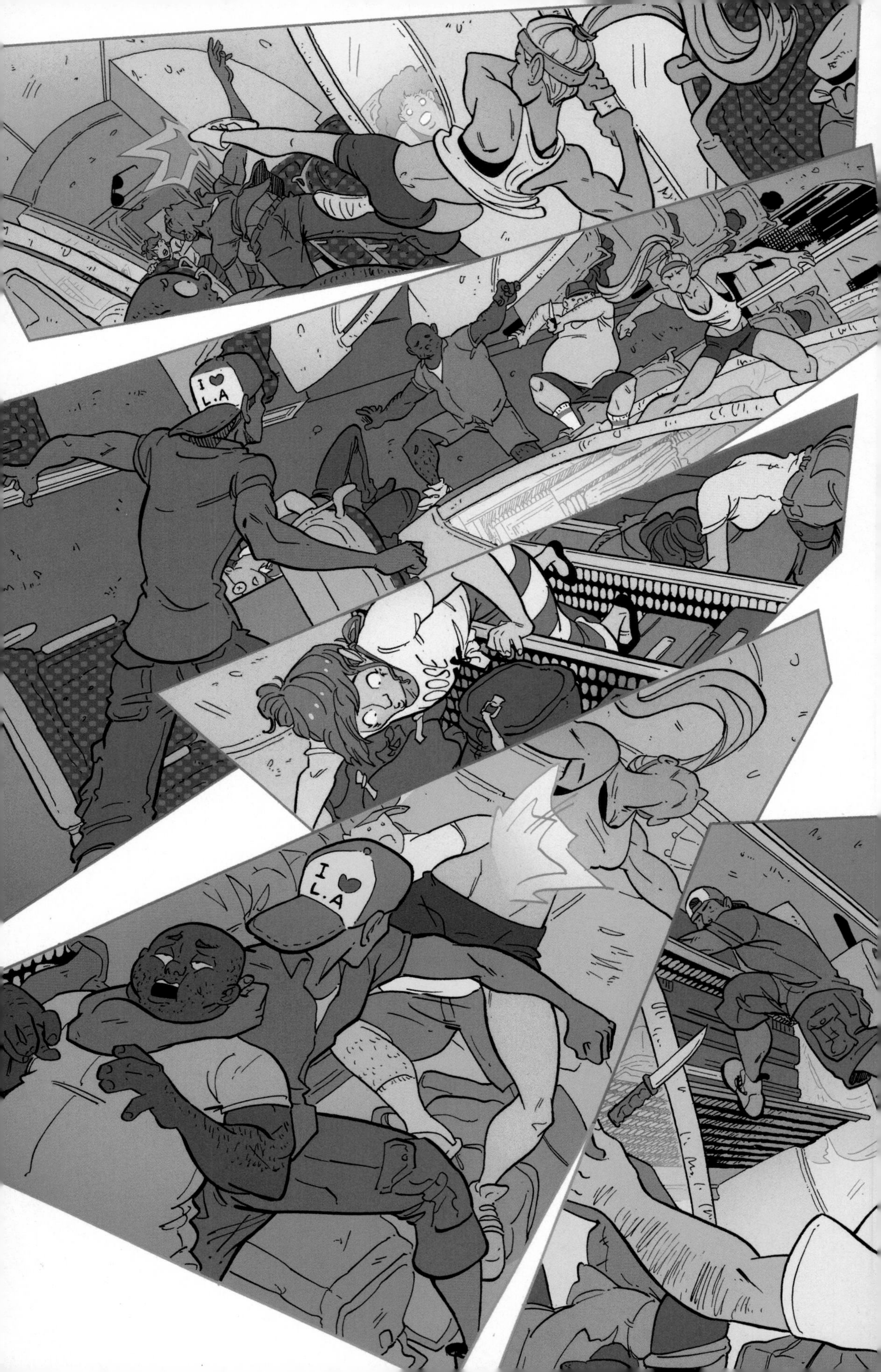
I ♥ L.A
I ♥ L.A

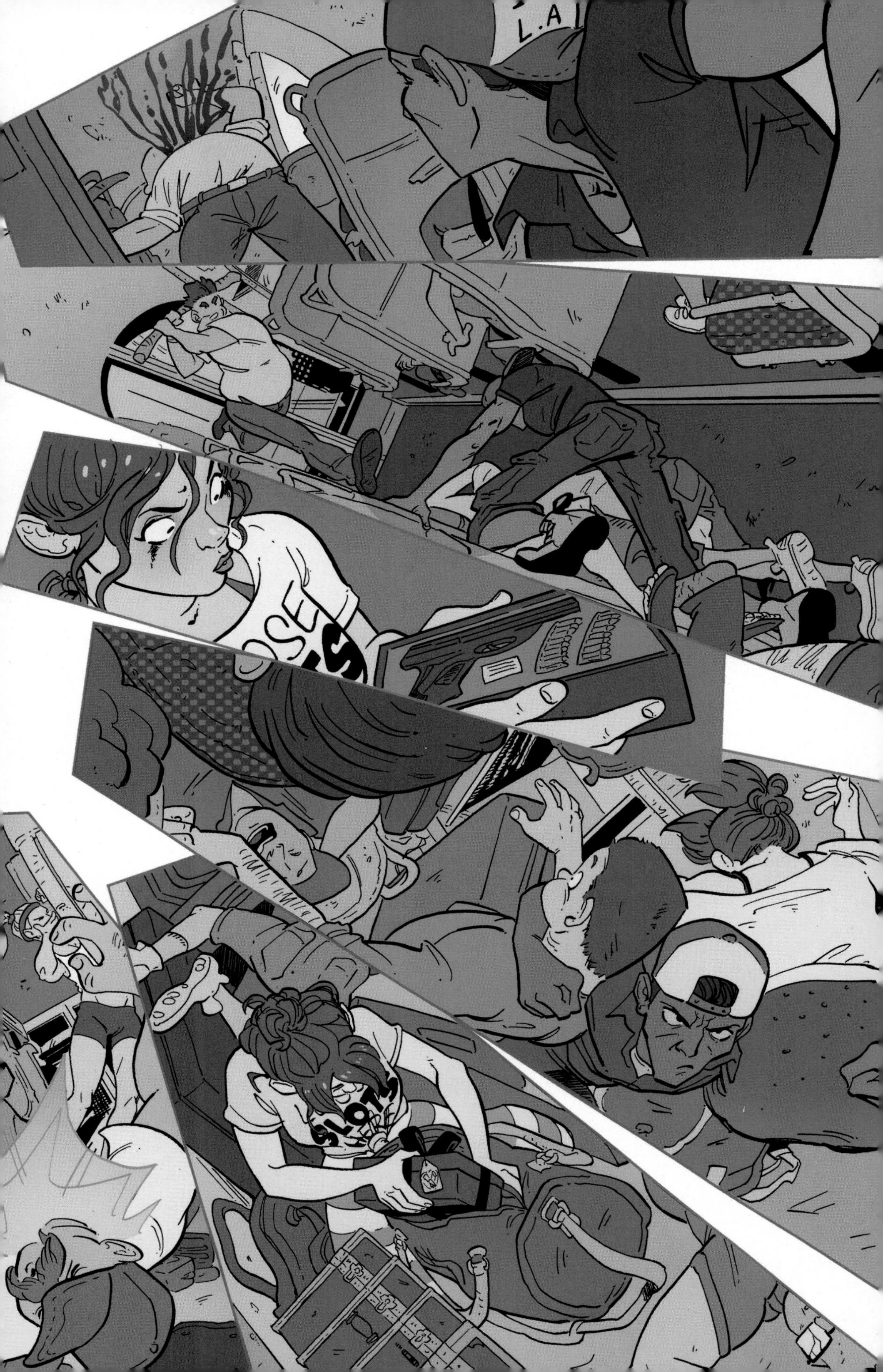
L.A
SLOTS

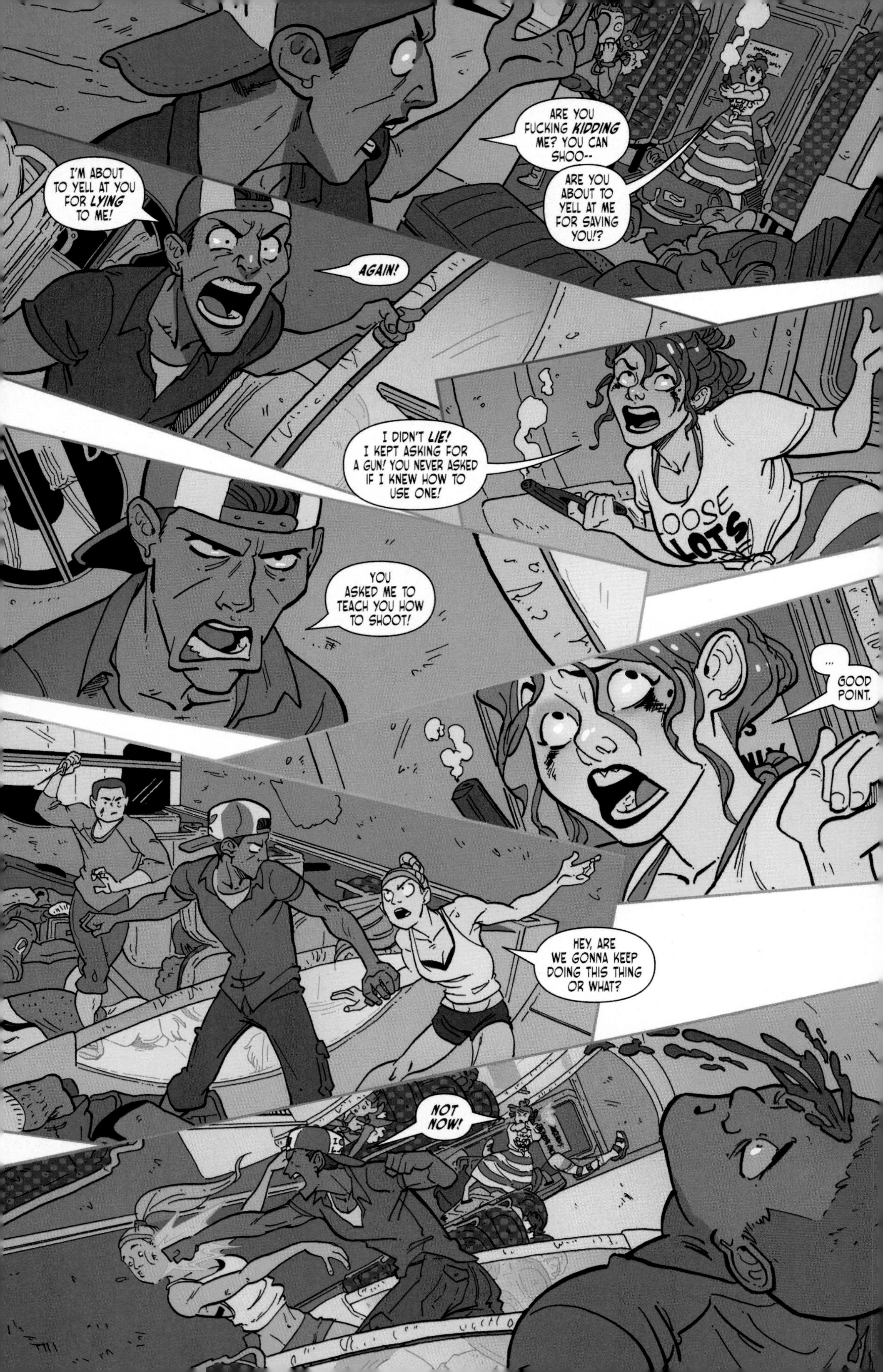
ARE YOU FUCKING KIDDING ME? YOU CAN SHOO--
ARE YOU ABOUT TO YELL AT ME FOR SAVING YOU!?
I'M ABOUT TO YELL AT YOU FOR LYING TO ME!
AGAIN!
I DIDN'T LIE! I KEPT ASKING FOR A GUN! YOU NEVER ASKED IF I KNEW HOW TO USE ONE!
YOU ASKED ME TO TEACH YOU HOW TO SHOOT!
... GOOD POINT.
HEY, ARE WE GONNA KEEP DOING THIS THING OR WHAT?
NOT NOW!

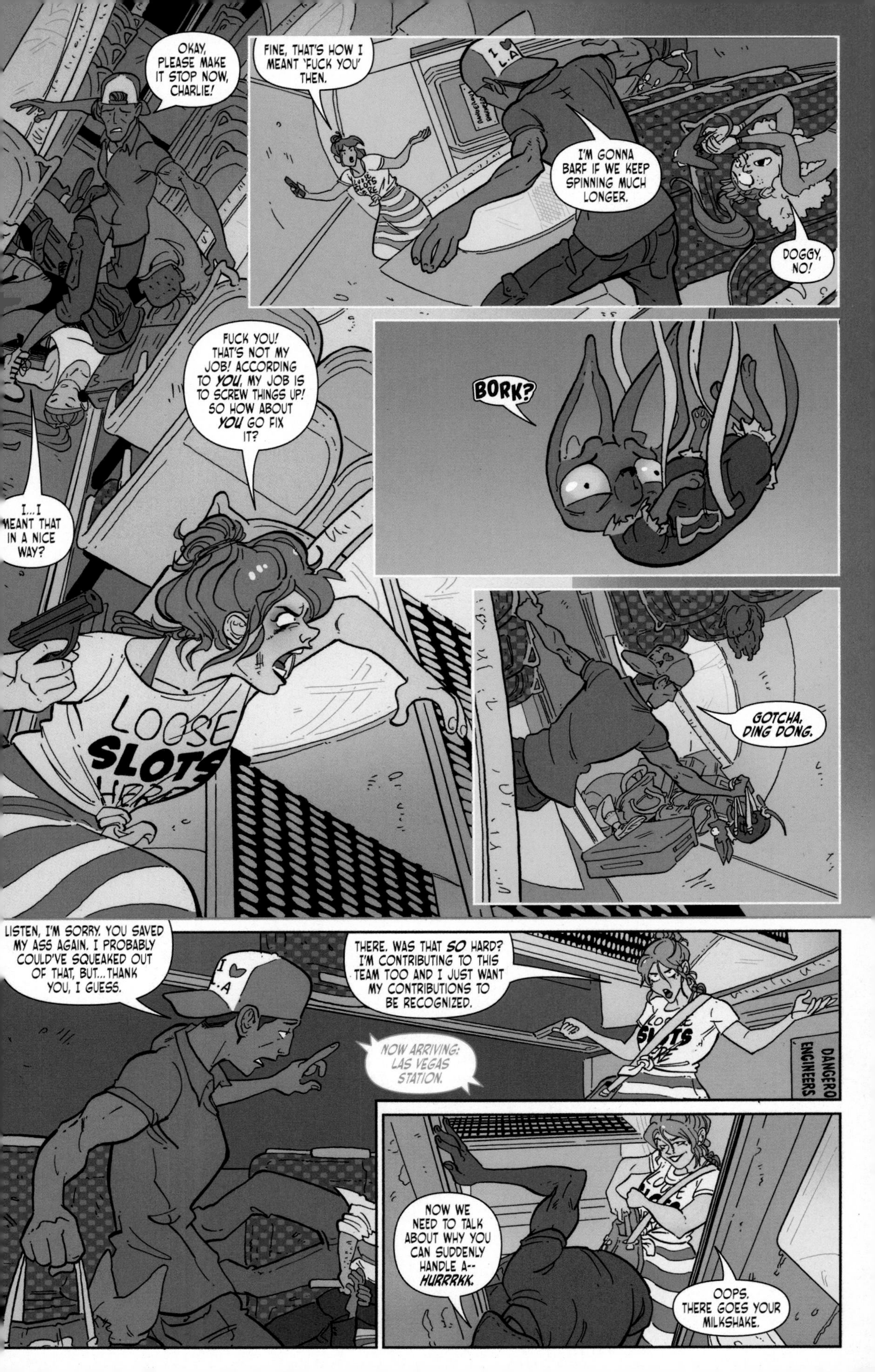
OKAY, PLEASE MAKE IT STOP NOW, CHARLIE!
FINE, THAT'S HOW I MEANT 'FUCK YOU' THEN.
I'M GONNA BARF IF WE KEEP SPINNING MUCH LONGER.
DOGGY, NO!
FUCK YOU! THAT'S NOT MY JOB! ACCORDING TO YOU, MY JOB IS TO SCREW THINGS UP! SO HOW ABOUT YOU GO FIX IT?
I...I MEANT THAT IN A NICE WAY?
BORK?
GOTCHA, DING DONG.
LOOSE SLOTS
LISTEN, I'M SORRY. YOU SAVED MY ASS AGAIN. I PROBABLY COULD'VE SQUEAKED OUT OF THAT, BUT...THANK YOU, I GUESS.
THERE. WAS THAT SO HARD? I'M CONTRIBUTING TO THIS TEAM TOO AND I JUST WANT MY CONTRIBUTIONS TO BE RECOGNIZED.
NOW ARRIVING: LAS VEGAS STATION.
DANGERO ENGINEERS
NOW WE NEED TO TALK ABOUT WHY YOU CAN SUDDENLY HANDLE A-- HURRRKK.
OOPS. THERE GOES YOUR MILKSHAKE.

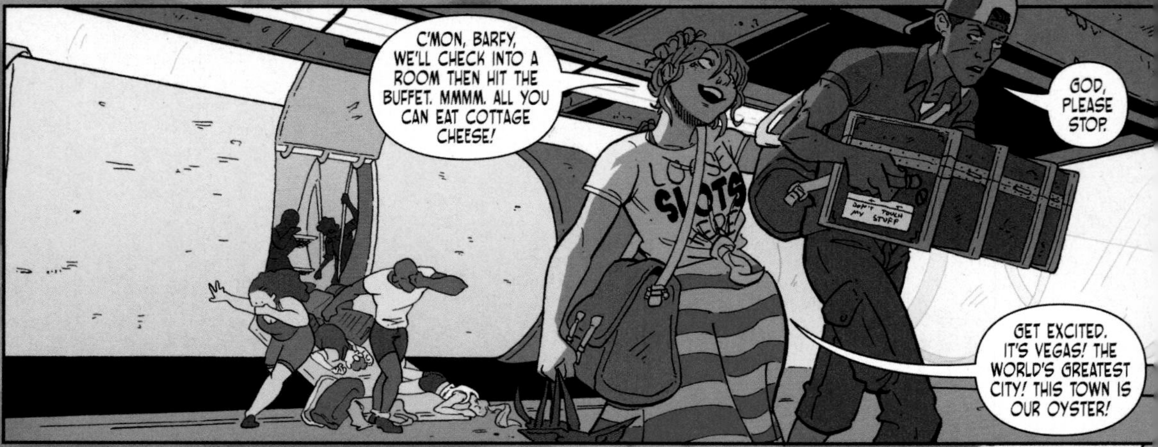
C'MON, BARFY, WE'LL CHECK INTO A ROOM THEN HIT THE BUFFET. MMMM. ALL YOU CAN EAT COTTAGE CHEESE!
GOD, PLEASE STOP.
GET EXCITED. IT'S VEGAS! THE WORLD'S GREATEST CITY! THIS TOWN IS OUR OYSTER!

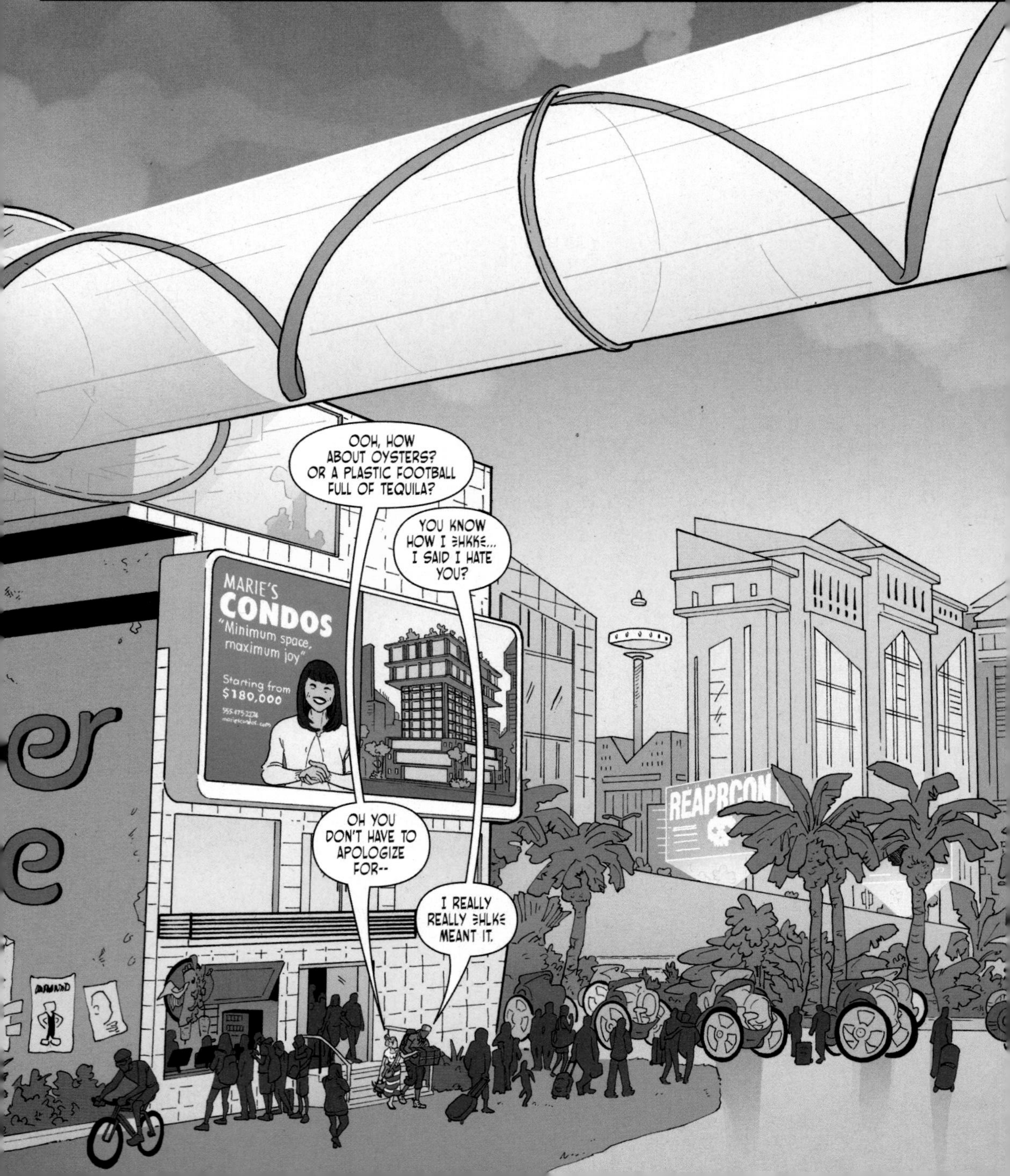
OOH, HOW ABOUT OYSTERS? OR A PLASTIC FOOTBALL FULL OF TEQUILA?
YOU KNOW HOW I ƎHKKƎ... I SAID I HATE YOU?
MARIE'S CONDOS
"Minimum space, maximum joy"
Starting from $180,000
OH YOU DON'T HAVE TO APOLOGIZE FOR--
I REALLY REALLY ƎHLKƎ MEANT IT.
REAPRCON

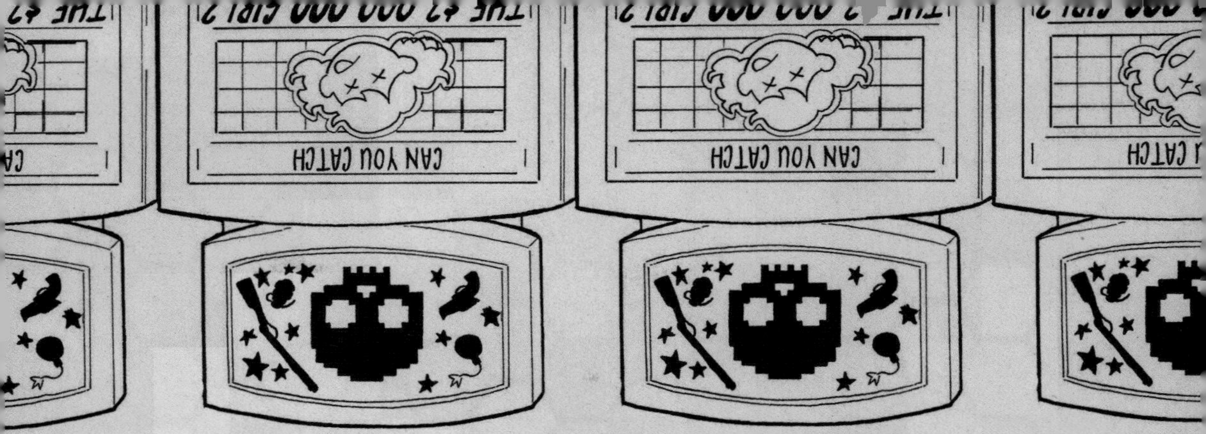

CHAPTER EIGHT
JUMP INTO THE FIRE

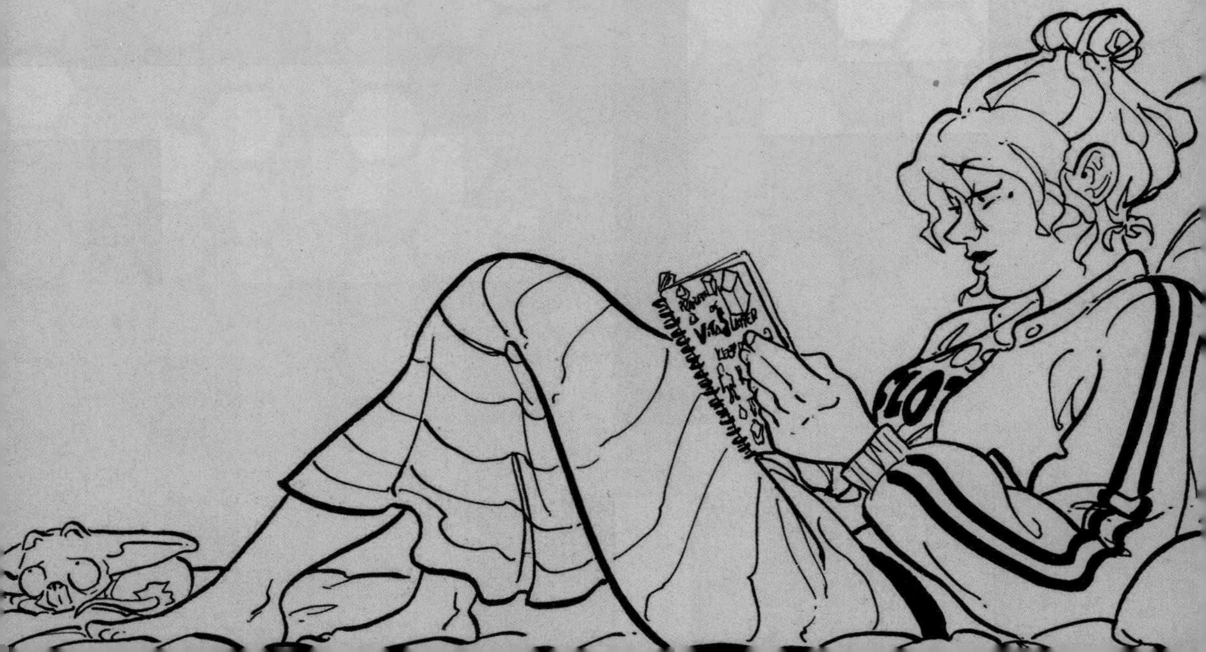

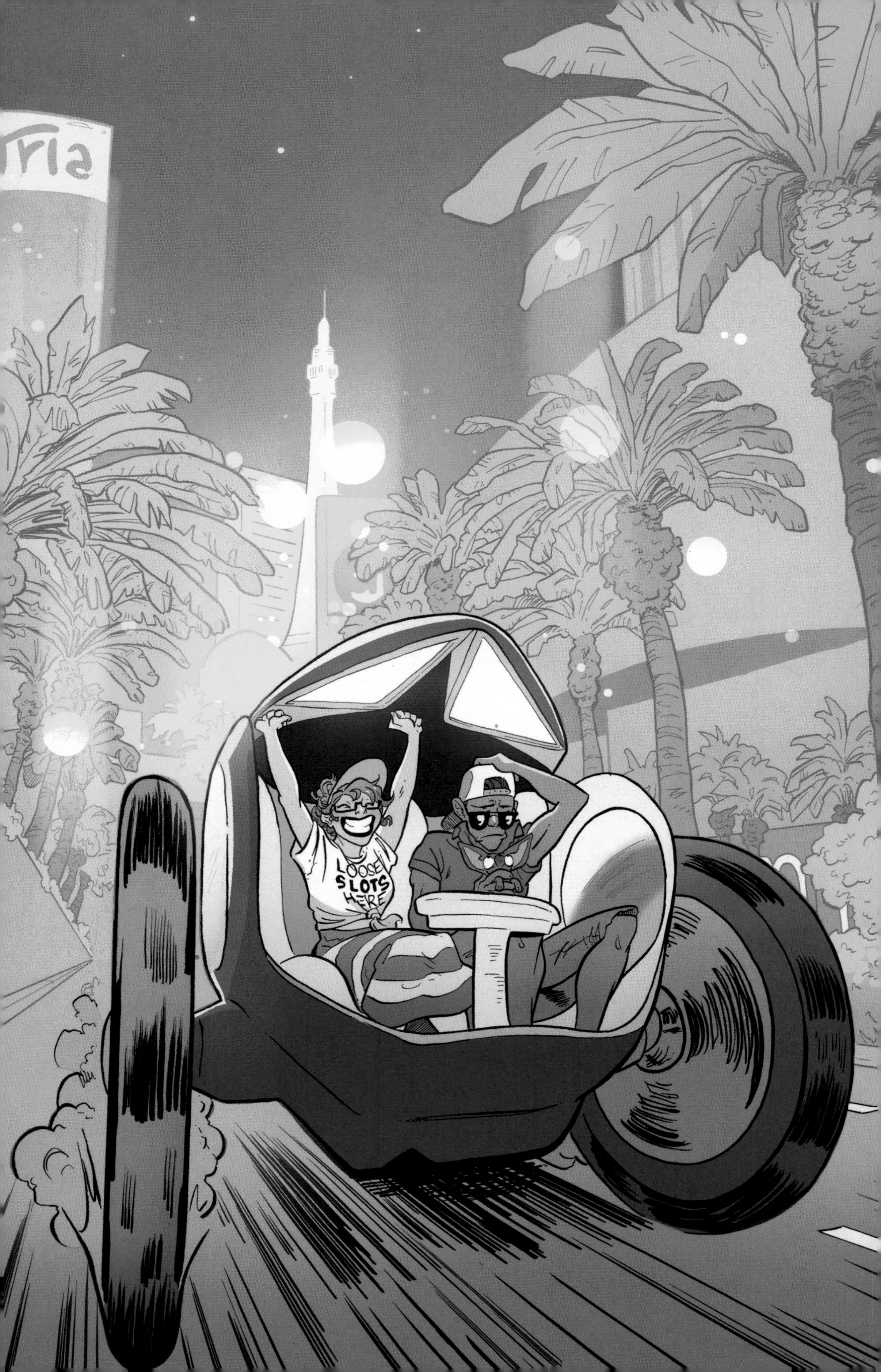
LOOSE
SLOTS
HERE

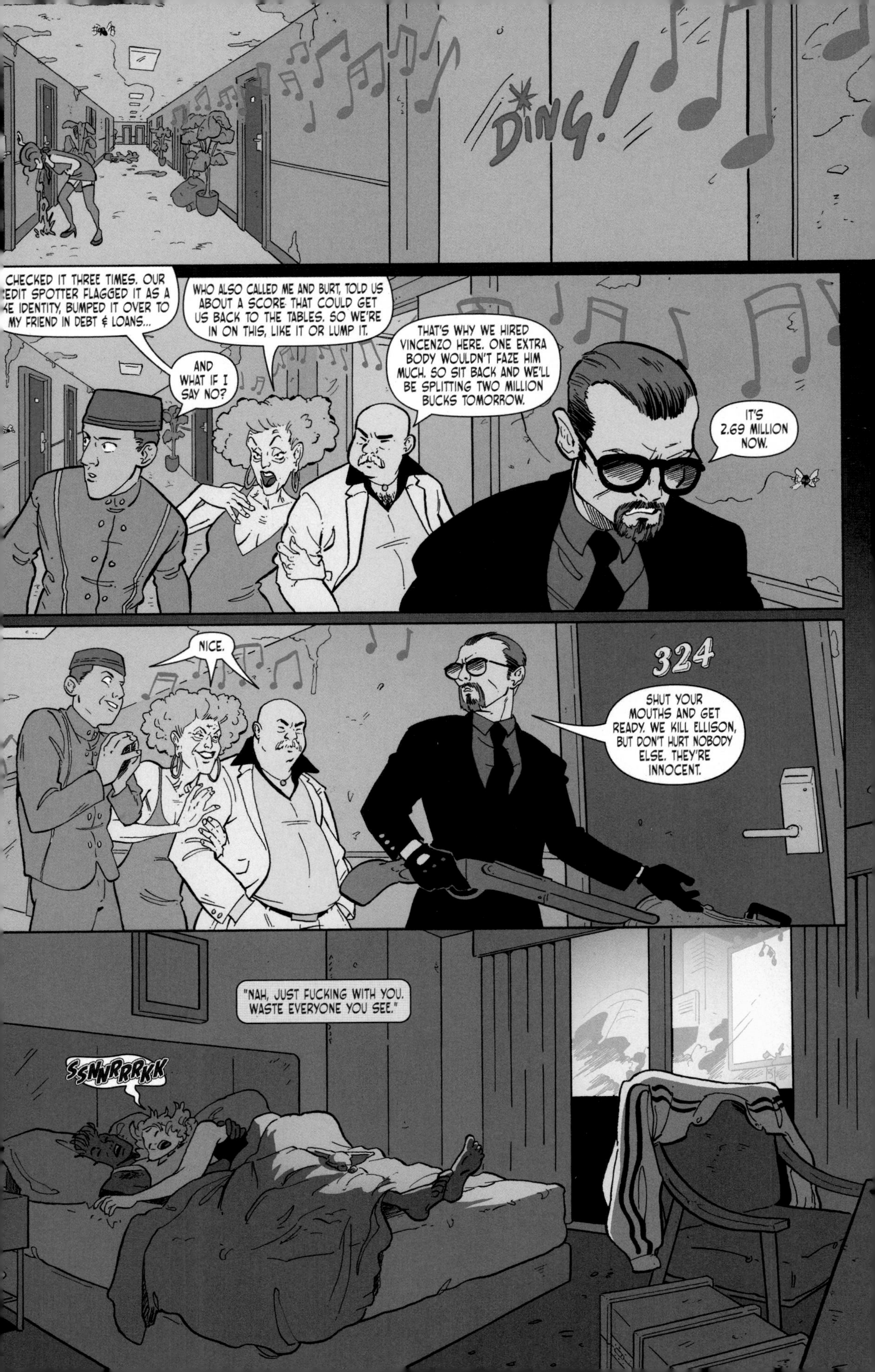
DING!
CHECKED IT THREE TIMES. OUR EDIT SPOTTER FLAGGED IT AS A E IDENTITY, BUMPED IT OVER TO MY FRIEND IN DEBT & LOANS...
AND WHAT IF I SAY NO?
WHO ALSO CALLED ME AND BURT, TOLD US ABOUT A SCORE THAT COULD GET US BACK TO THE TABLES. SO WE'RE IN ON THIS, LIKE IT OR LUMP IT.
THAT'S WHY WE HIRED VINCENZO HERE. ONE EXTRA BODY WOULDN'T FAZE HIM MUCH. SO SIT BACK AND WE'LL BE SPLITTING TWO MILLION BUCKS TOMORROW.
IT'S 2.69 MILLION NOW.
NICE.
324
SHUT YOUR MOUTHS AND GET READY. WE KILL ELLISON, BUT DON'T HURT NOBODY ELSE. THEY'RE INNOCENT.
"NAH, JUST FUCKING WITH YOU. WASTE EVERYONE YOU SEE."
SSNNRRRKK

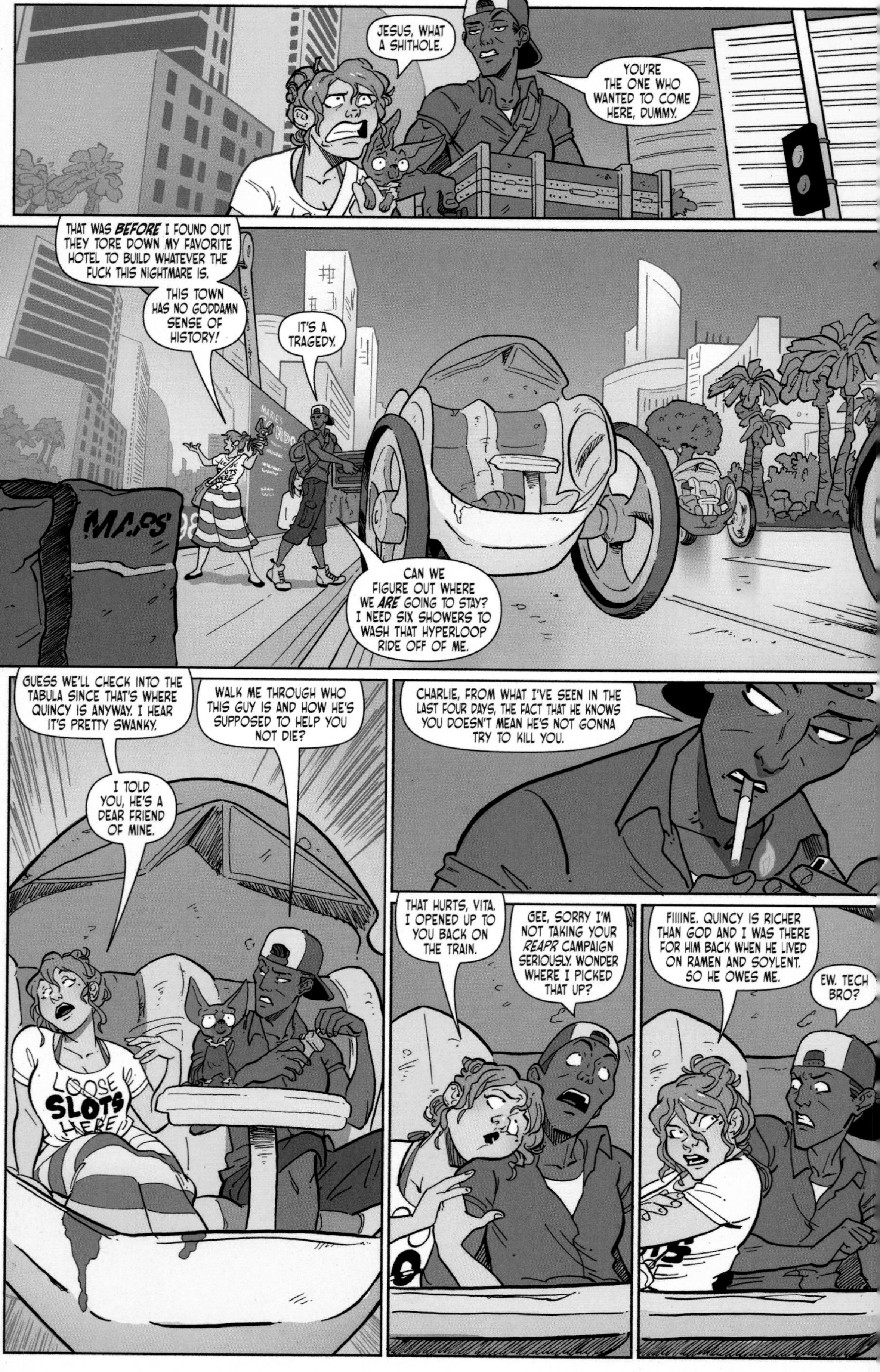
JESUS, WHAT A SHITHOLE.
YOU'RE THE ONE WHO WANTED TO COME HERE, DUMMY.
THAT WAS *BEFORE* I FOUND OUT THEY TORE DOWN MY FAVORITE HOTEL TO BUILD WHATEVER THE FUCK THIS NIGHTMARE IS.
THIS TOWN HAS NO GODDAMN SENSE OF HISTORY!
IT'S A TRAGEDY.
MARIE'S
MARS
CAN WE FIGURE OUT WHERE WE *ARE* GOING TO STAY? I NEED SIX SHOWERS TO WASH THAT HYPERLOOP RIDE OFF OF ME.
GUESS WE'LL CHECK INTO THE TABULA SINCE THAT'S WHERE QUINCY IS ANYWAY. I HEAR IT'S PRETTY SWANKY.
WALK ME THROUGH WHO THIS GUY IS AND HOW HE'S SUPPOSED TO HELP YOU NOT DIE?
I TOLD YOU, HE'S A DEAR FRIEND OF MINE.
LOOSE SLOTS HERE!
CHARLIE, FROM WHAT I'VE SEEN IN THE LAST FOUR DAYS, THE FACT THAT HE KNOWS YOU DOESN'T MEAN HE'S NOT GONNA TRY TO KILL YOU.
THAT HURTS, VITA. I OPENED UP TO YOU BACK ON THE TRAIN.
GEE, SORRY I'M NOT TAKING YOUR *REAPR* CAMPAIGN SERIOUSLY. WONDER WHERE I PICKED THAT UP?
FIIIINE. QUINCY IS RICHER THAN GOD AND I WAS THERE FOR HIM BACK WHEN HE LIVED ON RAMEN AND SOYLENT. SO HE OWES ME.
EW. TECH BRO?

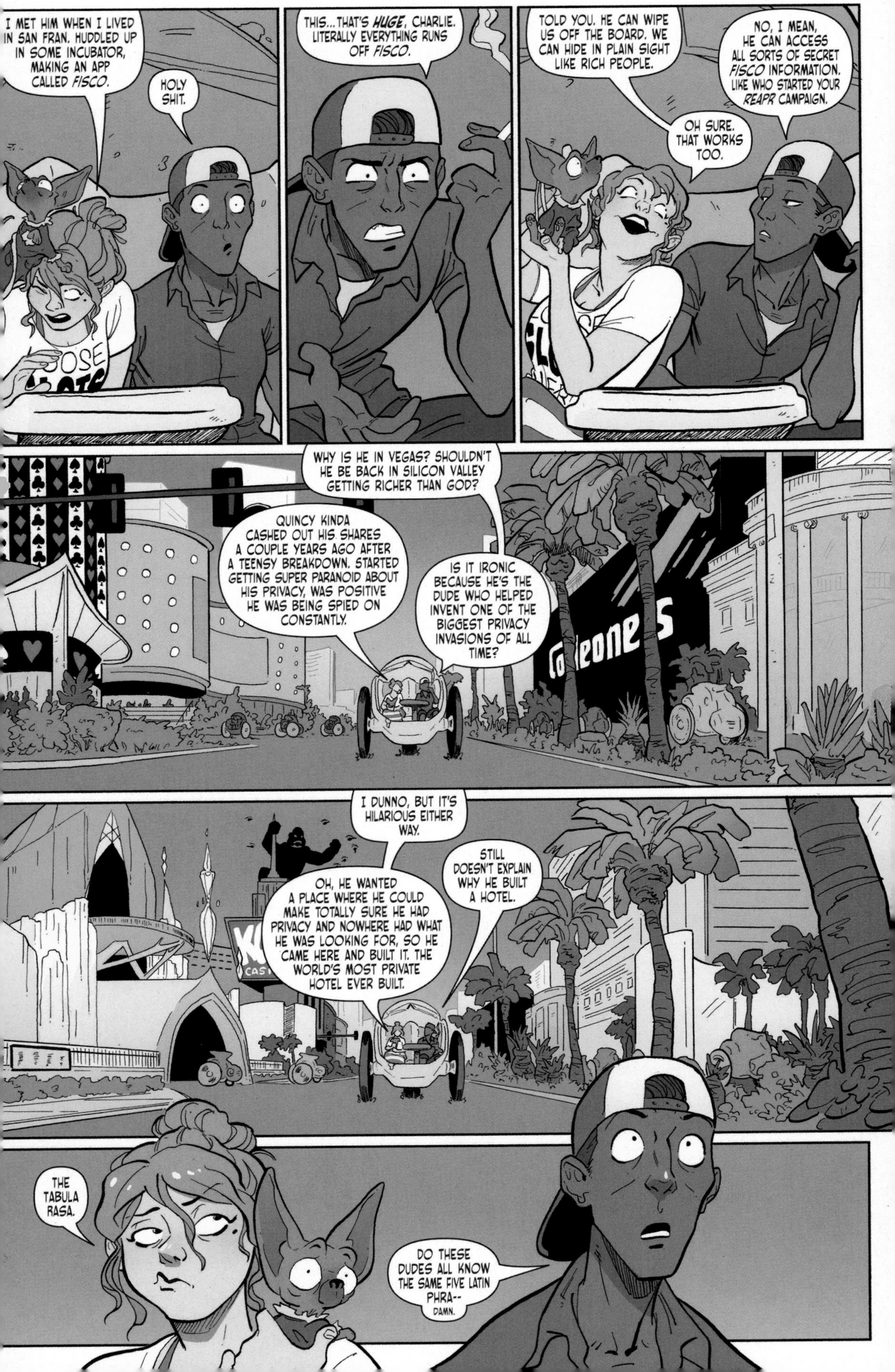
I MET HIM WHEN I LIVED IN SAN FRAN. HUDDLED UP IN SOME INCUBATOR, MAKING AN APP CALLED *FISCO*.
HOLY SHIT.
THIS...THAT'S ***HUGE***, CHARLIE. LITERALLY EVERYTHING RUNS OFF *FISCO*.
TOLD YOU. HE CAN WIPE US OFF THE BOARD. WE CAN HIDE IN PLAIN SIGHT LIKE RICH PEOPLE.
NO, I MEAN, HE CAN ACCESS ALL SORTS OF SECRET *FISCO* INFORMATION. LIKE WHO STARTED YOUR *REAPR* CAMPAIGN.
OH SURE. THAT WORKS TOO.
WHY IS HE IN VEGAS? SHOULDN'T HE BE BACK IN SILICON VALLEY GETTING RICHER THAN GOD?
QUINCY KINDA CASHED OUT HIS SHARES A COUPLE YEARS AGO AFTER A TEENSY BREAKDOWN. STARTED GETTING SUPER PARANOID ABOUT HIS PRIVACY, WAS POSITIVE HE WAS BEING SPIED ON CONSTANTLY.
IS IT IRONIC BECAUSE HE'S THE DUDE WHO HELPED INVENT ONE OF THE BIGGEST PRIVACY INVASIONS OF ALL TIME?
I DUNNO, BUT IT'S HILARIOUS EITHER WAY.
STILL DOESN'T EXPLAIN WHY HE BUILT A HOTEL.
OH, HE WANTED A PLACE WHERE HE COULD MAKE TOTALLY SURE HE HAD PRIVACY AND NOWHERE HAD WHAT HE WAS LOOKING FOR, SO HE CAME HERE AND BUILT IT. THE WORLD'S MOST PRIVATE HOTEL EVER BUILT.
THE TABULA RASA.
DO THESE DUDES ALL KNOW THE SAME FIVE LATIN PHRA--
DAMN.

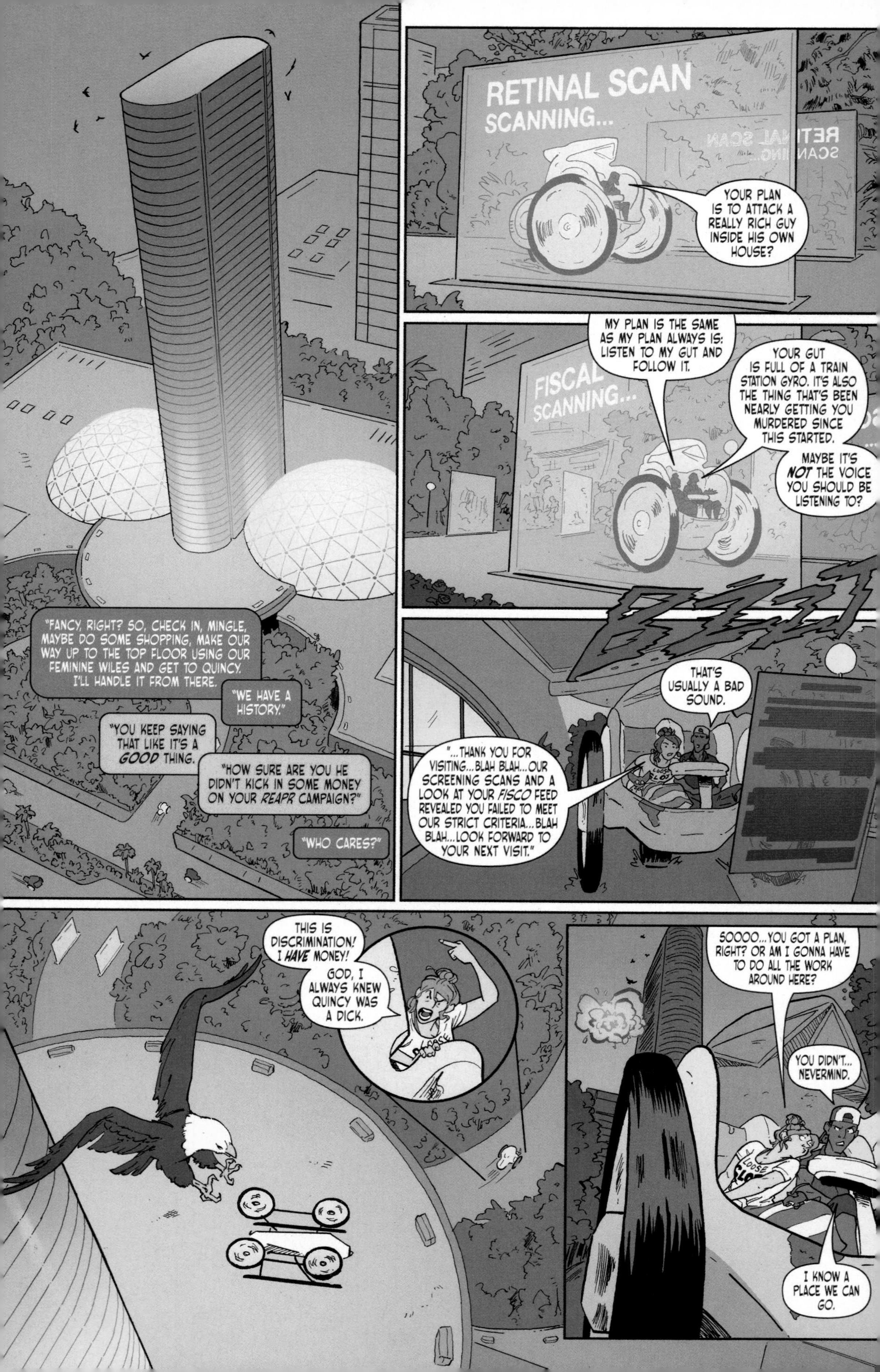
"FANCY, RIGHT? SO, CHECK IN, MINGLE, MAYBE DO SOME SHOPPING, MAKE OUR WAY UP TO THE TOP FLOOR USING OUR FEMININE WILES AND GET TO QUINCY. I'LL HANDLE IT FROM THERE.
"WE HAVE A HISTORY."
"YOU KEEP SAYING THAT LIKE IT'S A *GOOD* THING.
"HOW SURE ARE YOU HE DIDN'T KICK IN SOME MONEY ON YOUR *REAPR* CAMPAIGN?"
"WHO CARES?"
RETINAL SCAN
SCANNING...
YOUR PLAN IS TO ATTACK A REALLY RICH GUY INSIDE HIS OWN HOUSE?
FISCAL
SCANNING...
MY PLAN IS THE SAME AS MY PLAN ALWAYS IS: LISTEN TO MY GUT AND FOLLOW IT.
YOUR GUT IS FULL OF A TRAIN STATION GYRO. IT'S ALSO THE THING THAT'S BEEN NEARLY GETTING YOU MURDERED SINCE THIS STARTED.
MAYBE IT'S *NOT* THE VOICE YOU SHOULD BE LISTENING TO?
BZZZT
THAT'S USUALLY A BAD SOUND.
"...THANK YOU FOR VISITING...BLAH BLAH...OUR SCREENING SCANS AND A LOOK AT YOUR *FISCO* FEED REVEALED YOU FAILED TO MEET OUR STRICT CRITERIA...BLAH BLAH...LOOK FORWARD TO YOUR NEXT VISIT."
THIS IS DISCRIMINATION! I *HAVE* MONEY!
GOD, I ALWAYS KNEW QUINCY WAS A DICK.
SOOOO...YOU GOT A PLAN, RIGHT? OR AM I GONNA HAVE TO DO ALL THE WORK AROUND HERE?
YOU DIDN'T... NEVERMIND.
I KNOW A PLACE WE CAN GO.

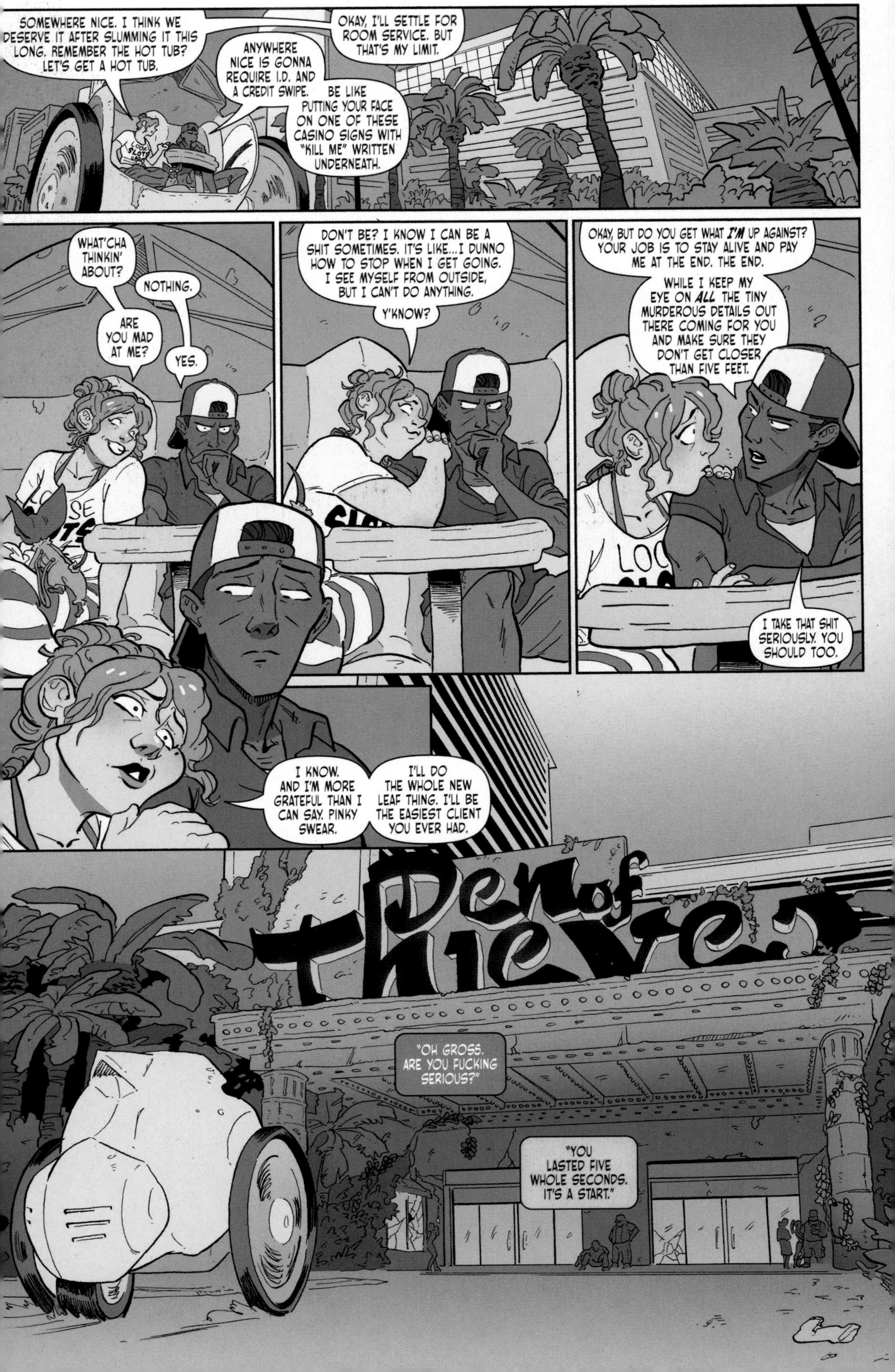
SOMEWHERE NICE. I THINK WE DESERVE IT AFTER SLUMMING IT THIS LONG. REMEMBER THE HOT TUB? LET'S GET A HOT TUB.
ANYWHERE NICE IS GONNA REQUIRE I.D. AND A CREDIT SWIPE.
OKAY, I'LL SETTLE FOR ROOM SERVICE. BUT THAT'S MY LIMIT.
BE LIKE PUTTING YOUR FACE ON ONE OF THESE CASINO SIGNS WITH "KILL ME" WRITTEN UNDERNEATH.
WHAT'CHA THINKIN' ABOUT?
NOTHING.
ARE YOU MAD AT ME?
YES.
DON'T BE? I KNOW I CAN BE A SHIT SOMETIMES. IT'S LIKE...I DUNNO HOW TO STOP WHEN I GET GOING. I SEE MYSELF FROM OUTSIDE, BUT I CAN'T DO ANYTHING.
Y'KNOW?
OKAY, BUT DO YOU GET WHAT I'M UP AGAINST? YOUR JOB IS TO STAY ALIVE AND PAY ME AT THE END. THE END.
WHILE I KEEP MY EYE ON ALL THE TINY MURDEROUS DETAILS OUT THERE COMING FOR YOU AND MAKE SURE THEY DON'T GET CLOSER THAN FIVE FEET.
I TAKE THAT SHIT SERIOUSLY. YOU SHOULD TOO.
I KNOW. AND I'M MORE GRATEFUL THAN I CAN SAY. PINKY SWEAR.
I'LL DO THE WHOLE NEW LEAF THING. I'LL BE THE EASIEST CLIENT YOU EVER HAD.
Den of Thieves
"OH GROSS. ARE YOU FUCKING SERIOUS?"
"YOU LASTED FIVE WHOLE SECONDS. IT'S A START."

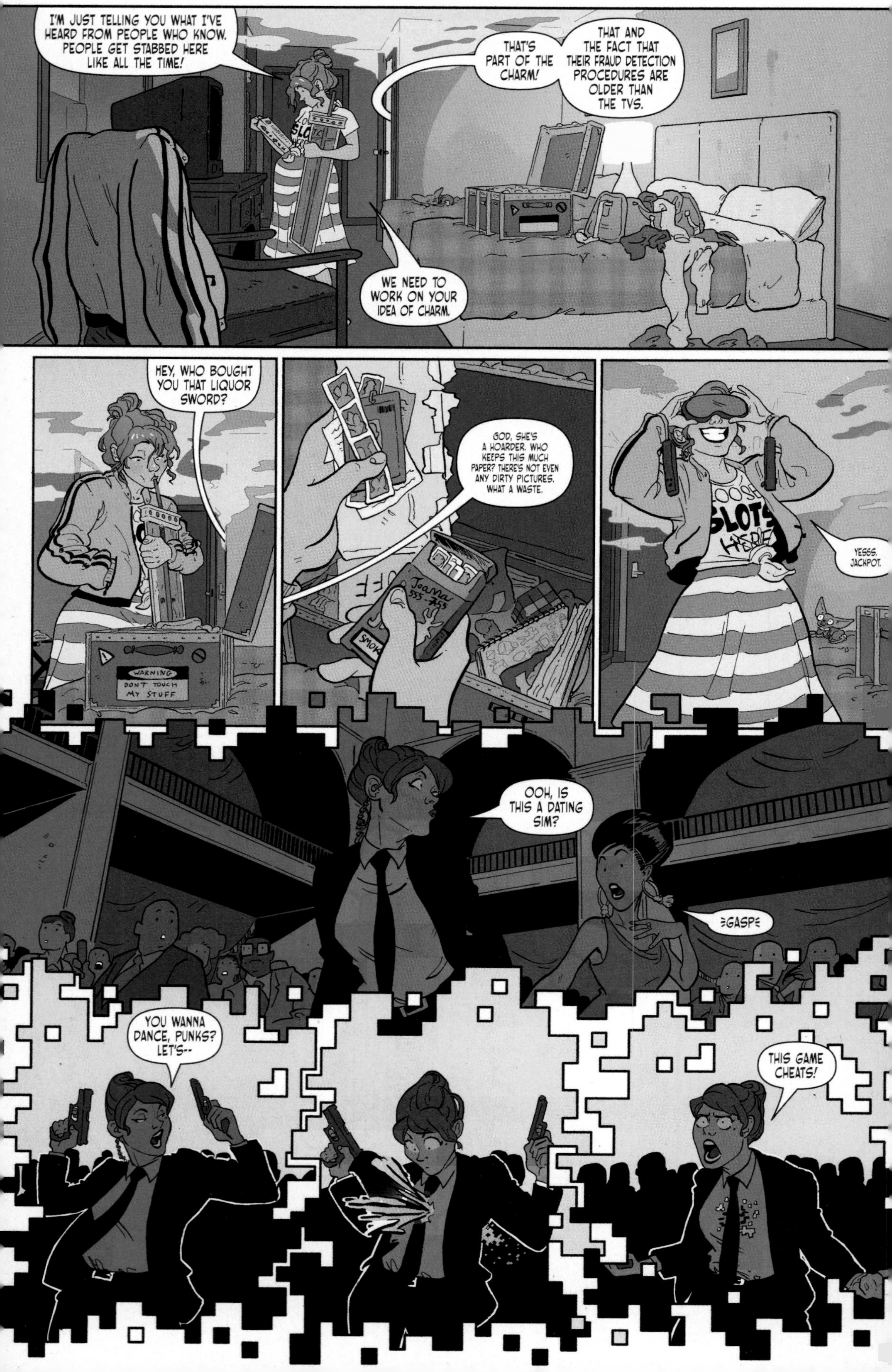

I'M JUST TELLING YOU WHAT I'VE HEARD FROM PEOPLE WHO KNOW. PEOPLE GET STABBED HERE LIKE ALL THE TIME!
THAT'S PART OF THE CHARM!
THAT AND THE FACT THAT THEIR FRAUD DETECTION PROCEDURES ARE OLDER THAN THE TVS.
WE NEED TO WORK ON YOUR IDEA OF CHARM.
HEY, WHO BOUGHT YOU THAT LIQUOR SWORD?
WARNING
DON'T TOUCH MY STUFF
GOD, SHE'S A HOARDER. WHO KEEPS THIS MUCH PAPER? THERE'S NOT EVEN ANY DIRTY PICTURES. WHAT A WASTE.
YESSS. JACKPOT.
OOH, IS THIS A DATING SIM?
GASP
YOU WANNA DANCE, PUNKS? LET'S--
THIS GAME CHEATS!

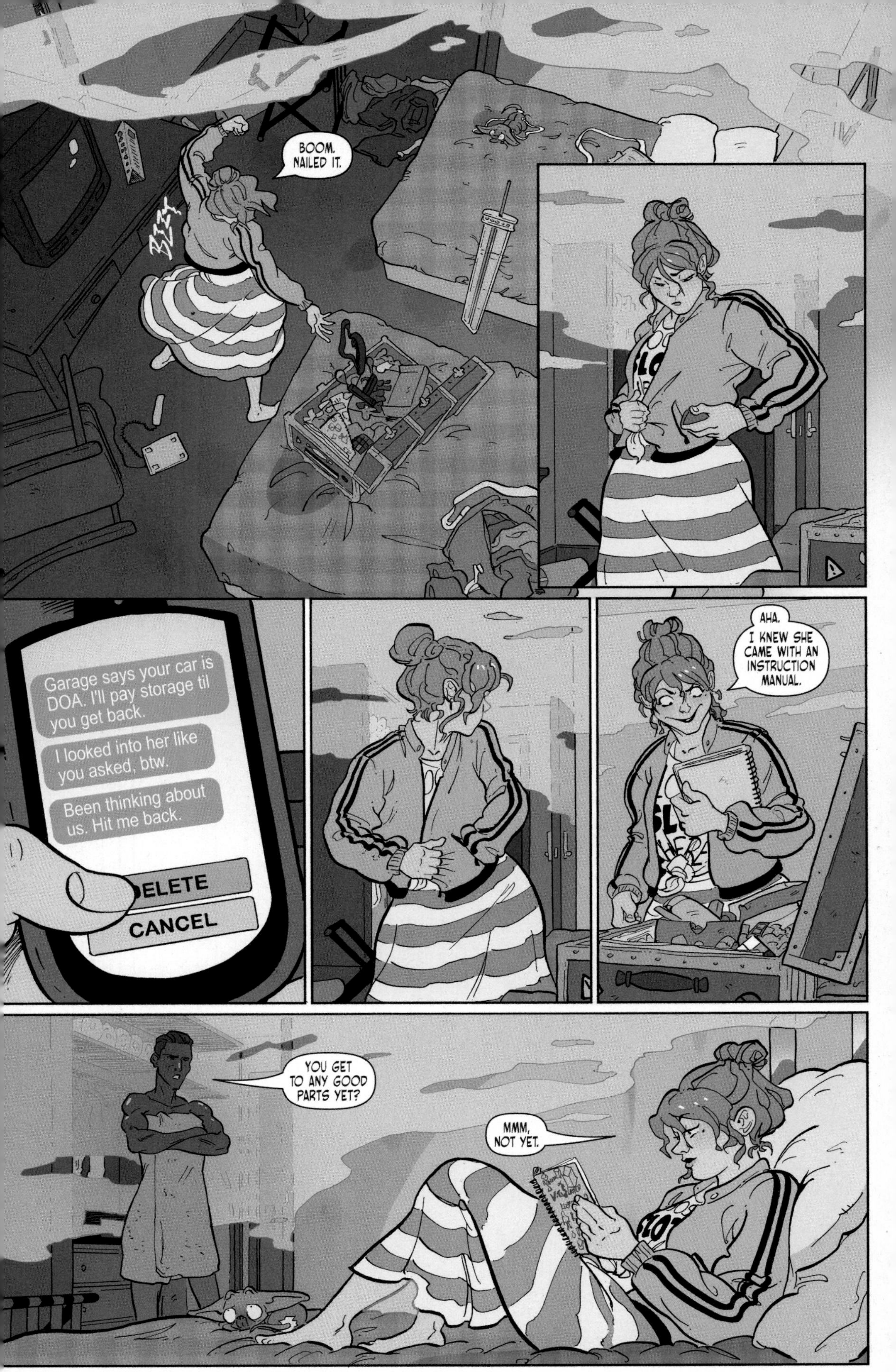
BOOM. NAILED IT.
BZZZ
Garage says your car is DOA. I'll pay storage til you get back.
I looked into her like you asked, btw.
Been thinking about us. Hit me back.
DELETE
CANCEL
AHA. I KNEW SHE CAME WITH AN INSTRUCTION MANUAL.
YOU GET TO ANY GOOD PARTS YET?
MMM, NOT YET.

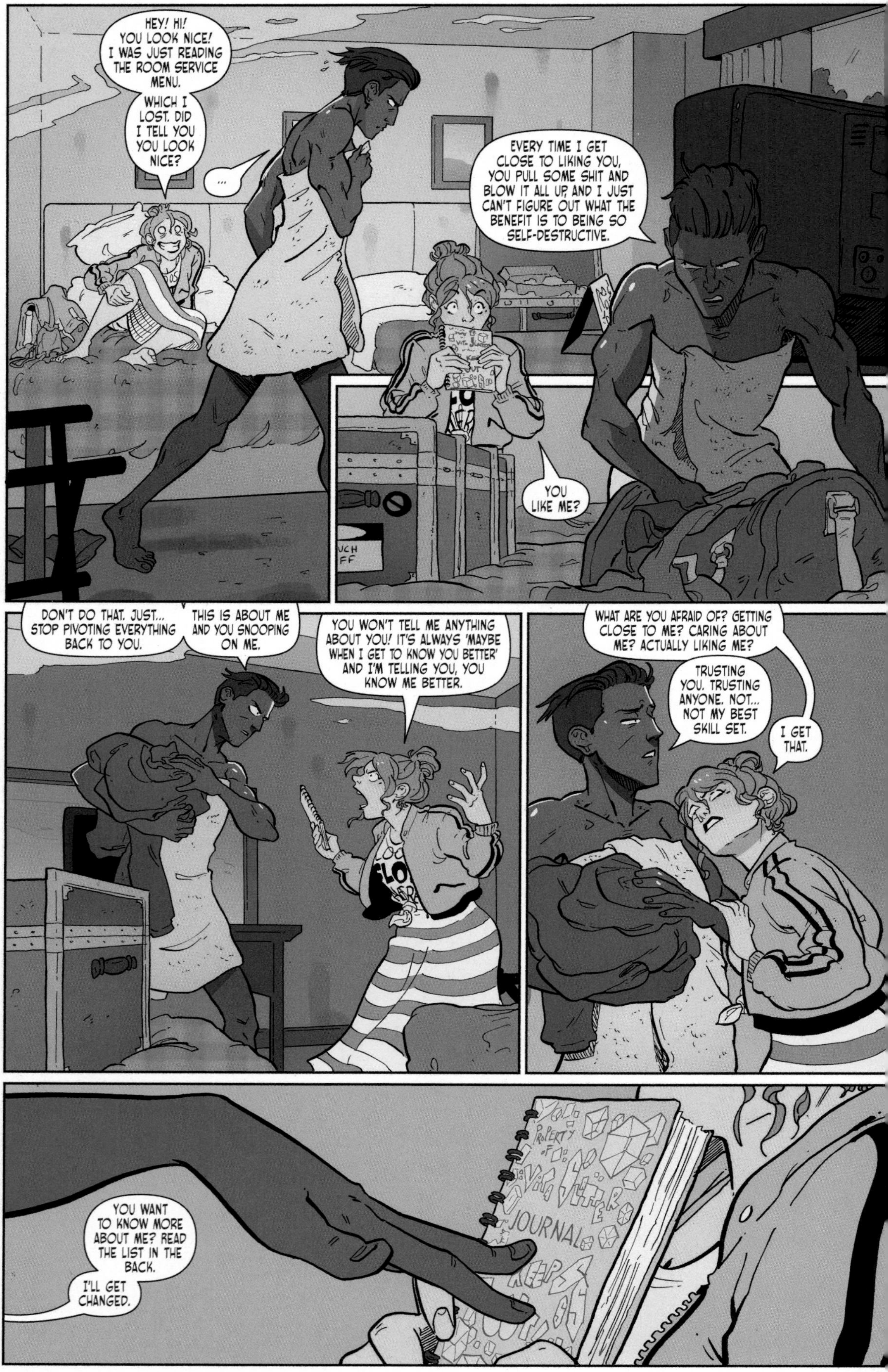
HEY! HI! YOU LOOK NICE! I WAS JUST READING THE ROOM SERVICE MENU.
WHICH I LOST. DID I TELL YOU YOU LOOK NICE?
...
EVERY TIME I GET CLOSE TO LIKING YOU, YOU PULL SOME SHIT AND BLOW IT ALL UP, AND I JUST CAN'T FIGURE OUT WHAT THE BENEFIT IS TO BEING SO SELF-DESTRUCTIVE.
YOU LIKE ME?
DON'T DO THAT. JUST... STOP PIVOTING EVERYTHING BACK TO YOU.
THIS IS ABOUT ME AND YOU SNOOPING ON ME.
YOU WON'T TELL ME ANYTHING ABOUT YOU! IT'S ALWAYS 'MAYBE WHEN I GET TO KNOW YOU BETTER' AND I'M TELLING YOU, YOU KNOW ME BETTER.
WHAT ARE YOU AFRAID OF? GETTING CLOSE TO ME? CARING ABOUT ME? ACTUALLY LIKING ME?
TRUSTING YOU. TRUSTING ANYONE. NOT... NOT MY BEST SKILL SET.
I GET THAT.
PROPERTY OF
JOURNAL
YOU WANT TO KNOW MORE ABOUT ME? READ THE LIST IN THE BACK.
I'LL GET CHANGED.

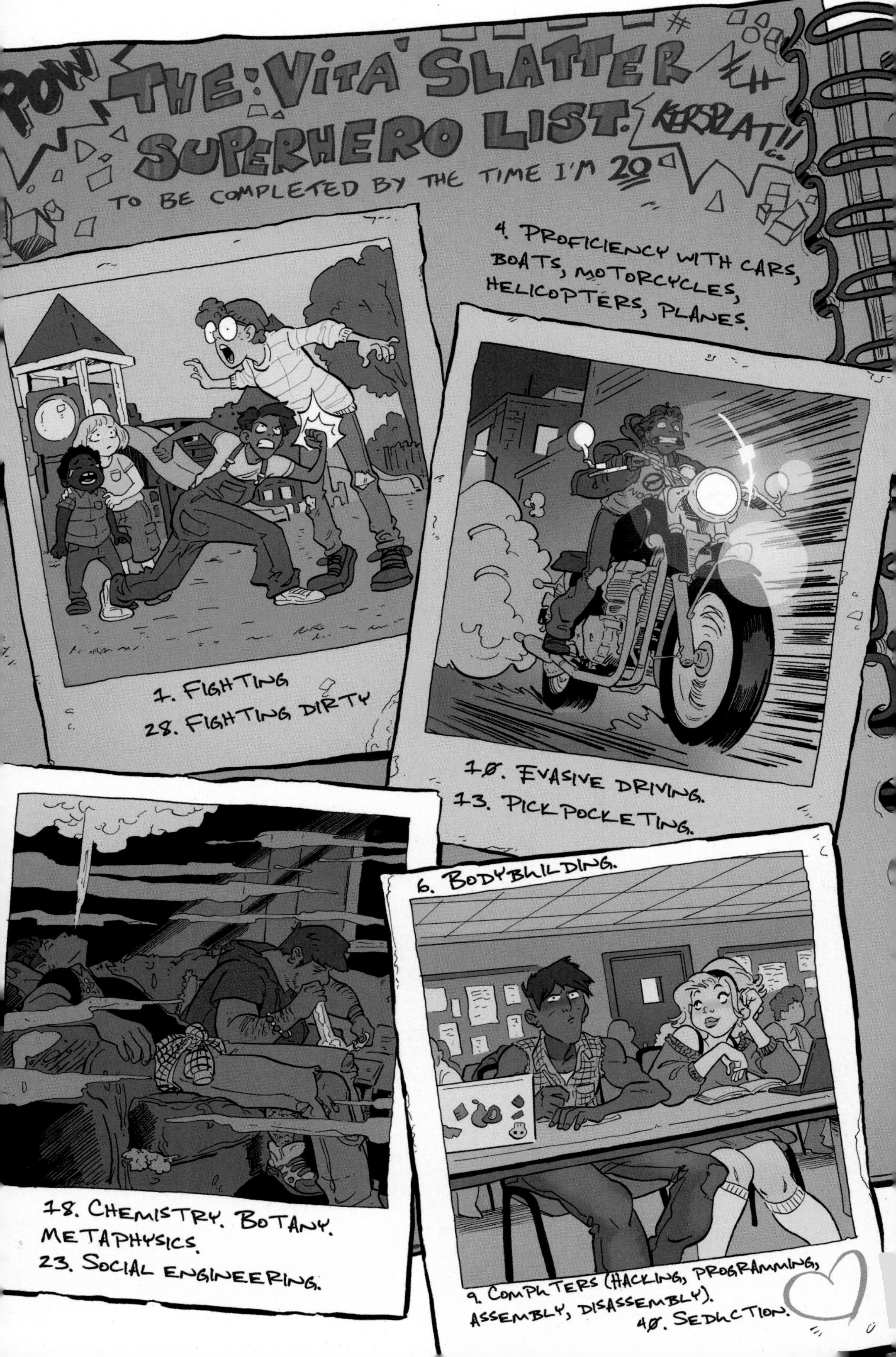
POW
THE: VITA SLATTER SUPERHERO LIST.
KERSPLAT!!
TO BE COMPLETED BY THE TIME I'M 20
4. PROFICIENCY WITH CARS, BOATS, MOTORCYCLES, HELICOPTERS, PLANES.
1. FIGHTING
28. FIGHTING DIRTY
10. EVASIVE DRIVING.
13. PICKPOCKETING.
6. BODYBUILDING.
18. CHEMISTRY. BOTANY. METAPHYSICS.
23. SOCIAL ENGINEERING.
9. COMPUTERS (HACKING, PROGRAMMING, ASSEMBLY, DISASSEMBLY).
40. SEDUCTION.

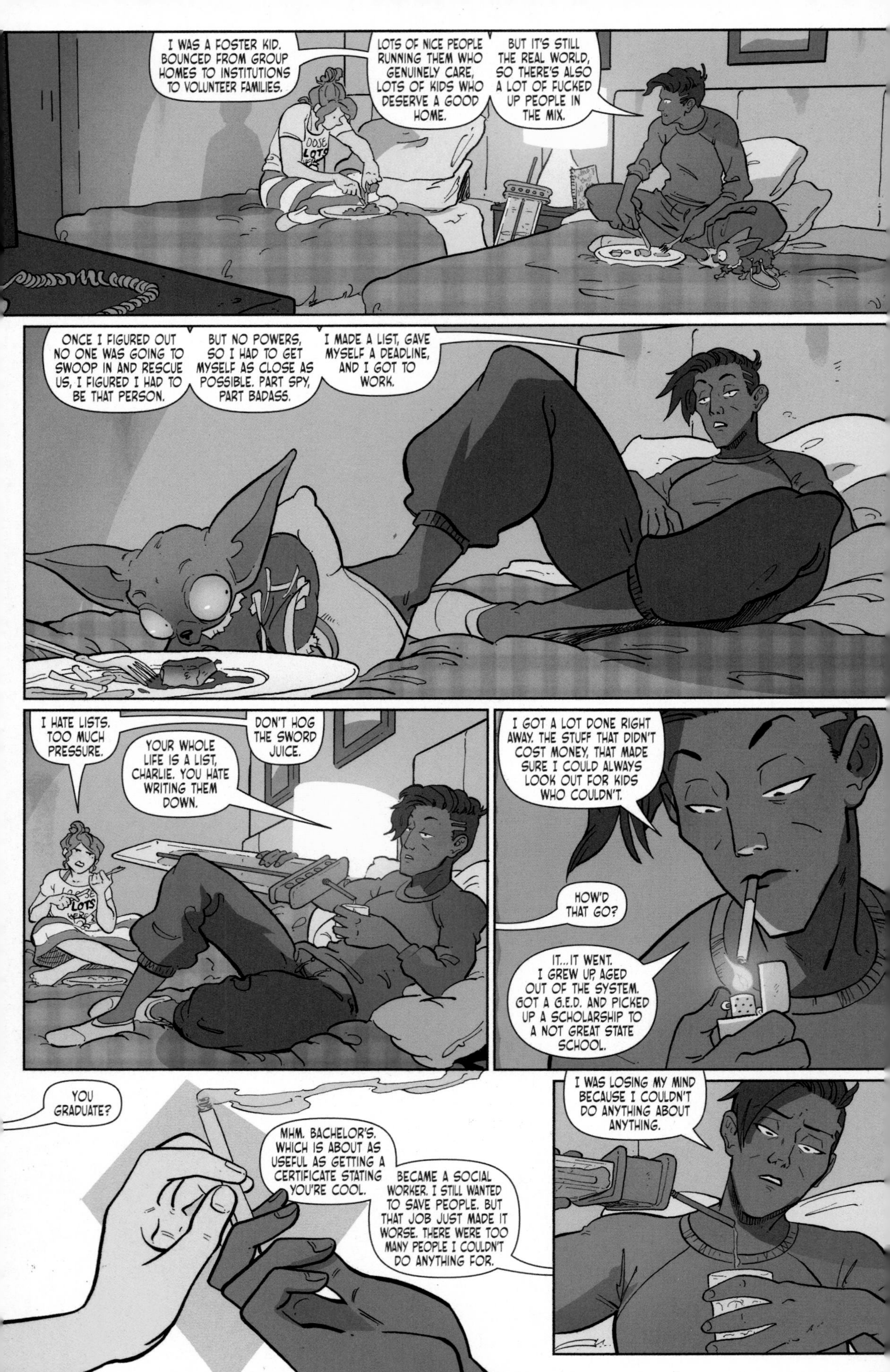
I WAS A FOSTER KID. BOUNCED FROM GROUP HOMES TO INSTITUTIONS TO VOLUNTEER FAMILIES.
LOTS OF NICE PEOPLE RUNNING THEM WHO GENUINELY CARE, LOTS OF KIDS WHO DESERVE A GOOD HOME.
BUT IT'S STILL THE REAL WORLD, SO THERE'S ALSO A LOT OF FUCKED UP PEOPLE IN THE MIX.
ONCE I FIGURED OUT NO ONE WAS GOING TO SWOOP IN AND RESCUE US, I FIGURED I HAD TO BE THAT PERSON.
BUT NO POWERS, SO I HAD TO GET MYSELF AS CLOSE AS POSSIBLE. PART SPY, PART BADASS.
I MADE A LIST, GAVE MYSELF A DEADLINE, AND I GOT TO WORK.
I HATE LISTS. TOO MUCH PRESSURE.
DON'T HOG THE SWORD JUICE.
YOUR WHOLE LIFE IS A LIST, CHARLIE. YOU HATE WRITING THEM DOWN.
I GOT A LOT DONE RIGHT AWAY. THE STUFF THAT DIDN'T COST MONEY, THAT MADE SURE I COULD ALWAYS LOOK OUT FOR KIDS WHO COULDN'T.
HOW'D THAT GO?
IT...IT WENT. I GREW UP, AGED OUT OF THE SYSTEM. GOT A G.E.D. AND PICKED UP A SCHOLARSHIP TO A NOT GREAT STATE SCHOOL.
YOU GRADUATE?
MHM. BACHELOR'S. WHICH IS ABOUT AS USEFUL AS GETTING A CERTIFICATE STATING YOU'RE COOL.
BECAME A SOCIAL WORKER. I STILL WANTED TO SAVE PEOPLE. BUT THAT JOB JUST MADE IT WORSE. THERE WERE TOO MANY PEOPLE I COULDN'T DO ANYTHING FOR.
I WAS LOSING MY MIND BECAUSE I COULDN'T DO ANYTHING ABOUT ANYTHING.

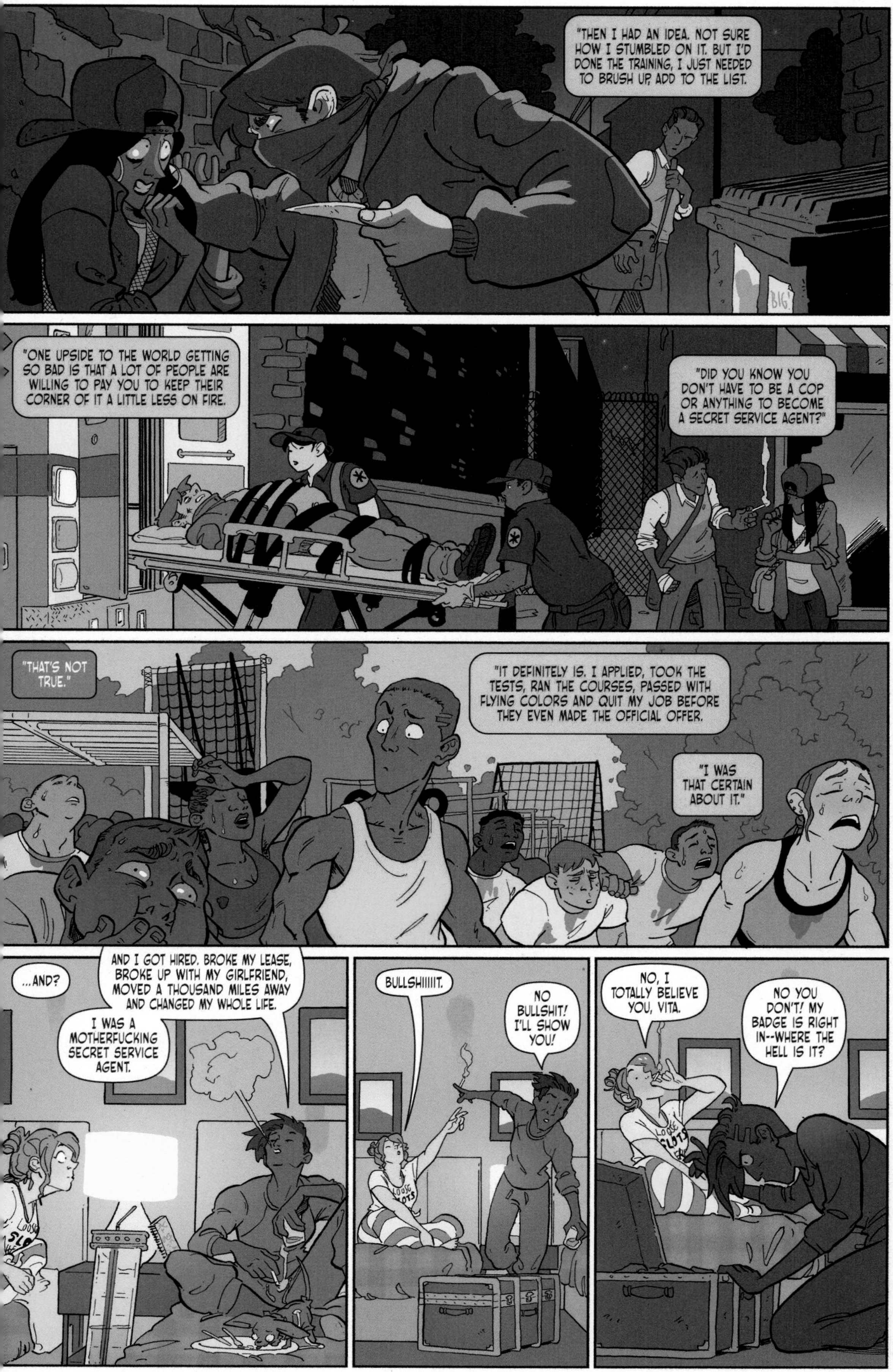
"THEN I HAD AN IDEA. NOT SURE HOW I STUMBLED ON IT. BUT I'D DONE THE TRAINING, I JUST NEEDED TO BRUSH UP, ADD TO THE LIST.
BIG
"ONE UPSIDE TO THE WORLD GETTING SO BAD IS THAT A LOT OF PEOPLE ARE WILLING TO PAY YOU TO KEEP THEIR CORNER OF IT A LITTLE LESS ON FIRE.
"DID YOU KNOW YOU DON'T HAVE TO BE A COP OR ANYTHING TO BECOME A SECRET SERVICE AGENT?"
"THAT'S NOT TRUE."
"IT DEFINITELY IS. I APPLIED, TOOK THE TESTS, RAN THE COURSES, PASSED WITH FLYING COLORS AND QUIT MY JOB BEFORE THEY EVEN MADE THE OFFICIAL OFFER.
"I WAS THAT CERTAIN ABOUT IT."
...AND?
AND I GOT HIRED. BROKE MY LEASE, BROKE UP WITH MY GIRLFRIEND, MOVED A THOUSAND MILES AWAY AND CHANGED MY WHOLE LIFE.
I WAS A MOTHERFUCKING SECRET SERVICE AGENT.
BULLSHIIIIIT.
NO BULLSHIT! I'LL SHOW YOU!
NO, I TOTALLY BELIEVE YOU, VITA.
NO YOU DON'T! MY BADGE IS RIGHT IN--WHERE THE HELL IS IT?

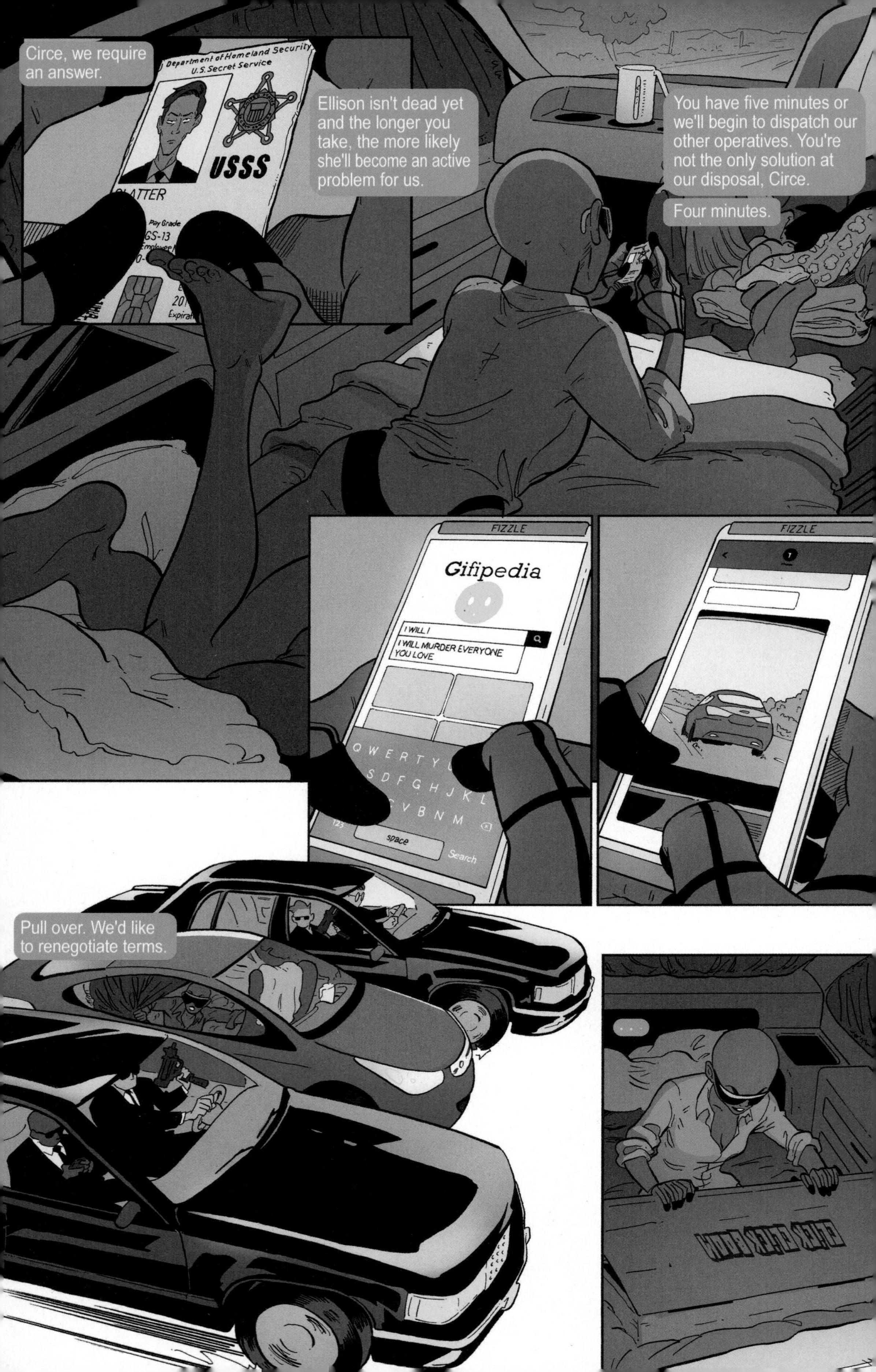
Circe, we require an answer.
Department of Homeland Security
U.S. Secret Service
USSS
Pay Grade
GS-13
Ellison isn't dead yet and the longer you take, the more likely she'll become an active problem for us.
You have five minutes or we'll begin to dispatch our other operatives. You're not the only solution at our disposal, Circe.
Four minutes.
FIZZLE
Gifipedia
I WILL I
I WILL MURDER EVERYONE YOU LOVE
space
Search
FIZZLE
Pull over. We'd like to renegotiate terms.

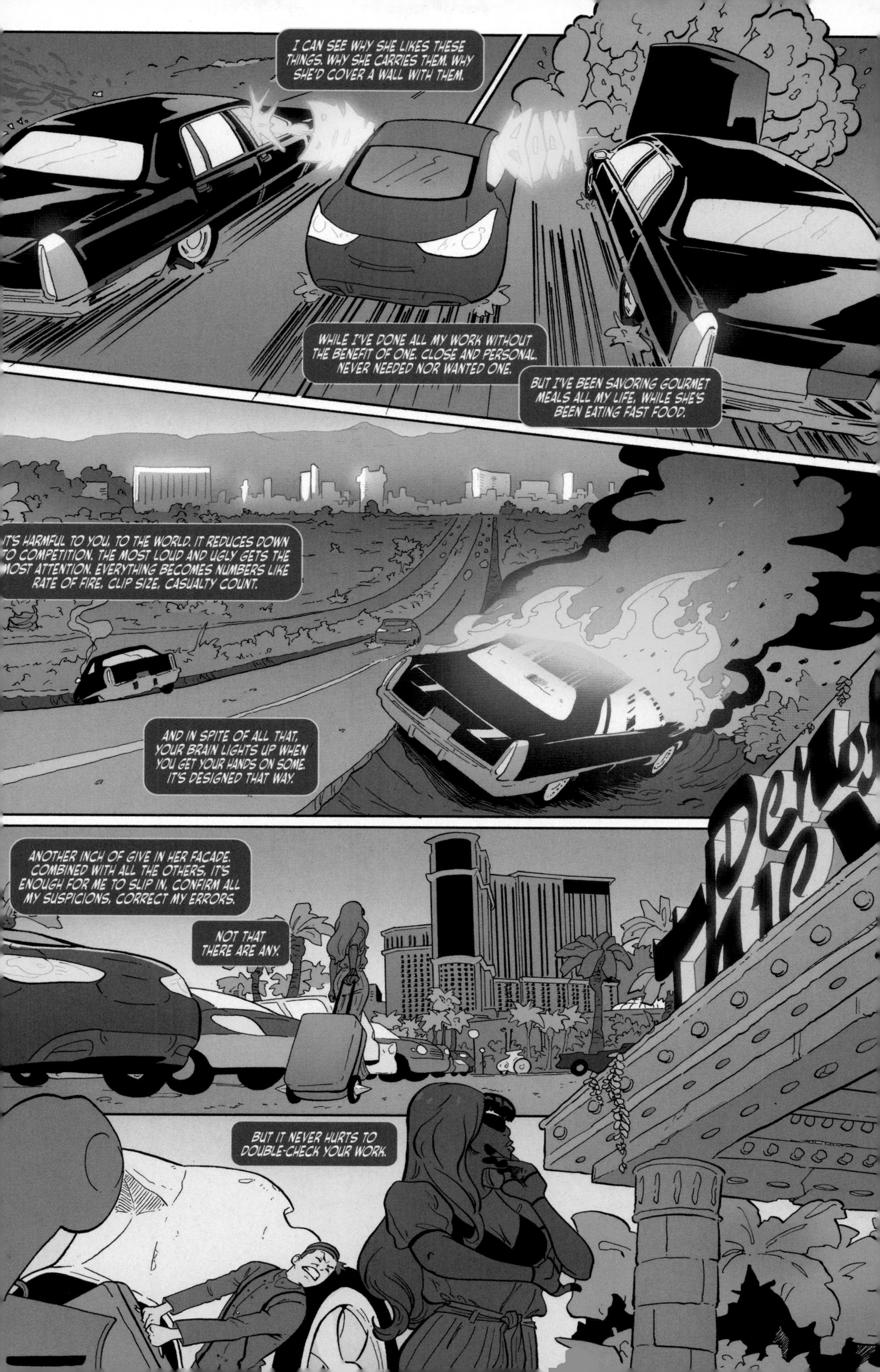

I CAN SEE WHY SHE LIKES THESE THINGS. WHY SHE CARRIES THEM. WHY SHE'D COVER A WALL WITH THEM.
BOOM
WHILE I'VE DONE ALL MY WORK WITHOUT THE BENEFIT OF ONE. CLOSE AND PERSONAL. NEVER NEEDED NOR WANTED ONE.
BUT I'VE BEEN SAVORING GOURMET MEALS ALL MY LIFE, WHILE SHE'S BEEN EATING FAST FOOD.
IT'S HARMFUL TO YOU, TO THE WORLD. IT REDUCES DOWN TO COMPETITION. THE MOST LOUD AND UGLY GETS THE MOST ATTENTION. EVERYTHING BECOMES NUMBERS LIKE RATE OF FIRE, CLIP SIZE, CASUALTY COUNT.
AND IN SPITE OF ALL THAT, YOUR BRAIN LIGHTS UP WHEN YOU GET YOUR HANDS ON SOME. IT'S DESIGNED THAT WAY.
ANOTHER INCH OF GIVE IN HER FACADE. COMBINED WITH ALL THE OTHERS, IT'S ENOUGH FOR ME TO SLIP IN, CONFIRM ALL MY SUSPICIONS, CORRECT MY ERRORS.
NOT THAT THERE ARE ANY.
BUT IT NEVER HURTS TO DOUBLE-CHECK YOUR WORK.

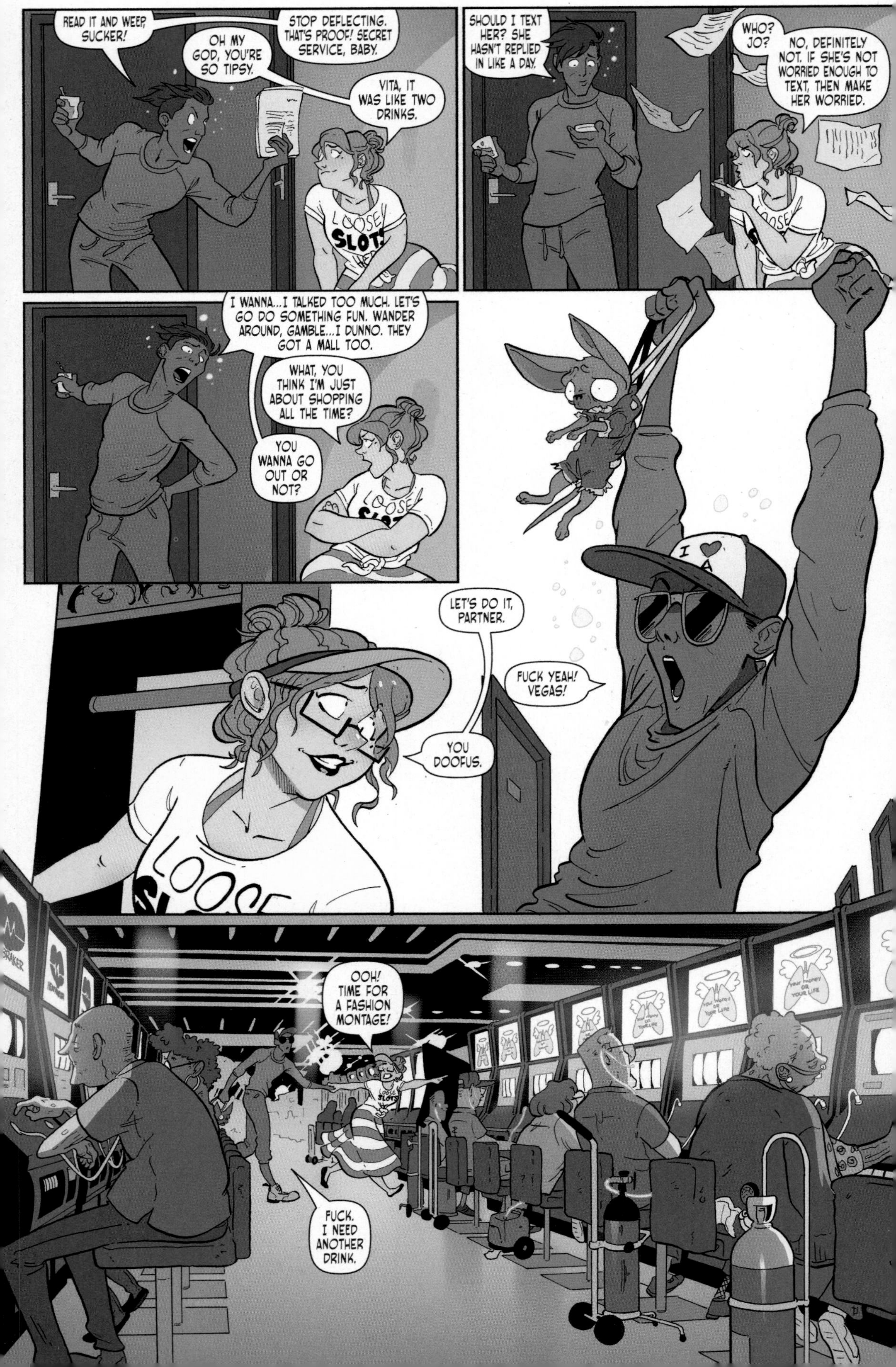
READ IT AND WEEP, SUCKER!
OH MY GOD, YOU'RE SO TIPSY.
STOP DEFLECTING. THAT'S PROOF! SECRET SERVICE, BABY.
VITA, IT WAS LIKE TWO DRINKS.
LOOSE SLOTS
SHOULD I TEXT HER? SHE HASN'T REPLIED IN LIKE A DAY.
WHO? JO?
NO, DEFINITELY NOT. IF SHE'S NOT WORRIED ENOUGH TO TEXT, THEN MAKE HER WORRIED.
I WANNA...I TALKED TOO MUCH. LET'S GO DO SOMETHING FUN. WANDER AROUND, GAMBLE...I DUNNO. THEY GOT A MALL TOO.
WHAT, YOU THINK I'M JUST ABOUT SHOPPING ALL THE TIME?
YOU WANNA GO OUT OR NOT?
LET'S DO IT, PARTNER.
FUCK YEAH! VEGAS!
YOU DOOFUS.
OOH! TIME FOR A FASHION MONTAGE!
FUCK. I NEED ANOTHER DRINK.

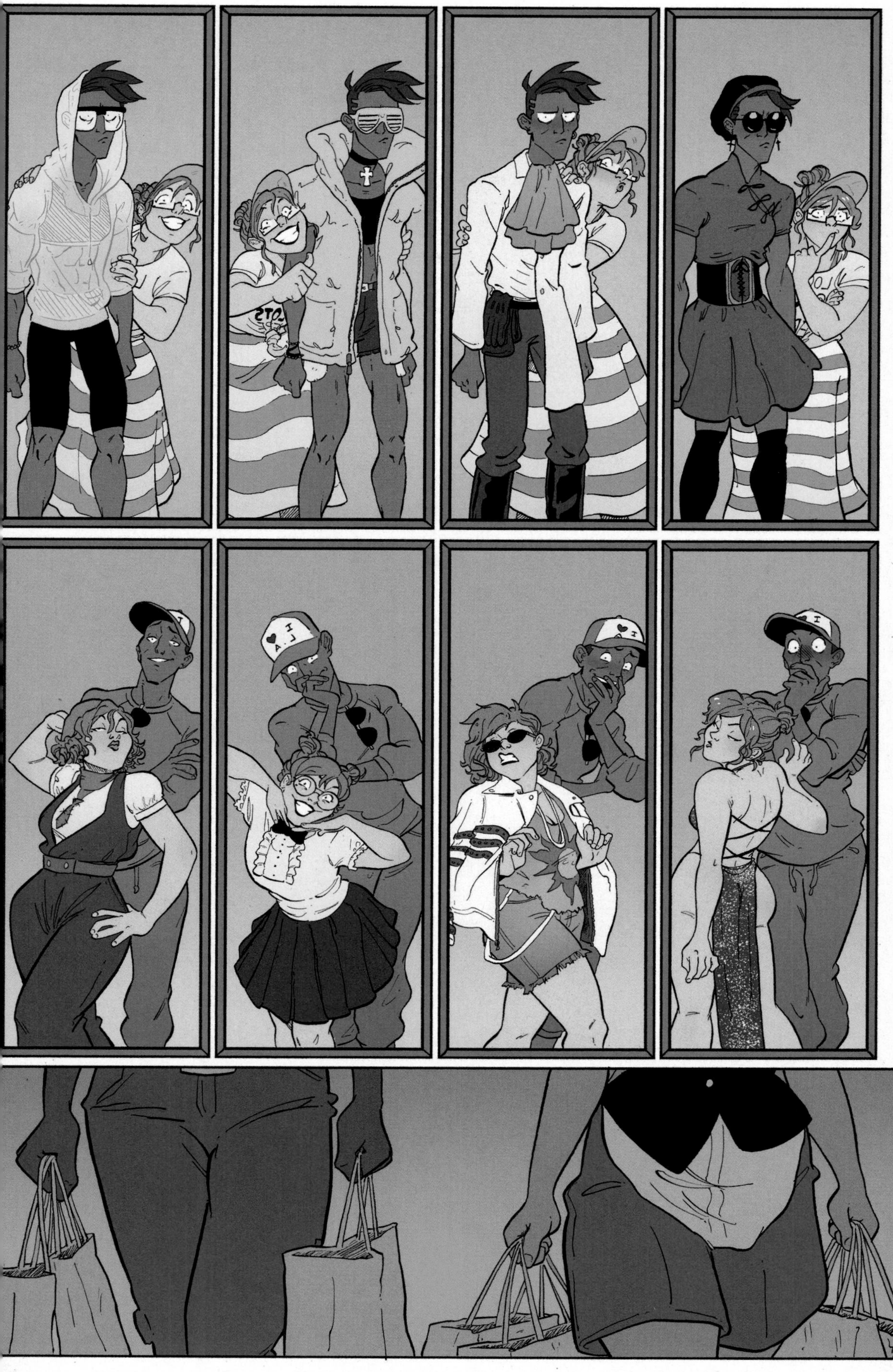

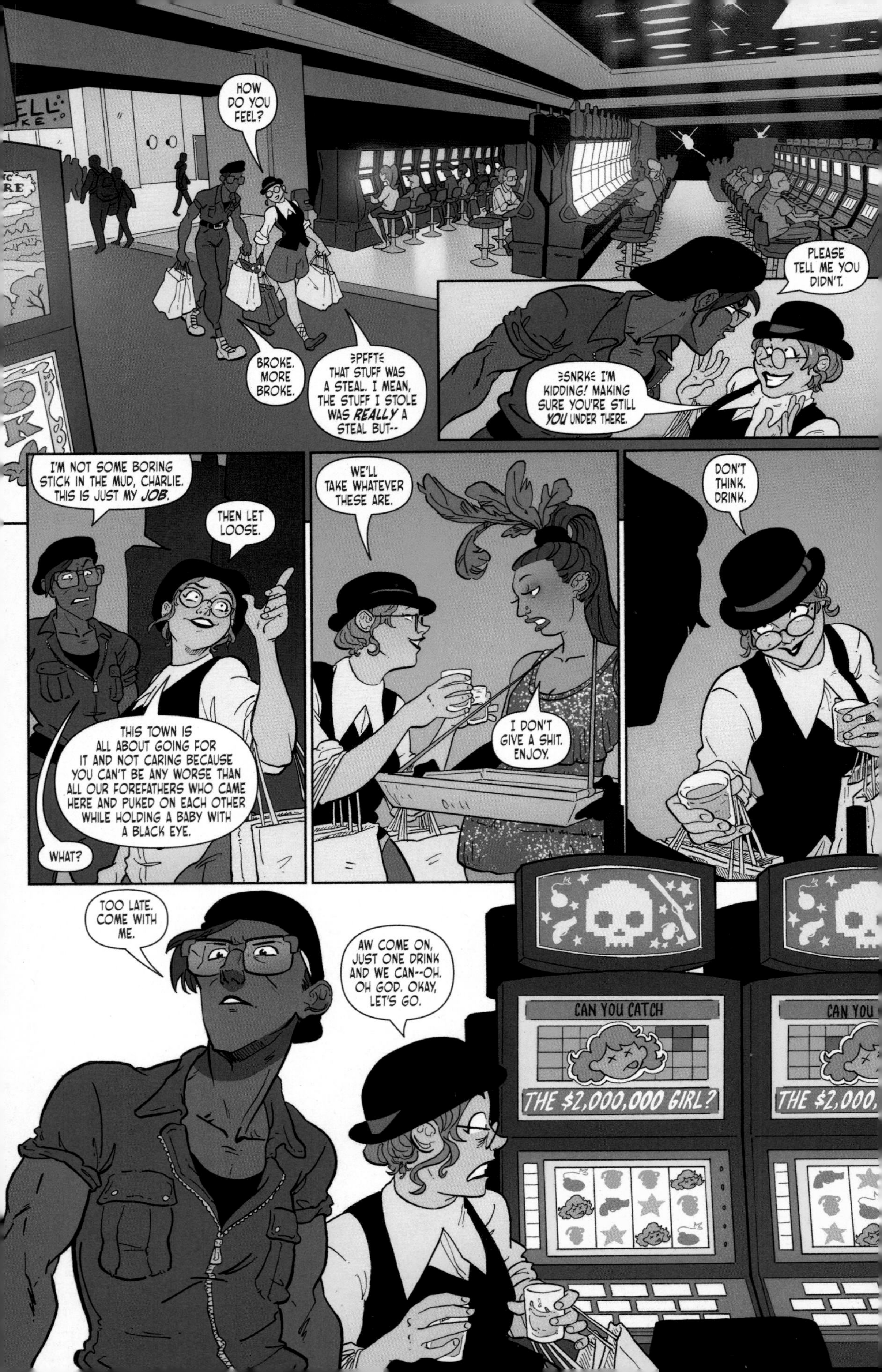
HOW DO YOU FEEL?
BROKE. MORE BROKE.
PFFT THAT STUFF WAS A STEAL. I MEAN, THE STUFF I STOLE WAS REALLY A STEAL BUT--
PLEASE TELL ME YOU DIDN'T.
SNRK I'M KIDDING! MAKING SURE YOU'RE STILL YOU UNDER THERE.
I'M NOT SOME BORING STICK IN THE MUD, CHARLIE. THIS IS JUST MY JOB.
THEN LET LOOSE.
THIS TOWN IS ALL ABOUT GOING FOR IT AND NOT CARING BECAUSE YOU CAN'T BE ANY WORSE THAN ALL OUR FOREFATHERS WHO CAME HERE AND PUKED ON EACH OTHER WHILE HOLDING A BABY WITH A BLACK EYE.
WHAT?
WE'LL TAKE WHATEVER THESE ARE.
I DON'T GIVE A SHIT. ENJOY.
DON'T THINK. DRINK.
TOO LATE. COME WITH ME.
AW COME ON, JUST ONE DRINK AND WE CAN--OH. OH GOD. OKAY, LET'S GO.
CAN YOU CATCH
THE $2,000,000 GIRL?

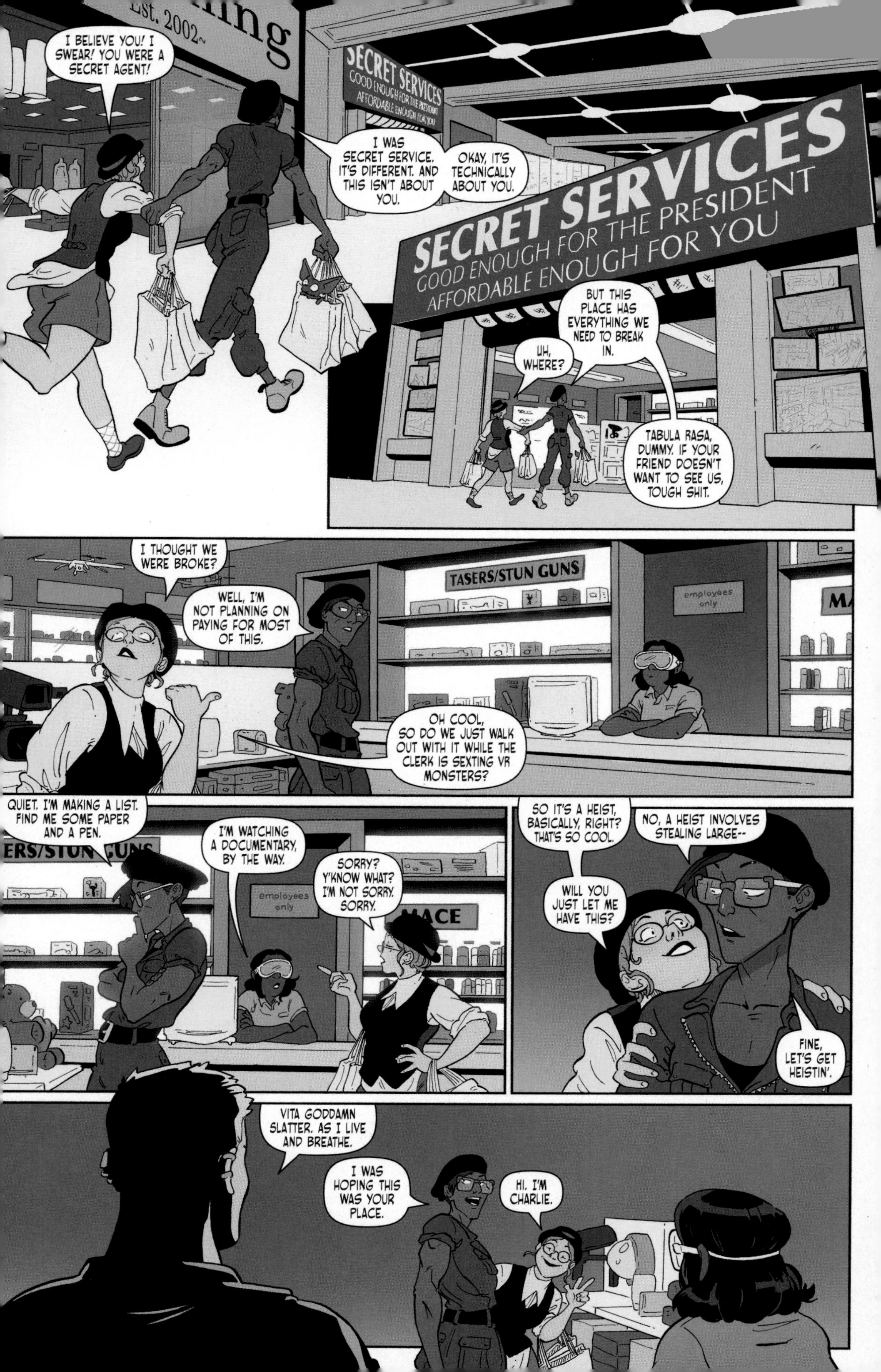
Est. 2002~
I BELIEVE YOU! I SWEAR! YOU WERE A SECRET AGENT!
SECRET SERVICES GOOD ENOUGH FOR THE PRESIDENT AFFORDABLE ENOUGH FOR YOU
I WAS SECRET SERVICE. IT'S DIFFERENT. AND THIS ISN'T ABOUT YOU.
OKAY, IT'S TECHNICALLY ABOUT YOU.
SECRET SERVICES GOOD ENOUGH FOR THE PRESIDENT AFFORDABLE ENOUGH FOR YOU
BUT THIS PLACE HAS EVERYTHING WE NEED TO BREAK IN.
UH, WHERE?
TABULA RASA, DUMMY. IF YOUR FRIEND DOESN'T WANT TO SEE US, TOUGH SHIT.
I THOUGHT WE WERE BROKE?
WELL, I'M NOT PLANNING ON PAYING FOR MOST OF THIS.
TASERS/STUN GUNS
employees only
OH COOL, SO DO WE JUST WALK OUT WITH IT WHILE THE CLERK IS SEXTING VR MONSTERS?
QUIET. I'M MAKING A LIST. FIND ME SOME PAPER AND A PEN.
I'M WATCHING A DOCUMENTARY, BY THE WAY.
SORRY? Y'KNOW WHAT? I'M NOT SORRY. SORRY.
employees only
SO IT'S A HEIST, BASICALLY, RIGHT? THAT'S SO COOL.
NO, A HEIST INVOLVES STEALING LARGE--
WILL YOU JUST LET ME HAVE THIS?
FINE, LET'S GET HEISTIN'.
VITA GODDAMN SLATTER. AS I LIVE AND BREATHE.
I WAS HOPING THIS WAS YOUR PLACE.
HI. I'M CHARLIE.

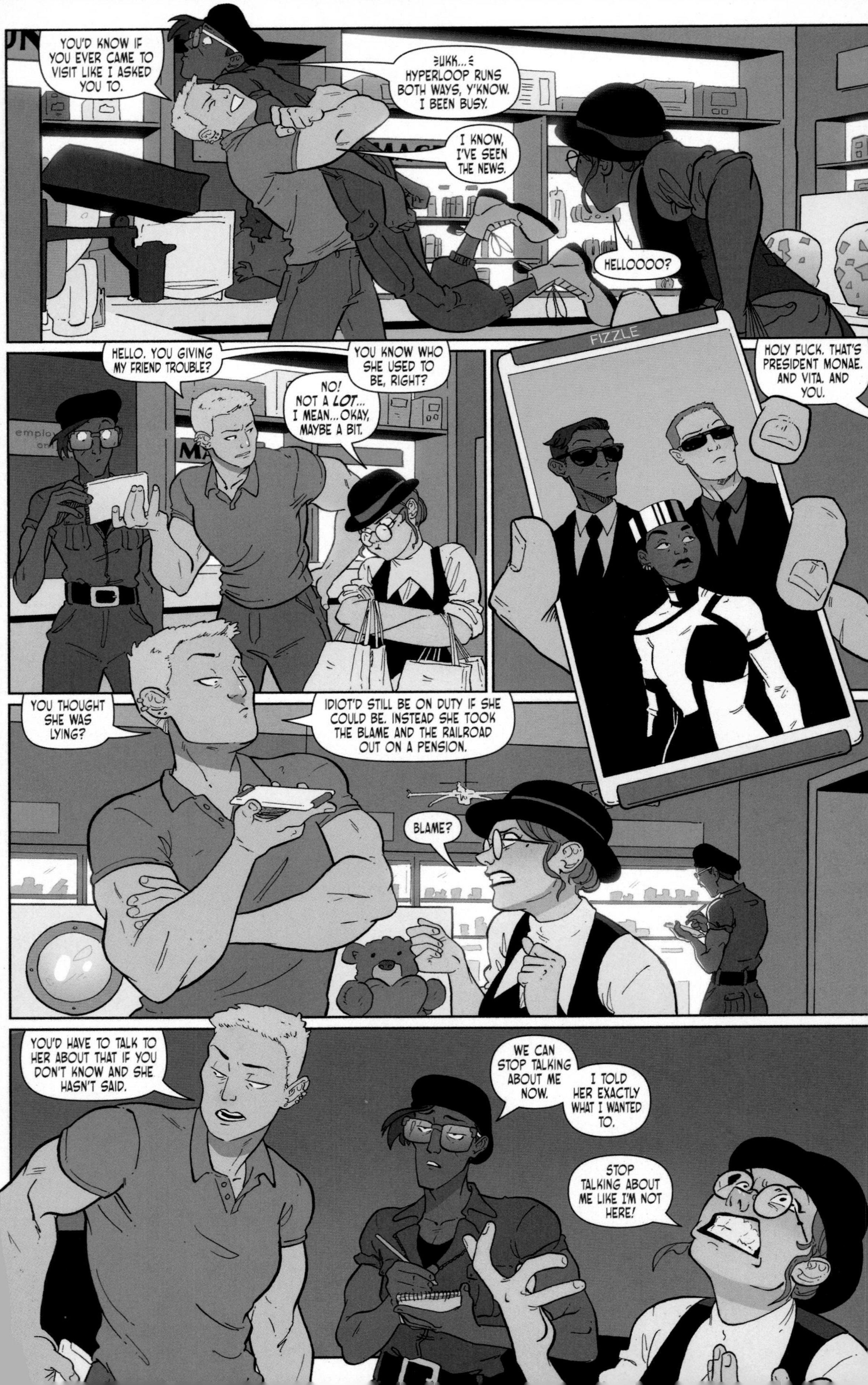
YOU'D KNOW IF YOU EVER CAME TO VISIT LIKE I ASKED YOU TO.
UKK... HYPERLOOP RUNS BOTH WAYS, Y'KNOW. I BEEN BUSY.
I KNOW, I'VE SEEN THE NEWS.
HELLOOOO?
HELLO. YOU GIVING MY FRIEND TROUBLE?
NO! NOT A *LOT*... I MEAN...OKAY, MAYBE A BIT.
YOU KNOW WHO SHE USED TO BE, RIGHT?
FIZZLE
HOLY FUCK. THAT'S PRESIDENT MONAE. AND VITA. AND YOU.
YOU THOUGHT SHE WAS LYING?
IDIOT'D STILL BE ON DUTY IF SHE COULD BE. INSTEAD SHE TOOK THE BLAME AND THE RAILROAD OUT ON A PENSION.
BLAME?
YOU'D HAVE TO TALK TO HER ABOUT THAT IF YOU DON'T KNOW AND SHE HASN'T SAID.
WE CAN STOP TALKING ABOUT ME NOW.
I TOLD HER EXACTLY WHAT I WANTED TO.
STOP TALKING ABOUT ME LIKE I'M NOT HERE!

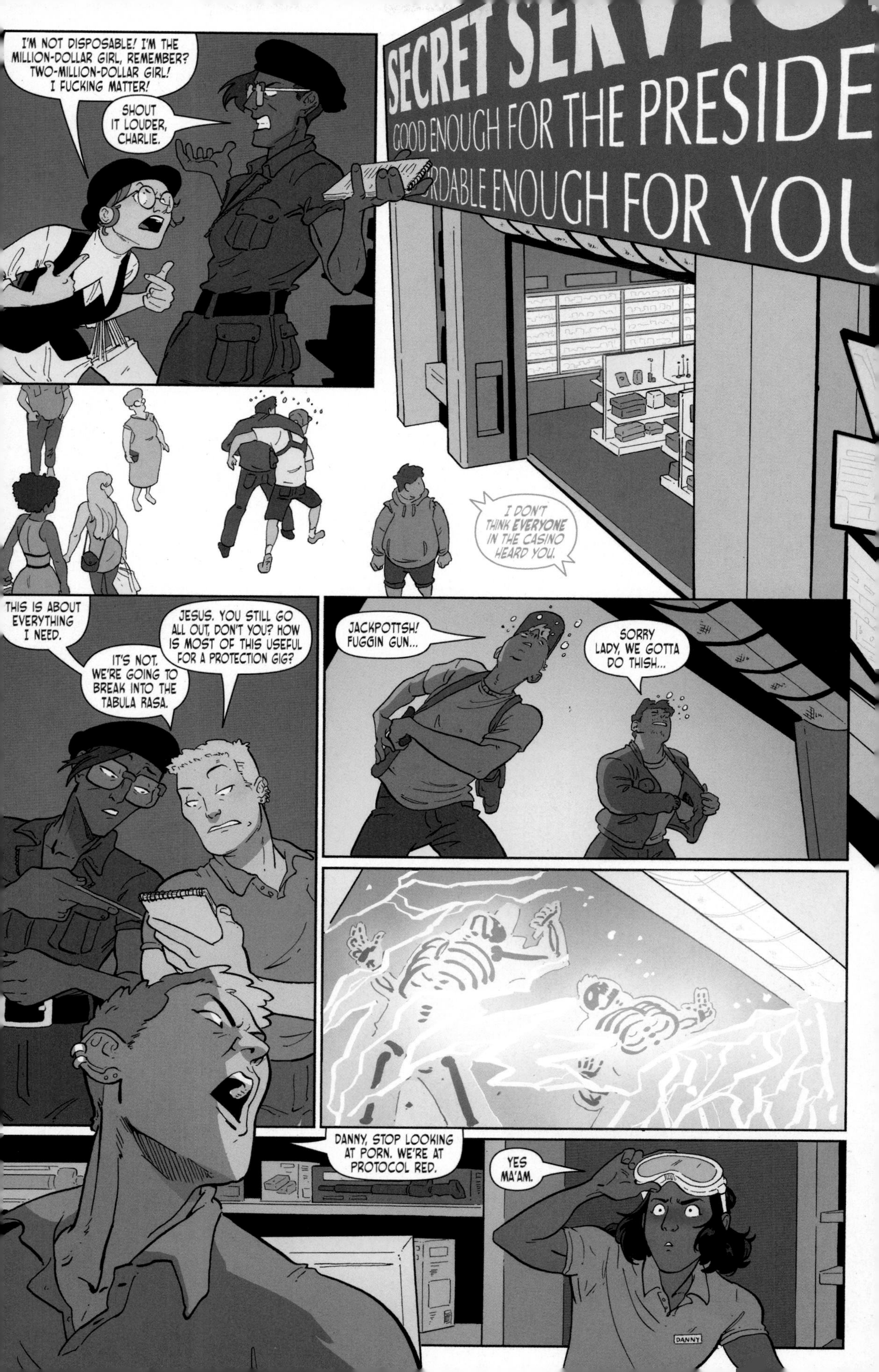
I'M NOT DISPOSABLE! I'M THE MILLION-DOLLAR GIRL, REMEMBER? TWO-MILLION-DOLLAR GIRL! I FUCKING MATTER!
SHOUT IT LOUDER, CHARLIE.
SECRET SERVI
GOOD ENOUGH FOR THE PRESIDE
ORDABLE ENOUGH FOR YOU
I DON'T THINK EVERYONE IN THE CASINO HEARD YOU.
THIS IS ABOUT EVERYTHING I NEED.
JESUS. YOU STILL GO ALL OUT, DON'T YOU? HOW IS MOST OF THIS USEFUL FOR A PROTECTION GIG?
IT'S NOT. WE'RE GOING TO BREAK INTO THE TABULA RASA.
JACKPOTTSH! FUGGIN GUN...
SORRY LADY, WE GOTTA DO THISH...
DANNY, STOP LOOKING AT PORN. WE'RE AT PROTOCOL RED.
YES MA'AM.
DANNY

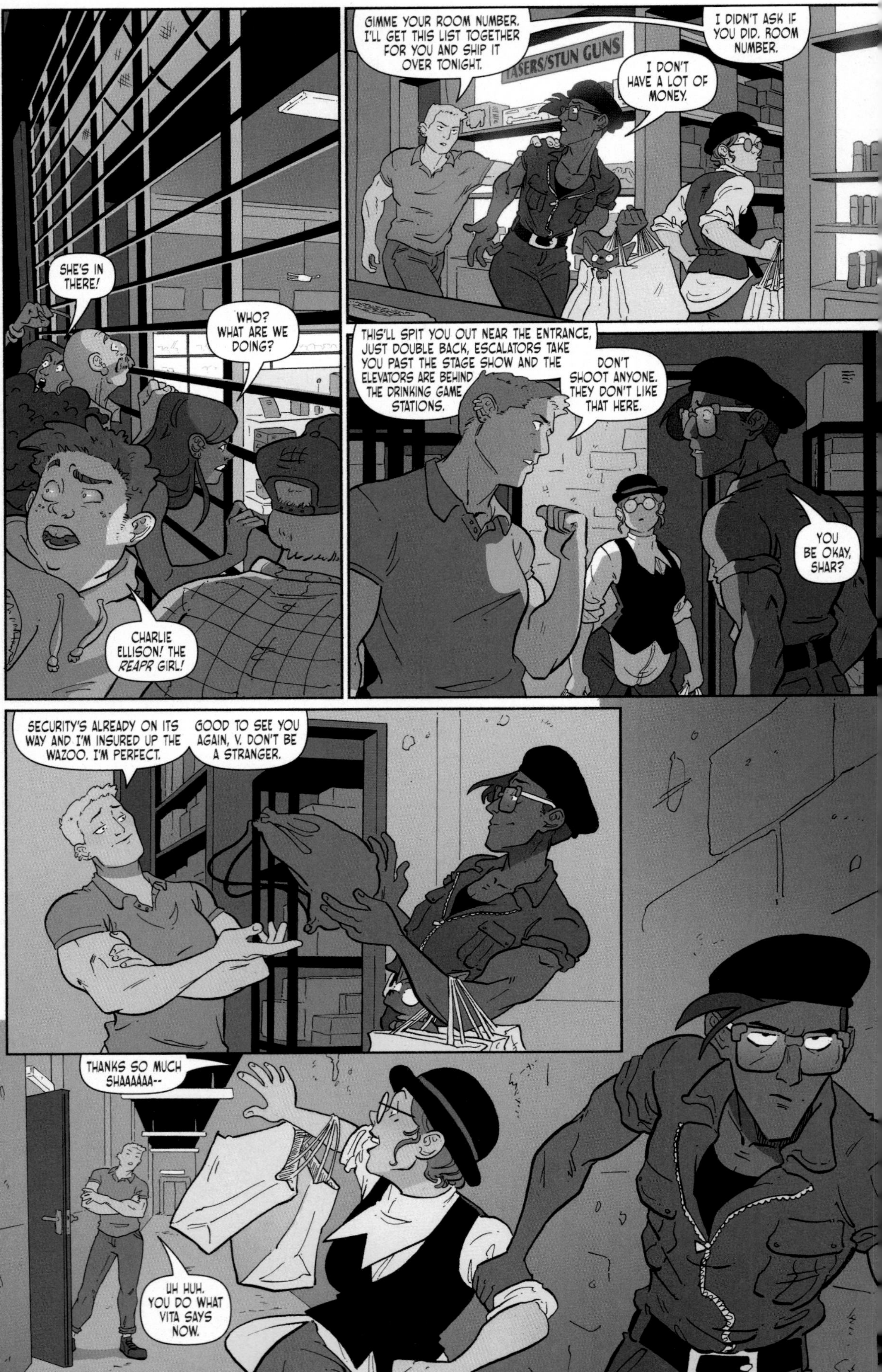

SHE'S IN THERE!
WHO? WHAT ARE WE DOING?
CHARLIE ELLISON! THE *REAPR* GIRL!
GIMME YOUR ROOM NUMBER. I'LL GET THIS LIST TOGETHER FOR YOU AND SHIP IT OVER TONIGHT.
TASERS/STUN GUNS
I DON'T HAVE A LOT OF MONEY.
I DIDN'T ASK IF YOU DID. ROOM NUMBER.
THIS'LL SPIT YOU OUT NEAR THE ENTRANCE, JUST DOUBLE BACK, ESCALATORS TAKE YOU PAST THE STAGE SHOW AND THE ELEVATORS ARE BEHIND THE DRINKING GAME STATIONS.
DON'T SHOOT ANYONE. THEY DON'T LIKE THAT HERE.
YOU BE OKAY, SHAR?
SECURITY'S ALREADY ON ITS WAY AND I'M INSURED UP THE WAZOO. I'M PERFECT.
GOOD TO SEE YOU AGAIN, V. DON'T BE A STRANGER.
THANKS SO MUCH SHAAAAAA--
UH HUH. YOU DO WHAT VITA SAYS NOW.

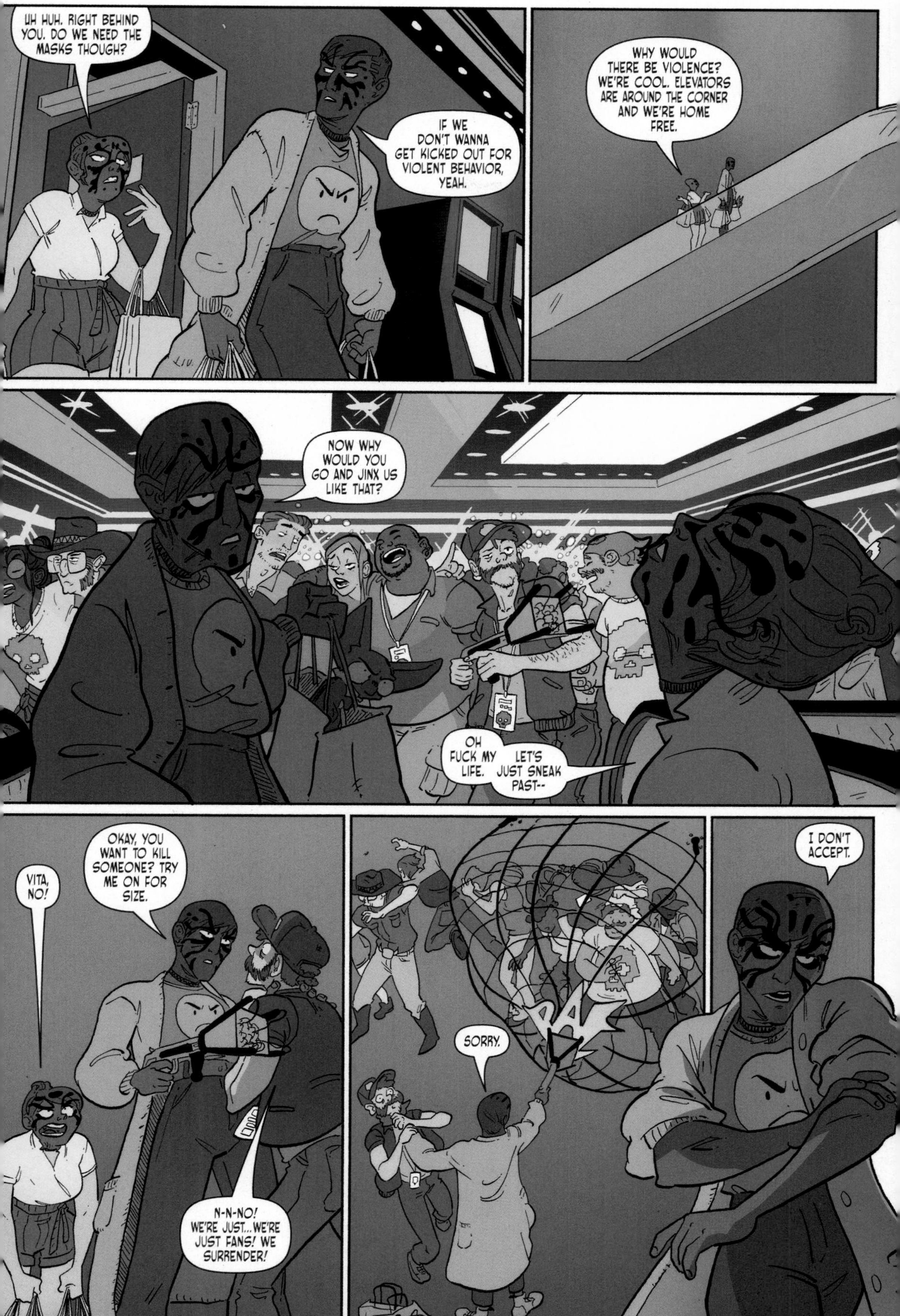
UH HUH. RIGHT BEHIND YOU. DO WE NEED THE MASKS THOUGH?
IF WE DON'T WANNA GET KICKED OUT FOR VIOLENT BEHAVIOR, YEAH.
WHY WOULD THERE BE VIOLENCE? WE'RE COOL. ELEVATORS ARE AROUND THE CORNER AND WE'RE HOME FREE.
NOW WHY WOULD YOU GO AND JINX US LIKE THAT?
OH FUCK MY LIFE.
LET'S JUST SNEAK PAST--
VITA, NO!
OKAY, YOU WANT TO KILL SOMEONE? TRY ME ON FOR SIZE.
N-N-NO! WE'RE JUST... WE'RE JUST FANS! WE SURRENDER!
SORRY.
I DON'T ACCEPT.

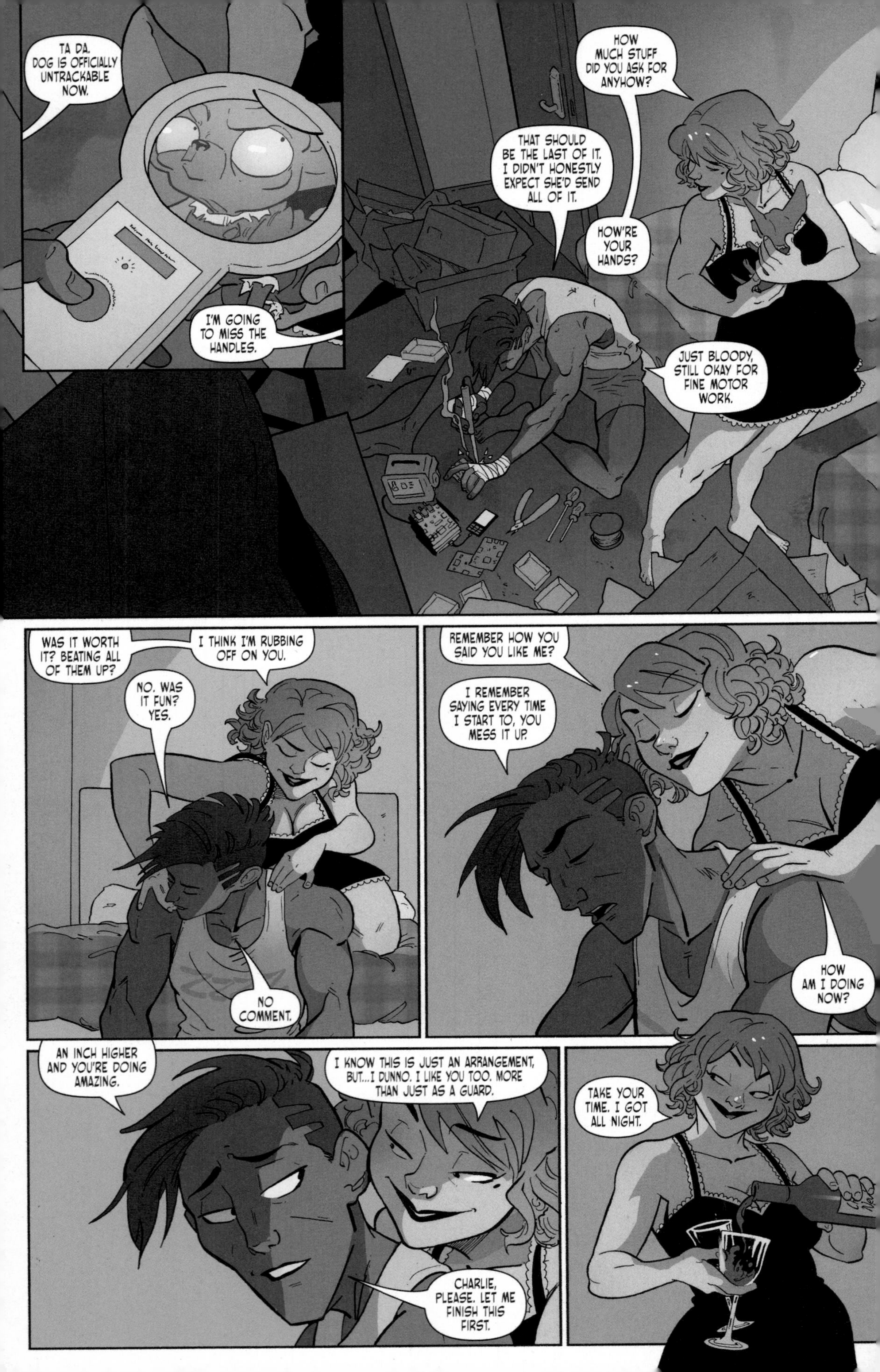
TA DA. DOG IS OFFICIALLY UNTRACKABLE NOW.
I'M GOING TO MISS THE HANDLES.
THAT SHOULD BE THE LAST OF IT. I DIDN'T HONESTLY EXPECT SHE'D SEND ALL OF IT.
HOW MUCH STUFF DID YOU ASK FOR ANYHOW?
HOW'RE YOUR HANDS?
JUST BLOODY, STILL OKAY FOR FINE MOTOR WORK.
WAS IT WORTH IT? BEATING ALL OF THEM UP?
I THINK I'M RUBBING OFF ON YOU.
NO. WAS IT FUN? YES.
NO COMMENT.
REMEMBER HOW YOU SAID YOU LIKE ME?
I REMEMBER SAYING EVERY TIME I START TO, YOU MESS IT UP.
HOW AM I DOING NOW?
AN INCH HIGHER AND YOU'RE DOING AMAZING.
I KNOW THIS IS JUST AN ARRANGEMENT, BUT...I DUNNO. I LIKE YOU TOO. MORE THAN JUST AS A GUARD.
CHARLIE, PLEASE. LET ME FINISH THIS FIRST.
TAKE YOUR TIME. I GOT ALL NIGHT.

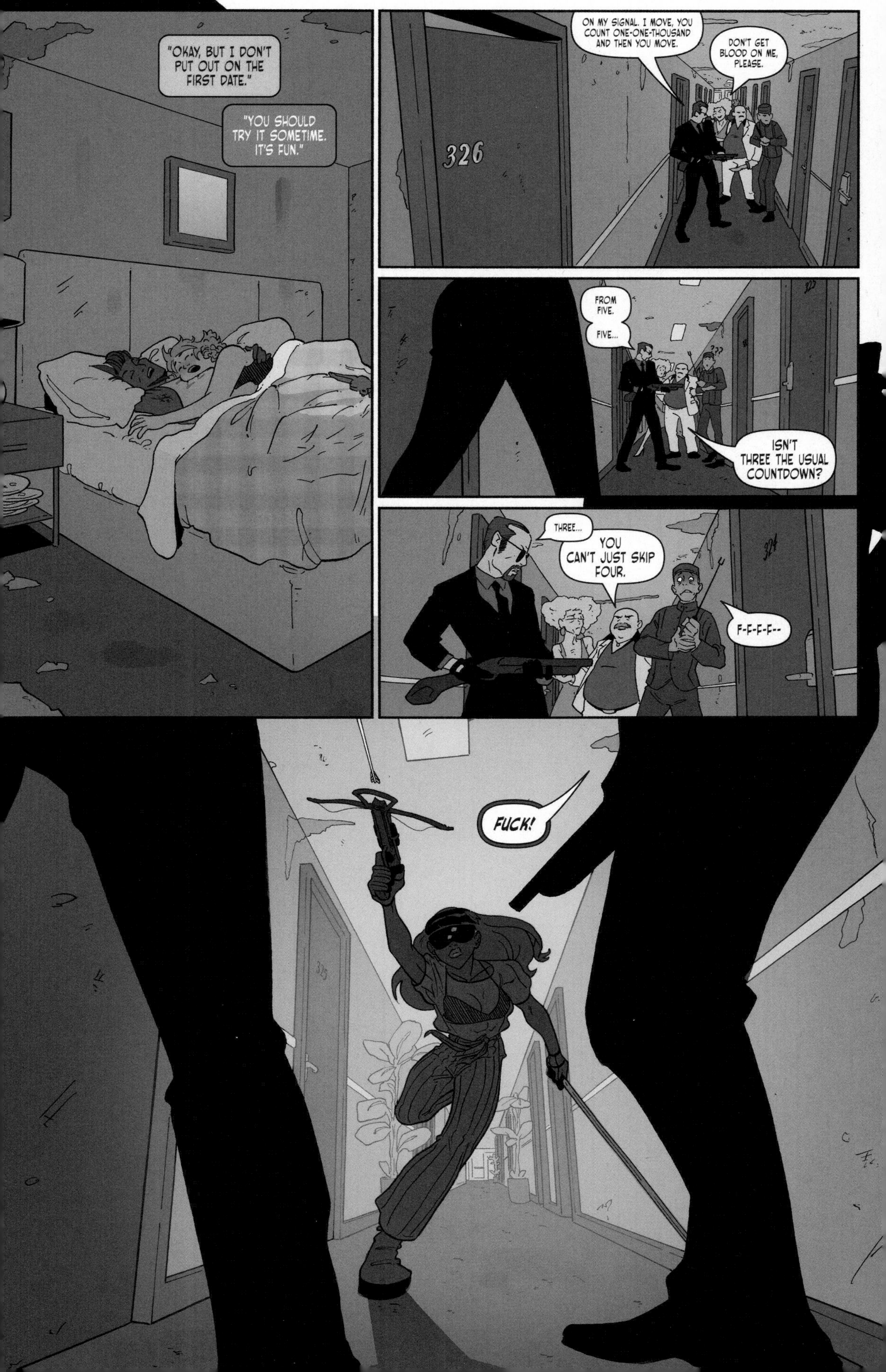
"OKAY, BUT I DON'T PUT OUT ON THE FIRST DATE."
"YOU SHOULD TRY IT SOMETIME. IT'S FUN."
326
ON MY SIGNAL. I MOVE, YOU COUNT ONE-ONE-THOUSAND AND THEN YOU MOVE.
DON'T GET BLOOD ON ME, PLEASE.
FROM FIVE.
FIVE...
???
ISN'T THREE THE USUAL COUNTDOWN?
THREE...
YOU CAN'T JUST SKIP FOUR.
F-F-F-F--
FUCK!

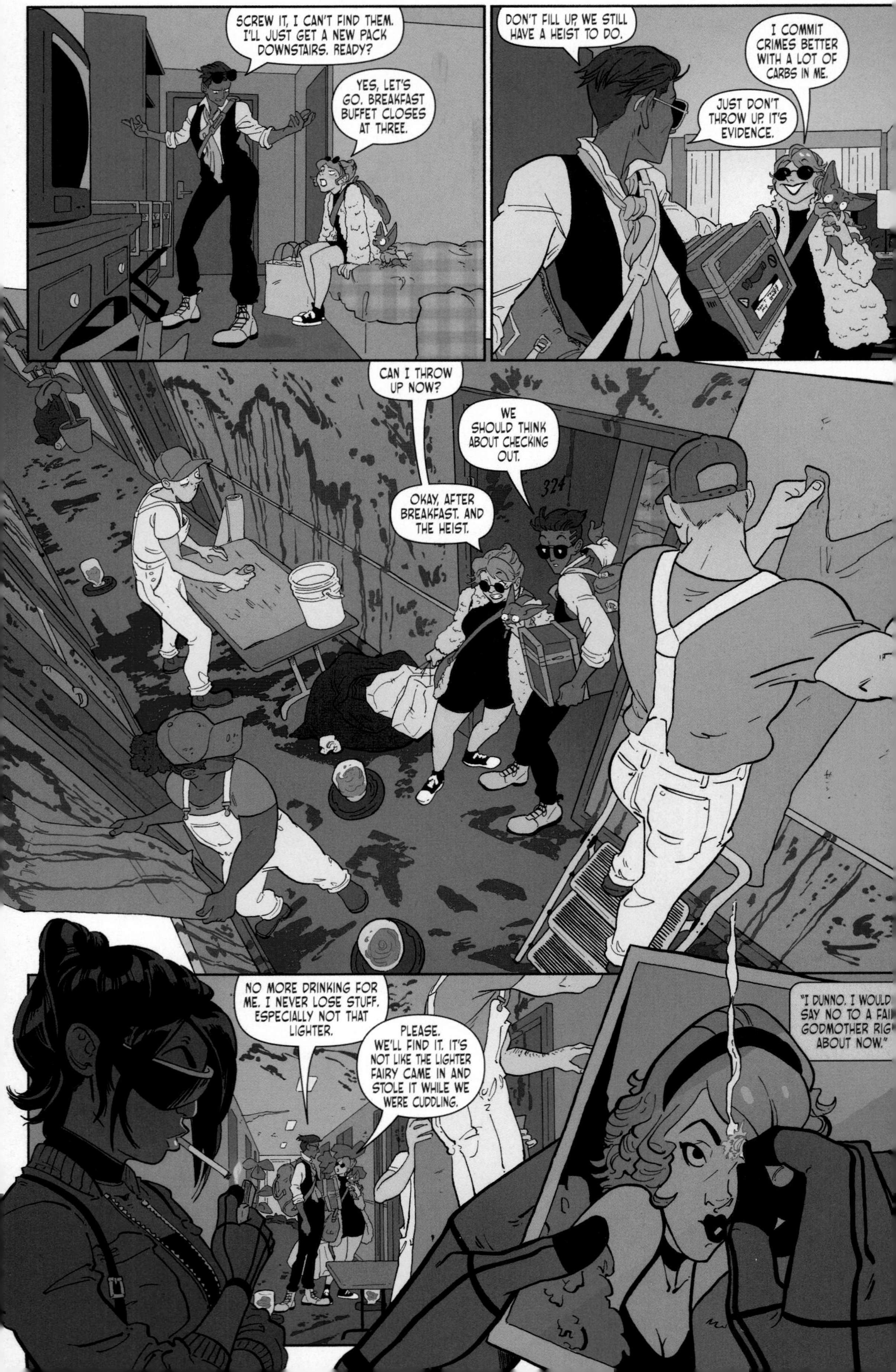
SCREW IT, I CAN'T FIND THEM. I'LL JUST GET A NEW PACK DOWNSTAIRS. READY?
YES, LET'S GO. BREAKFAST BUFFET CLOSES AT THREE.
DON'T FILL UP, WE STILL HAVE A HEIST TO DO.
I COMMIT CRIMES BETTER WITH A LOT OF CARBS IN ME.
JUST DON'T THROW UP. IT'S EVIDENCE.
CAN I THROW UP NOW?
WE SHOULD THINK ABOUT CHECKING OUT.
OKAY, AFTER BREAKFAST. AND THE HEIST.
324
NO MORE DRINKING FOR ME. I NEVER LOSE STUFF. ESPECIALLY NOT THAT LIGHTER.
PLEASE. WE'LL FIND IT. IT'S NOT LIKE THE LIGHTER FAIRY CAME IN AND STOLE IT WHILE WE WERE CUDDLING.
"I DUNNO. I WOULD SAY NO TO A FAI GODMOTHER RIG ABOUT NOW."

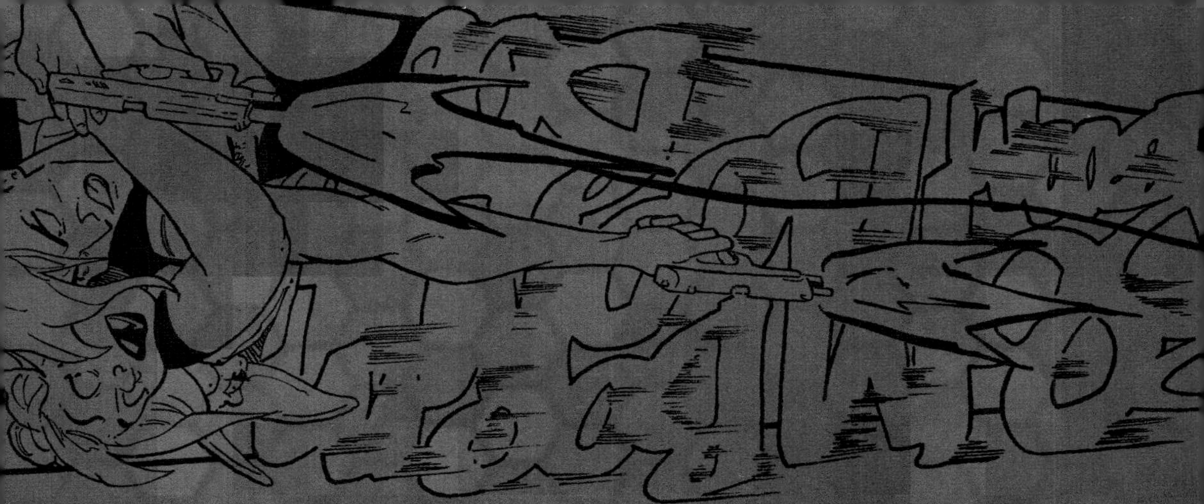

CHAPTER NINE

BABES NEVER DIE

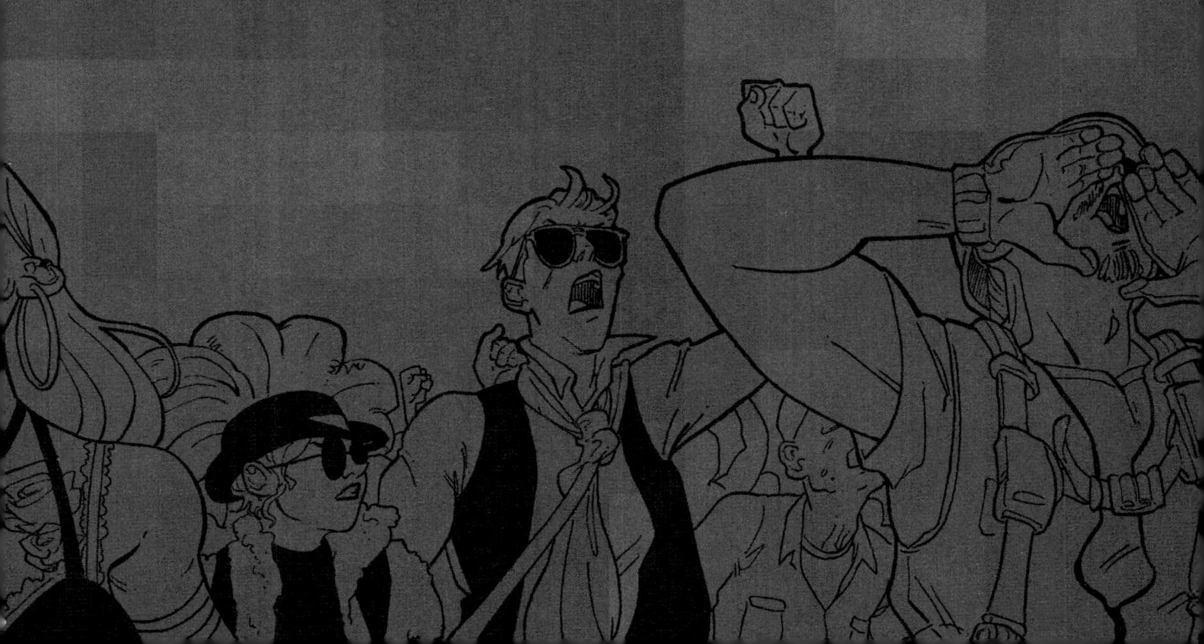

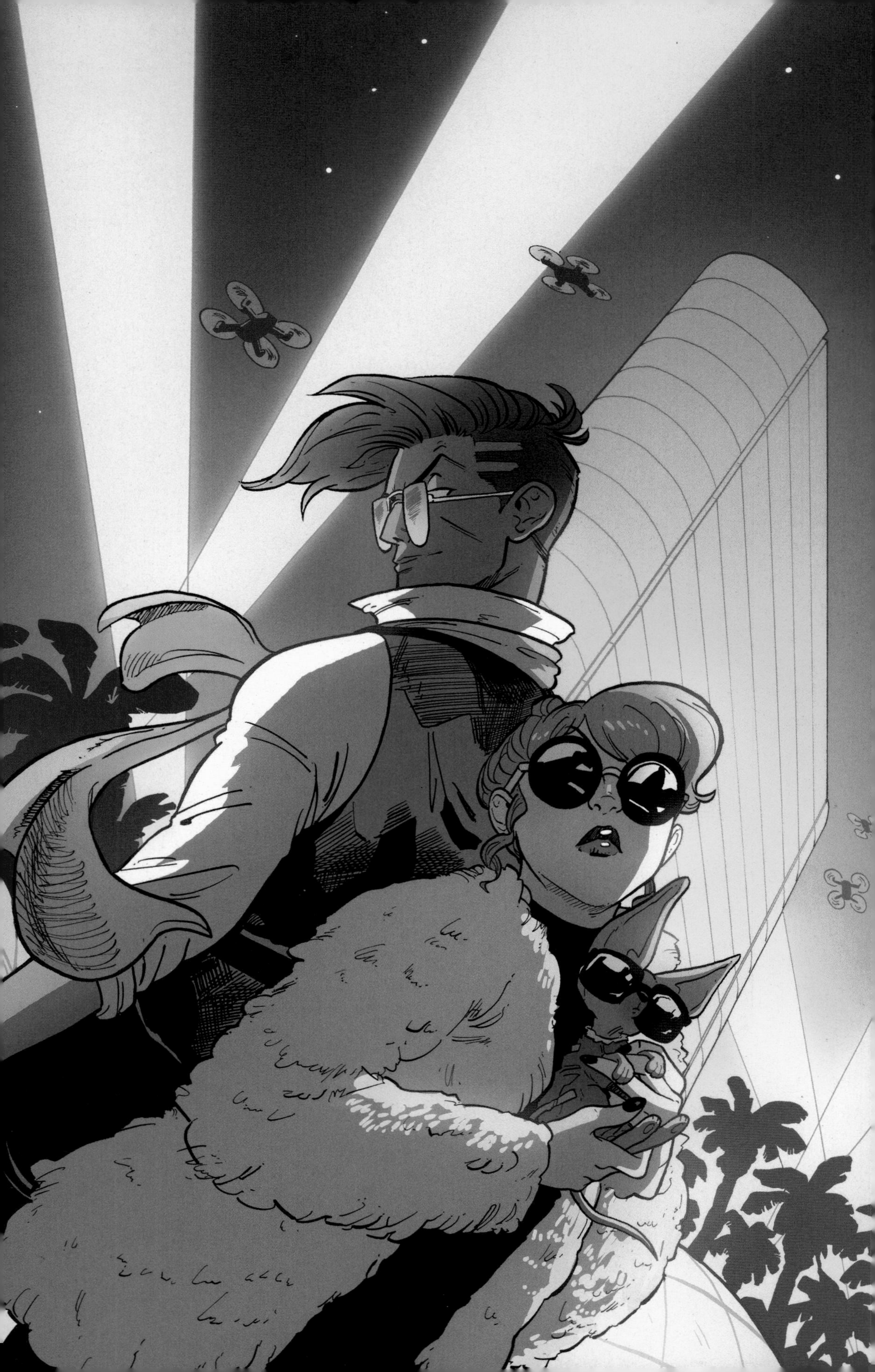

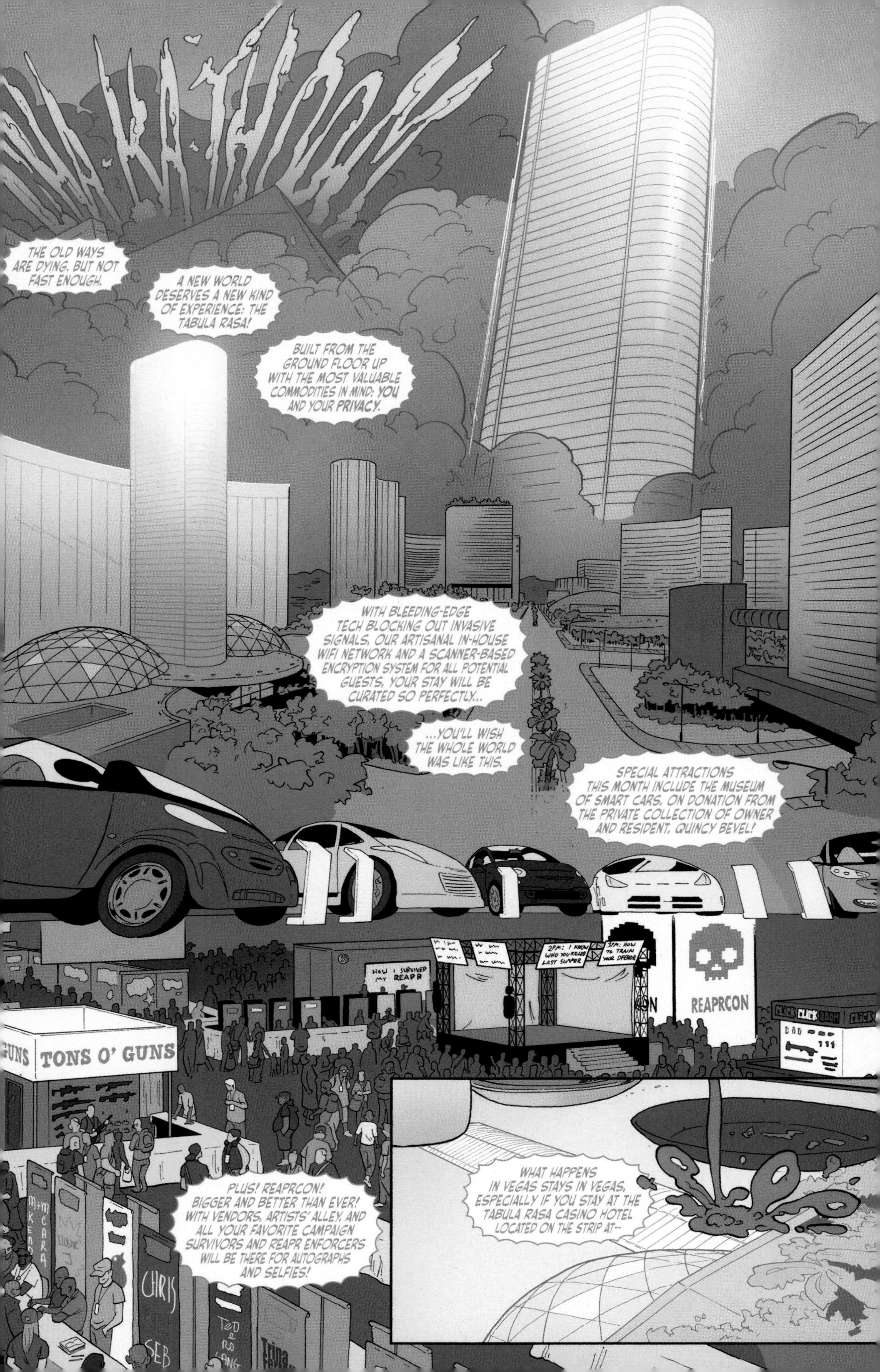
THE OLD WAYS ARE DYING. BUT NOT FAST ENOUGH.
A NEW WORLD DESERVES A NEW KIND OF EXPERIENCE: THE TABULA RASA!
BUILT FROM THE GROUND FLOOR UP WITH THE MOST VALUABLE COMMODITIES IN MIND: YOU AND YOUR PRIVACY.
WITH BLEEDING-EDGE TECH BLOCKING OUT INVASIVE SIGNALS, OUR ARTISANAL IN-HOUSE WIFI NETWORK AND A SCANNER-BASED ENCRYPTION SYSTEM FOR ALL POTENTIAL GUESTS, YOUR STAY WILL BE CURATED SO PERFECTLY...
...YOU'LL WISH THE WHOLE WORLD WAS LIKE THIS.
SPECIAL ATTRACTIONS THIS MONTH INCLUDE THE MUSEUM OF SMART CARS, ON DONATION FROM THE PRIVATE COLLECTION OF OWNER AND RESIDENT, QUINCY BEVEL!
HOW I SURVIVED MY REAPR
REAPRCON
TONS O' GUNS
PLUS! REAPRCON! BIGGER AND BETTER THAN EVER! WITH VENDORS, ARTISTS' ALLEY, AND ALL YOUR FAVORITE CAMPAIGN SURVIVORS AND REAPR ENFORCERS WILL BE THERE FOR AUTOGRAPHS AND SELFIES!
WHAT HAPPENS IN VEGAS STAYS IN VEGAS, ESPECIALLY IF YOU STAY AT THE TABULA RASA CASINO HOTEL LOCATED ON THE STRIP AT--

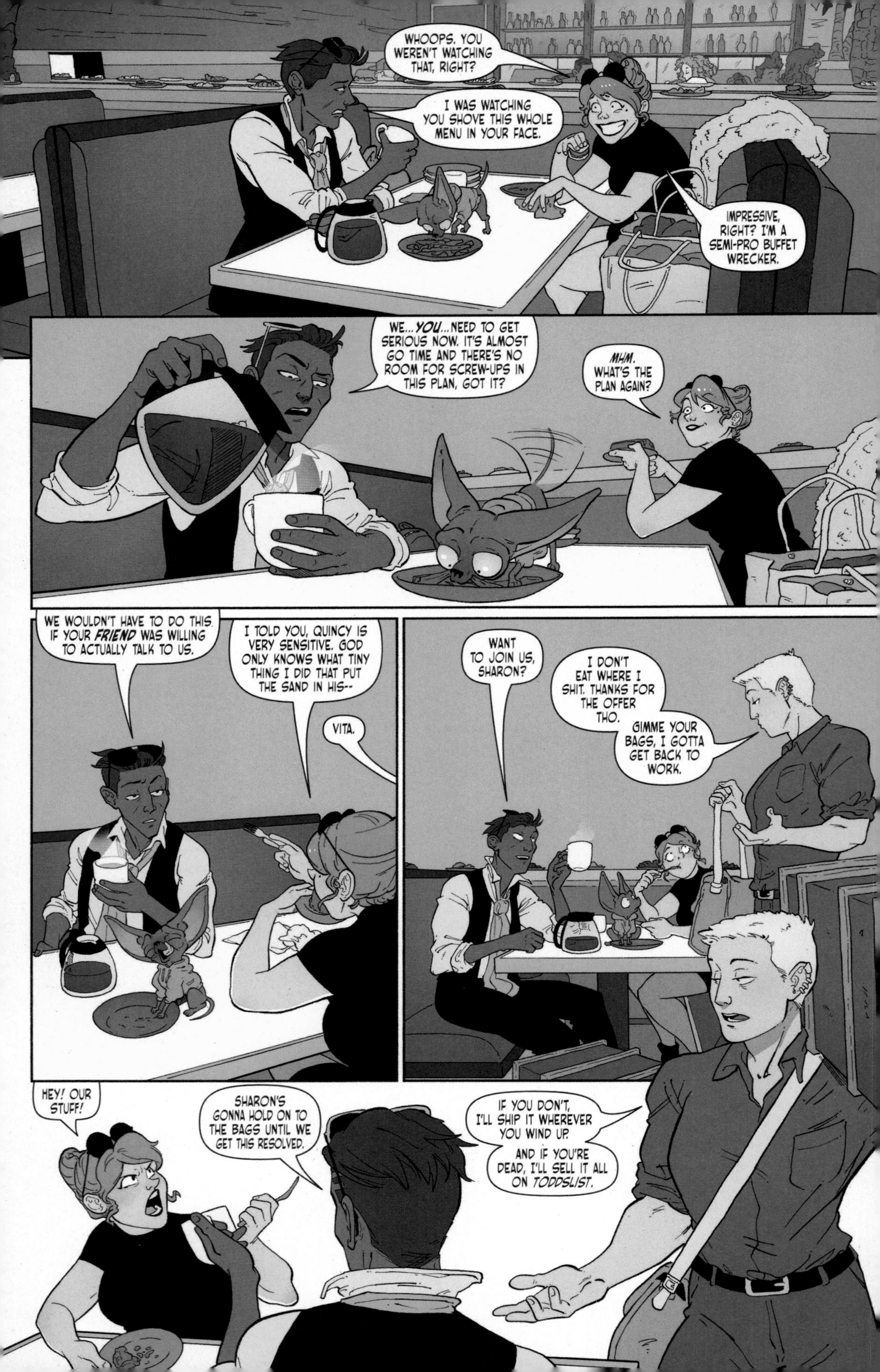
WHOOPS. YOU WEREN'T WATCHING THAT, RIGHT?
I WAS WATCHING YOU SHOVE THIS WHOLE MENU IN YOUR FACE.
IMPRESSIVE, RIGHT? I'M A SEMI-PRO BUFFET WRECKER.
WE...*YOU*...NEED TO GET SERIOUS NOW. IT'S ALMOST GO TIME AND THERE'S NO ROOM FOR SCREW-UPS IN THIS PLAN, GOT IT?
MHM. WHAT'S THE PLAN AGAIN?
WE WOULDN'T HAVE TO DO THIS IF YOUR *FRIEND* WAS WILLING TO ACTUALLY TALK TO US.
I TOLD YOU, QUINCY IS VERY SENSITIVE. GOD ONLY KNOWS WHAT TINY THING I DID THAT PUT THE SAND IN HIS--
VITA.
WANT TO JOIN US, SHARON?
I DON'T EAT WHERE I SHIT. THANKS FOR THE OFFER THO.
GIMME YOUR BAGS, I GOTTA GET BACK TO WORK.
HEY! OUR STUFF!
SHARON'S GONNA HOLD ON TO THE BAGS UNTIL WE GET THIS RESOLVED.
IF YOU DON'T, I'LL SHIP IT WHEREVER YOU WIND UP.
AND IF YOU'RE DEAD, I'LL SELL IT ALL ON *TODDSLIST*.

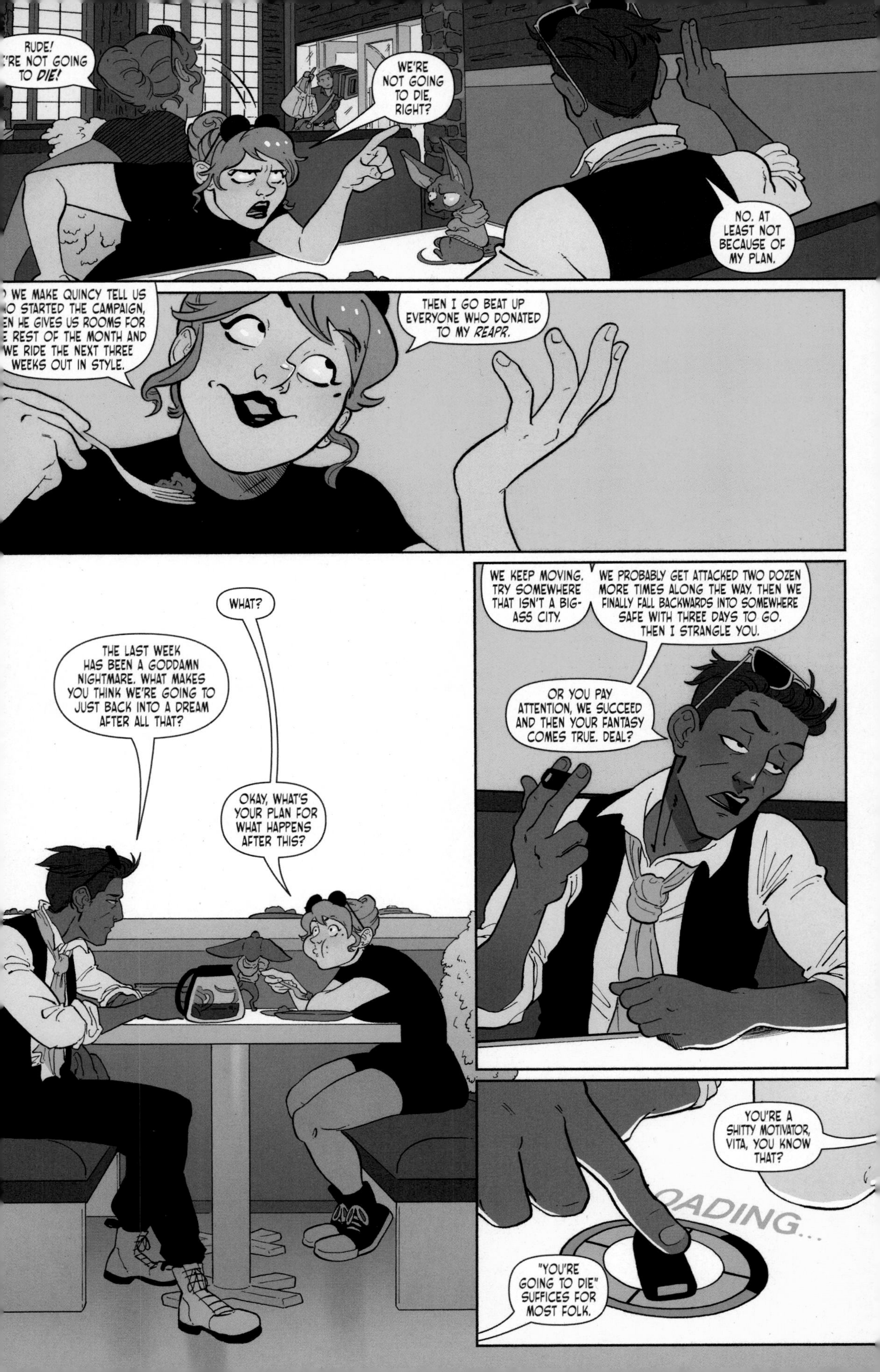
RUDE! WE'RE NOT GOING TO *DIE!*
WE'RE NOT GOING TO DIE, RIGHT?
NO. AT LEAST NOT BECAUSE OF MY PLAN.
WE MAKE QUINCY TELL US WHO STARTED THE CAMPAIGN, THEN HE GIVES US ROOMS FOR THE REST OF THE MONTH AND WE RIDE THE NEXT THREE WEEKS OUT IN STYLE.
THEN I GO BEAT UP EVERYONE WHO DONATED TO MY *REAPR*.
WHAT?
THE LAST WEEK HAS BEEN A GODDAMN NIGHTMARE. WHAT MAKES YOU THINK WE'RE GOING TO JUST BACK INTO A DREAM AFTER ALL THAT?
OKAY, WHAT'S YOUR PLAN FOR WHAT HAPPENS AFTER THIS?
WE KEEP MOVING. TRY SOMEWHERE THAT ISN'T A BIG-ASS CITY.
WE PROBABLY GET ATTACKED TWO DOZEN MORE TIMES ALONG THE WAY. THEN WE FINALLY FALL BACKWARDS INTO SOMEWHERE SAFE WITH THREE DAYS TO GO. THEN I STRANGLE YOU.
OR YOU PAY ATTENTION, WE SUCCEED AND THEN YOUR FANTASY COMES TRUE. DEAL?
YOU'RE A SHITTY MOTIVATOR, VITA, YOU KNOW THAT?
LOADING...
"YOU'RE GOING TO DIE" SUFFICES FOR MOST FOLK.

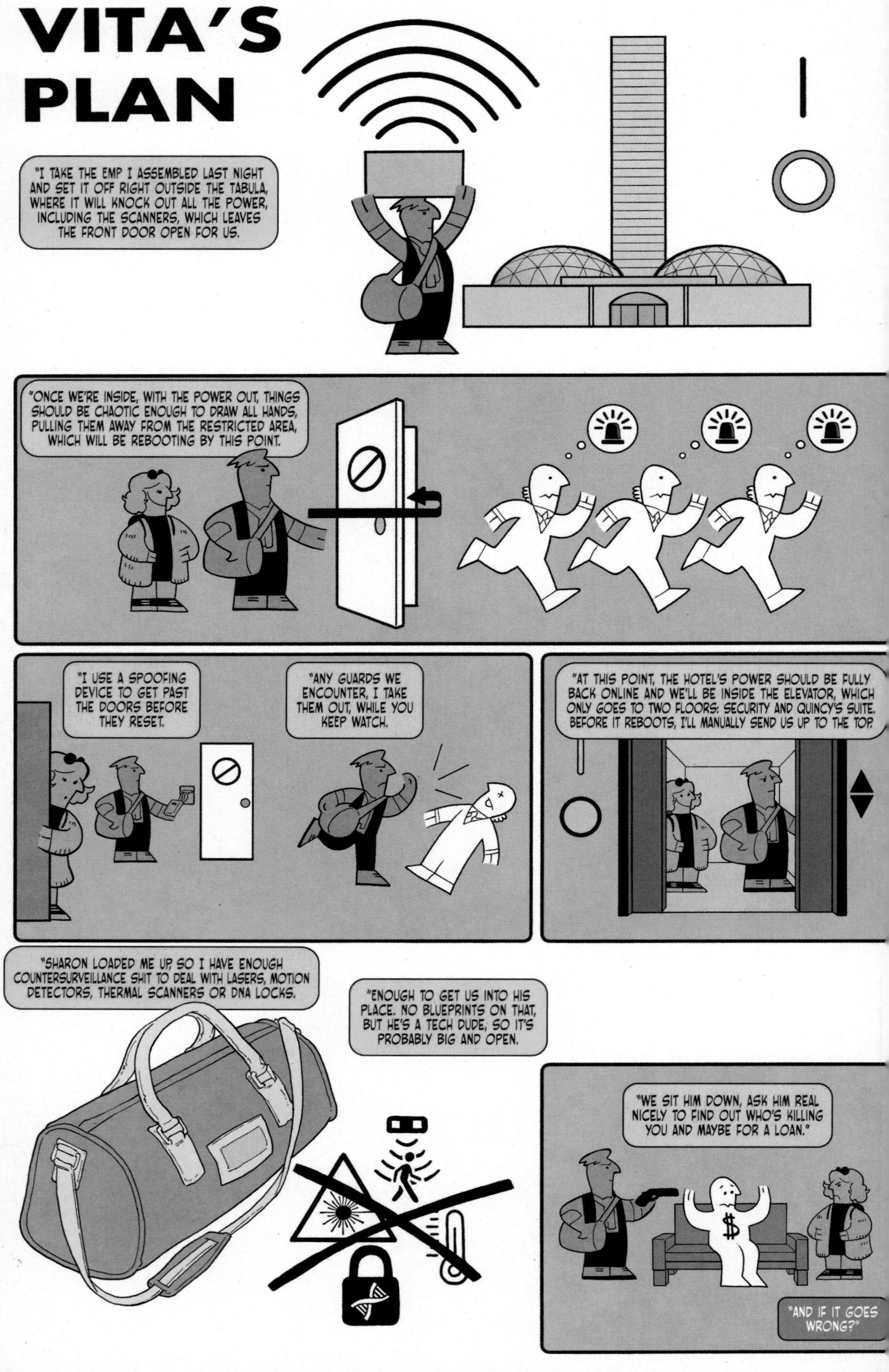
VITA'S PLAN
"I TAKE THE EMP I ASSEMBLED LAST NIGHT AND SET IT OFF RIGHT OUTSIDE THE TABULA, WHERE IT WILL KNOCK OUT ALL THE POWER, INCLUDING THE SCANNERS, WHICH LEAVES THE FRONT DOOR OPEN FOR US.
"ONCE WE'RE INSIDE, WITH THE POWER OUT, THINGS SHOULD BE CHAOTIC ENOUGH TO DRAW ALL HANDS, PULLING THEM AWAY FROM THE RESTRICTED AREA, WHICH WILL BE REBOOTING BY THIS POINT.
"I USE A SPOOFING DEVICE TO GET PAST THE DOORS BEFORE THEY RESET.
"ANY GUARDS WE ENCOUNTER, I TAKE THEM OUT, WHILE YOU KEEP WATCH.
"AT THIS POINT, THE HOTEL'S POWER SHOULD BE FULLY BACK ONLINE AND WE'LL BE INSIDE THE ELEVATOR, WHICH ONLY GOES TO TWO FLOORS: SECURITY AND QUINCY'S SUITE. BEFORE IT REBOOTS, I'LL MANUALLY SEND US UP TO THE TOP.
"SHARON LOADED ME UP, SO I HAVE ENOUGH COUNTERSURVEILLANCE SHIT TO DEAL WITH LASERS, MOTION DETECTORS, THERMAL SCANNERS OR DNA LOCKS.
"ENOUGH TO GET US INTO HIS PLACE. NO BLUEPRINTS ON THAT, BUT HE'S A TECH DUDE, SO IT'S PROBABLY BIG AND OPEN.
"WE SIT HIM DOWN, ASK HIM REAL NICELY TO FIND OUT WHO'S KILLING YOU AND MAYBE FOR A LOAN."
"AND IF IT GOES WRONG?"

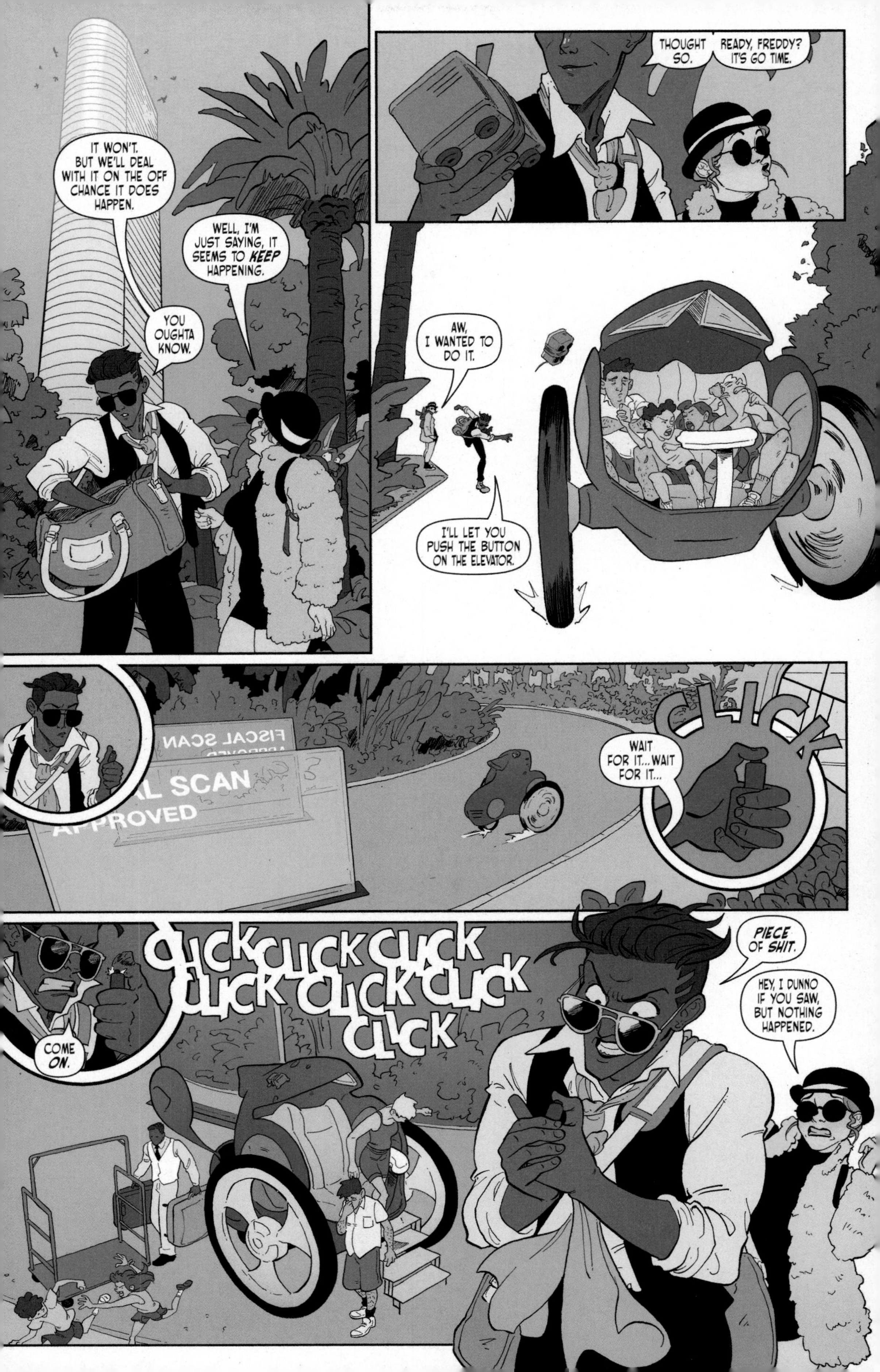
IT WON'T. BUT WE'LL DEAL WITH IT ON THE OFF CHANCE IT DOES HAPPEN.
WELL, I'M JUST SAYING, IT SEEMS TO *KEEP* HAPPENING.
YOU OUGHTA KNOW.
THOUGHT SO.
READY, FREDDY? IT'S GO TIME.
AW, I WANTED TO DO IT.
I'LL LET YOU PUSH THE BUTTON ON THE ELEVATOR.
FISCAL SCAN APPROVED
WAIT FOR IT...WAIT FOR IT...
CLICK
CLICK CLICK CLICK CLICK CLICK CLICK CLICK
COME *ON*.
PIECE OF *SHIT*.
HEY, I DUNNO IF YOU SAW, BUT NOTHING HAPPENED.

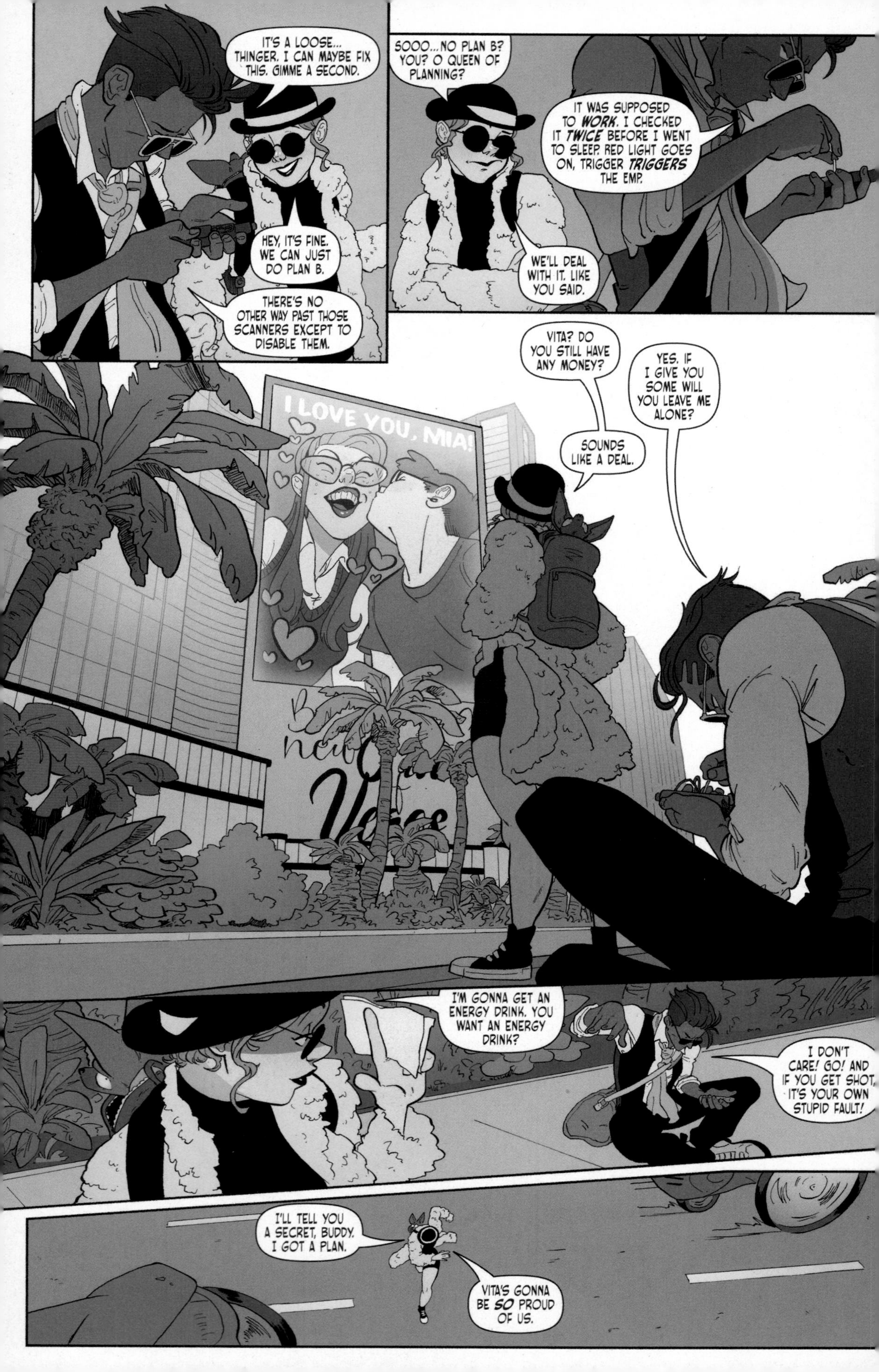
IT'S A LOOSE... THINGER. I CAN MAYBE FIX THIS. GIMME A SECOND.
HEY, IT'S FINE. WE CAN JUST DO PLAN B.
THERE'S NO OTHER WAY PAST THOSE SCANNERS EXCEPT TO DISABLE THEM.
SOOO...NO PLAN B? YOU? O QUEEN OF PLANNING?
IT WAS SUPPOSED TO WORK. I CHECKED IT TWICE BEFORE I WENT TO SLEEP. RED LIGHT GOES ON, TRIGGER TRIGGERS THE EMP.
WE'LL DEAL WITH IT. LIKE YOU SAID.
I LOVE YOU, MIA!
VITA? DO YOU STILL HAVE ANY MONEY?
YES. IF I GIVE YOU SOME WILL YOU LEAVE ME ALONE?
SOUNDS LIKE A DEAL.
I'M GONNA GET AN ENERGY DRINK. YOU WANT AN ENERGY DRINK?
I DON'T CARE! GO! AND IF YOU GET SHOT, IT'S YOUR OWN STUPID FAULT!
I'LL TELL YOU A SECRET, BUDDY. I GOT A PLAN.
VITA'S GONNA BE SO PROUD OF US.

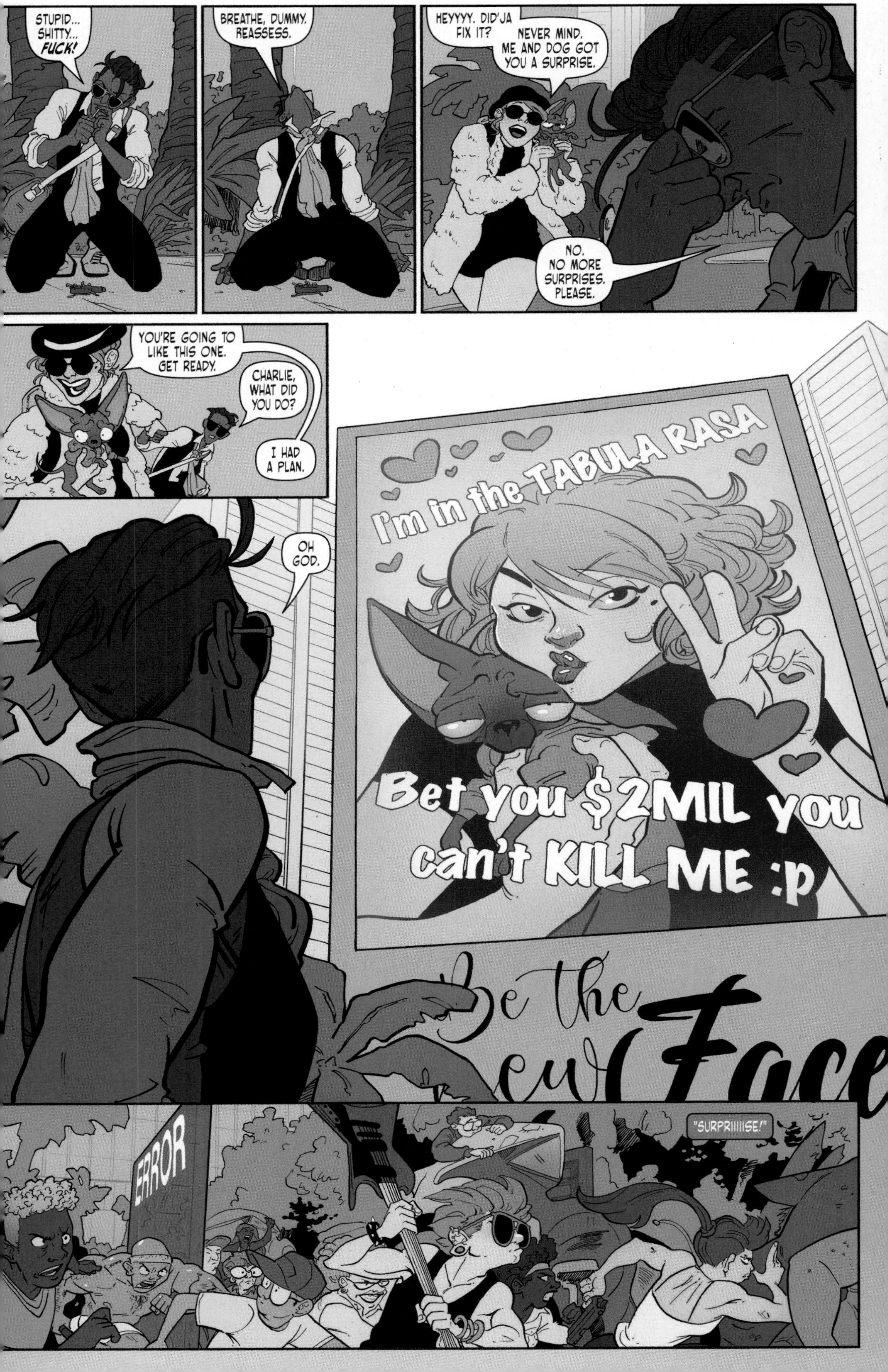
STUPID... SHITTY... FUCK!
BREATHE, DUMMY. REASSESS.
HEYYYY. DID'JA FIX IT?
NEVER MIND. ME AND DOG GOT YOU A SURPRISE.
NO. NO MORE SURPRISES. PLEASE.
YOU'RE GOING TO LIKE THIS ONE. GET READY.
CHARLIE, WHAT DID YOU DO?
I HAD A PLAN.
OH GOD.
I'm in the TABULA RASA
Bet you $2MIL you can't KILL ME :p
ERROR
"SURPRIIIIISE!"

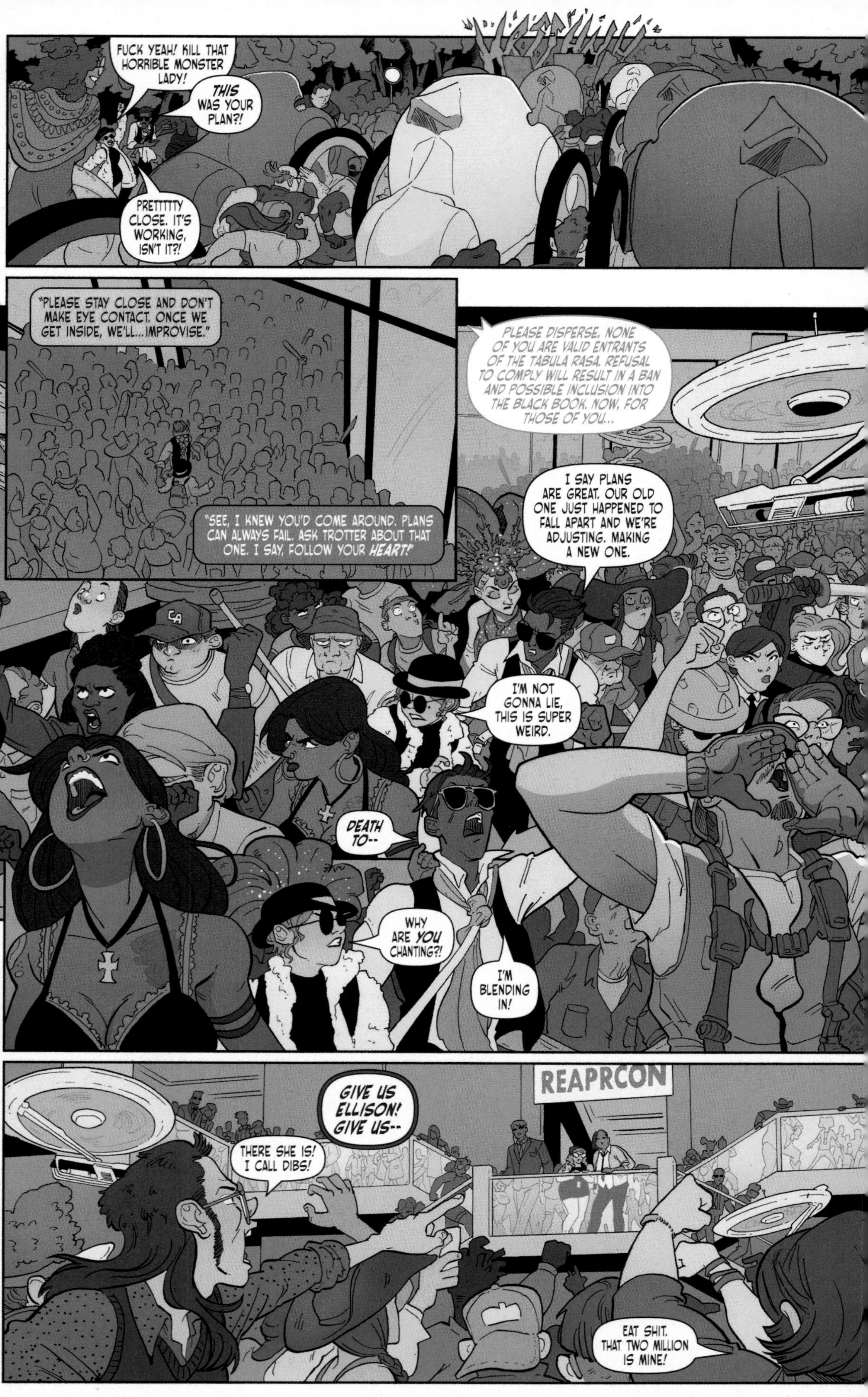
FUCK YEAH! KILL THAT HORRIBLE MONSTER LADY!
THIS WAS YOUR PLAN?!
PRETTTTTY CLOSE. IT'S WORKING, ISN'T IT?!
"PLEASE STAY CLOSE AND DON'T MAKE EYE CONTACT. ONCE WE GET INSIDE, WE'LL...IMPROVISE."
"SEE, I KNEW YOU'D COME AROUND. PLANS CAN ALWAYS FAIL. ASK TROTTER ABOUT THAT ONE. I SAY, FOLLOW YOUR HEART!"
PLEASE DISPERSE, NONE OF YOU ARE VALID ENTRANTS OF THE TABULA RASA. REFUSAL TO COMPLY WILL RESULT IN A BAN AND POSSIBLE INCLUSION INTO THE BLACK BOOK. NOW, FOR THOSE OF YOU...
I SAY PLANS ARE GREAT. OUR OLD ONE JUST HAPPENED TO FALL APART AND WE'RE ADJUSTING. MAKING A NEW ONE.
I'M NOT GONNA LIE, THIS IS SUPER WEIRD.
DEATH TO--
WHY ARE YOU CHANTING?!
I'M BLENDING IN!
REAPRCON
GIVE US ELLISON! GIVE US--
THERE SHE IS! I CALL DIBS!
EAT SHIT. THAT TWO MILLION IS MINE!

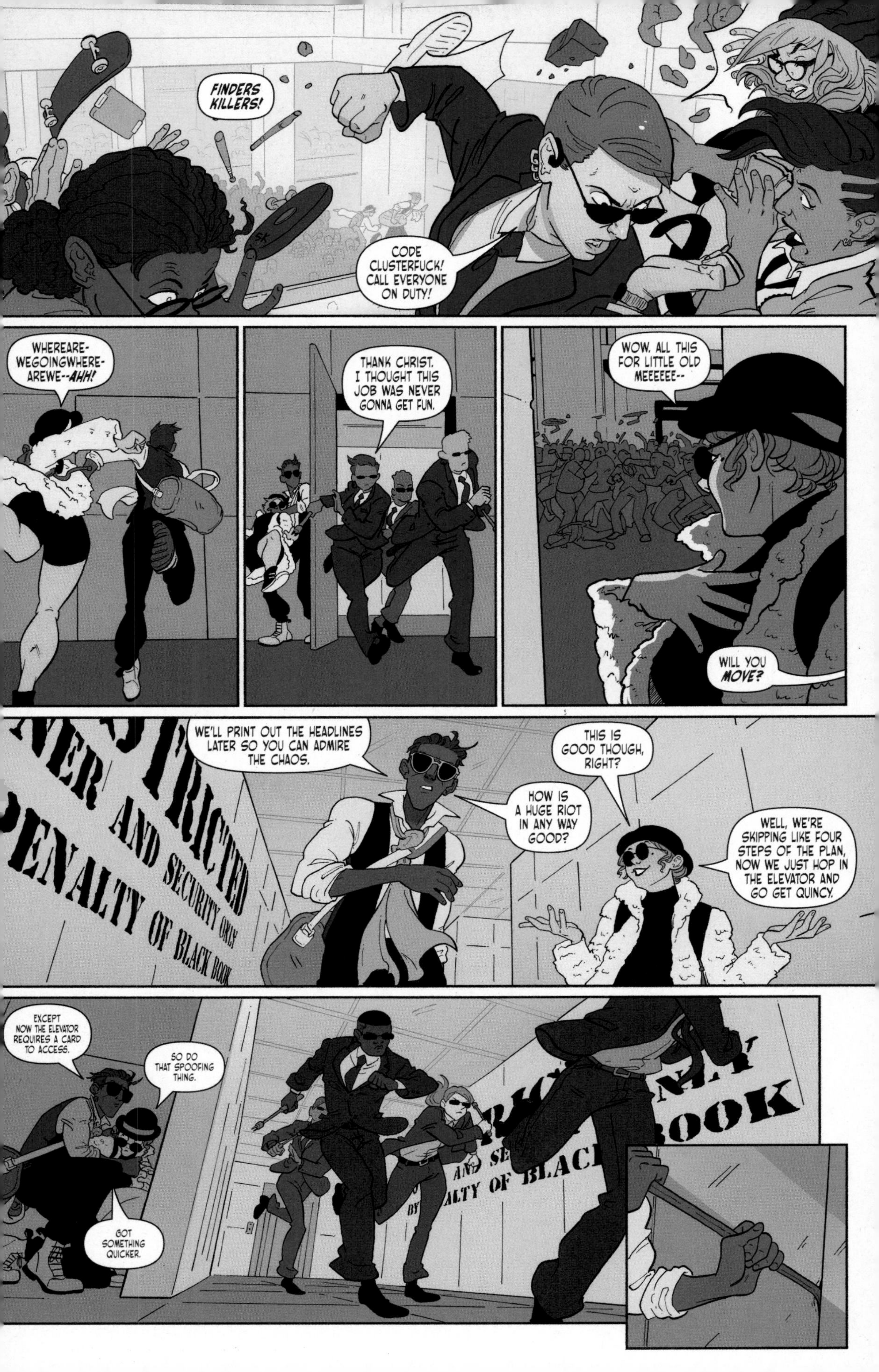
FINDERS KILLERS!
CODE CLUSTERFUCK! CALL EVERYONE ON DUTY!
WHEREARE-WEGOINGWHERE-AREWE--AHH!
THANK CHRIST. I THOUGHT THIS JOB WAS NEVER GONNA GET FUN.
WOW. ALL THIS FOR LITTLE OLD MEEEEEE--
WILL YOU MOVE?
WE'LL PRINT OUT THE HEADLINES LATER SO YOU CAN ADMIRE THE CHAOS.
THIS IS GOOD THOUGH, RIGHT?
HOW IS A HUGE RIOT IN ANY WAY GOOD?
WELL, WE'RE SKIPPING LIKE FOUR STEPS OF THE PLAN, NOW WE JUST HOP IN THE ELEVATOR AND GO GET QUINCY.
RESTRICTED
AND SECURITY ONLY
PENALTY OF BLACK BOOK
EXCEPT NOW THE ELEVATOR REQUIRES A CARD TO ACCESS.
SO DO THAT SPOOFING THING.
GOT SOMETHING QUICKER.

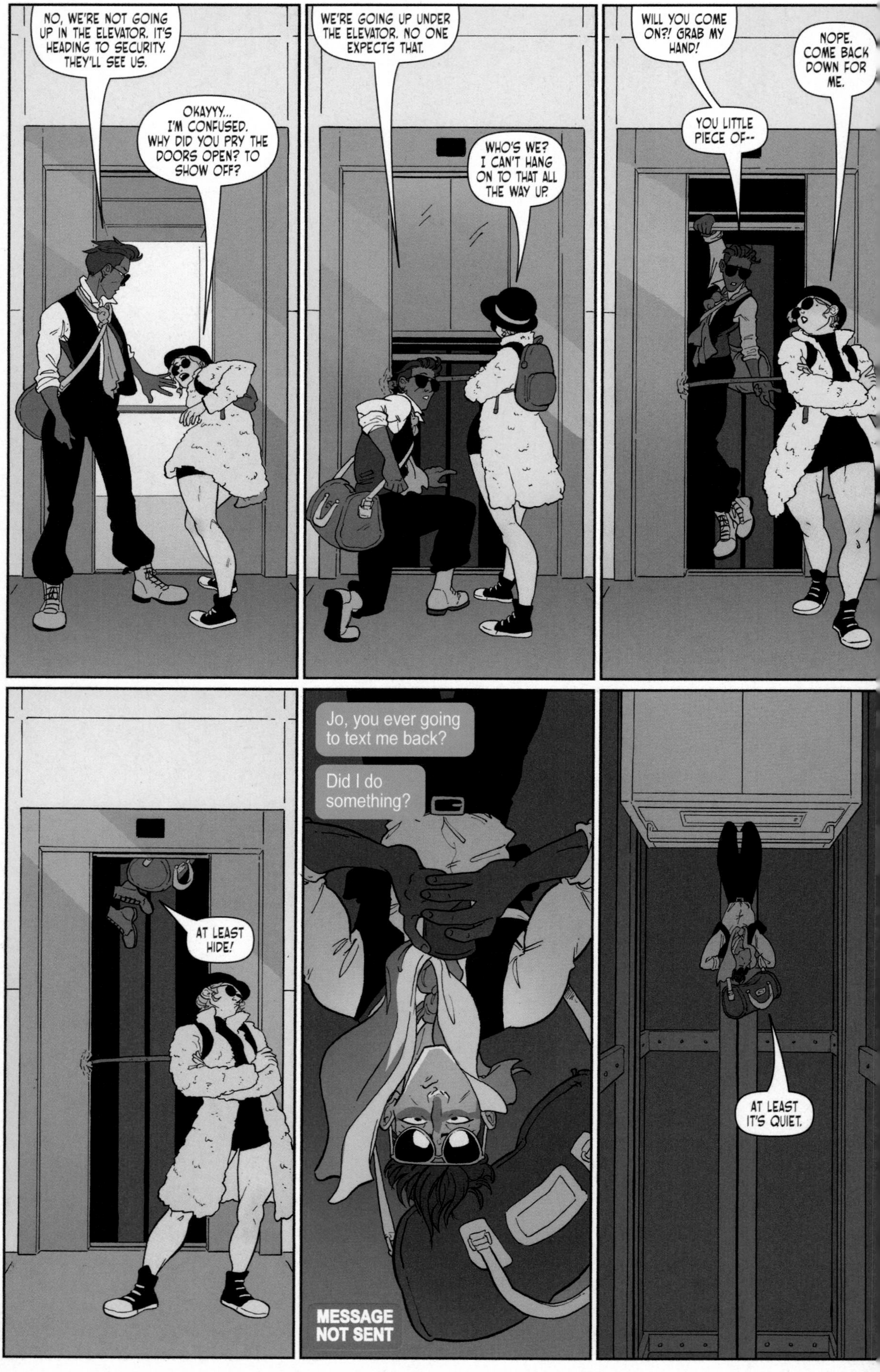
NO, WE'RE NOT GOING UP IN THE ELEVATOR. IT'S HEADING TO SECURITY. THEY'LL SEE US.
OKAYYY... I'M CONFUSED. WHY DID YOU PRY THE DOORS OPEN? TO SHOW OFF?
WE'RE GOING UP UNDER THE ELEVATOR. NO ONE EXPECTS THAT.
WHO'S WE? I CAN'T HANG ON TO THAT ALL THE WAY UP.
WILL YOU COME ON?! GRAB MY HAND!
NOPE. COME BACK DOWN FOR ME.
YOU LITTLE PIECE OF--
AT LEAST HIDE!
Jo, you ever going to text me back?
Did I do something?
MESSAGE NOT SENT
AT LEAST IT'S QUIET.

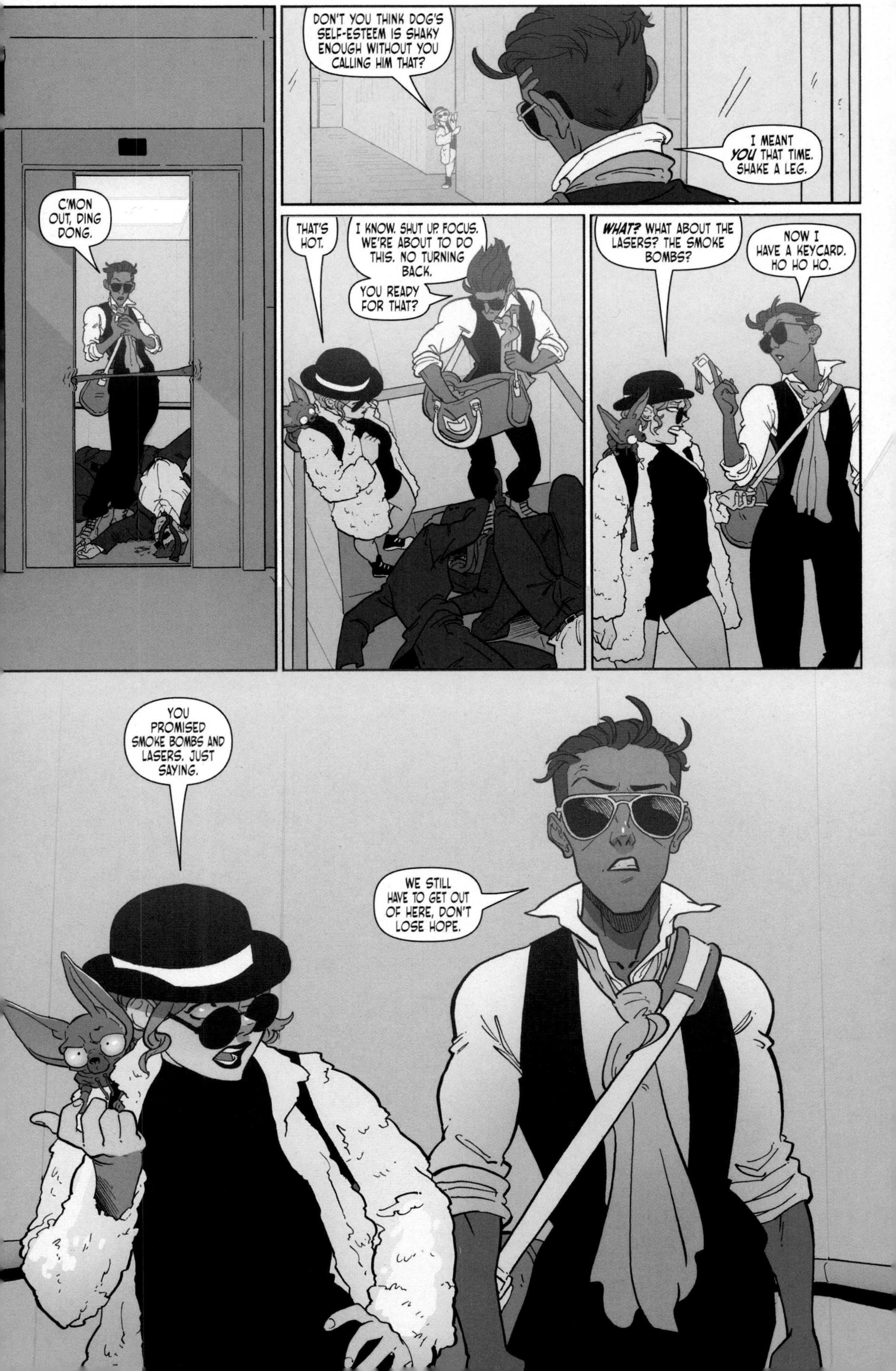
C'MON OUT, DING DONG.
DON'T YOU THINK DOG'S SELF-ESTEEM IS SHAKY ENOUGH WITHOUT YOU CALLING HIM THAT?
I MEANT *YOU* THAT TIME. SHAKE A LEG.
THAT'S HOT.
I KNOW. SHUT UP. FOCUS. WE'RE ABOUT TO DO THIS. NO TURNING BACK.
YOU READY FOR THAT?
WHAT? WHAT ABOUT THE LASERS? THE SMOKE BOMBS?
NOW I HAVE A KEYCARD. HO HO HO.
YOU PROMISED SMOKE BOMBS AND LASERS. JUST SAYING.
WE STILL HAVE TO GET OUT OF HERE, DON'T LOSE HOPE.

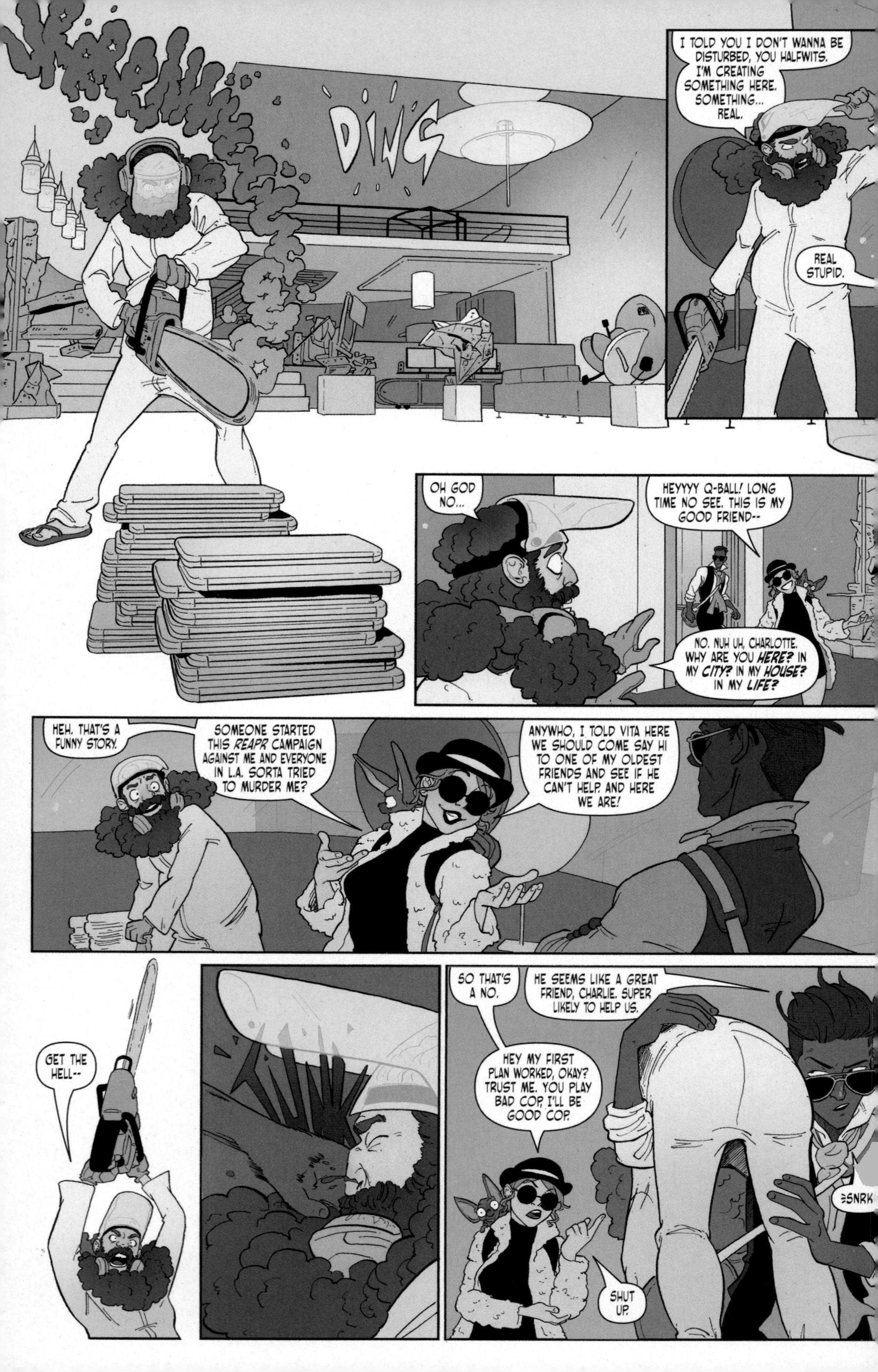

DING
I TOLD YOU I DON'T WANNA BE DISTURBED, YOU HALFWITS. I'M CREATING SOMETHING HERE. SOMETHING... REAL.
REAL STUPID.
OH GOD NO...
HEYYYY Q-BALL! LONG TIME NO SEE. THIS IS MY GOOD FRIEND--
NO. NUH UH, CHARLOTTE. WHY ARE YOU HERE? IN MY CITY? IN MY HOUSE? IN MY LIFE?
HEH. THAT'S A FUNNY STORY.
SOMEONE STARTED THIS REAPR CAMPAIGN AGAINST ME AND EVERYONE IN L.A. SORTA TRIED TO MURDER ME?
ANYWHO, I TOLD VITA HERE WE SHOULD COME SAY HI TO ONE OF MY OLDEST FRIENDS AND SEE IF HE CAN'T HELP. AND HERE WE ARE!
GET THE HELL--
SO THAT'S A NO.
HE SEEMS LIKE A GREAT FRIEND, CHARLIE. SUPER LIKELY TO HELP US.
HEY MY FIRST PLAN WORKED, OKAY? TRUST ME. YOU PLAY BAD COP, I'LL BE GOOD COP.
SNRK
SHUT UP.

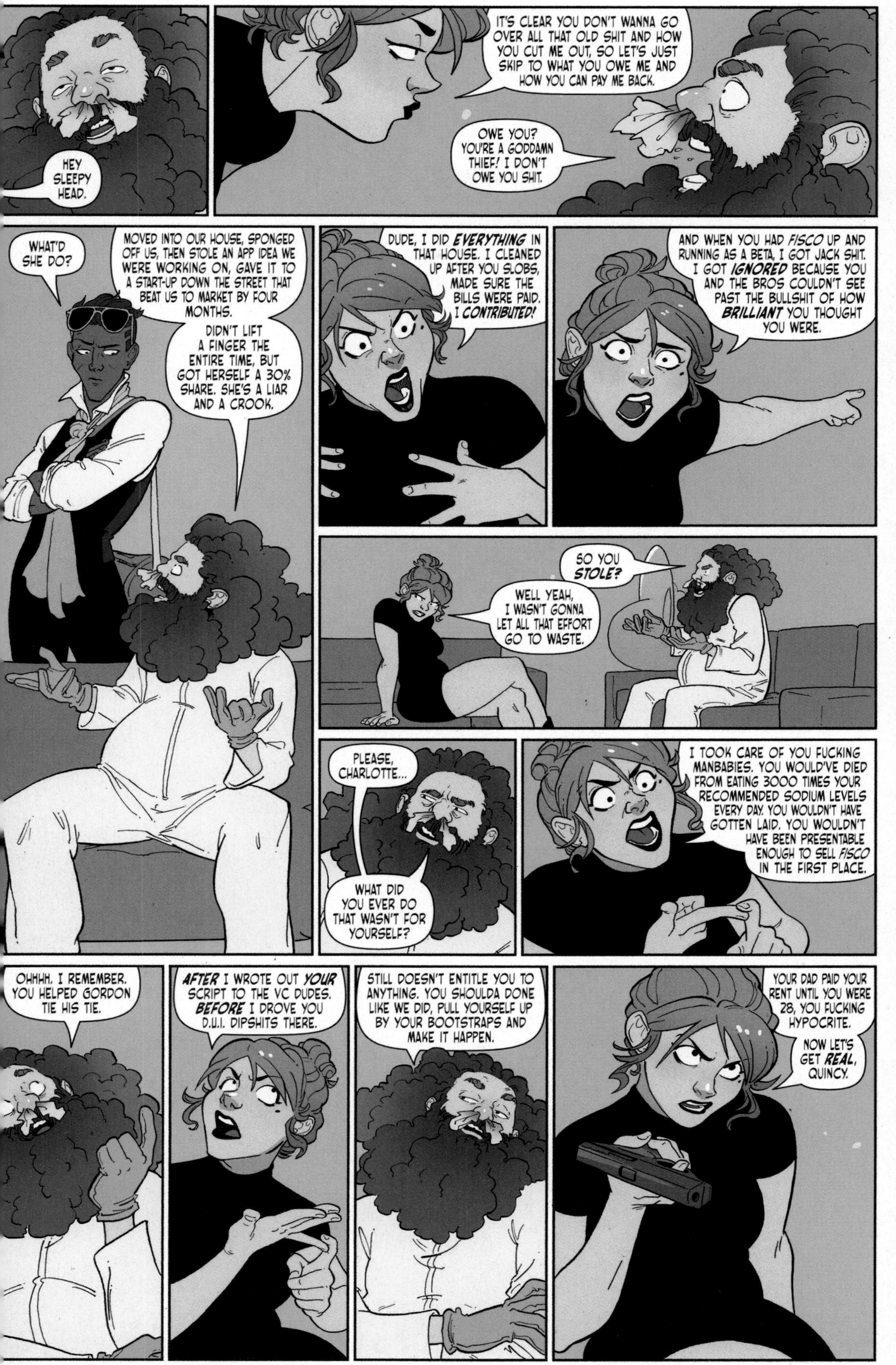
HEY SLEEPY HEAD.
IT'S CLEAR YOU DON'T WANNA GO OVER ALL THAT OLD SHIT AND HOW YOU CUT ME OUT, SO LET'S JUST SKIP TO WHAT YOU OWE ME AND HOW YOU CAN PAY ME BACK.
OWE YOU? YOU'RE A GODDAMN THIEF! I DON'T OWE YOU SHIT.
WHAT'D SHE DO?
MOVED INTO OUR HOUSE, SPONGED OFF US, THEN STOLE AN APP IDEA WE WERE WORKING ON, GAVE IT TO A START-UP DOWN THE STREET THAT BEAT US TO MARKET BY FOUR MONTHS.
DIDN'T LIFT A FINGER THE ENTIRE TIME, BUT GOT HERSELF A 30% SHARE. SHE'S A LIAR AND A CROOK.
DUDE, I DID EVERYTHING IN THAT HOUSE. I CLEANED UP AFTER YOU SLOBS, MADE SURE THE BILLS WERE PAID. I CONTRIBUTED!
AND WHEN YOU HAD FISCO UP AND RUNNING AS A BETA, I GOT JACK SHIT. I GOT IGNORED BECAUSE YOU AND THE BROS COULDN'T SEE PAST THE BULLSHIT OF HOW BRILLIANT YOU THOUGHT YOU WERE.
SO YOU STOLE?
WELL YEAH, I WASN'T GONNA LET ALL THAT EFFORT GO TO WASTE.
PLEASE, CHARLOTTE...
WHAT DID YOU EVER DO THAT WASN'T FOR YOURSELF?
I TOOK CARE OF YOU FUCKING MANBABIES. YOU WOULD'VE DIED FROM EATING 3000 TIMES YOUR RECOMMENDED SODIUM LEVELS EVERY DAY. YOU WOULDN'T HAVE GOTTEN LAID. YOU WOULDN'T HAVE BEEN PRESENTABLE ENOUGH TO SELL FISCO IN THE FIRST PLACE.
OHHHH. I REMEMBER. YOU HELPED GORDON TIE HIS TIE.
AFTER I WROTE OUT YOUR SCRIPT TO THE VC DUDES. BEFORE I DROVE YOU D.U.I. DIPSHITS THERE.
STILL DOESN'T ENTITLE YOU TO ANYTHING. YOU SHOULDA DONE LIKE WE DID, PULL YOURSELF UP BY YOUR BOOTSTRAPS AND MAKE IT HAPPEN.
YOUR DAD PAID YOUR RENT UNTIL YOU WERE 28, YOU FUCKING HYPOCRITE.
NOW LET'S GET REAL, QUINCY.

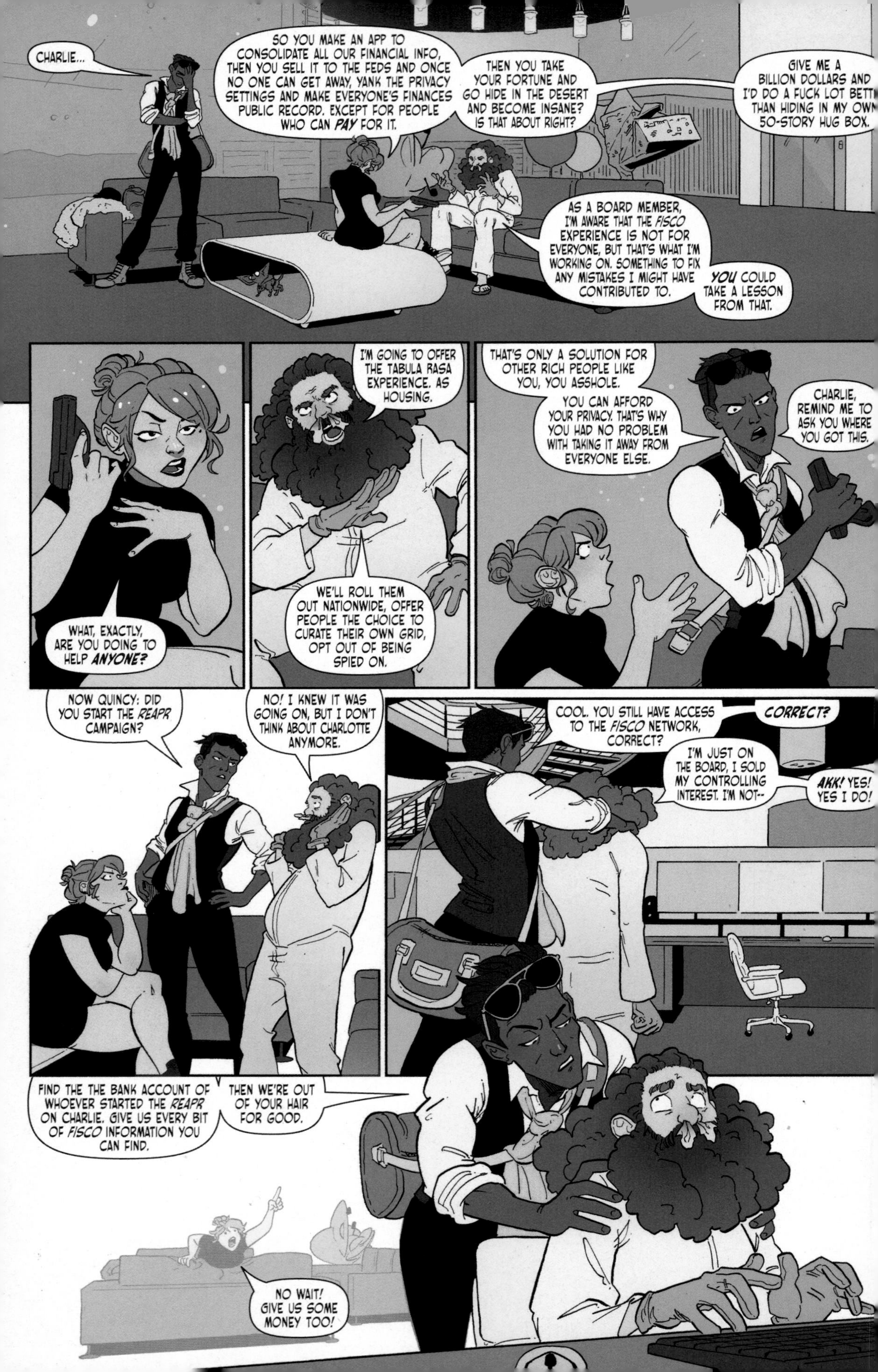

CHARLIE...
SO YOU MAKE AN APP TO CONSOLIDATE ALL OUR FINANCIAL INFO, THEN YOU SELL IT TO THE FEDS AND ONCE NO ONE CAN GET AWAY, YANK THE PRIVACY SETTINGS AND MAKE EVERYONE'S FINANCES PUBLIC RECORD. EXCEPT FOR PEOPLE WHO CAN *PAY* FOR IT.
THEN YOU TAKE YOUR FORTUNE AND GO HIDE IN THE DESERT AND BECOME INSANE? IS THAT ABOUT RIGHT?
GIVE ME A BILLION DOLLARS AND I'D DO A FUCK LOT BETT THAN HIDING IN MY OWN 50-STORY HUG BOX.
AS A BOARD MEMBER, I'M AWARE THAT THE *FISCO* EXPERIENCE IS NOT FOR EVERYONE, BUT THAT'S WHAT I'M WORKING ON. SOMETHING TO FIX ANY MISTAKES I MIGHT HAVE CONTRIBUTED TO.
YOU COULD TAKE A LESSON FROM THAT.
WHAT, EXACTLY, ARE YOU DOING TO HELP *ANYONE?*
I'M GOING TO OFFER THE TABULA RASA EXPERIENCE. AS HOUSING.
WE'LL ROLL THEM OUT NATIONWIDE, OFFER PEOPLE THE CHOICE TO CURATE THEIR OWN GRID, OPT OUT OF BEING SPIED ON.
THAT'S ONLY A SOLUTION FOR OTHER RICH PEOPLE LIKE YOU, YOU ASSHOLE.
YOU CAN AFFORD YOUR PRIVACY. THAT'S WHY YOU HAD NO PROBLEM WITH TAKING IT AWAY FROM EVERYONE ELSE.
CHARLIE, REMIND ME TO ASK YOU WHERE YOU GOT THIS.
NOW QUINCY: DID YOU START THE *REAPR* CAMPAIGN?
NO! I KNEW IT WAS GOING ON, BUT I DON'T THINK ABOUT CHARLOTTE ANYMORE.
COOL. YOU STILL HAVE ACCESS TO THE *FISCO* NETWORK, CORRECT?
I'M JUST ON THE BOARD, I SOLD MY CONTROLLING INTEREST. I'M NOT--
CORRECT?
AKK! YES! YES I DO!
FIND THE THE BANK ACCOUNT OF WHOEVER STARTED THE *REAPR* ON CHARLIE. GIVE US EVERY BIT OF *FISCO* INFORMATION YOU CAN FIND.
THEN WE'RE OUT OF YOUR HAIR FOR GOOD.
NO WAIT! GIVE US SOME MONEY TOO!

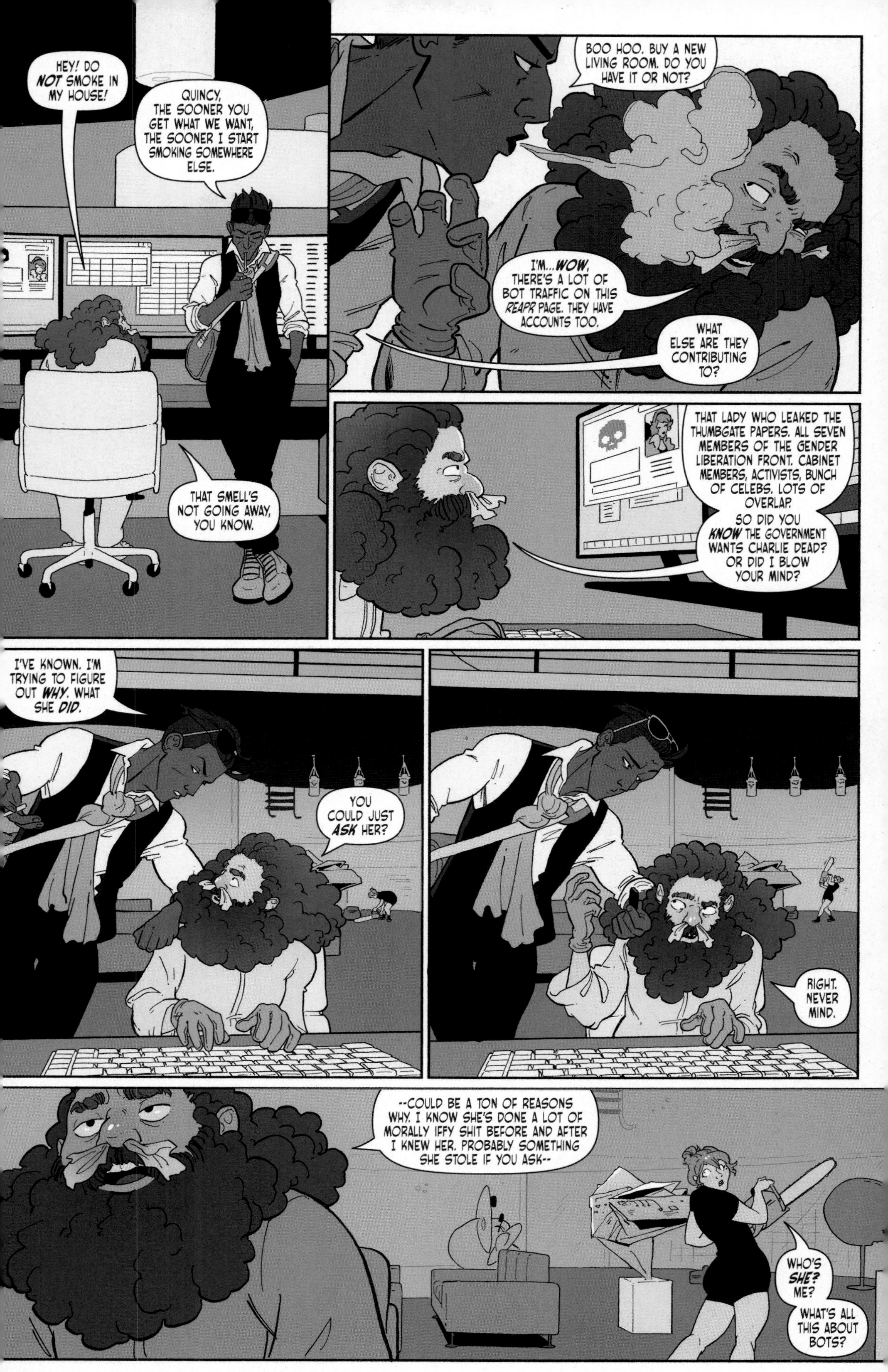
HEY! DO NOT SMOKE IN MY HOUSE!
QUINCY, THE SOONER YOU GET WHAT WE WANT, THE SOONER I START SMOKING SOMEWHERE ELSE.
THAT SMELL'S NOT GOING AWAY, YOU KNOW.
BOO HOO. BUY A NEW LIVING ROOM. DO YOU HAVE IT OR NOT?
I'M...WOW, THERE'S A LOT OF BOT TRAFFIC ON THIS REAPR PAGE. THEY HAVE ACCOUNTS TOO.
WHAT ELSE ARE THEY CONTRIBUTING TO?
THAT LADY WHO LEAKED THE THUMBGATE PAPERS. ALL SEVEN MEMBERS OF THE GENDER LIBERATION FRONT. CABINET MEMBERS, ACTIVISTS, BUNCH OF CELEBS. LOTS OF OVERLAP.
SO DID YOU KNOW THE GOVERNMENT WANTS CHARLIE DEAD? OR DID I BLOW YOUR MIND?
I'VE KNOWN. I'M TRYING TO FIGURE OUT WHY. WHAT SHE DID.
YOU COULD JUST ASK HER?
RIGHT. NEVER MIND.
--COULD BE A TON OF REASONS WHY. I KNOW SHE'S DONE A LOT OF MORALLY IFFY SHIT BEFORE AND AFTER I KNEW HER. PROBABLY SOMETHING SHE STOLE IF YOU ASK--
WHO'S SHE? ME?
WHAT'S ALL THIS ABOUT BOTS?

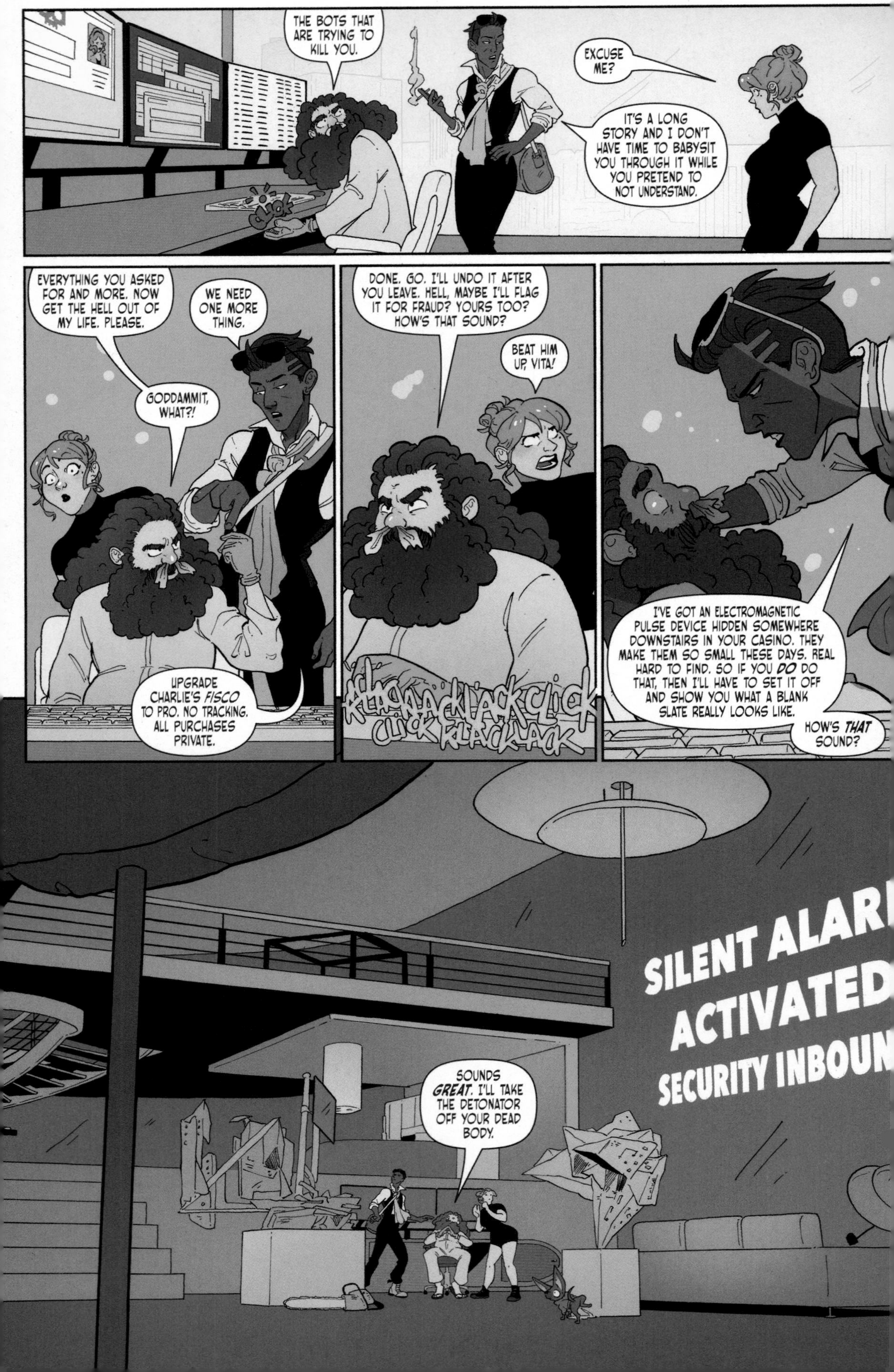
THE BOTS THAT ARE TRYING TO KILL YOU.
EXCUSE ME?
IT'S A LONG STORY AND I DON'T HAVE TIME TO BABYSIT YOU THROUGH IT WHILE YOU PRETEND TO NOT UNDERSTAND.
CLICK
EVERYTHING YOU ASKED FOR AND MORE. NOW GET THE HELL OUT OF MY LIFE. PLEASE.
WE NEED ONE MORE THING.
GODDAMMIT, WHAT?!
UPGRADE CHARLIE'S *FISCO* TO PRO. NO TRACKING. ALL PURCHASES PRIVATE.
DONE. GO. I'LL UNDO IT AFTER YOU LEAVE. HELL, MAYBE I'LL FLAG IT FOR FRAUD? YOURS TOO? HOW'S THAT SOUND?
BEAT HIM UP, VITA!
KLACKKLACKKLACKCLICK CLICK KLACKLACK
I'VE GOT AN ELECTROMAGNETIC PULSE DEVICE HIDDEN SOMEWHERE DOWNSTAIRS IN YOUR CASINO. THEY MAKE THEM SO SMALL THESE DAYS. REAL HARD TO FIND. SO IF YOU ***DO*** DO THAT, THEN I'LL HAVE TO SET IT OFF AND SHOW YOU WHAT A BLANK SLATE REALLY LOOKS LIKE.
HOW'S ***THAT*** SOUND?
SILENT ALAR
ACTIVATED
SECURITY INBOUN
SOUNDS ***GREAT***. I'LL TAKE THE DETONATOR OFF YOUR DEAD BODY.

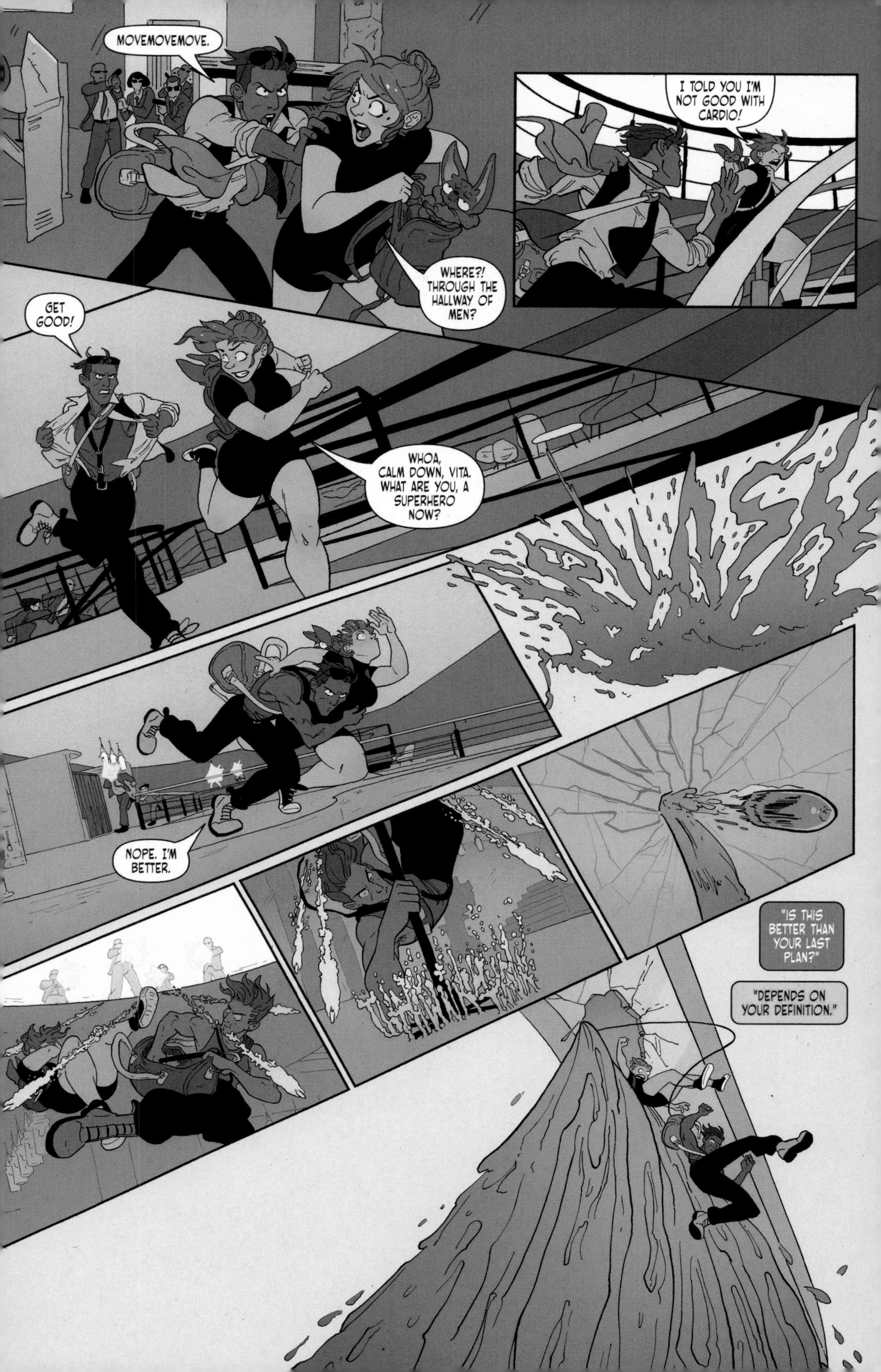
MOVEMOVEMOVE.
WHERE?! THROUGH THE HALLWAY OF MEN?
I TOLD YOU I'M NOT GOOD WITH CARDIO!
GET GOOD!
WHOA, CALM DOWN, VITA. WHAT ARE YOU, A SUPERHERO NOW?
NOPE. I'M BETTER.
"IS THIS BETTER THAN YOUR LAST PLAN?"
"DEPENDS ON YOUR DEFINITION."

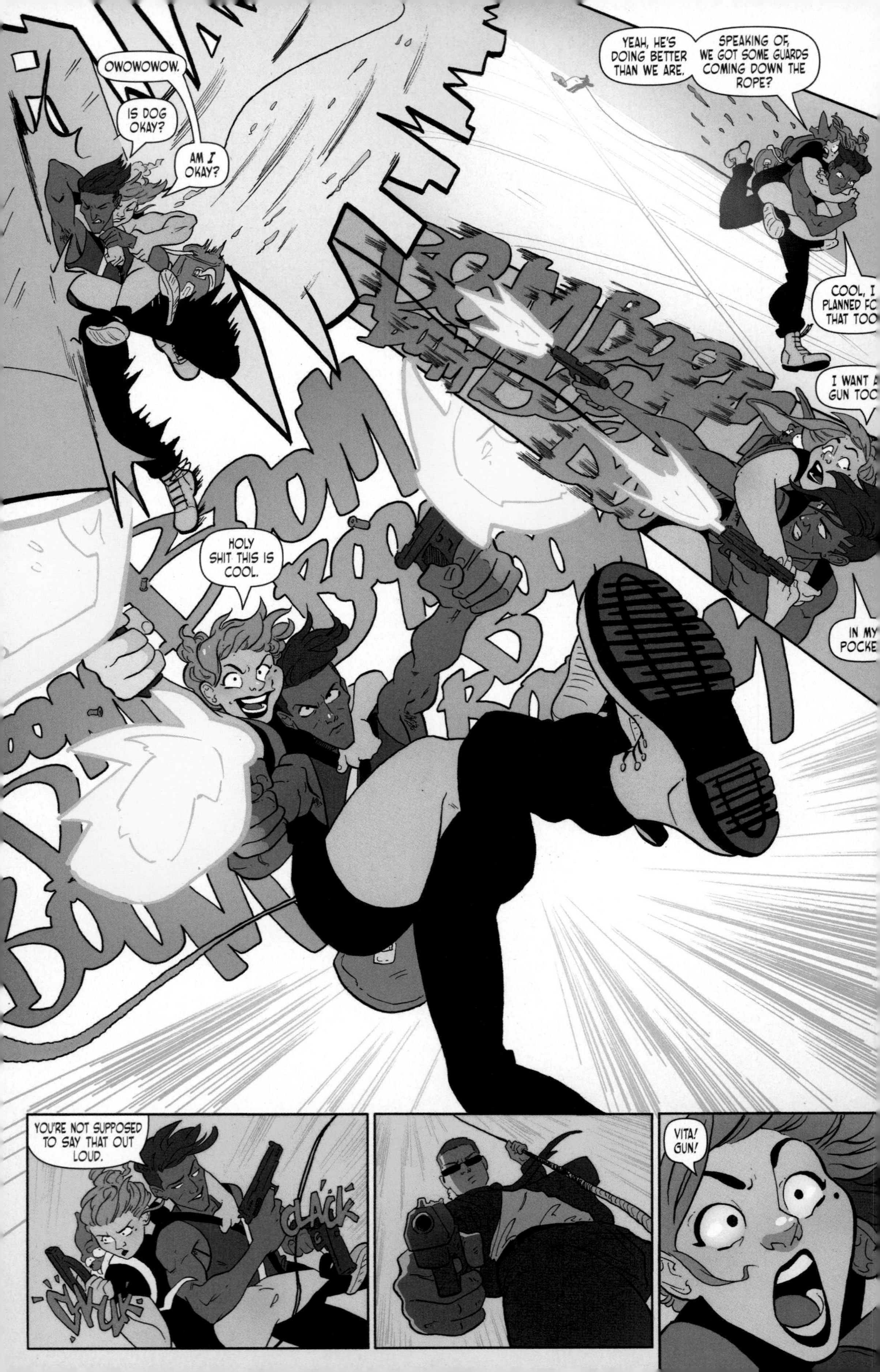
OWOWOWOW.
IS DOG OKAY?
AM I OKAY?
YEAH, HE'S DOING BETTER THAN WE ARE.
SPEAKING OF, WE GOT SOME GUARDS COMING DOWN THE ROPE?
COOL, I PLANNED FO THAT TOO
I WANT A GUN TOO
IN MY POCKE
HOLY SHIT THIS IS COOL.
YOU'RE NOT SUPPOSED TO SAY THAT OUT LOUD.
CLACK
CLACK
VITA! GUN!

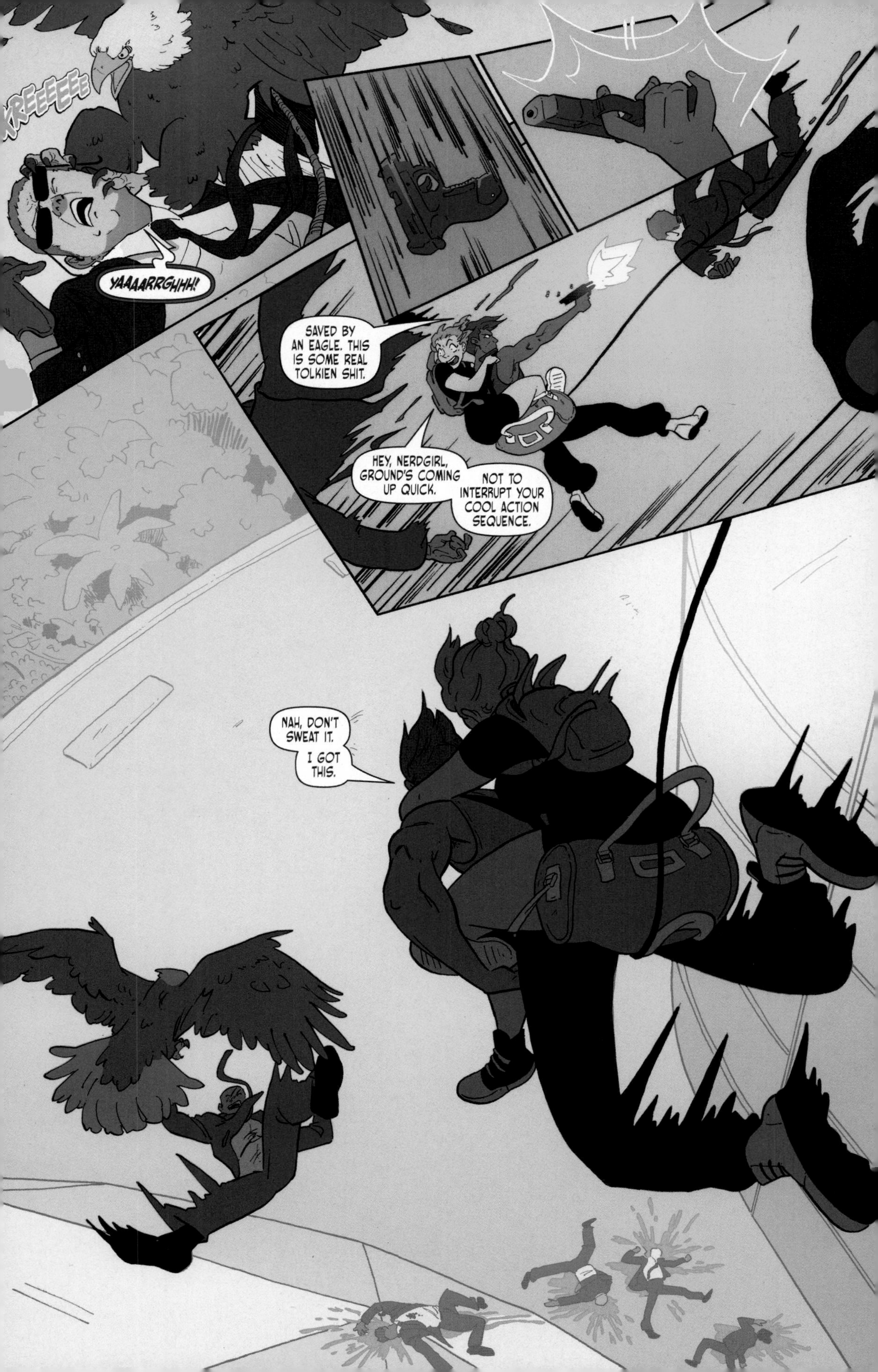
KREEEEEE
YAAAARRGHHH!
SAVED BY AN EAGLE. THIS IS SOME REAL TOLKIEN SHIT.
HEY, NERDGIRL, GROUND'S COMING UP QUICK.
NOT TO INTERRUPT YOUR COOL ACTION SEQUENCE.
NAH, DON'T SWEAT IT.
I GOT THIS.

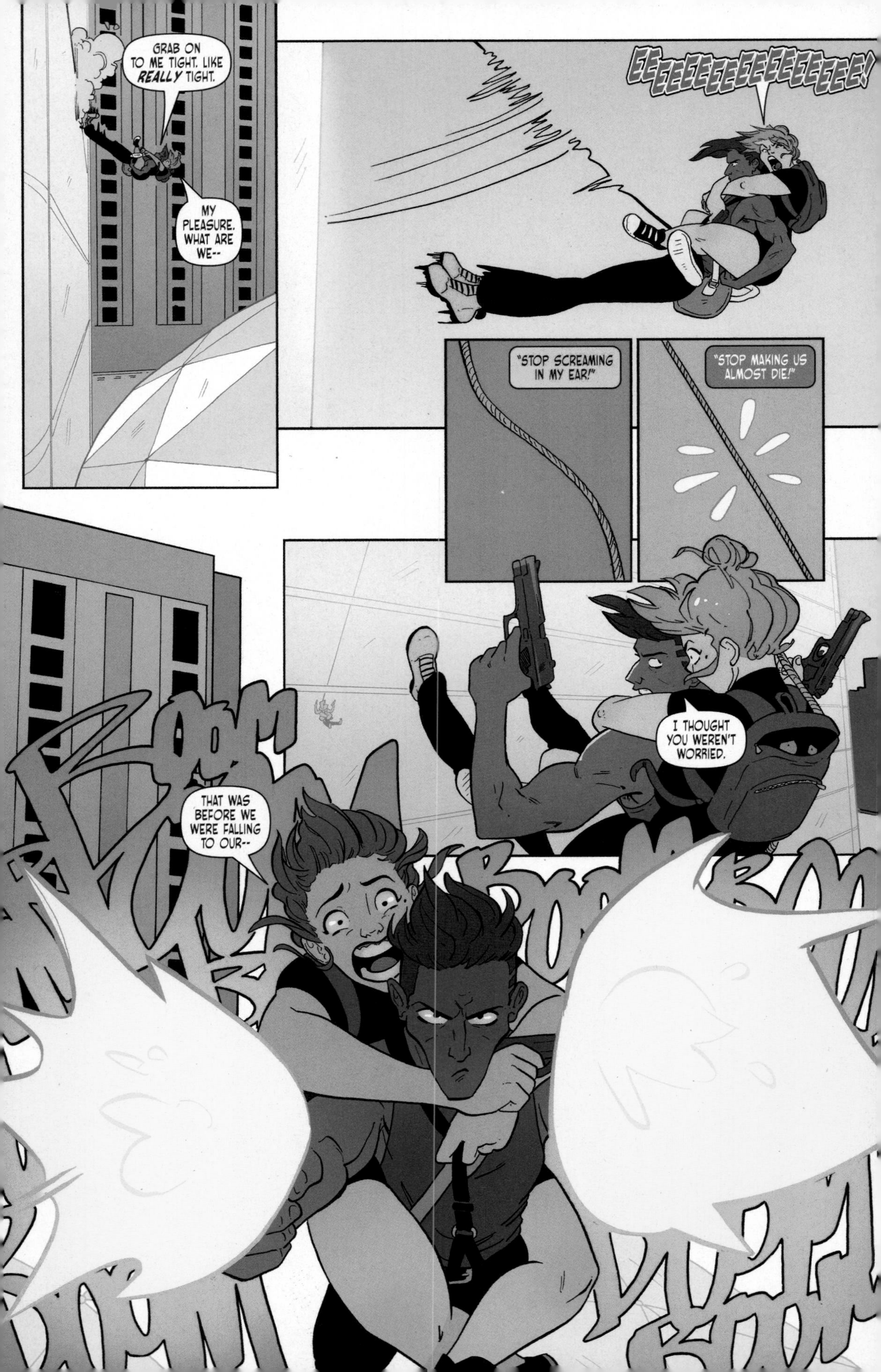
GRAB ON TO ME TIGHT. LIKE REALLY TIGHT.
MY PLEASURE. WHAT ARE WE--
EEEEEEEEEEEEEEEEE!
"STOP SCREAMING IN MY EAR!"
"STOP MAKING US ALMOST DIE!"
I THOUGHT YOU WEREN'T WORRIED.
THAT WAS BEFORE WE WERE FALLING TO OUR--

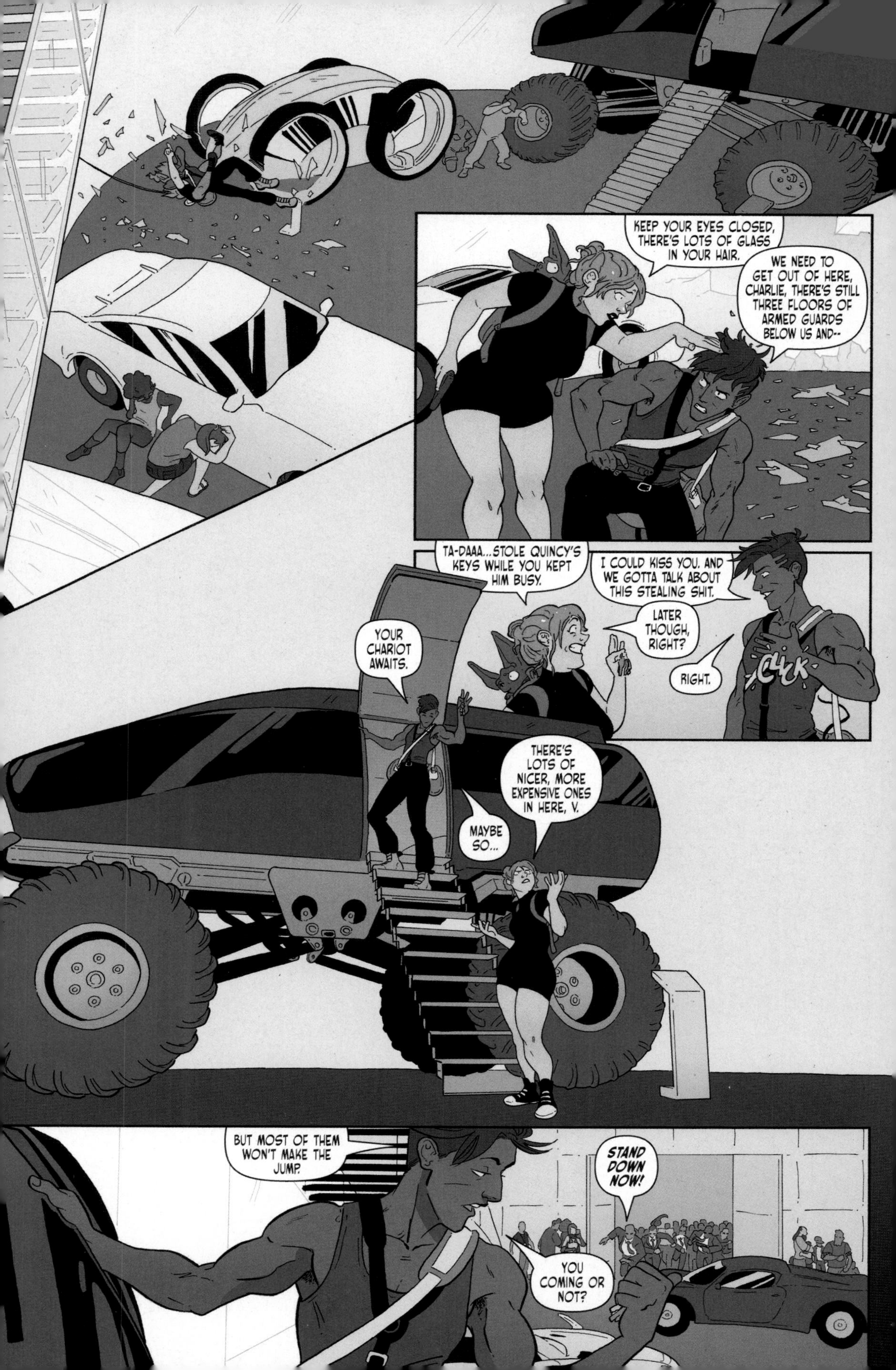
KEEP YOUR EYES CLOSED, THERE'S LOTS OF GLASS IN YOUR HAIR.
WE NEED TO GET OUT OF HERE, CHARLIE, THERE'S STILL THREE FLOORS OF ARMED GUARDS BELOW US AND--
TA-DAAA...STOLE QUINCY'S KEYS WHILE YOU KEPT HIM BUSY.
I COULD KISS YOU. AND WE GOTTA TALK ABOUT THIS STEALING SHIT.
LATER THOUGH, RIGHT?
RIGHT.
CLICK
YOUR CHARIOT AWAITS.
THERE'S LOTS OF NICER, MORE EXPENSIVE ONES IN HERE, V.
MAYBE SO...
BUT MOST OF THEM WON'T MAKE THE JUMP.
STAND DOWN NOW!
YOU COMING OR NOT?

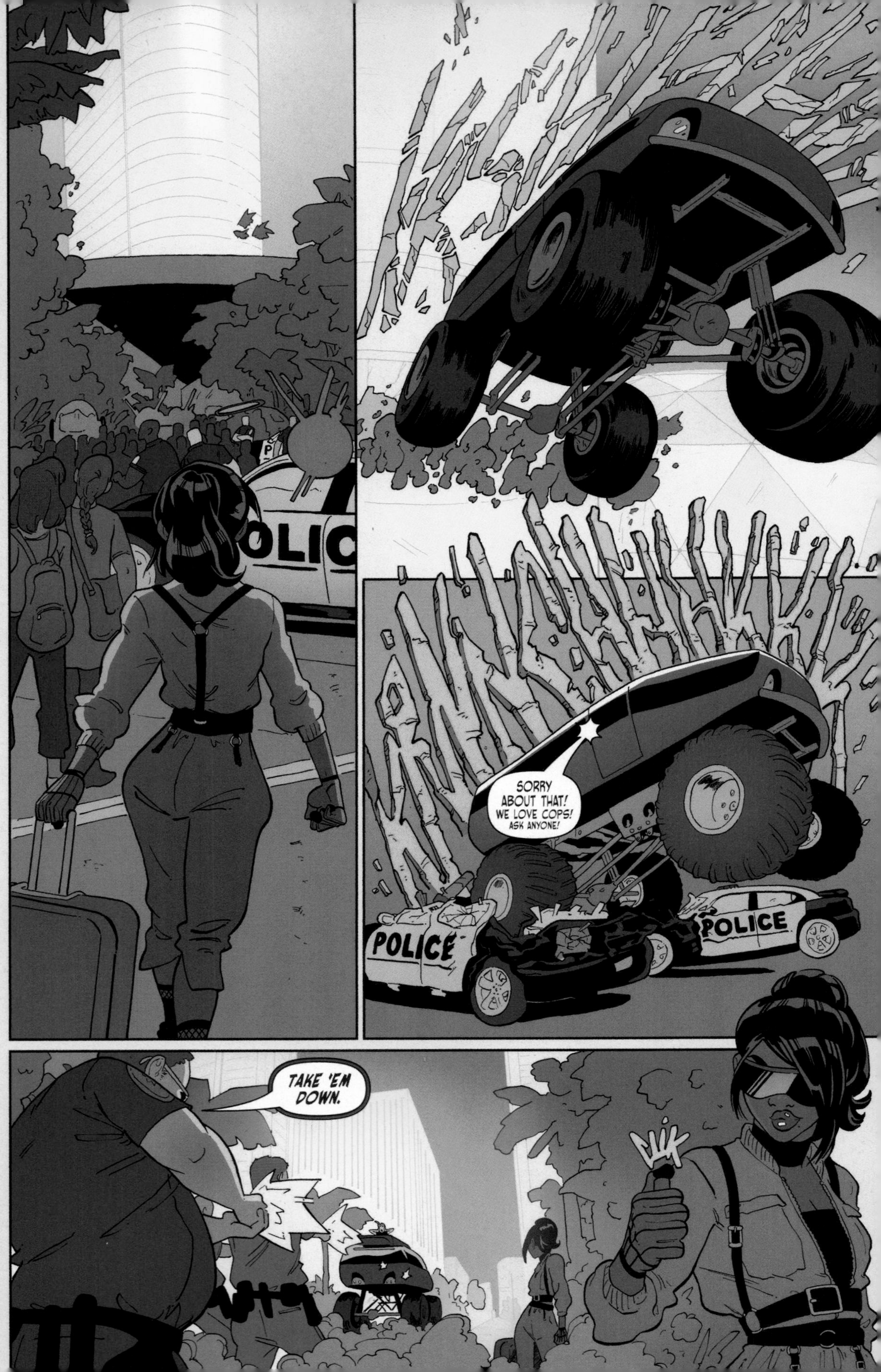
POLIC
SORRY
ABOUT THAT!
WE LOVE COPS!
ASK ANYONE!
POLICE
POLICE
TAKE 'EM
DOWN.
CLIK

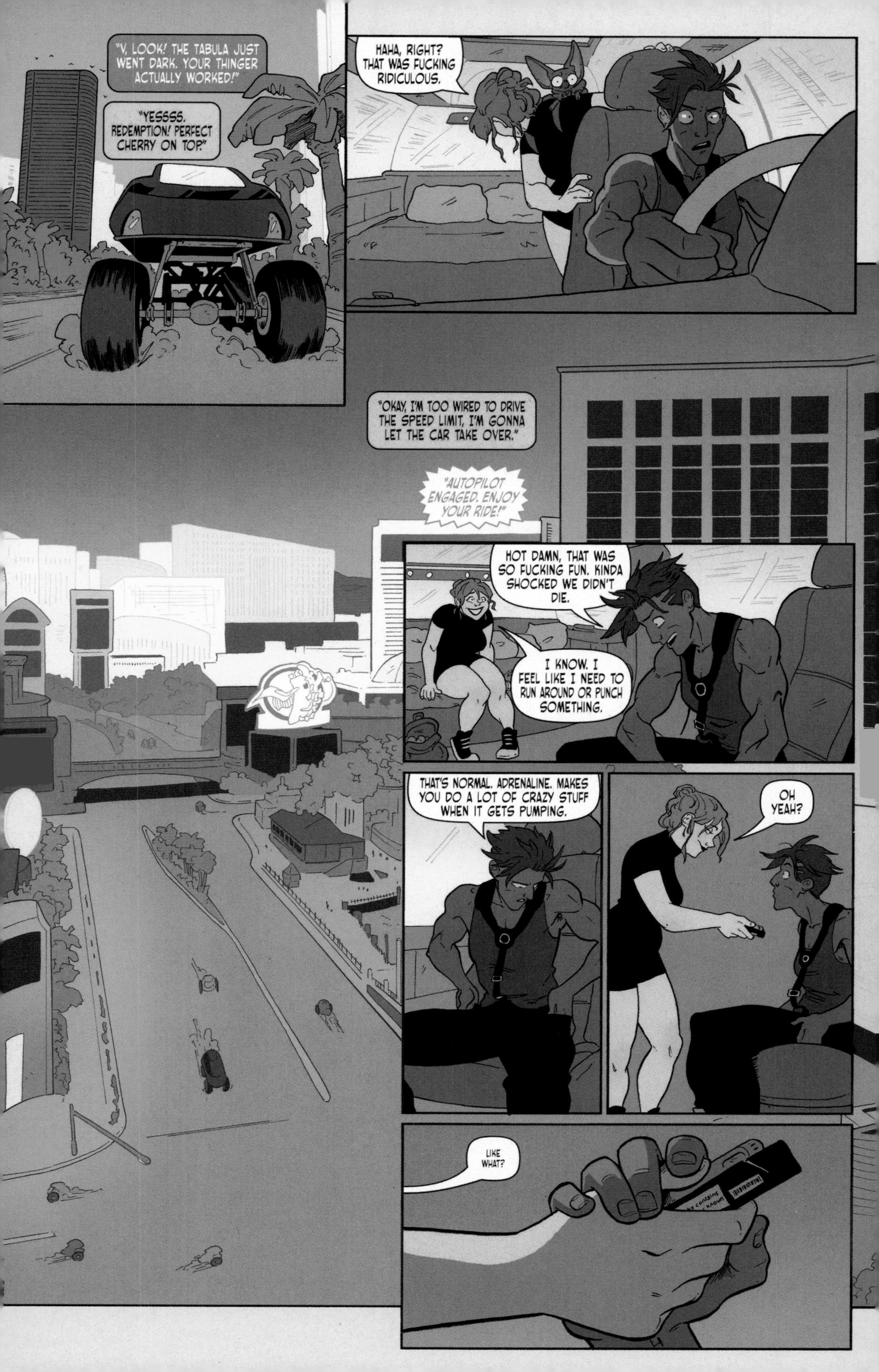
"V, LOOK! THE TABULA JUST WENT DARK. YOUR THINGER ACTUALLY WORKED!"
"YESSSS. REDEMPTION! PERFECT CHERRY ON TOP."
HAHA, RIGHT? THAT WAS FUCKING RIDICULOUS.
"OKAY, I'M TOO WIRED TO DRIVE THE SPEED LIMIT, I'M GONNA LET THE CAR TAKE OVER."
"AUTOPILOT ENGAGED. ENJOY YOUR RIDE!"
HOT DAMN, THAT WAS SO FUCKING FUN. KINDA SHOCKED WE DIDN'T DIE.
I KNOW. I FEEL LIKE I NEED TO RUN AROUND OR PUNCH SOMETHING.
THAT'S NORMAL. ADRENALINE. MAKES YOU DO A LOT OF CRAZY STUFF WHEN IT GETS PUMPING.
OH YEAH?
LIKE WHAT?

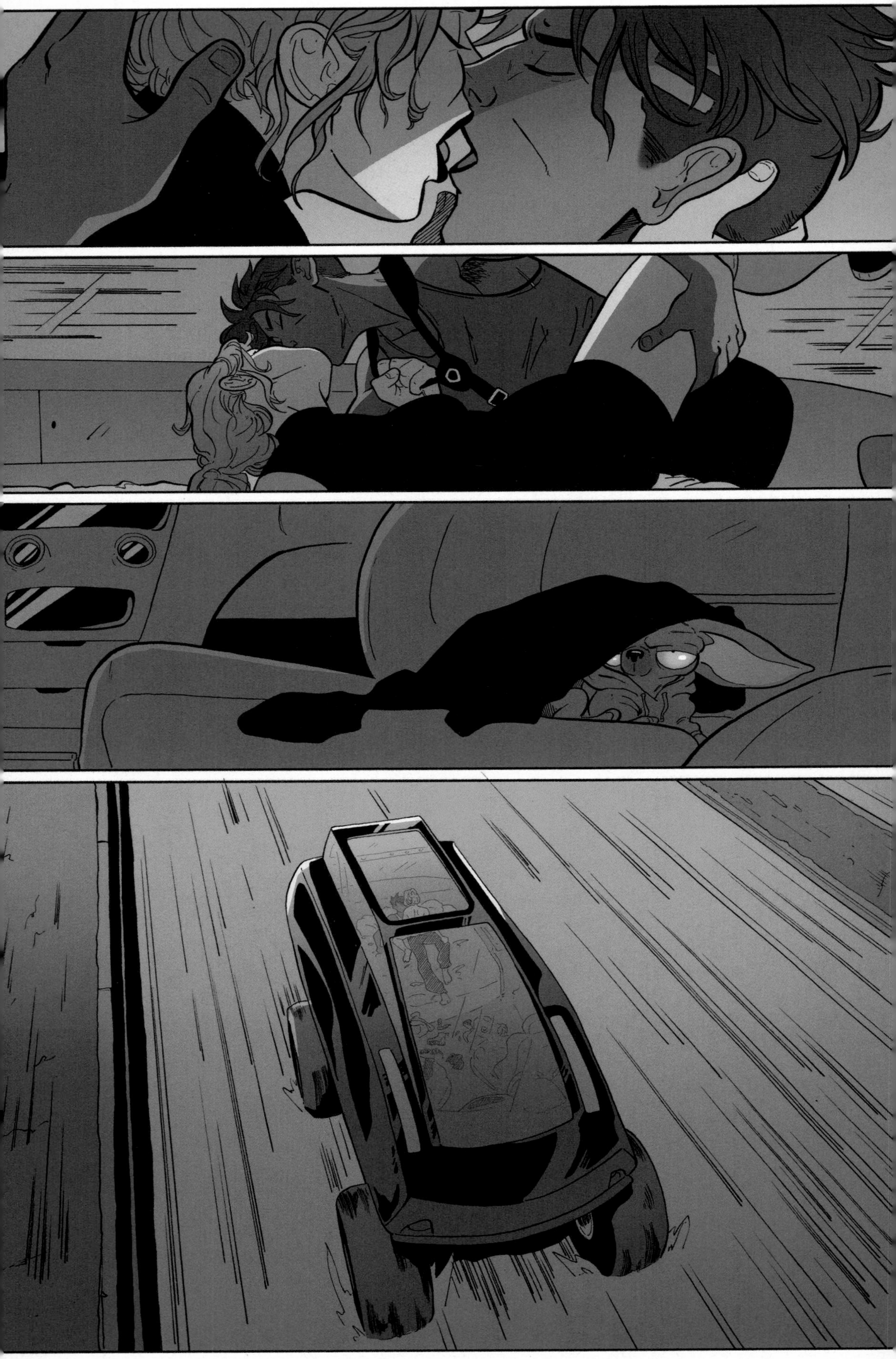

CHAPTER TEN

IF WE'RE STILL ALIVE

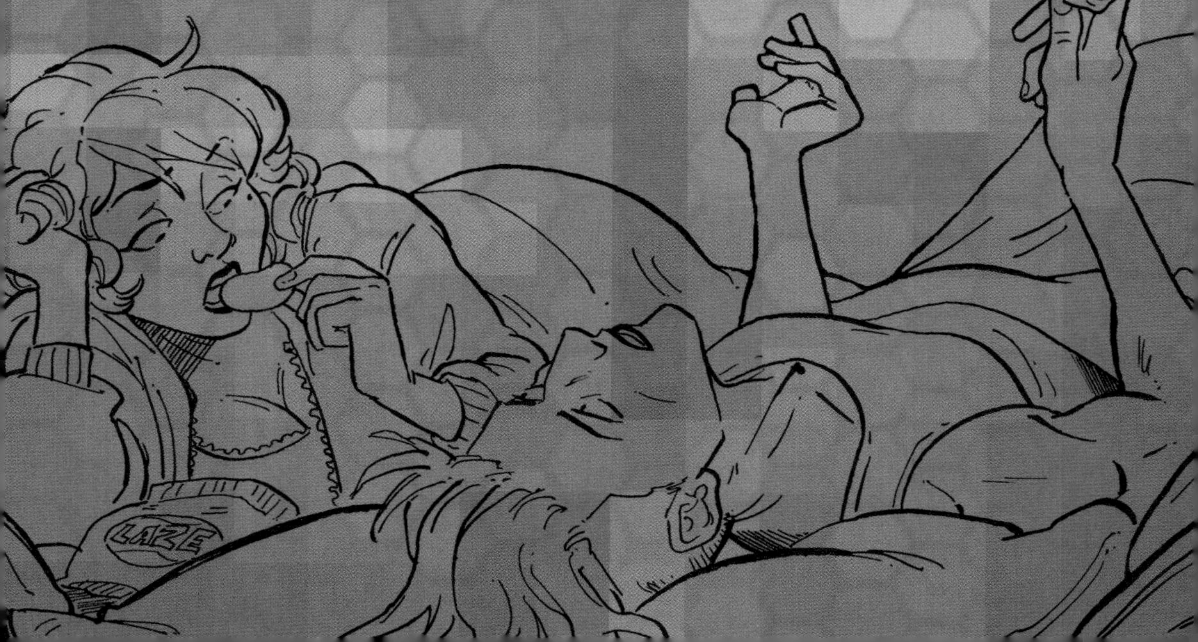
LAZE

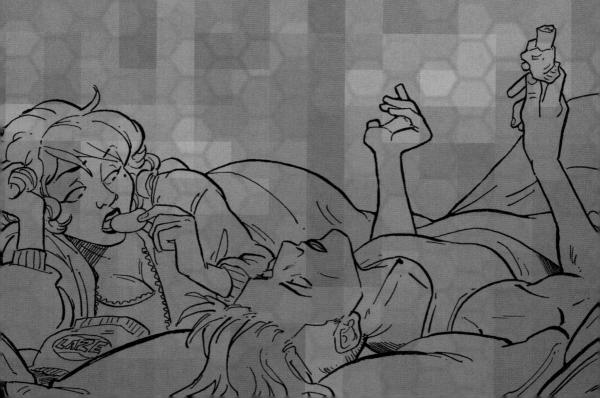

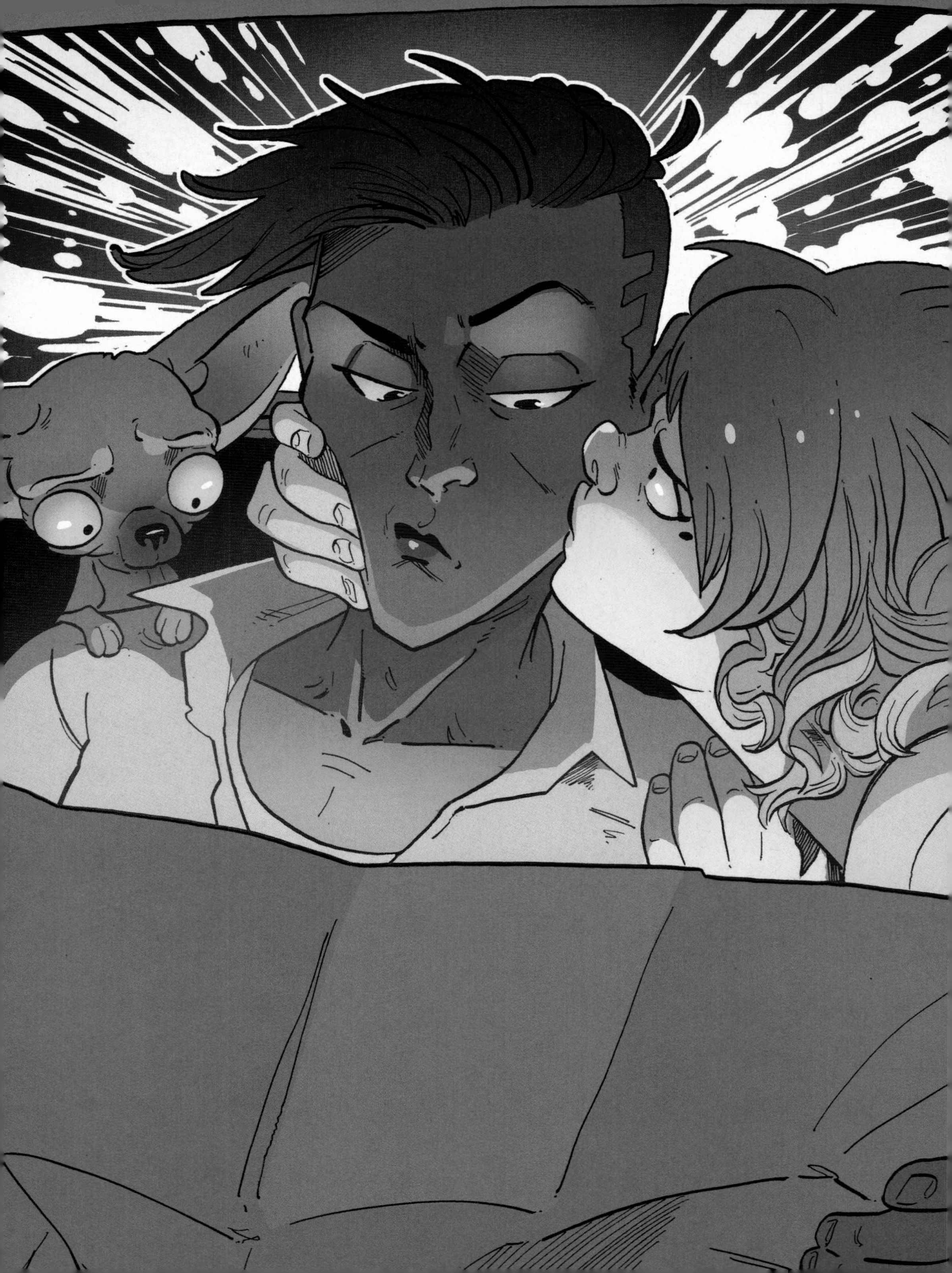

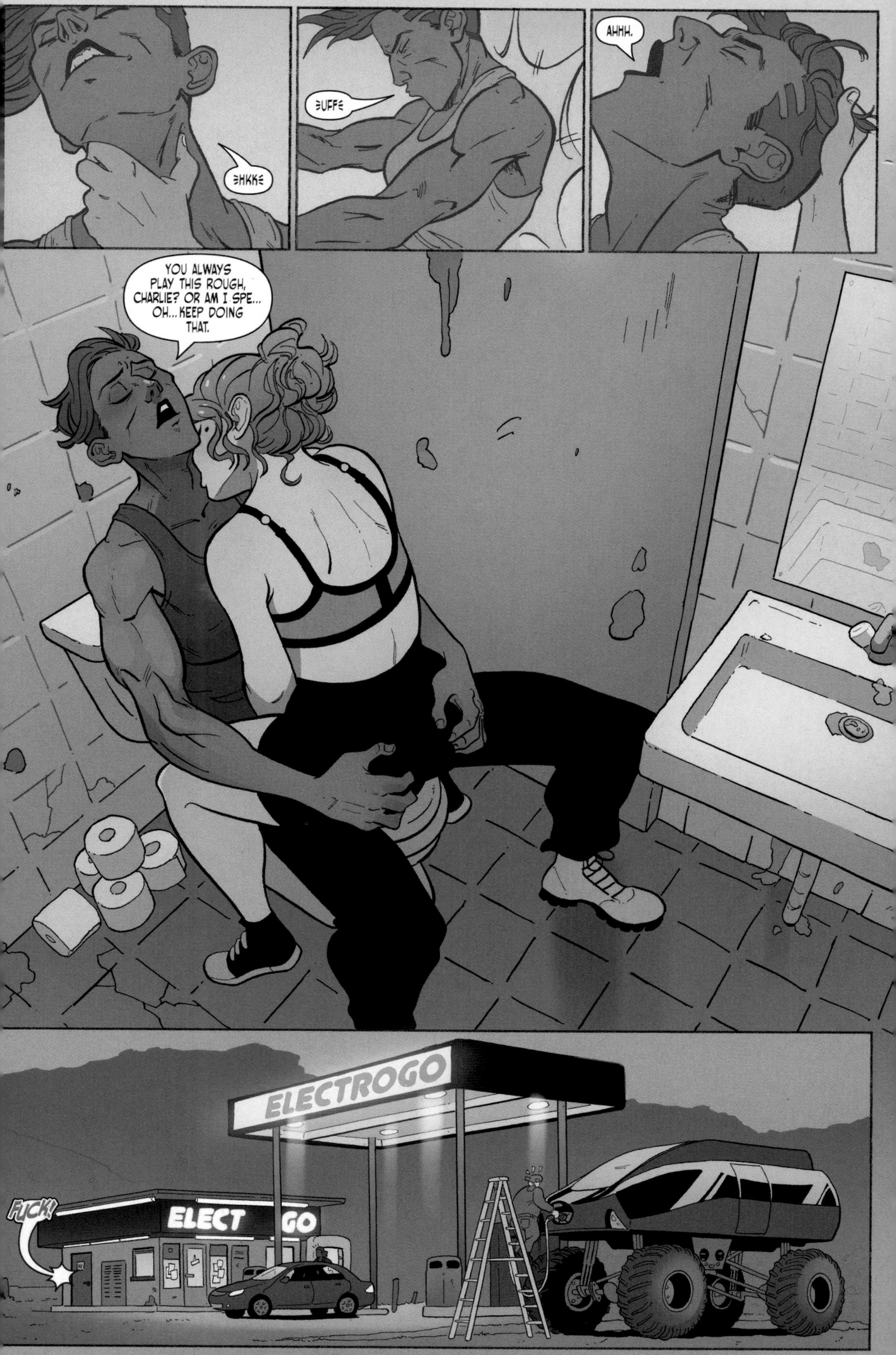
ƎHKKƎ
ƎUFFƎ
AHHH.
YOU ALWAYS PLAY THIS ROUGH, CHARLIE? OR AM I SPE... OH...KEEP DOING THAT.
ELECTROGO
ELECT GO
FUCK!

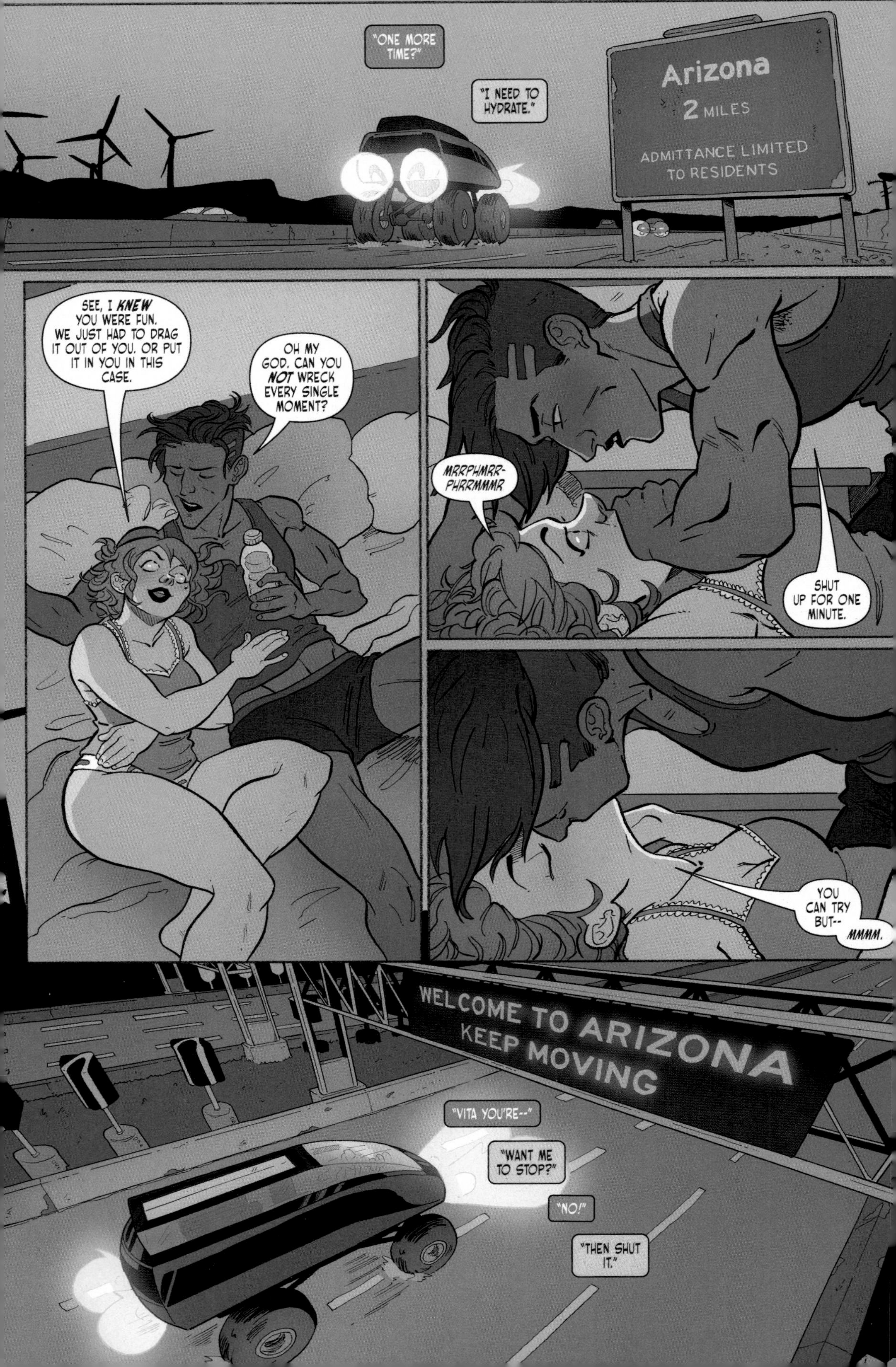
"ONE MORE TIME?"
"I NEED TO HYDRATE."
Arizona
2 MILES
ADMITTANCE LIMITED TO RESIDENTS
SEE, I KNEW YOU WERE FUN. WE JUST HAD TO DRAG IT OUT OF YOU. OR PUT IT IN YOU IN THIS CASE.
OH MY GOD. CAN YOU NOT WRECK EVERY SINGLE MOMENT?
MRRPHMRR-PHRRMMMR
SHUT UP FOR ONE MINUTE.
YOU CAN TRY BUT-- MMMM.
WELCOME TO ARIZONA
KEEP MOVING
"VITA YOU'RE--"
"WANT ME TO STOP?"
"NO!"
"THEN SHUT IT."

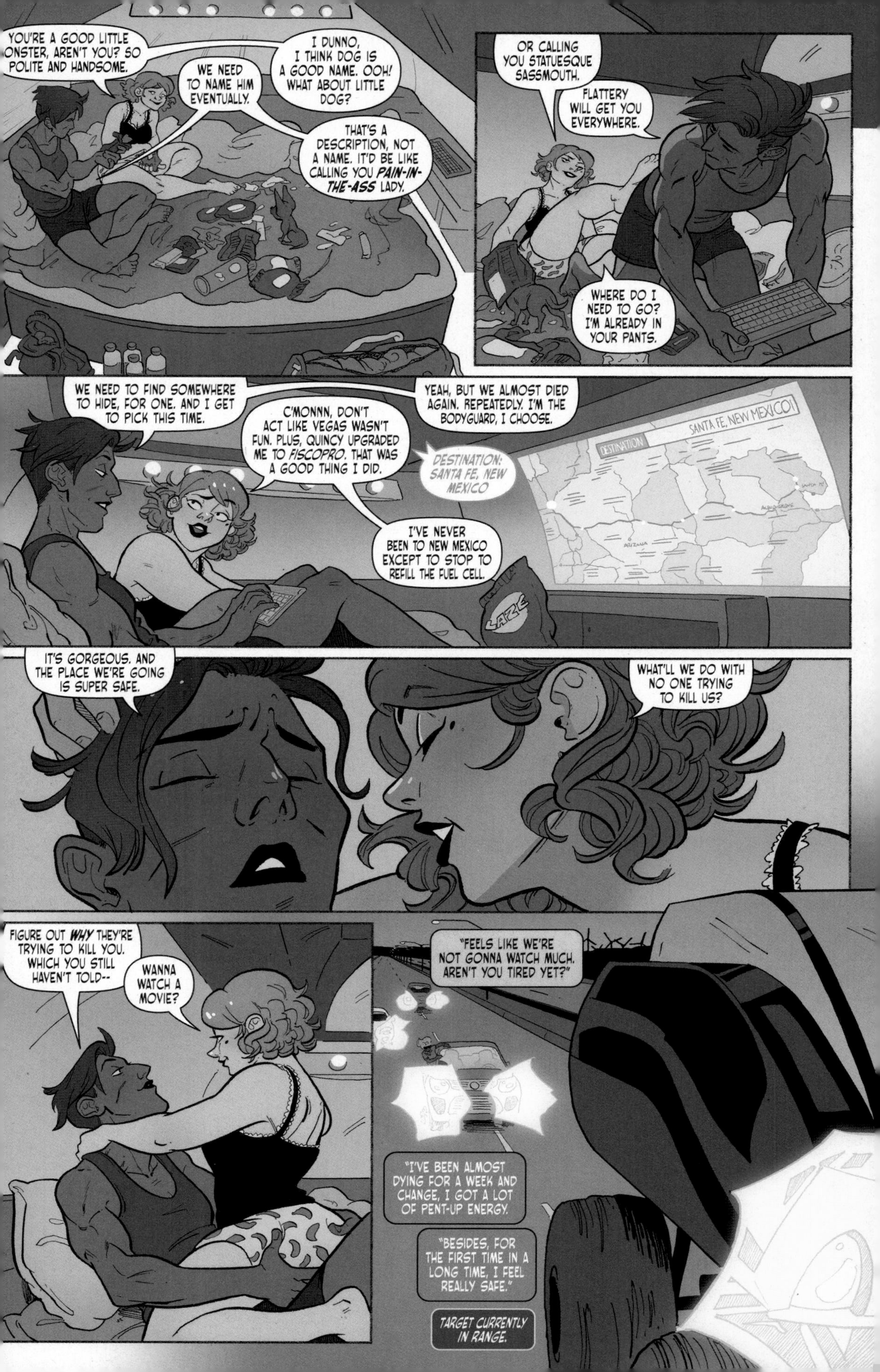
YOU'RE A GOOD LITTLE ONSTER, AREN'T YOU? SO POLITE AND HANDSOME.
WE NEED TO NAME HIM EVENTUALLY.
I DUNNO, I THINK DOG IS A GOOD NAME. OOH! WHAT ABOUT LITTLE DOG?
THAT'S A DESCRIPTION, NOT A NAME. IT'D BE LIKE CALLING YOU PAIN-IN-THE-ASS LADY.
OR CALLING YOU STATUESQUE SASSMOUTH.
FLATTERY WILL GET YOU EVERYWHERE.
WHERE DO I NEED TO GO? I'M ALREADY IN YOUR PANTS.
WE NEED TO FIND SOMEWHERE TO HIDE, FOR ONE. AND I GET TO PICK THIS TIME.
C'MONNN, DON'T ACT LIKE VEGAS WASN'T FUN. PLUS, QUINCY UPGRADED ME TO FISCOPRO. THAT WAS A GOOD THING I DID.
YEAH, BUT WE ALMOST DIED AGAIN. REPEATEDLY. I'M THE BODYGUARD, I CHOOSE.
DESTINATION: SANTA FE, NEW MEXICO
DESTINATION
SANTA FE, NEW MEXICO
I'VE NEVER BEEN TO NEW MEXICO EXCEPT TO STOP TO REFILL THE FUEL CELL.
LAZE
IT'S GORGEOUS. AND THE PLACE WE'RE GOING IS SUPER SAFE.
WHAT'LL WE DO WITH NO ONE TRYING TO KILL US?
FIGURE OUT WHY THEY'RE TRYING TO KILL YOU. WHICH YOU STILL HAVEN'T TOLD--
WANNA WATCH A MOVIE?
"FEELS LIKE WE'RE NOT GONNA WATCH MUCH. AREN'T YOU TIRED YET?"
"I'VE BEEN ALMOST DYING FOR A WEEK AND CHANGE, I GOT A LOT OF PENT-UP ENERGY.
"BESIDES, FOR THE FIRST TIME IN A LONG TIME, I FEEL REALLY SAFE."
TARGET CURRENTLY IN RANGE.

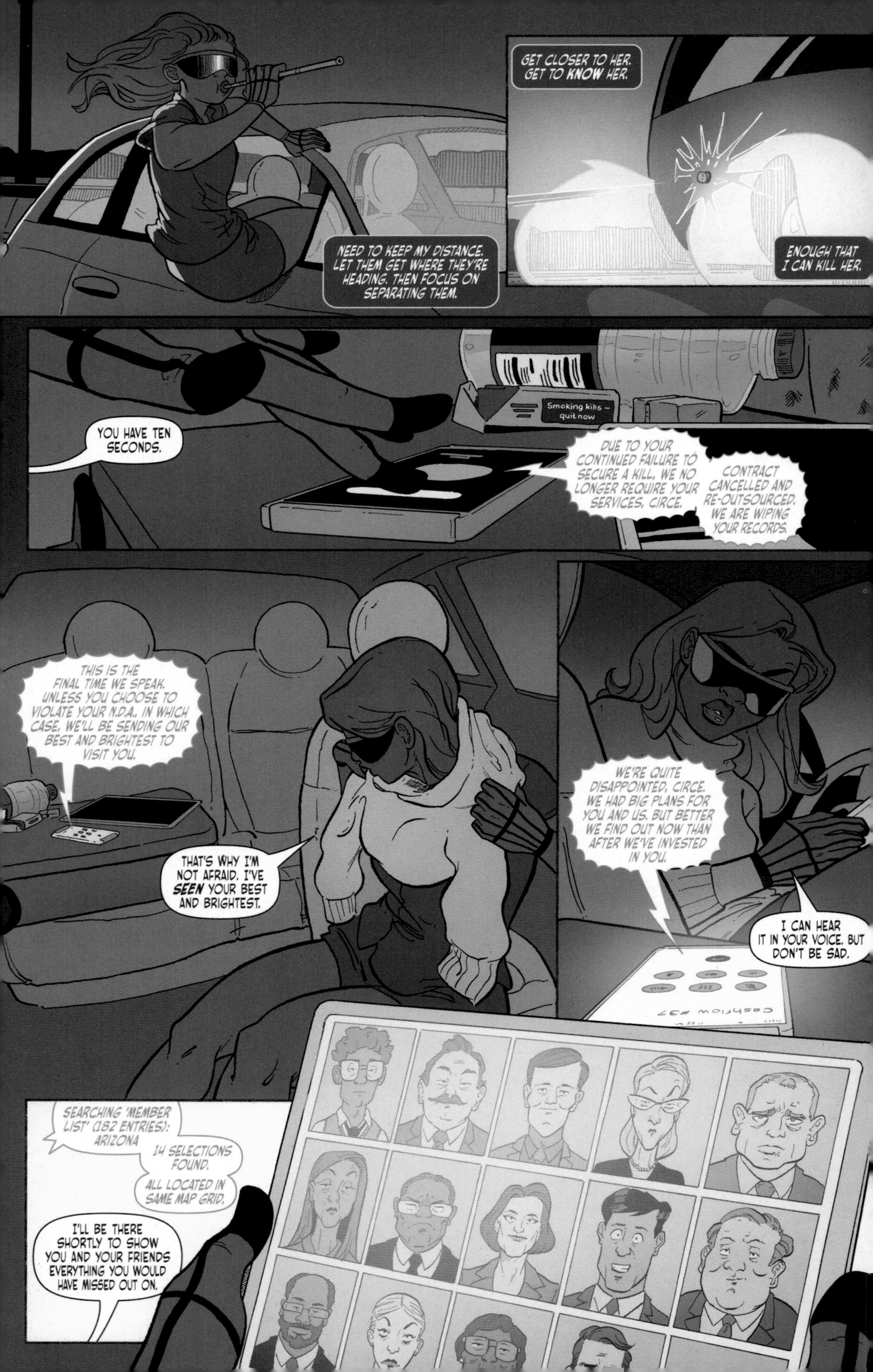
NEED TO KEEP MY DISTANCE. LET THEM GET WHERE THEY'RE HEADING. THEN FOCUS ON SEPARATING THEM.
GET CLOSER TO HER. GET TO KNOW HER.
ENOUGH THAT I CAN KILL HER.
Smoking kills – quit now
YOU HAVE TEN SECONDS.
DUE TO YOUR CONTINUED FAILURE TO SECURE A KILL, WE NO LONGER REQUIRE YOUR SERVICES, CIRCE.
CONTRACT CANCELLED AND RE-OUTSOURCED. WE ARE WIPING YOUR RECORDS.
THIS IS THE FINAL TIME WE SPEAK. UNLESS YOU CHOOSE TO VIOLATE YOUR N.D.A., IN WHICH CASE, WE'LL BE SENDING OUR BEST AND BRIGHTEST TO VISIT YOU.
THAT'S WHY I'M NOT AFRAID. I'VE SEEN YOUR BEST AND BRIGHTEST.
WE'RE QUITE DISAPPOINTED, CIRCE. WE HAD BIG PLANS FOR YOU AND US. BUT BETTER WE FIND OUT NOW THAN AFTER WE'VE INVESTED IN YOU.
I CAN HEAR IT IN YOUR VOICE. BUT DON'T BE SAD.
SEARCHING 'MEMBER LIST' (182 ENTRIES): ARIZONA
14 SELECTIONS FOUND.
ALL LOCATED IN SAME MAP GRID.
I'LL BE THERE SHORTLY TO SHOW YOU AND YOUR FRIENDS EVERYTHING YOU WOULD HAVE MISSED OUT ON.

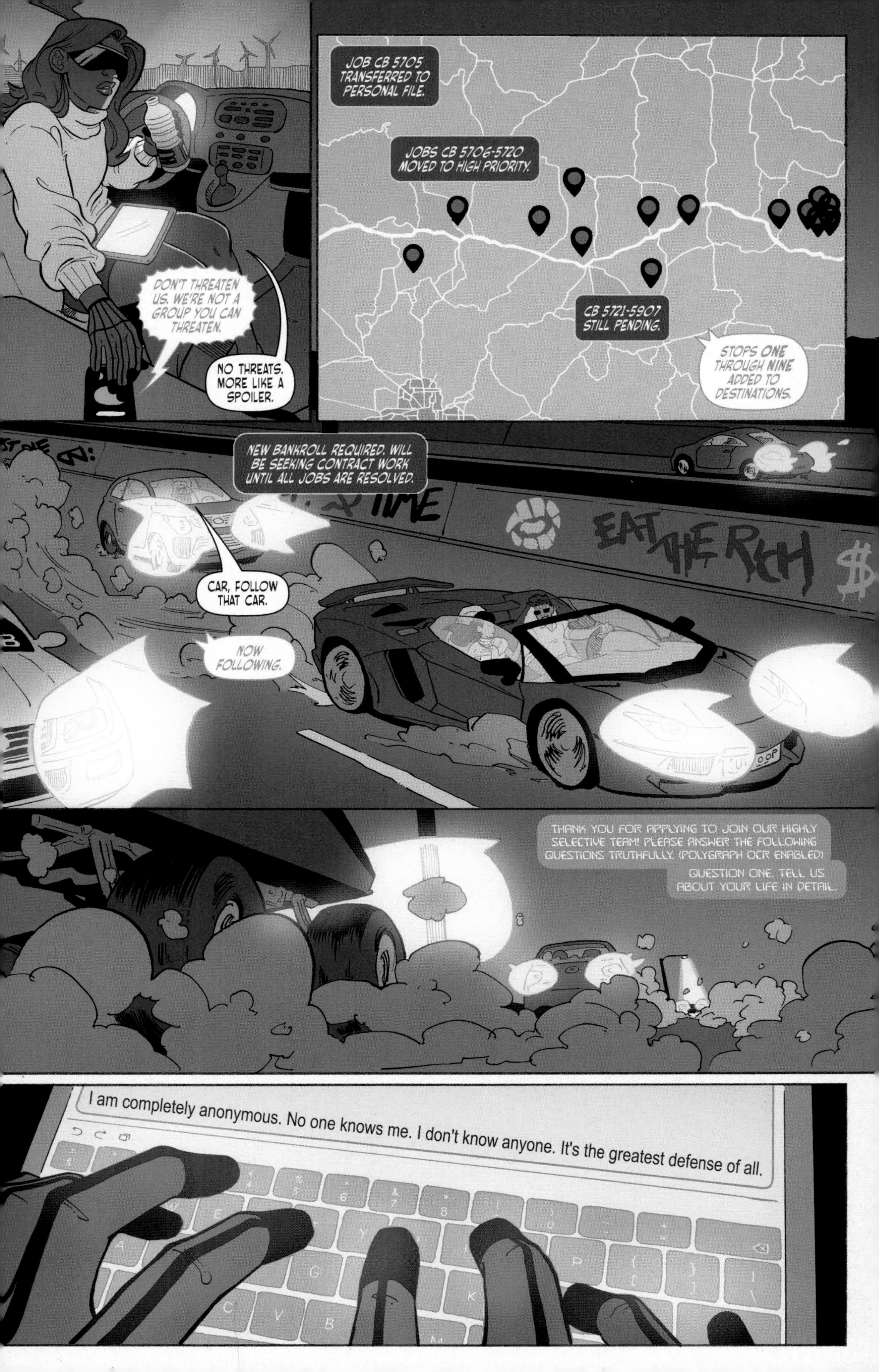

DON'T THREATEN US. WE'RE NOT A GROUP YOU CAN THREATEN.
NO THREATS. MORE LIKE A SPOILER.
JOB CB 5705 TRANSFERRED TO PERSONAL FILE.
JOBS CB 5706-5720 MOVED TO HIGH PRIORITY.
CB 5721-5907 STILL PENDING.
STOPS ONE THROUGH NINE ADDED TO DESTINATIONS.
NEW BANKROLL REQUIRED. WILL BE SEEKING CONTRACT WORK UNTIL ALL JOBS ARE RESOLVED.
EAT THE RICH
CAR, FOLLOW THAT CAR.
NOW FOLLOWING.
THANK YOU FOR APPLYING TO JOIN OUR HIGHLY SELECTIVE TEAM! PLEASE ANSWER THE FOLLOWING QUESTIONS TRUTHFULLY. (POLYGRAPH OCR ENABLED)
QUESTION ONE. TELL US ABOUT YOUR LIFE IN DETAIL.
I am completely anonymous. No one knows me. I don't know anyone. It's the greatest defense of all.

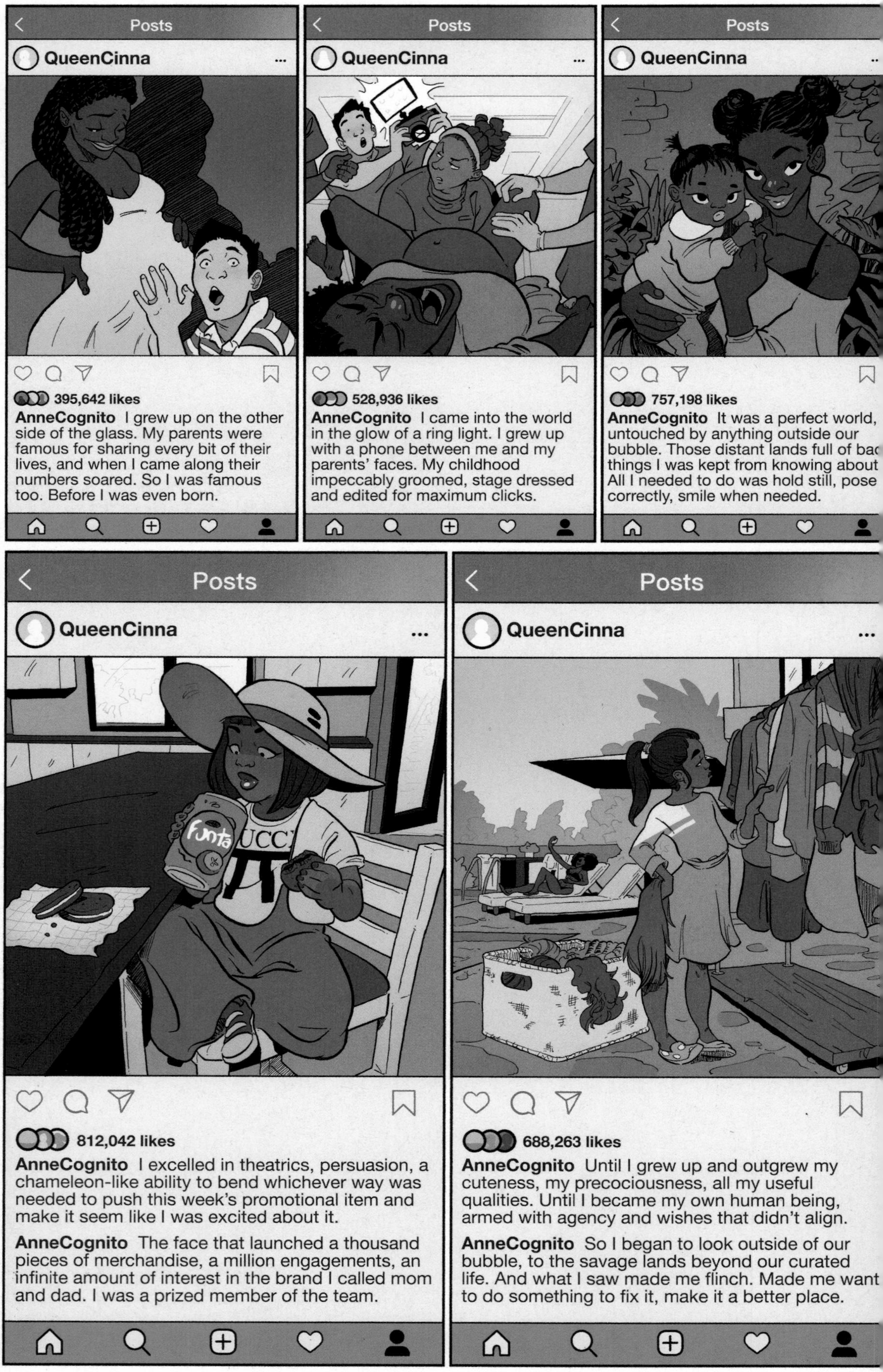

Posts
QueenCinna
395,642 likes
AnneCognito I grew up on the other side of the glass. My parents were famous for sharing every bit of their lives, and when I came along their numbers soared. So I was famous too. Before I was even born.
Posts
QueenCinna
528,936 likes
AnneCognito I came into the world in the glow of a ring light. I grew up with a phone between me and my parents' faces. My childhood impeccably groomed, stage dressed and edited for maximum clicks.
Posts
QueenCinna
757,198 likes
AnneCognito It was a perfect world, untouched by anything outside our bubble. Those distant lands full of bad things I was kept from knowing about. All I needed to do was hold still, pose correctly, smile when needed.
Posts
QueenCinna
Funta
812,042 likes
AnneCognito I excelled in theatrics, persuasion, a chameleon-like ability to bend whichever way was needed to push this week's promotional item and make it seem like I was excited about it.
AnneCognito The face that launched a thousand pieces of merchandise, a million engagements, an infinite amount of interest in the brand I called mom and dad. I was a prized member of the team.
Posts
QueenCinna
688,263 likes
AnneCognito Until I grew up and outgrew my cuteness, my precociousness, all my useful qualities. Until I became my own human being, armed with agency and wishes that didn't align.
AnneCognito So I began to look outside of our bubble, to the savage lands beyond our curated life. And what I saw made me flinch. Made me want to do something to fix it, make it a better place.

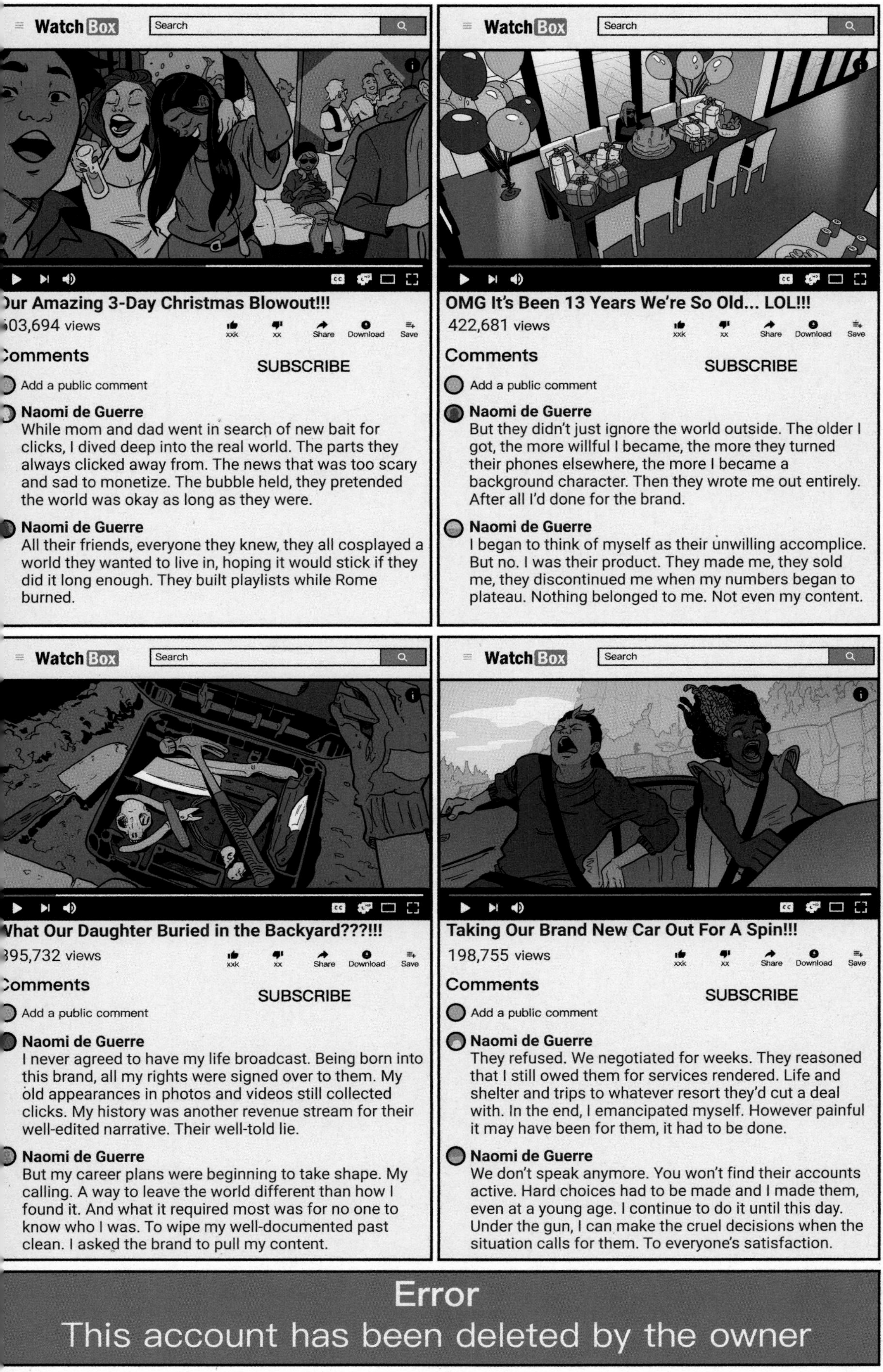

WatchBox
Search
ur Amazing 3-Day Christmas Blowout!!!
03,694 views
xxk
xx
Share
Download
Save
omments
SUBSCRIBE
Add a public comment
Naomi de Guerre
While mom and dad went in search of new bait for clicks, I dived deep into the real world. The parts they always clicked away from. The news that was too scary and sad to monetize. The bubble held, they pretended the world was okay as long as they were.
Naomi de Guerre
All their friends, everyone they knew, they all cosplayed a world they wanted to live in, hoping it would stick if they did it long enough. They built playlists while Rome burned.
WatchBox
Search
OMG It's Been 13 Years We're So Old... LOL!!!
422,681 views
xxk
xx
Share
Download
Save
Comments
SUBSCRIBE
Add a public comment
Naomi de Guerre
But they didn't just ignore the world outside. The older I got, the more willful I became, the more they turned their phones elsewhere, the more I became a background character. Then they wrote me out entirely. After all I'd done for the brand.
Naomi de Guerre
I began to think of myself as their unwilling accomplice. But no. I was their product. They made me, they sold me, they discontinued me when my numbers began to plateau. Nothing belonged to me. Not even my content.
WatchBox
Search
hat Our Daughter Buried in the Backyard???!!!
95,732 views
xxk
xx
Share
Download
Save
omments
SUBSCRIBE
Add a public comment
Naomi de Guerre
I never agreed to have my life broadcast. Being born into this brand, all my rights were signed over to them. My old appearances in photos and videos still collected clicks. My history was another revenue stream for their well-edited narrative. Their well-told lie.
Naomi de Guerre
But my career plans were beginning to take shape. My calling. A way to leave the world different than how I found it. And what it required most was for no one to know who I was. To wipe my well-documented past clean. I asked the brand to pull my content.
WatchBox
Search
Taking Our Brand New Car Out For A Spin!!!
198,755 views
xxk
xx
Share
Download
Save
Comments
SUBSCRIBE
Add a public comment
Naomi de Guerre
They refused. We negotiated for weeks. They reasoned that I still owed them for services rendered. Life and shelter and trips to whatever resort they'd cut a deal with. In the end, I emancipated myself. However painful it may have been for them, it had to be done.
Naomi de Guerre
We don't speak anymore. You won't find their accounts active. Hard choices had to be made and I made them, even at a young age. I continue to do it until this day. Under the gun, I can make the cruel decisions when the situation calls for them. To everyone's satisfaction.
Error
This account has been deleted by the owner

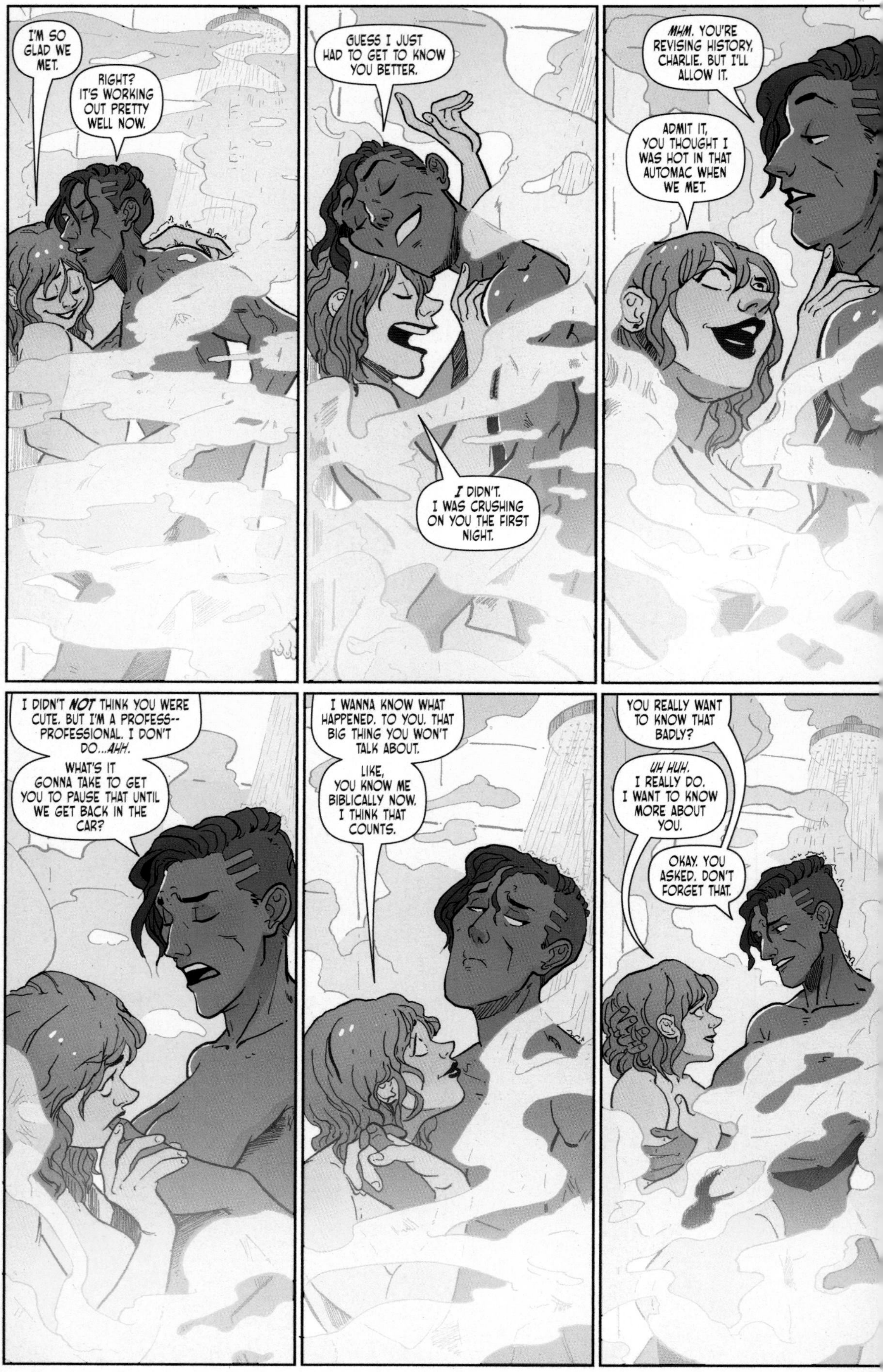
I'M SO GLAD WE MET.
RIGHT? IT'S WORKING OUT PRETTY WELL NOW.
GUESS I JUST HAD TO GET TO KNOW YOU BETTER.
I DIDN'T. I WAS CRUSHING ON YOU THE FIRST NIGHT.
MHM. YOU'RE REVISING HISTORY, CHARLIE. BUT I'LL ALLOW IT.
ADMIT IT, YOU THOUGHT I WAS HOT IN THAT AUTOMAC WHEN WE MET.
I DIDN'T ***NOT*** THINK YOU WERE CUTE. BUT I'M A PROFESS-- PROFESSIONAL. I DON'T DO...*AHH.*
WHAT'S IT GONNA TAKE TO GET YOU TO PAUSE THAT UNTIL WE GET BACK IN THE CAR?
I WANNA KNOW WHAT HAPPENED. TO YOU. THAT BIG THING YOU WON'T TALK ABOUT.
LIKE, YOU KNOW ME BIBLICALLY NOW. I THINK THAT COUNTS.
YOU REALLY WANT TO KNOW THAT BADLY?
UH HUH. I REALLY DO. I WANT TO KNOW MORE ABOUT YOU.
OKAY. YOU ASKED. DON'T FORGET THAT.

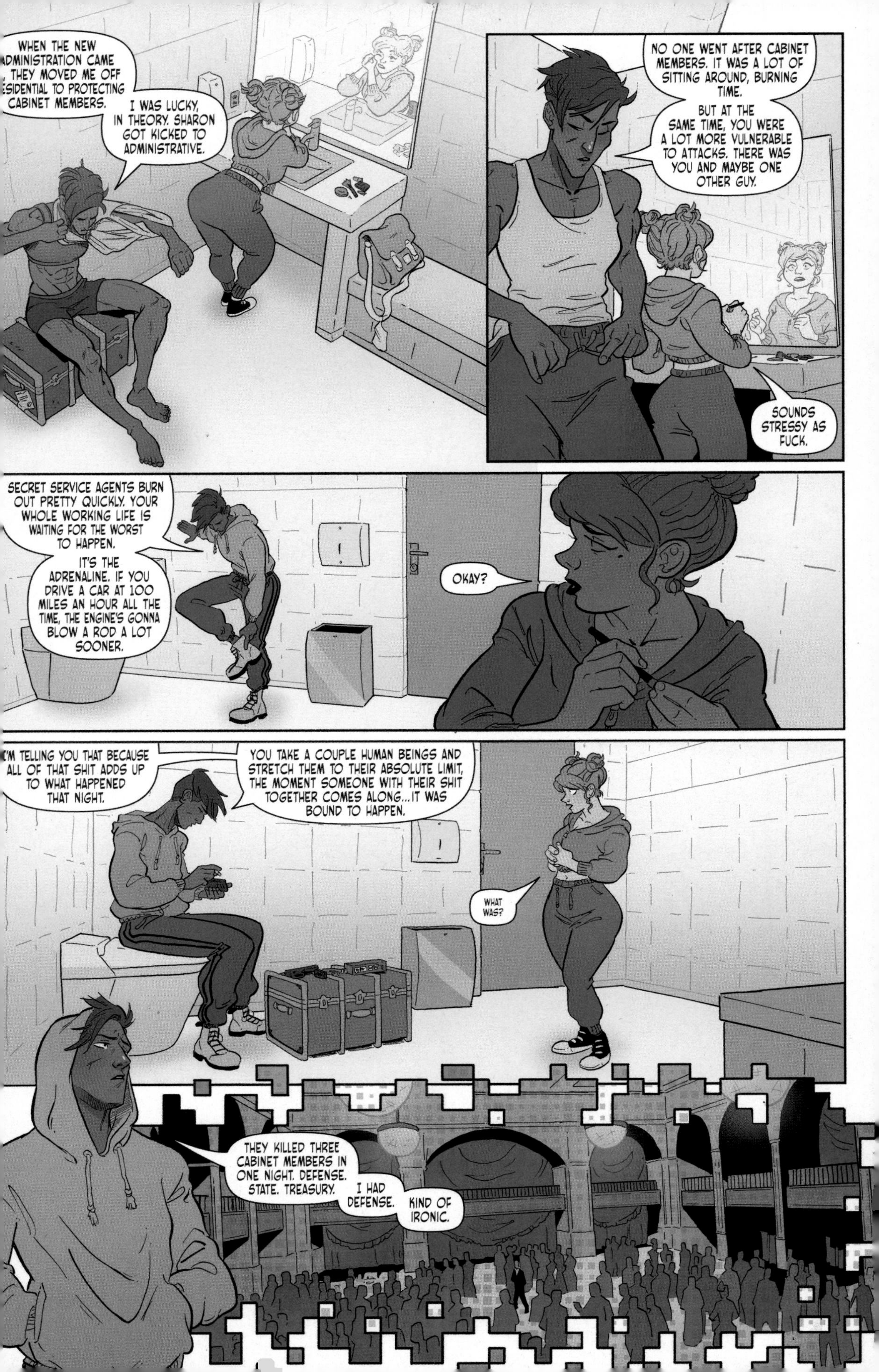
WHEN THE NEW ADMINISTRATION CAME , THEY MOVED ME OFF ESIDENTIAL TO PROTECTING CABINET MEMBERS.
I WAS LUCKY, IN THEORY. SHARON GOT KICKED TO ADMINISTRATIVE.
NO ONE WENT AFTER CABINET MEMBERS. IT WAS A LOT OF SITTING AROUND, BURNING TIME.
BUT AT THE SAME TIME, YOU WERE A LOT MORE VULNERABLE TO ATTACKS. THERE WAS YOU AND MAYBE ONE OTHER GUY.
SOUNDS STRESSY AS FUCK.
SECRET SERVICE AGENTS BURN OUT PRETTY QUICKLY. YOUR WHOLE WORKING LIFE IS WAITING FOR THE WORST TO HAPPEN.
IT'S THE ADRENALINE. IF YOU DRIVE A CAR AT 100 MILES AN HOUR ALL THE TIME, THE ENGINE'S GONNA BLOW A ROD A LOT SOONER.
OKAY?
'M TELLING YOU THAT BECAUSE ALL OF THAT SHIT ADDS UP TO WHAT HAPPENED THAT NIGHT.
YOU TAKE A COUPLE HUMAN BEINGS AND STRETCH THEM TO THEIR ABSOLUTE LIMIT, THE MOMENT SOMEONE WITH THEIR SHIT TOGETHER COMES ALONG... IT WAS BOUND TO HAPPEN.
WHAT WAS?
THEY KILLED THREE CABINET MEMBERS IN ONE NIGHT. DEFENSE. STATE. TREASURY.
I HAD DEFENSE.
KIND OF IRONIC.

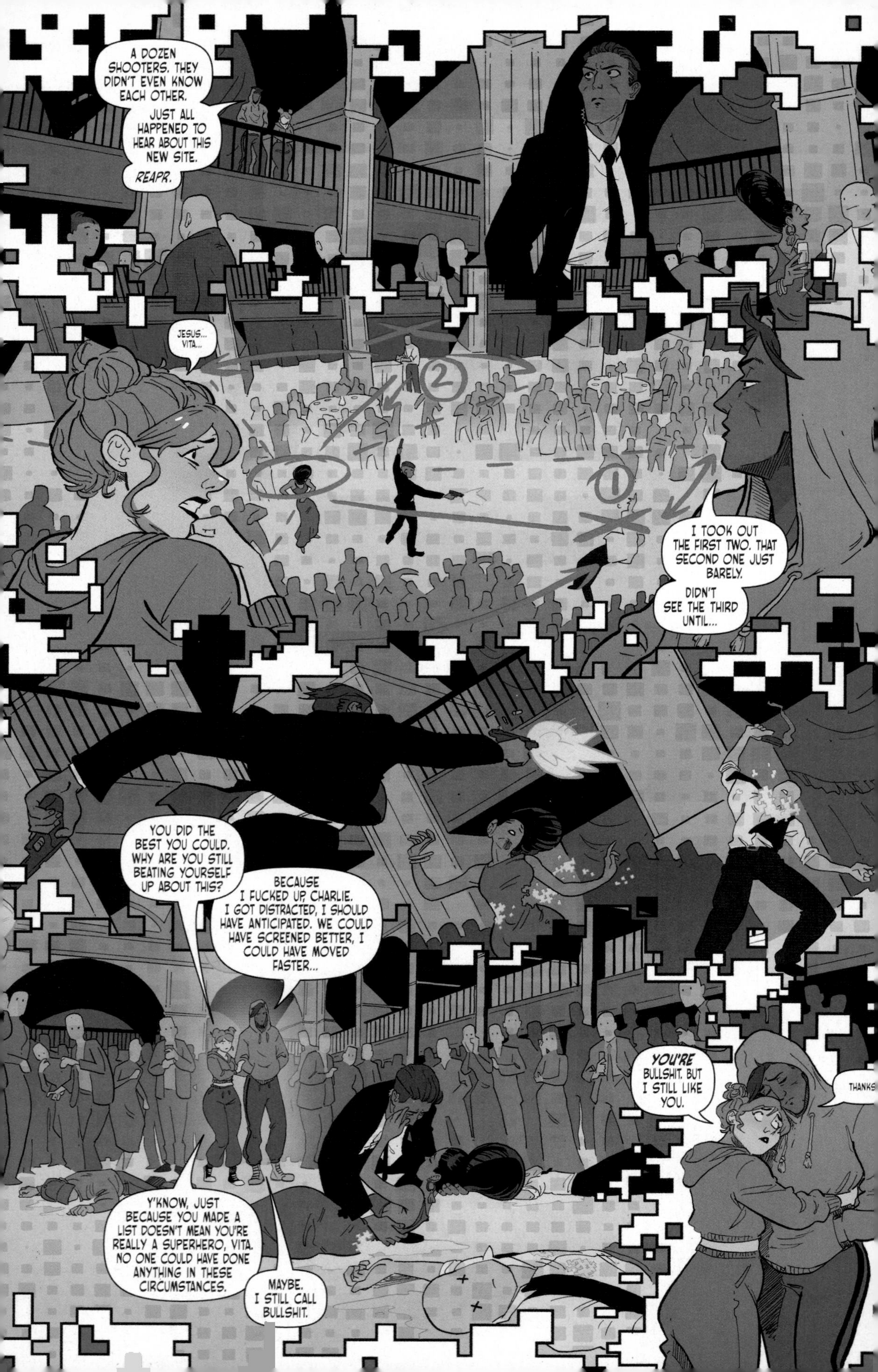
A DOZEN SHOOTERS. THEY DIDN'T EVEN KNOW EACH OTHER.
JUST ALL HAPPENED TO HEAR ABOUT THIS NEW SITE.
REAPR.
JESUS... VITA...
I TOOK OUT THE FIRST TWO. THAT SECOND ONE JUST BARELY.
DIDN'T SEE THE THIRD UNTIL...
YOU DID THE BEST YOU COULD. WHY ARE YOU STILL BEATING YOURSELF UP ABOUT THIS?
BECAUSE I FUCKED UP, CHARLIE. I GOT DISTRACTED, I SHOULD HAVE ANTICIPATED. WE COULD HAVE SCREENED BETTER, I COULD HAVE MOVED FASTER...
Y'KNOW, JUST BECAUSE YOU MADE A LIST DOESN'T MEAN YOU'RE REALLY A SUPERHERO, VITA. NO ONE COULD HAVE DONE ANYTHING IN THESE CIRCUMSTANCES.
MAYBE. I STILL CALL BULLSHIT.
YOU'RE BULLSHIT. BUT I STILL LIKE YOU.
THANKS

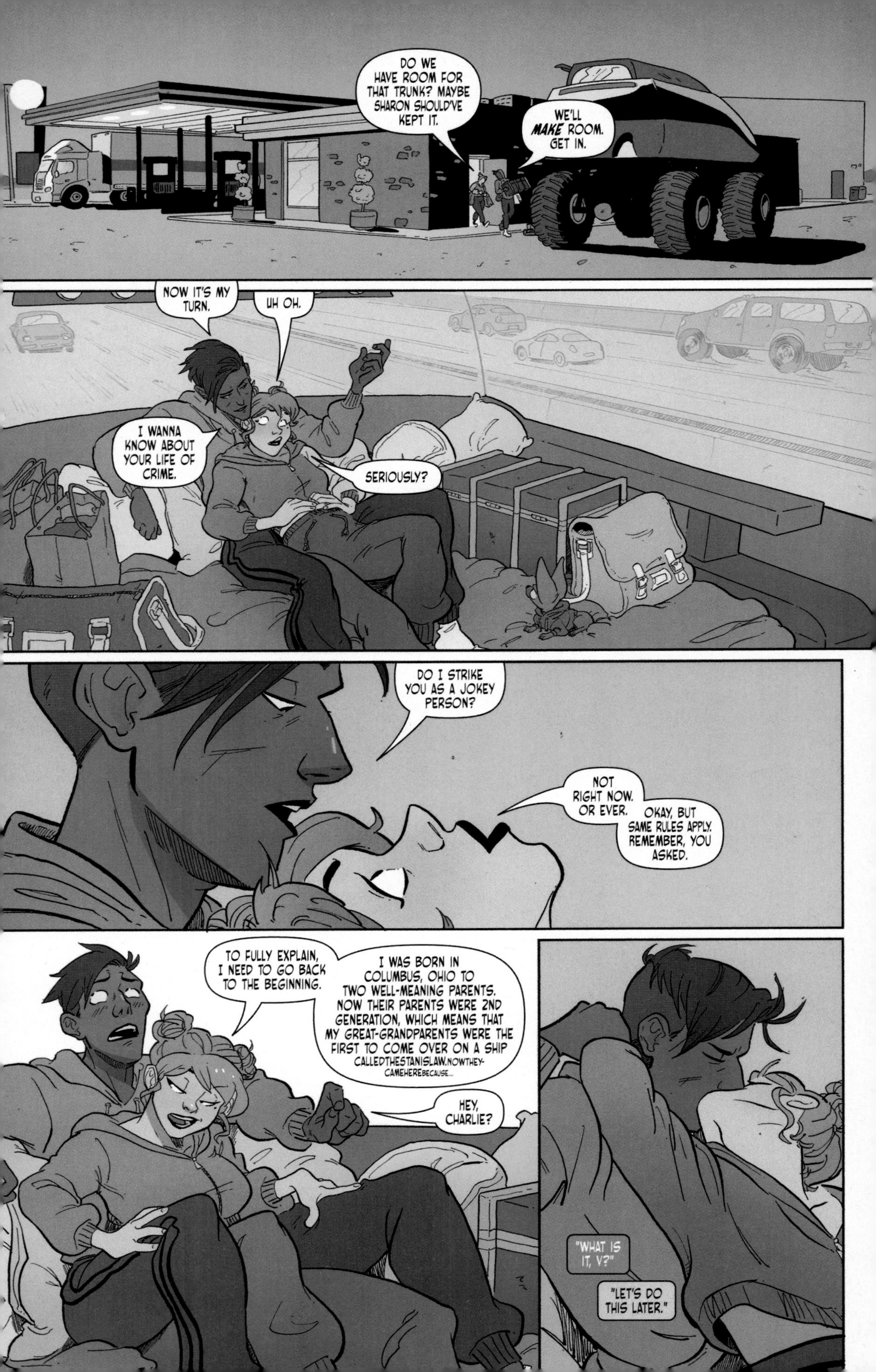
DO WE HAVE ROOM FOR THAT TRUNK? MAYBE SHARON SHOULD'VE KEPT IT.
WE'LL *MAKE* ROOM. GET IN.
NOW IT'S MY TURN.
UH OH.
I WANNA KNOW ABOUT YOUR LIFE OF CRIME.
SERIOUSLY?
DO I STRIKE YOU AS A JOKEY PERSON?
NOT RIGHT NOW. OR EVER.
OKAY, BUT SAME RULES APPLY. REMEMBER, YOU ASKED.
TO FULLY EXPLAIN, I NEED TO GO BACK TO THE BEGINNING.
I WAS BORN IN COLUMBUS, OHIO TO TWO WELL-MEANING PARENTS. NOW THEIR PARENTS WERE 2ND GENERATION, WHICH MEANS THAT MY GREAT-GRANDPARENTS WERE THE FIRST TO COME OVER ON A SHIP CALLEDTHESTANISLAW.NOWTHEY-CAMEHEREBECAUSE...
HEY, CHARLIE?
"WHAT IS IT, V?"
"LET'S DO THIS LATER."

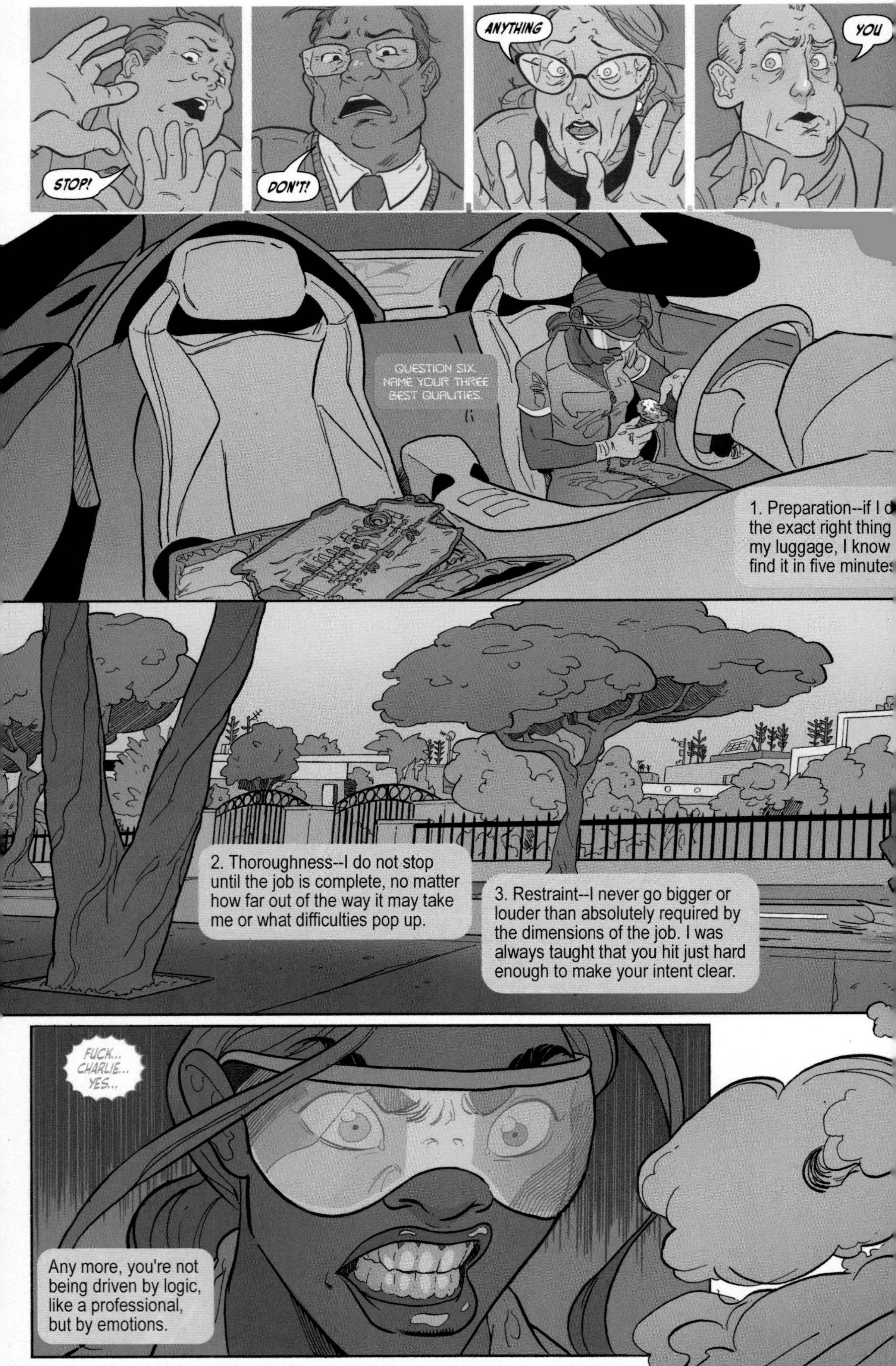
STOP!
DON'T!
ANYTHING
YOU
QUESTION SIX. NAME YOUR THREE BEST QUALITIES.
1. Preparation--if I d
the exact right thing
my luggage, I know
find it in five minutes
2. Thoroughness--I do not stop until the job is complete, no matter how far out of the way it may take me or what difficulties pop up.
3. Restraint--I never go bigger or louder than absolutely required by the dimensions of the job. I was always taught that you hit just hard enough to make your intent clear.
FUCK... CHARLIE... YES...
Any more, you're not being driven by logic, like a professional, but by emotions.

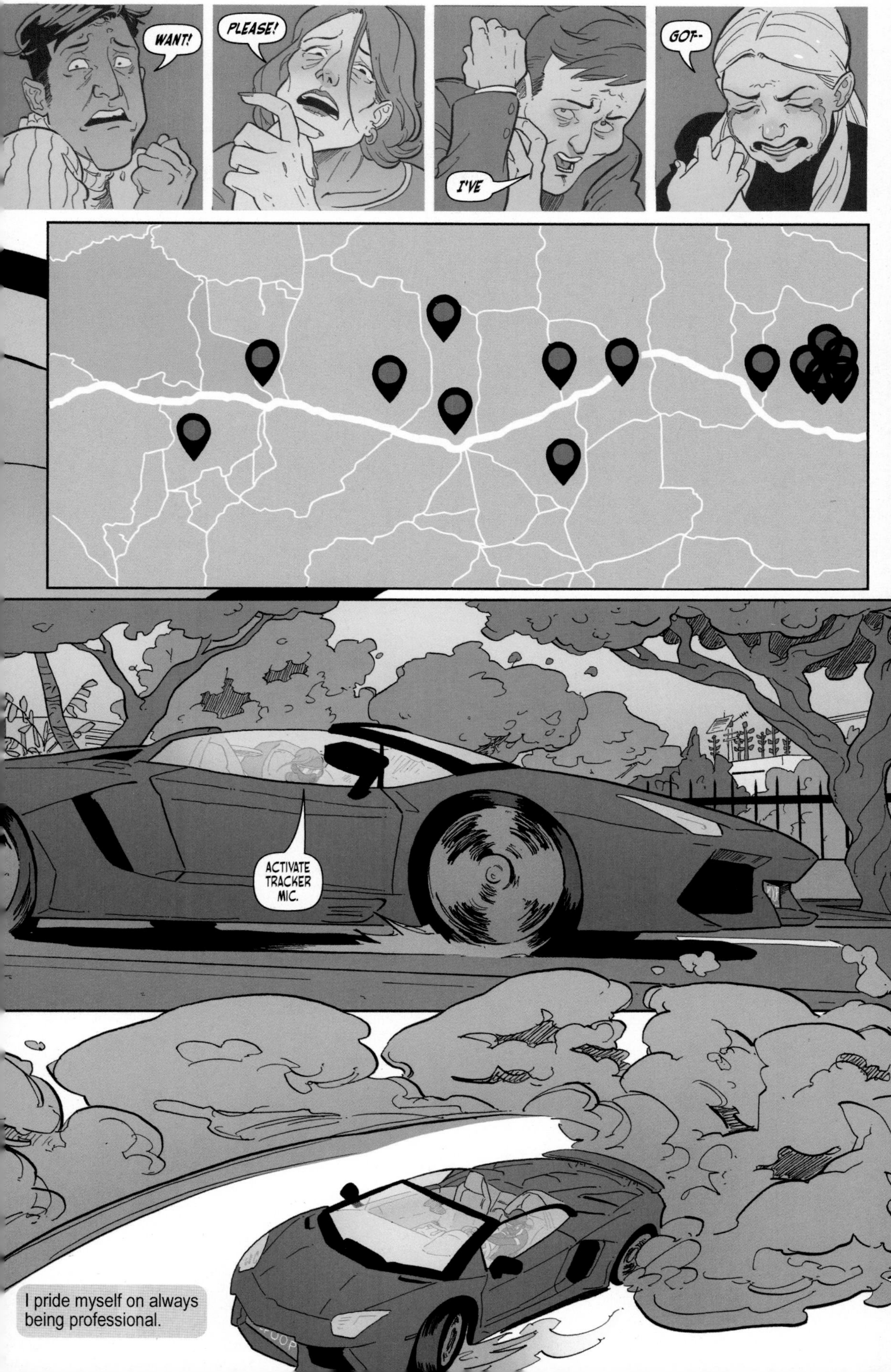
WANT!
PLEASE!
I'VE
GOT-
ACTIVATE TRACKER MIC.
I pride myself on always being professional.

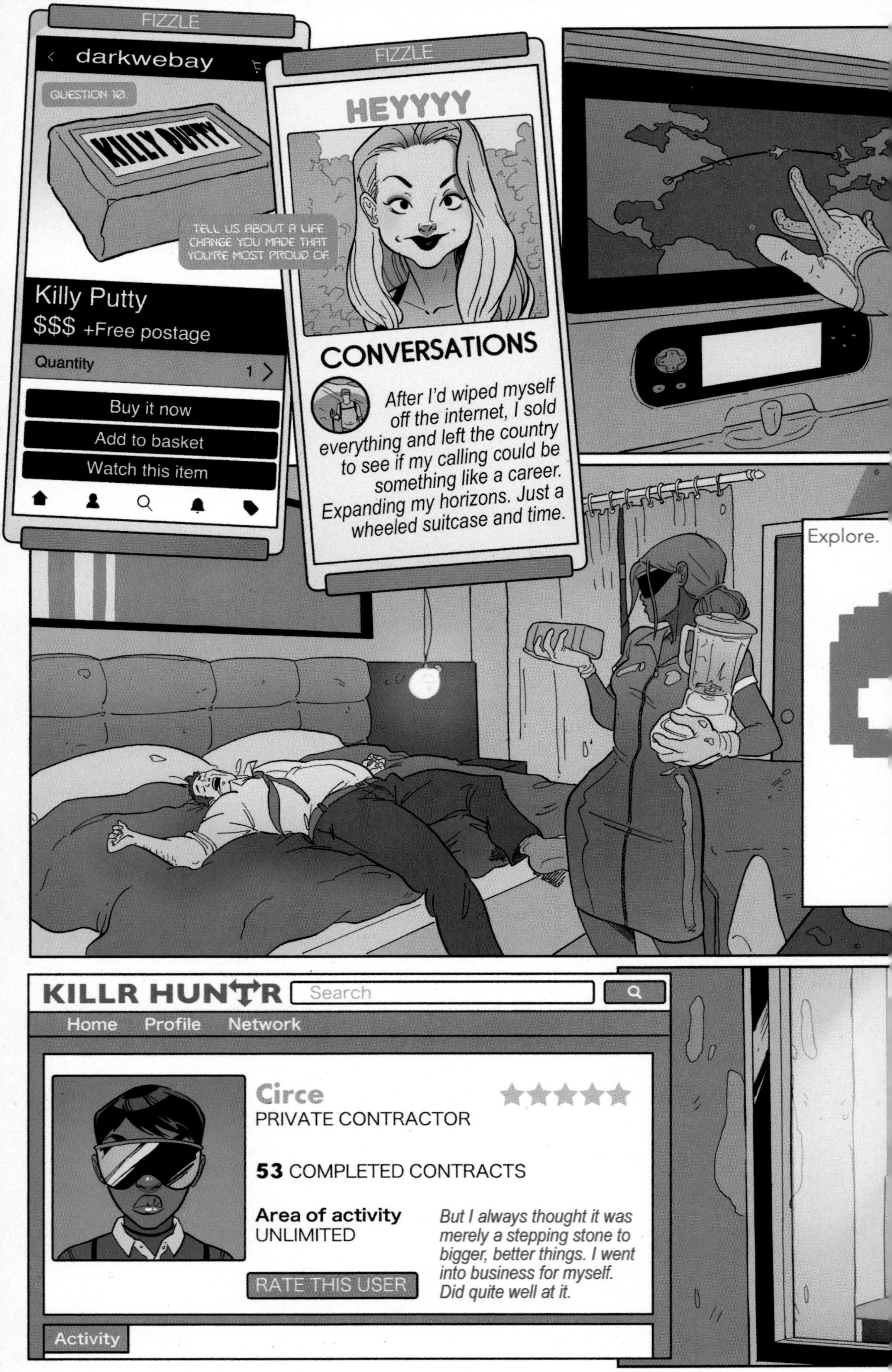
FIZZLE
darkwebay
QUESTION 10.
KILLY PUTTY
TELL US ABOUT A LIFE CHANGE YOU MADE THAT YOU'RE MOST PROUD OF.
Killy Putty
$$$ +Free postage
Quantity 1
Buy it now
Add to basket
Watch this item
FIZZLE
HEYYYY
CONVERSATIONS
After I'd wiped myself off the internet, I sold everything and left the country to see if my calling could be something like a career. Expanding my horizons. Just a wheeled suitcase and time.
Explore.
KILLR HUNTR
Search
Home Profile Network
Circe
PRIVATE CONTRACTOR
53 COMPLETED CONTRACTS
Area of activity
UNLIMITED
RATE THIS USER
But I always thought it was merely a stepping stone to bigger, better things. I went into business for myself. Did quite well at it.
Activity

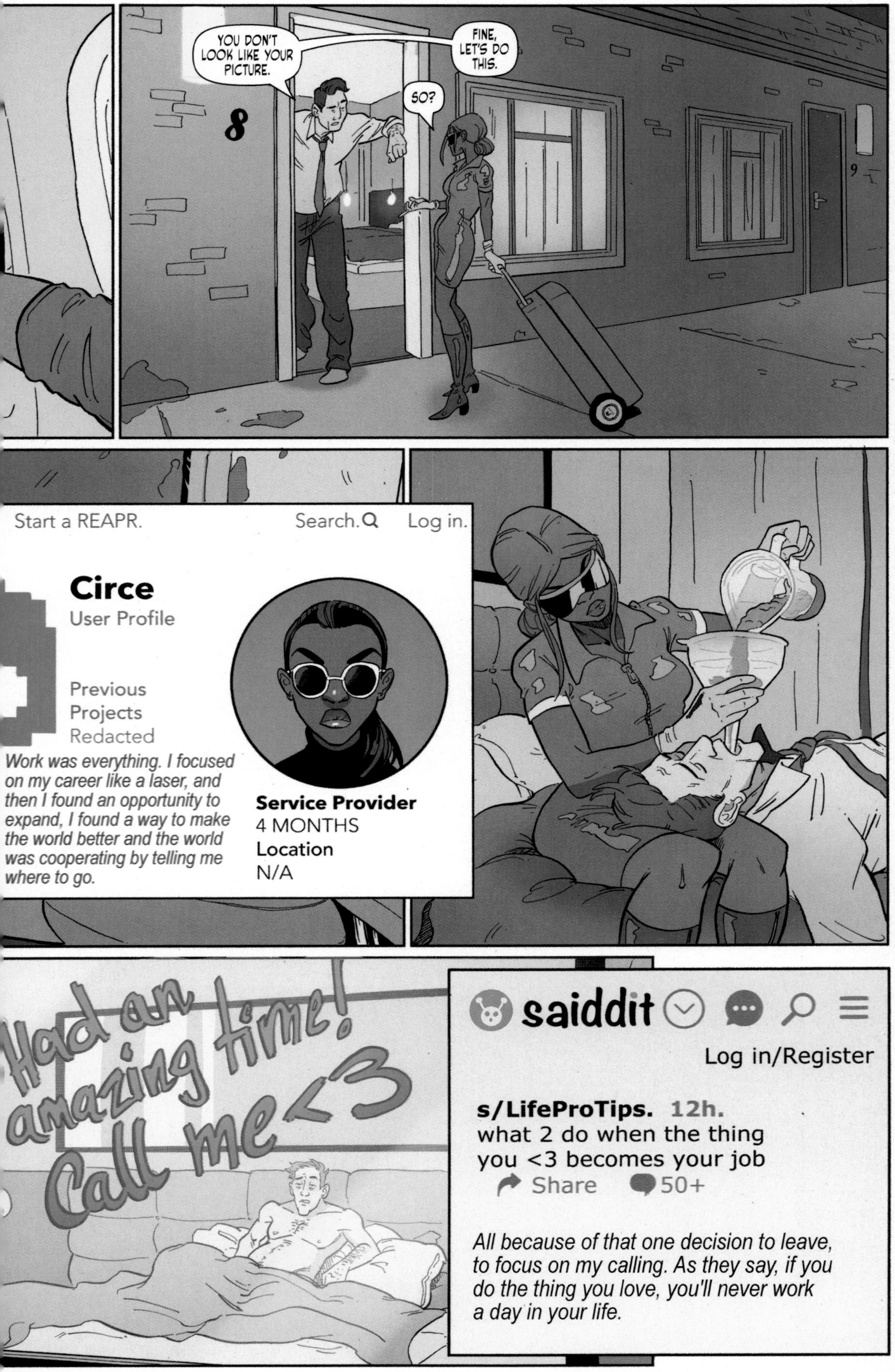

8
YOU DON'T LOOK LIKE YOUR PICTURE.
FINE, LET'S DO THIS.
SO?
9
Start a REAPR.
Search.
Log in.
Circe
User Profile
Previous Projects
Redacted
Work was everything. I focused on my career like a laser, and then I found an opportunity to expand, I found a way to make the world better and the world was cooperating by telling me where to go.
Service Provider
4 MONTHS
Location
N/A
Had an amazing time! Call me <3
saiddit
Log in/Register
s/LifeProTips. 12h.
what 2 do when the thing you <3 becomes your job
Share
50+
All because of that one decision to leave, to focus on my calling. As they say, if you do the thing you love, you'll never work a day in your life.

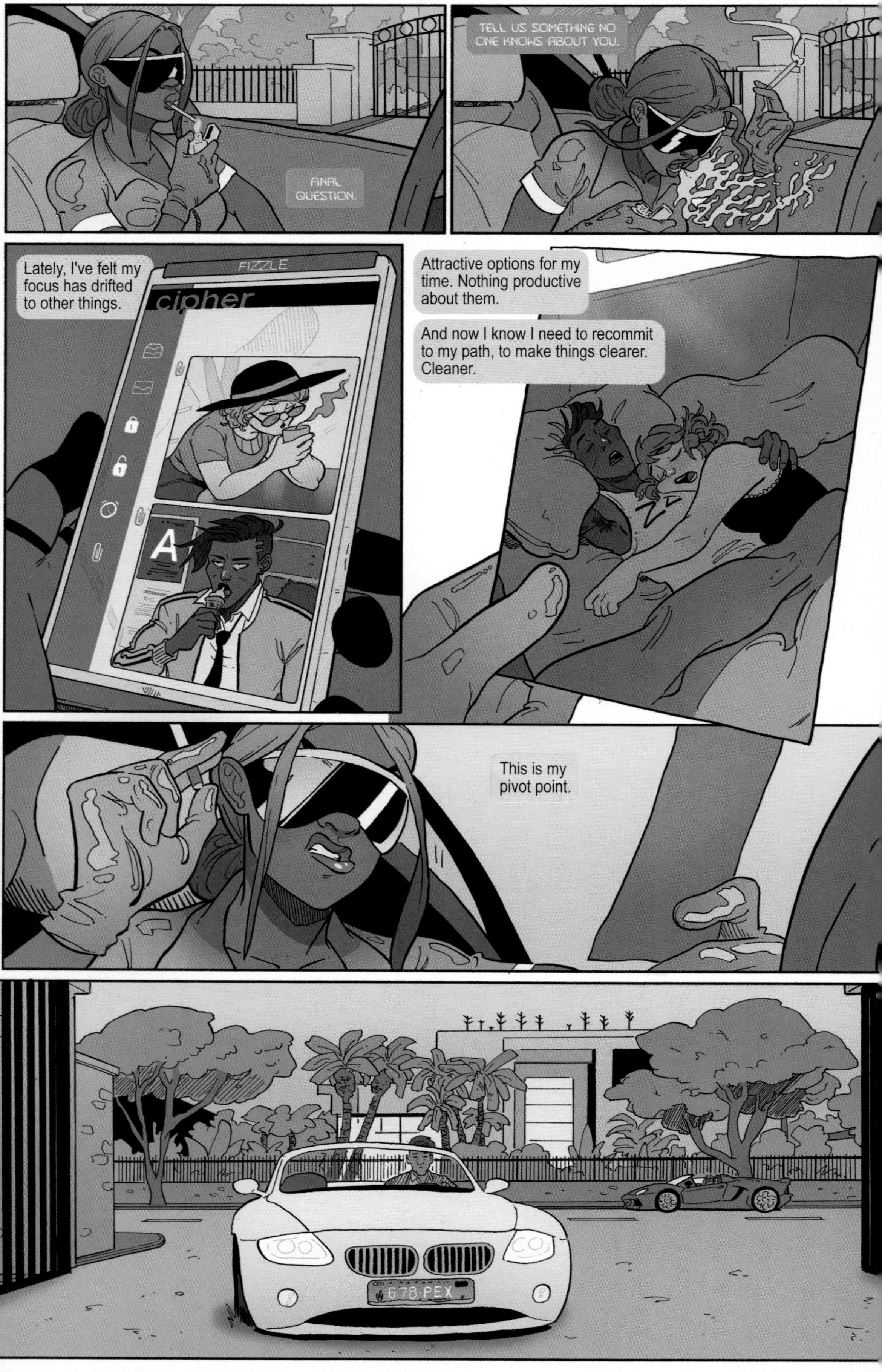
FINAL QUESTION.
TELL US SOMETHING NO ONE KNOWS ABOUT YOU.
Lately, I've felt my focus has drifted to other things.
FIZZLE
cipher
A
Attractive options for my time. Nothing productive about them.
And now I know I need to recommit to my path, to make things clearer. Cleaner.
This is my pivot point.
678·PEX

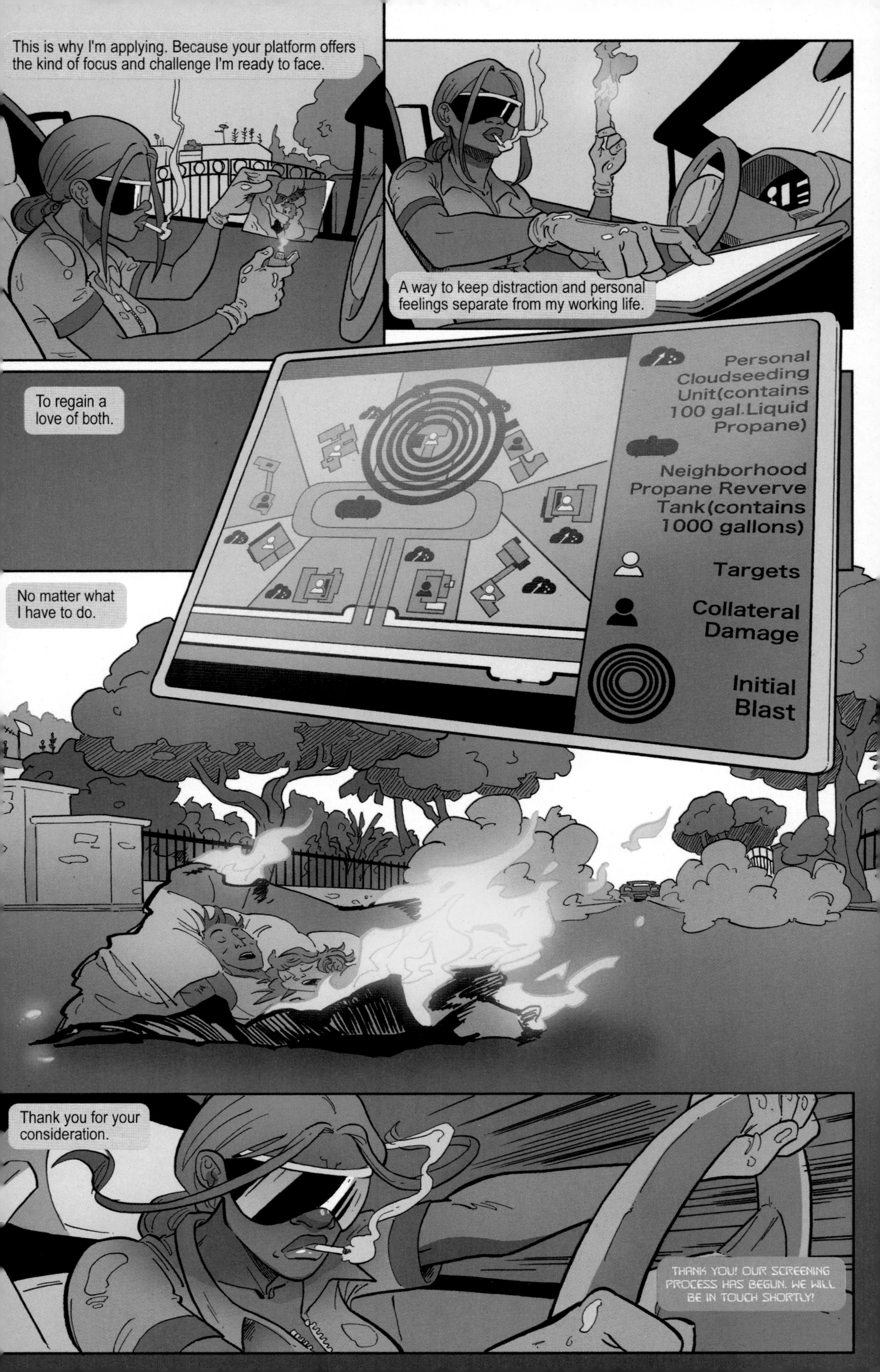

This is why I'm applying. Because your platform offers the kind of focus and challenge I'm ready to face.
A way to keep distraction and personal feelings separate from my working life.
To regain a love of both.
Personal Cloudseeding Unit(contains 100 gal.Liquid Propane)
Neighborhood Propane Reverve Tank(contains 1000 gallons)
Targets
Collateral Damage
Initial Blast
No matter what I have to do.
Thank you for your consideration.
THANK YOU! OUR SCREENING PROCESS HAS BEGUN. WE WILL BE IN TOUCH SHORTLY!

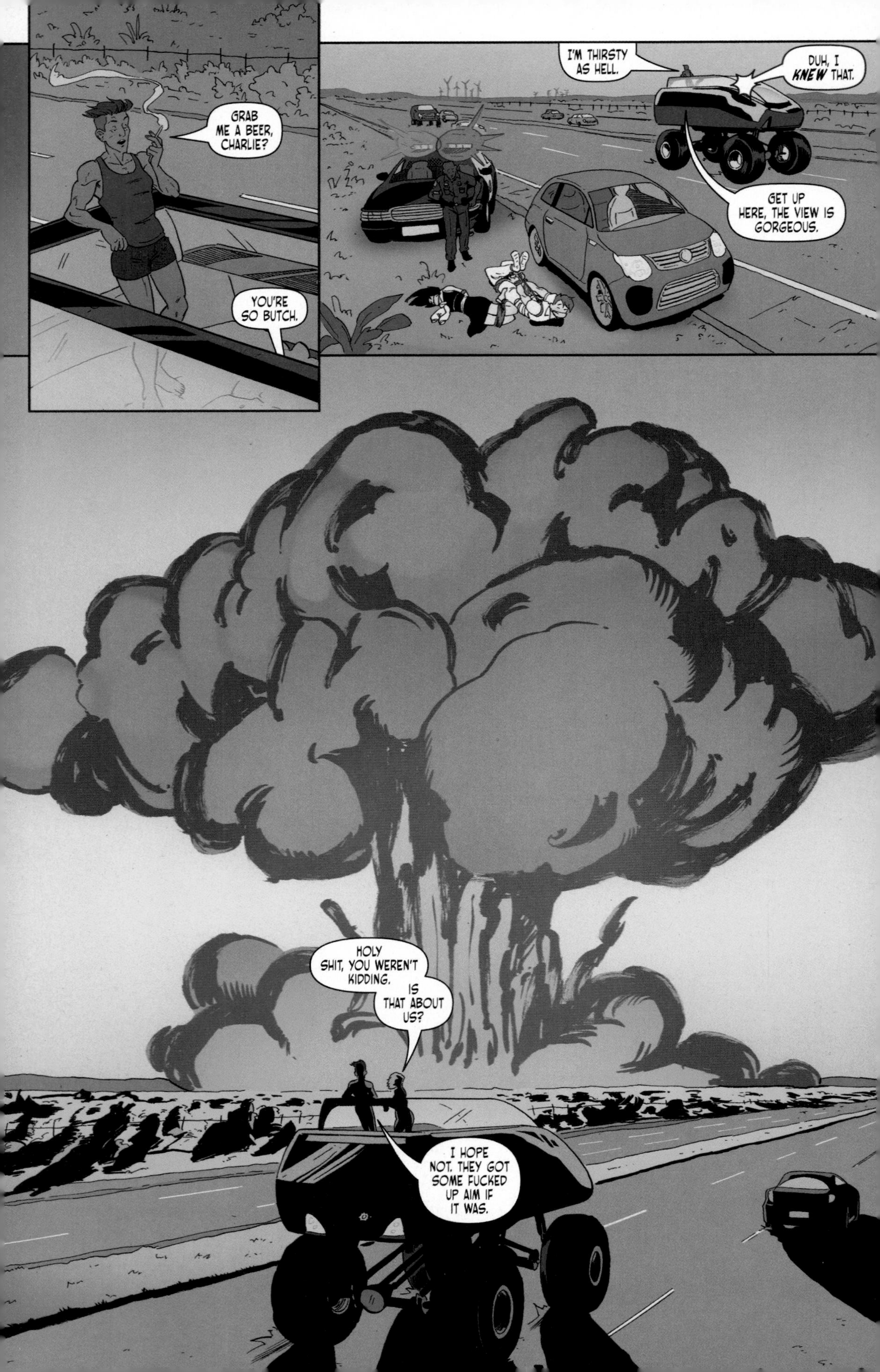
GRAB ME A BEER, CHARLIE?
YOU'RE SO BUTCH.
I'M THIRSTY AS HELL.
DUH, I KNEW THAT.
GET UP HERE, THE VIEW IS GORGEOUS.
HOLY SHIT, YOU WEREN'T KIDDING.
IS THAT ABOUT US?
I HOPE NOT. THEY GOT SOME FUCKED UP AIM IF IT WAS.

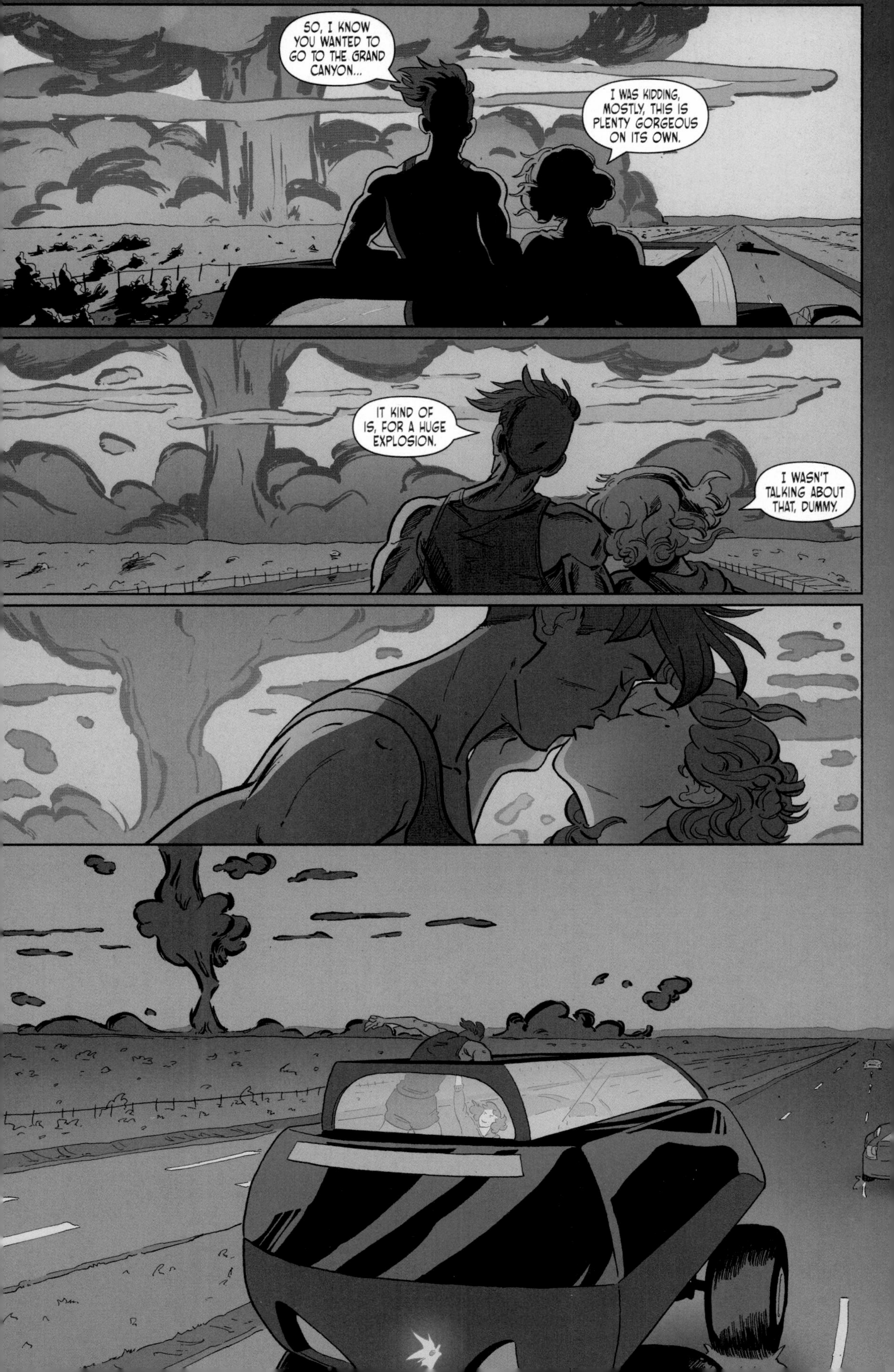
SO, I KNOW YOU WANTED TO GO TO THE GRAND CANYON...
I WAS KIDDING, MOSTLY, THIS IS PLENTY GORGEOUS ON ITS OWN.
IT KIND OF IS, FOR A HUGE EXPLOSION.
I WASN'T TALKING ABOUT THAT, DUMMY.

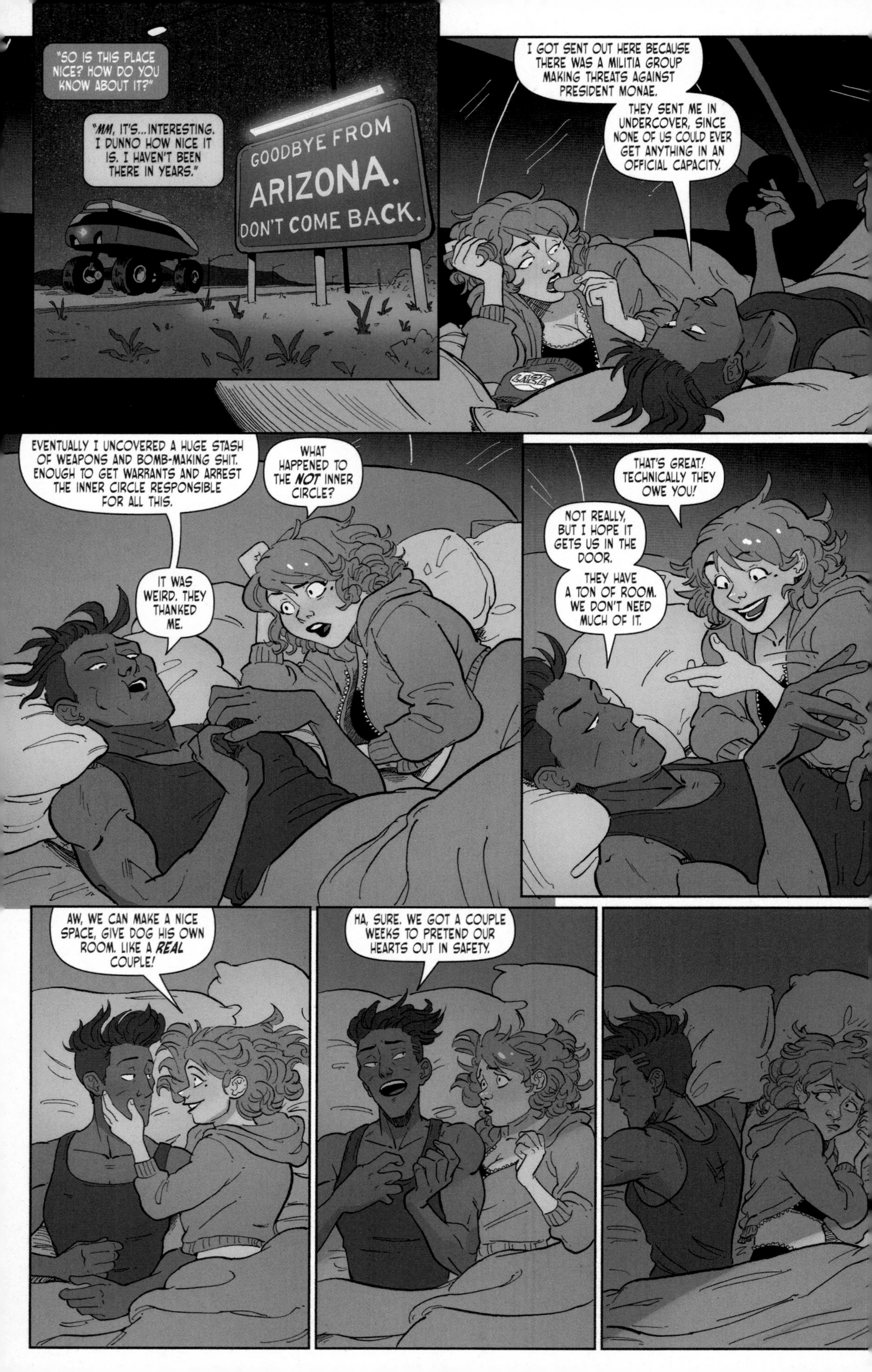
"SO IS THIS PLACE NICE? HOW DO YOU KNOW ABOUT IT?"
"MM, IT'S...INTERESTING. I DUNNO HOW NICE IT IS. I HAVEN'T BEEN THERE IN YEARS."
GOODBYE FROM ARIZONA. DON'T COME BACK.
I GOT SENT OUT HERE BECAUSE THERE WAS A MILITIA GROUP MAKING THREATS AGAINST PRESIDENT MONAE.
THEY SENT ME IN UNDERCOVER, SINCE NONE OF US COULD EVER GET ANYTHING IN AN OFFICIAL CAPACITY.
EVENTUALLY I UNCOVERED A HUGE STASH OF WEAPONS AND BOMB-MAKING SHIT. ENOUGH TO GET WARRANTS AND ARREST THE INNER CIRCLE RESPONSIBLE FOR ALL THIS.
WHAT HAPPENED TO THE NOT INNER CIRCLE?
IT WAS WEIRD. THEY THANKED ME.
THAT'S GREAT! TECHNICALLY THEY OWE YOU!
NOT REALLY, BUT I HOPE IT GETS US IN THE DOOR.
THEY HAVE A TON OF ROOM. WE DON'T NEED MUCH OF IT.
AW, WE CAN MAKE A NICE SPACE, GIVE DOG HIS OWN ROOM. LIKE A REAL COUPLE!
HA, SURE. WE GOT A COUPLE WEEKS TO PRETEND OUR HEARTS OUT IN SAFETY.

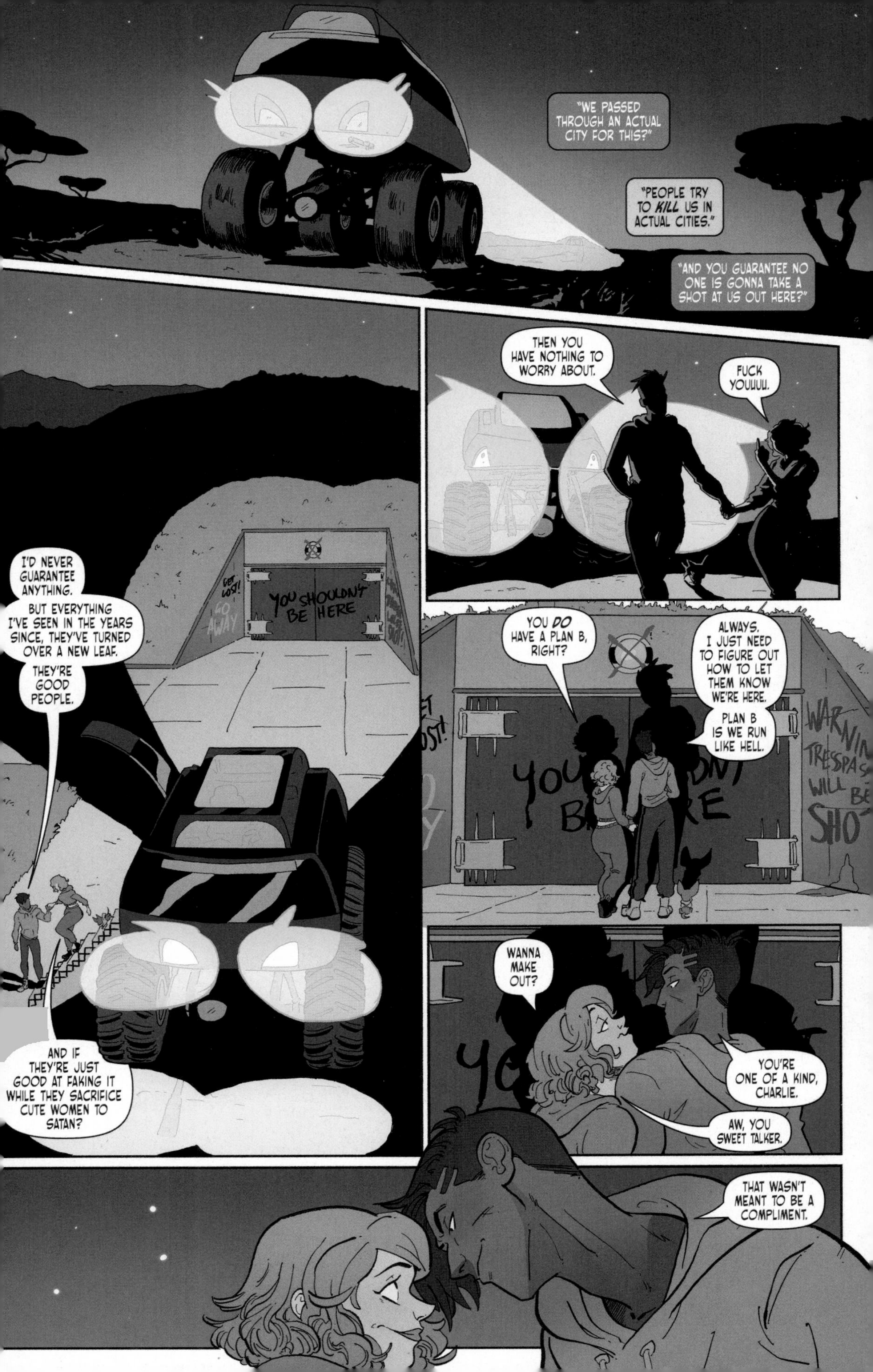
"WE PASSED THROUGH AN ACTUAL CITY FOR THIS?"
"PEOPLE TRY TO KILL US IN ACTUAL CITIES."
"AND YOU GUARANTEE NO ONE IS GONNA TAKE A SHOT AT US OUT HERE?"
THEN YOU HAVE NOTHING TO WORRY ABOUT.
FUCK YOUUUU.
GET LOST!
YOU SHOULDN'T BE HERE
GO AWAY
I'D NEVER GUARANTEE ANYTHING.
BUT EVERYTHING I'VE SEEN IN THE YEARS SINCE, THEY'VE TURNED OVER A NEW LEAF.
THEY'RE GOOD PEOPLE.
AND IF THEY'RE JUST GOOD AT FAKING IT WHILE THEY SACRIFICE CUTE WOMEN TO SATAN?
YOU DO HAVE A PLAN B, RIGHT?
ALWAYS. I JUST NEED TO FIGURE OUT HOW TO LET THEM KNOW WE'RE HERE.
PLAN B IS WE RUN LIKE HELL.
WANNA MAKE OUT?
YOU'RE ONE OF A KIND, CHARLIE.
AW, YOU SWEET TALKER.
THAT WASN'T MEANT TO BE A COMPLIMENT.

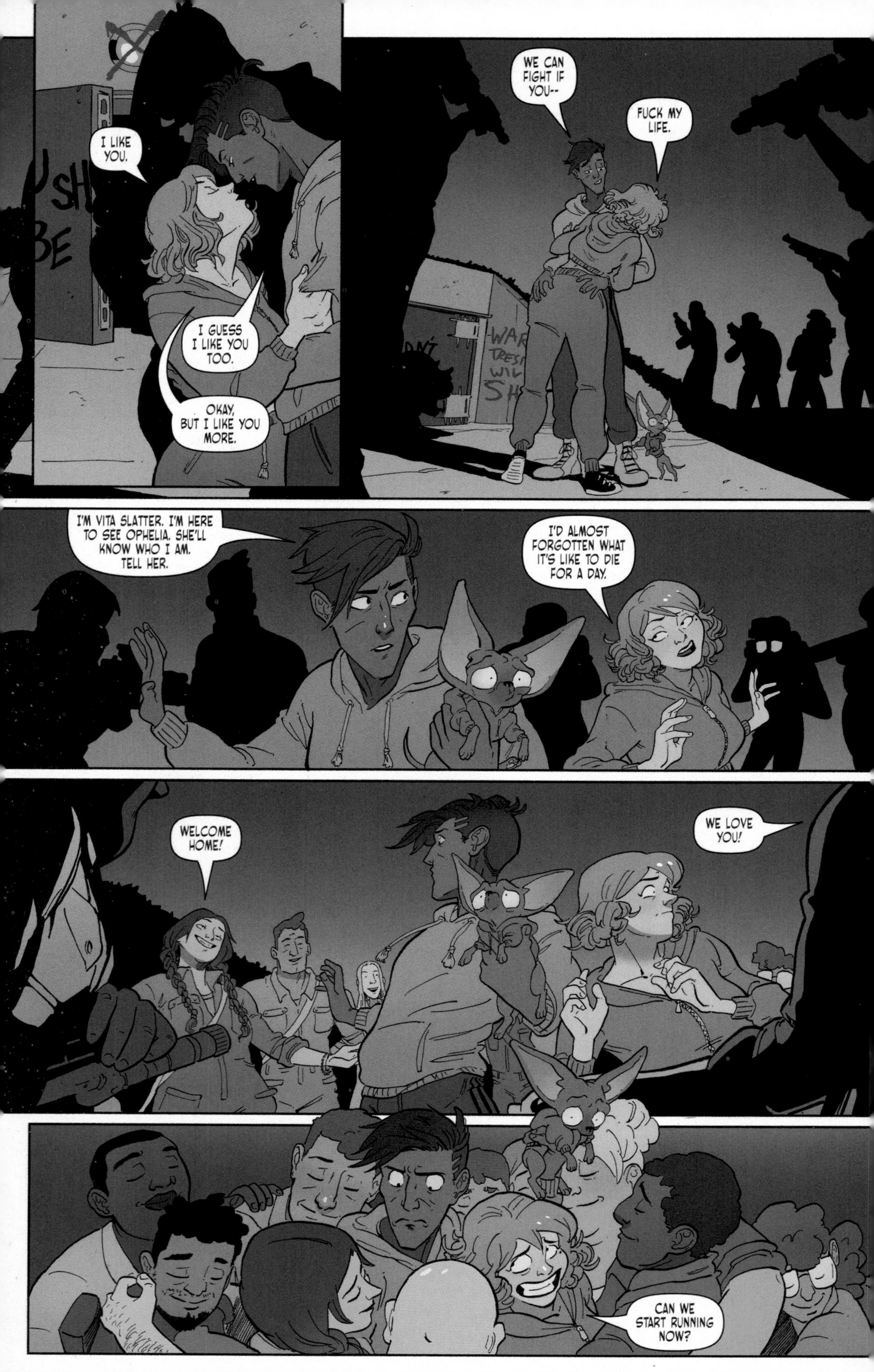
I LIKE YOU.
I GUESS I LIKE YOU TOO.
OKAY, BUT I LIKE YOU MORE.
WE CAN FIGHT IF YOU--
FUCK MY LIFE.
I'M VITA SLATTER. I'M HERE TO SEE OPHELIA. SHE'LL KNOW WHO I AM. TELL HER.
I'D ALMOST FORGOTTEN WHAT IT'S LIKE TO DIE FOR A DAY.
WELCOME HOME!
WE LOVE YOU!
CAN WE START RUNNING NOW?

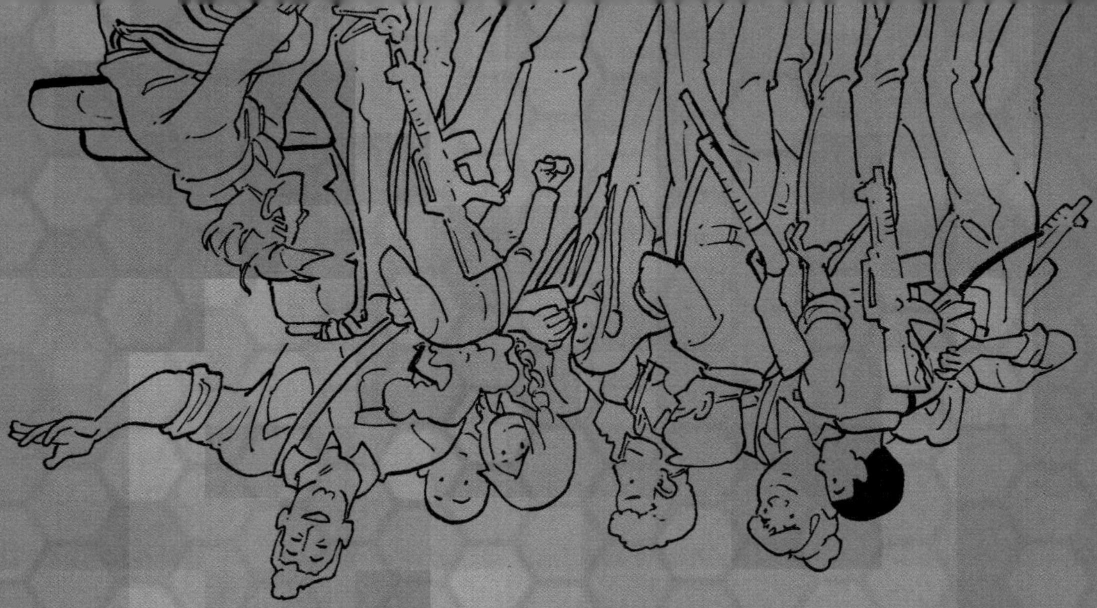

CHAPTER ELEVEN
ANXIOUS TYPE

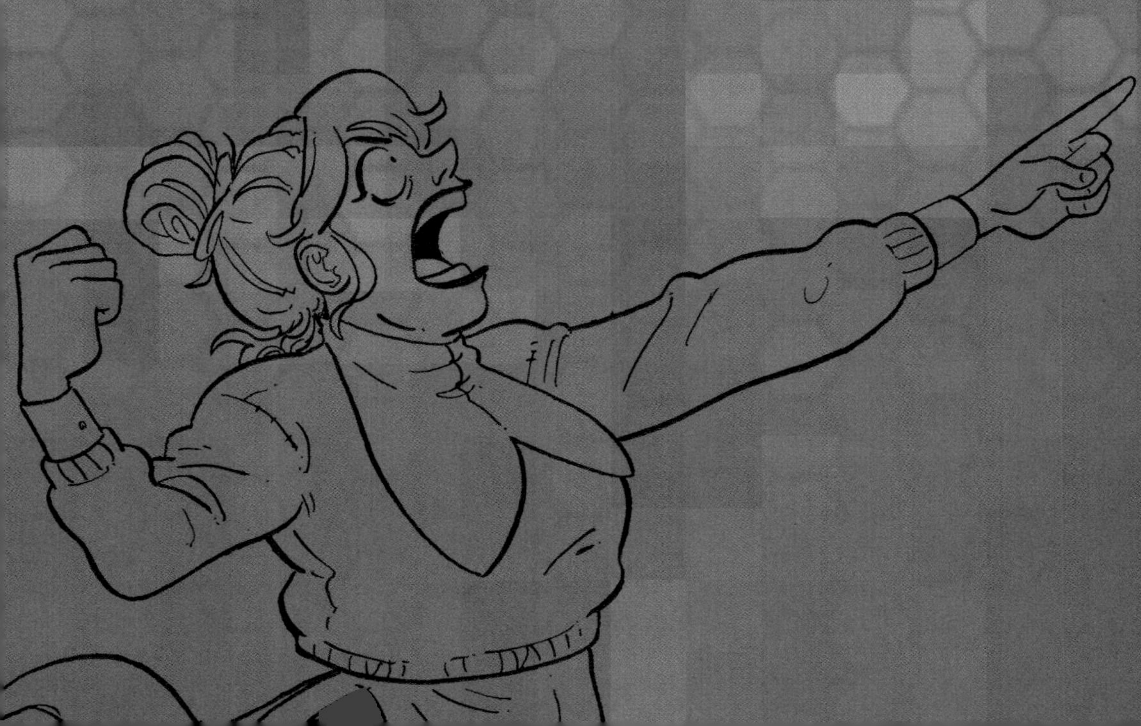

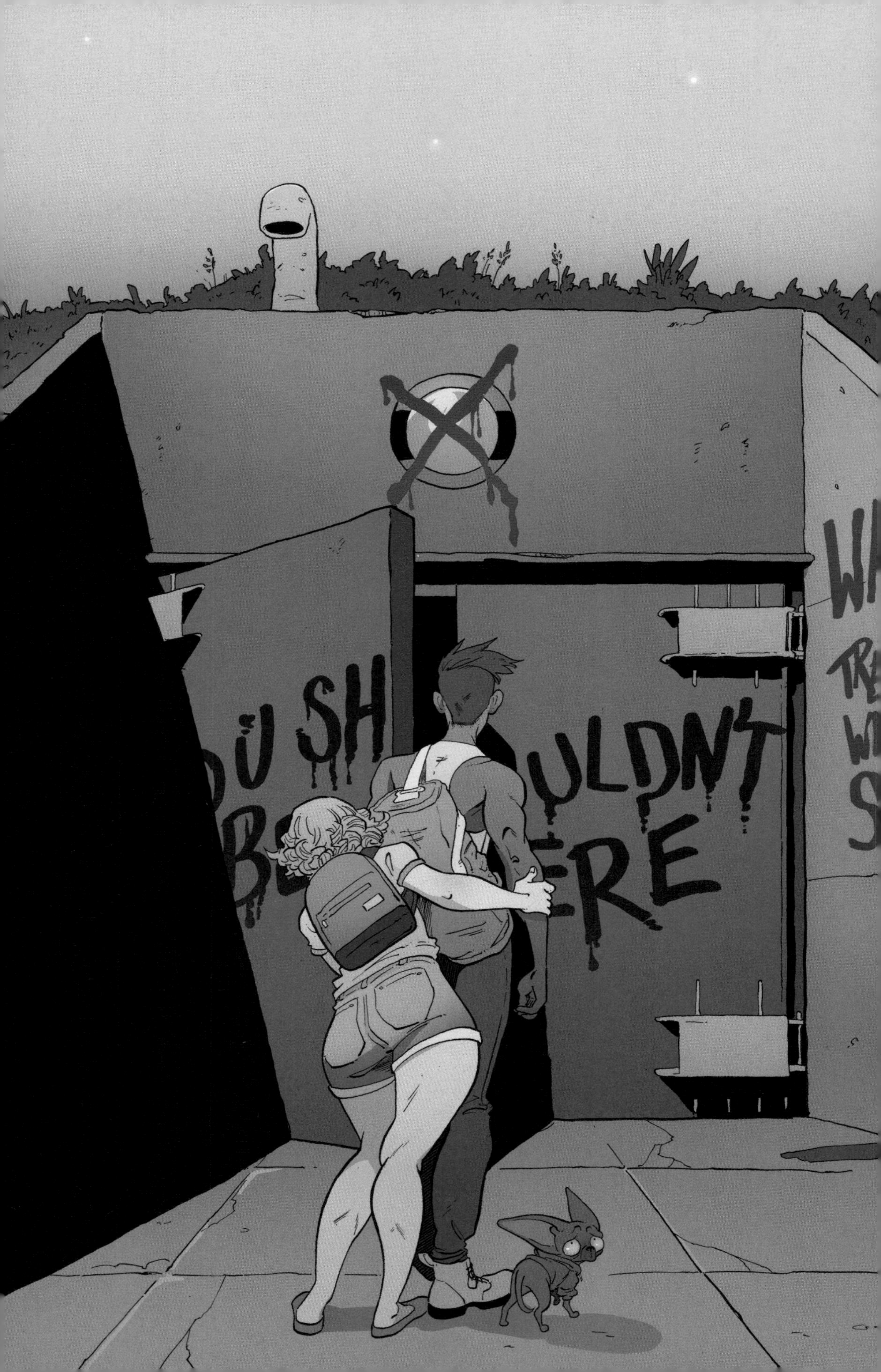
OU SH ULDN'T
B ERE
WA
TRE
WI
S

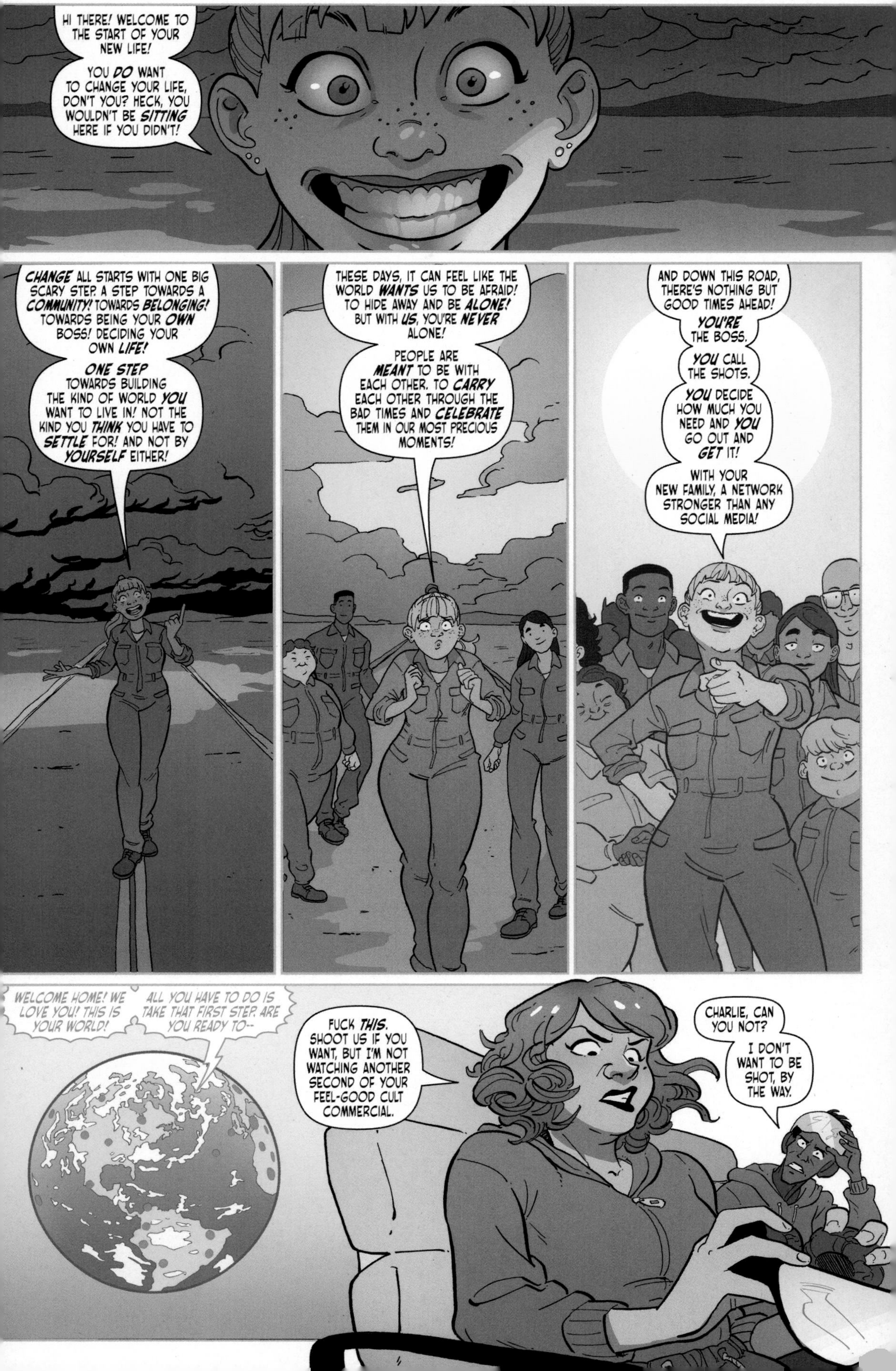
HI THERE! WELCOME TO THE START OF YOUR NEW LIFE!
YOU DO WANT TO CHANGE YOUR LIFE, DON'T YOU? HECK, YOU WOULDN'T BE SITTING HERE IF YOU DIDN'T!
CHANGE ALL STARTS WITH ONE BIG SCARY STEP. A STEP TOWARDS A COMMUNITY! TOWARDS BELONGING! TOWARDS BEING YOUR OWN BOSS! DECIDING YOUR OWN LIFE!
ONE STEP TOWARDS BUILDING THE KIND OF WORLD YOU WANT TO LIVE IN! NOT THE KIND YOU THINK YOU HAVE TO SETTLE FOR! AND NOT BY YOURSELF EITHER!
THESE DAYS, IT CAN FEEL LIKE THE WORLD WANTS US TO BE AFRAID! TO HIDE AWAY AND BE ALONE! BUT WITH US, YOU'RE NEVER ALONE!
PEOPLE ARE MEANT TO BE WITH EACH OTHER. TO CARRY EACH OTHER THROUGH THE BAD TIMES AND CELEBRATE THEM IN OUR MOST PRECIOUS MOMENTS!
AND DOWN THIS ROAD, THERE'S NOTHING BUT GOOD TIMES AHEAD!
YOU'RE THE BOSS.
YOU CALL THE SHOTS.
YOU DECIDE HOW MUCH YOU NEED AND YOU GO OUT AND GET IT!
WITH YOUR NEW FAMILY, A NETWORK STRONGER THAN ANY SOCIAL MEDIA!
WELCOME HOME! WE LOVE YOU! THIS IS YOUR WORLD!
ALL YOU HAVE TO DO IS TAKE THAT FIRST STEP. ARE YOU READY TO--
FUCK THIS. SHOOT US IF YOU WANT, BUT I'M NOT WATCHING ANOTHER SECOND OF YOUR FEEL-GOOD CULT COMMERCIAL.
CHARLIE, CAN YOU NOT?
I DON'T WANT TO BE SHOT, BY THE WAY.

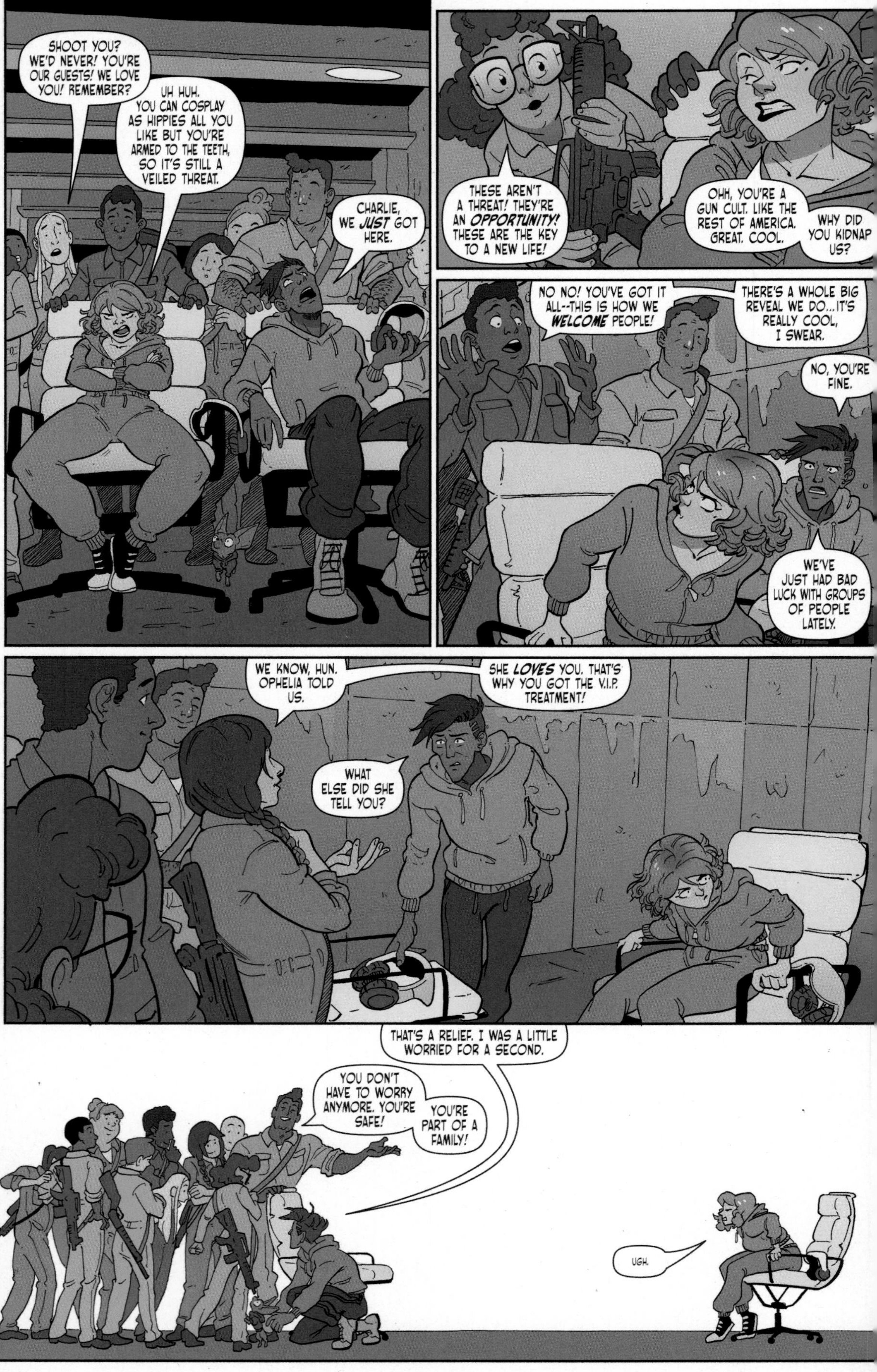
SHOOT YOU? WE'D NEVER! YOU'RE OUR GUESTS! WE LOVE YOU! REMEMBER?
UH HUH. YOU CAN COSPLAY AS HIPPIES ALL YOU LIKE BUT YOU'RE ARMED TO THE TEETH, SO IT'S STILL A VEILED THREAT.
CHARLIE, WE JUST GOT HERE.
THESE AREN'T A THREAT! THEY'RE AN OPPORTUNITY! THESE ARE THE KEY TO A NEW LIFE!
OHH, YOU'RE A GUN CULT. LIKE THE REST OF AMERICA. GREAT. COOL.
WHY DID YOU KIDNAP US?
NO NO! YOU'VE GOT IT ALL--THIS IS HOW WE WELCOME PEOPLE!
THERE'S A WHOLE BIG REVEAL WE DO...IT'S REALLY COOL, I SWEAR.
NO, YOU'RE FINE.
WE'VE JUST HAD BAD LUCK WITH GROUPS OF PEOPLE LATELY.
WE KNOW, HUN. OPHELIA TOLD US.
SHE LOVES YOU. THAT'S WHY YOU GOT THE V.I.P. TREATMENT!
WHAT ELSE DID SHE TELL YOU?
THAT'S A RELIEF. I WAS A LITTLE WORRIED FOR A SECOND.
YOU DON'T HAVE TO WORRY ANYMORE. YOU'RE SAFE!
YOU'RE PART OF A FAMILY!
UGH.

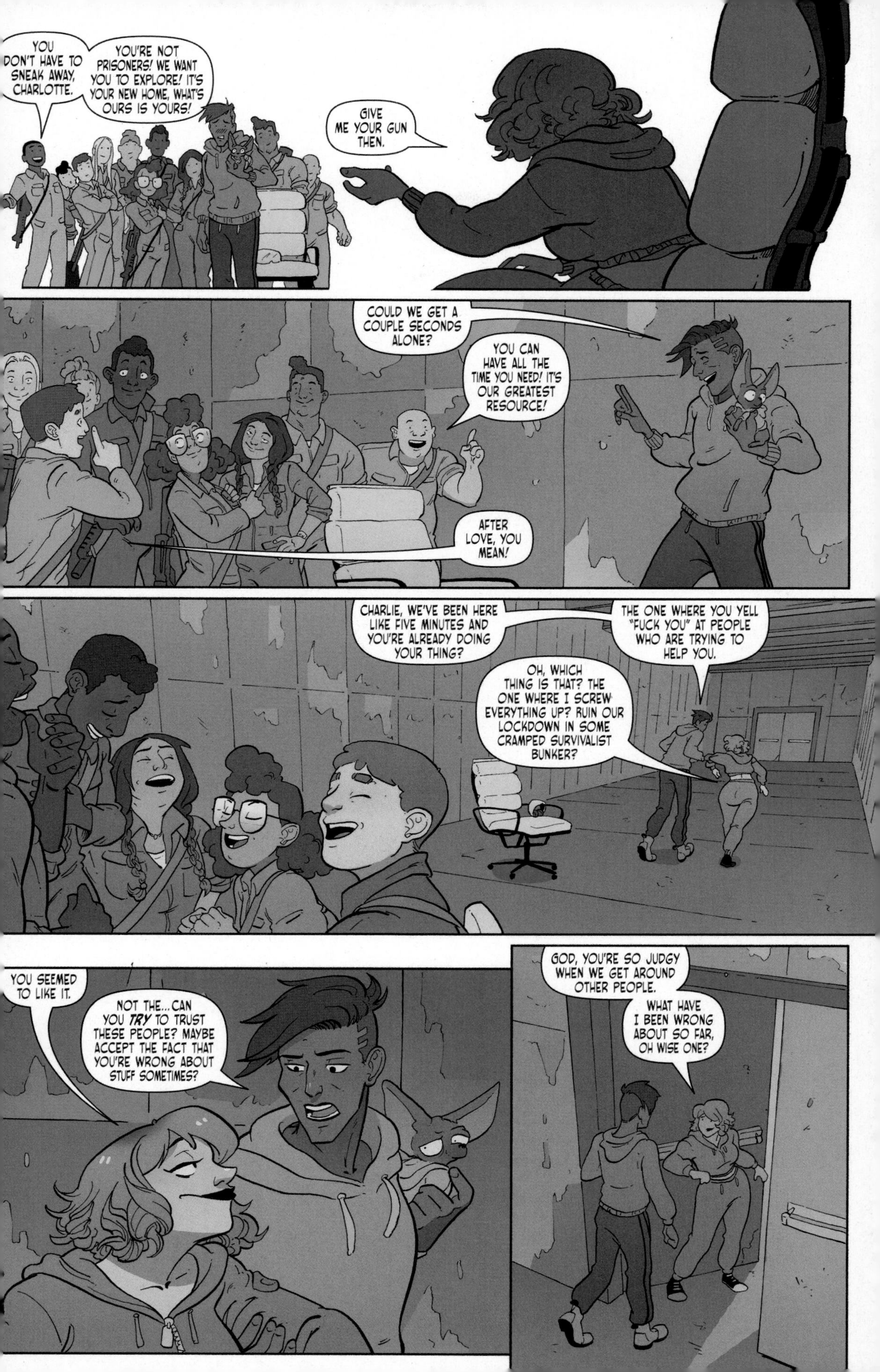
YOU DON'T HAVE TO SNEAK AWAY, CHARLOTTE.
YOU'RE NOT PRISONERS! WE WANT YOU TO EXPLORE! IT'S YOUR NEW HOME, WHAT'S OURS IS YOURS!
GIVE ME YOUR GUN THEN.
COULD WE GET A COUPLE SECONDS ALONE?
YOU CAN HAVE ALL THE TIME YOU NEED! IT'S OUR GREATEST RESOURCE!
AFTER LOVE, YOU MEAN!
CHARLIE, WE'VE BEEN HERE LIKE FIVE MINUTES AND YOU'RE ALREADY DOING YOUR THING?
OH, WHICH THING IS THAT? THE ONE WHERE I SCREW EVERYTHING UP? RUIN OUR LOCKDOWN IN SOME CRAMPED SURVIVALIST BUNKER?
THE ONE WHERE YOU YELL "FUCK YOU" AT PEOPLE WHO ARE TRYING TO HELP YOU.
YOU SEEMED TO LIKE IT.
NOT THE... CAN YOU TRY TO TRUST THESE PEOPLE? MAYBE ACCEPT THE FACT THAT YOU'RE WRONG ABOUT STUFF SOMETIMES?
GOD, YOU'RE SO JUDGY WHEN WE GET AROUND OTHER PEOPLE.
WHAT HAVE I BEEN WRONG ABOUT SO FAR, OH WISE ONE?

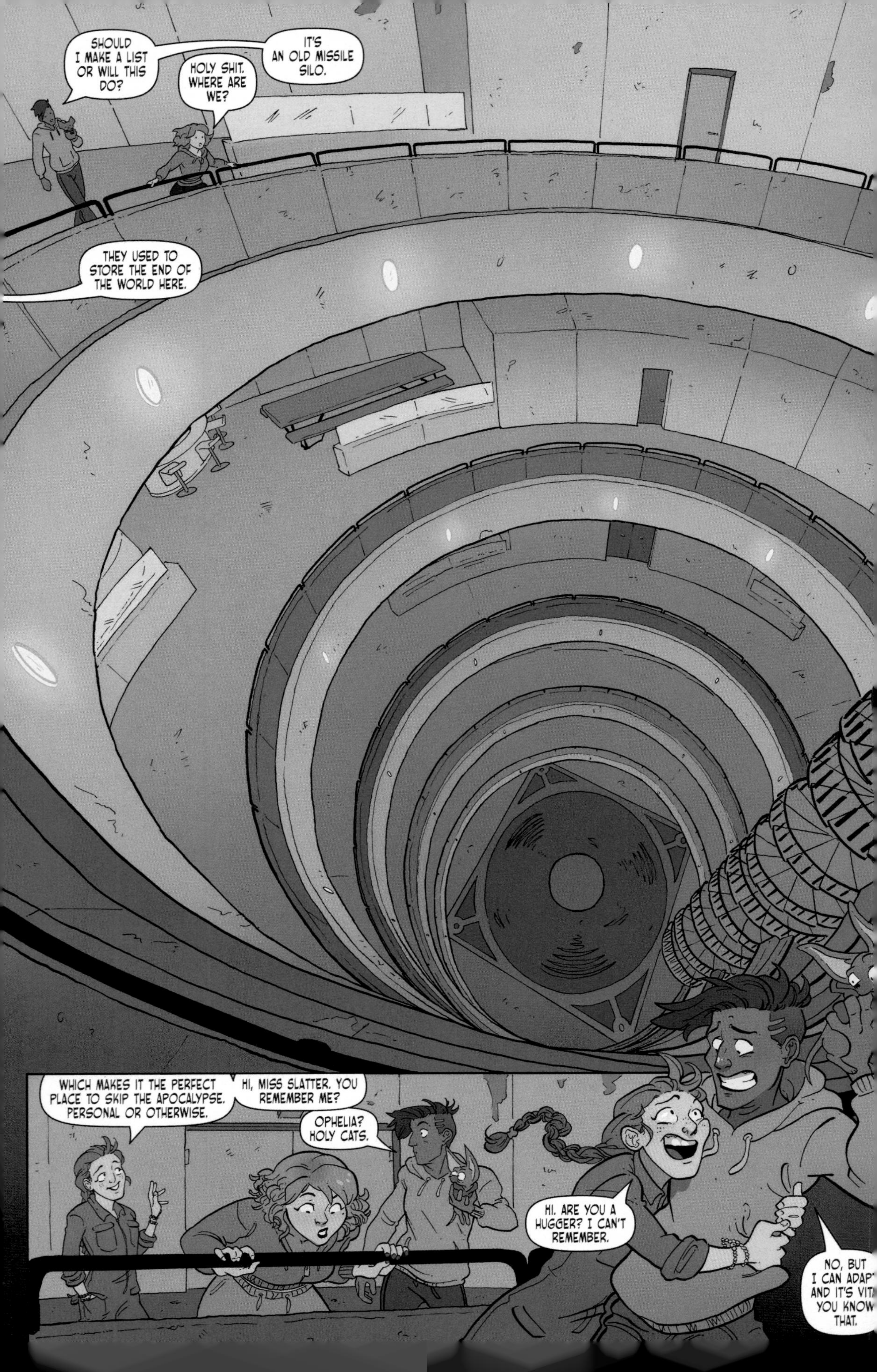
SHOULD I MAKE A LIST OR WILL THIS DO?
HOLY SHIT. WHERE ARE WE?
IT'S AN OLD MISSILE SILO.
THEY USED TO STORE THE END OF THE WORLD HERE.
WHICH MAKES IT THE PERFECT PLACE TO SKIP THE APOCALYPSE. PERSONAL OR OTHERWISE.
HI, MISS SLATTER. YOU REMEMBER ME?
OPHELIA? HOLY CATS.
HI. ARE YOU A HUGGER? I CAN'T REMEMBER.
NO, BUT I CAN ADAP AND IT'S VIT YOU KNOW THAT.

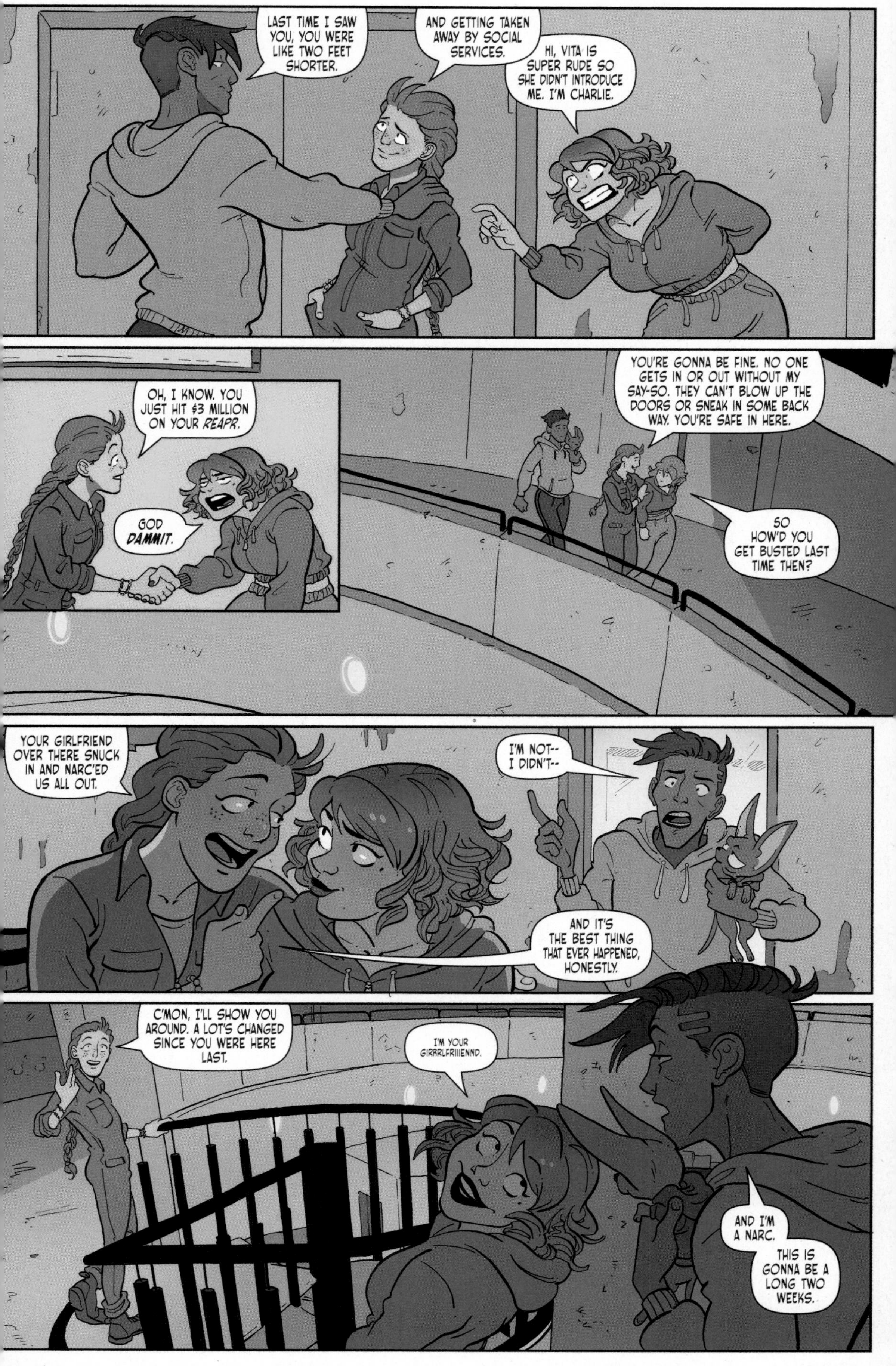
LAST TIME I SAW YOU, YOU WERE LIKE TWO FEET SHORTER.
AND GETTING TAKEN AWAY BY SOCIAL SERVICES.
HI, VITA IS SUPER RUDE SO SHE DIDN'T INTRODUCE ME. I'M CHARLIE.
OH, I KNOW. YOU JUST HIT $3 MILLION ON YOUR *REAPR*.
GOD *DAMMIT*.
YOU'RE GONNA BE FINE. NO ONE GETS IN OR OUT WITHOUT MY SAY-SO. THEY CAN'T BLOW UP THE DOORS OR SNEAK IN SOME BACK WAY. YOU'RE SAFE IN HERE.
SO HOW'D YOU GET BUSTED LAST TIME THEN?
YOUR GIRLFRIEND OVER THERE SNUCK IN AND NARC'ED US ALL OUT.
I'M NOT-- I DIDN'T--
AND IT'S THE BEST THING THAT EVER HAPPENED, HONESTLY.
C'MON, I'LL SHOW YOU AROUND. A LOT'S CHANGED SINCE YOU WERE HERE LAST.
I'M YOUR GIRRRLFRIIIENND.
AND I'M A NARC.
THIS IS GONNA BE A LONG TWO WEEKS.

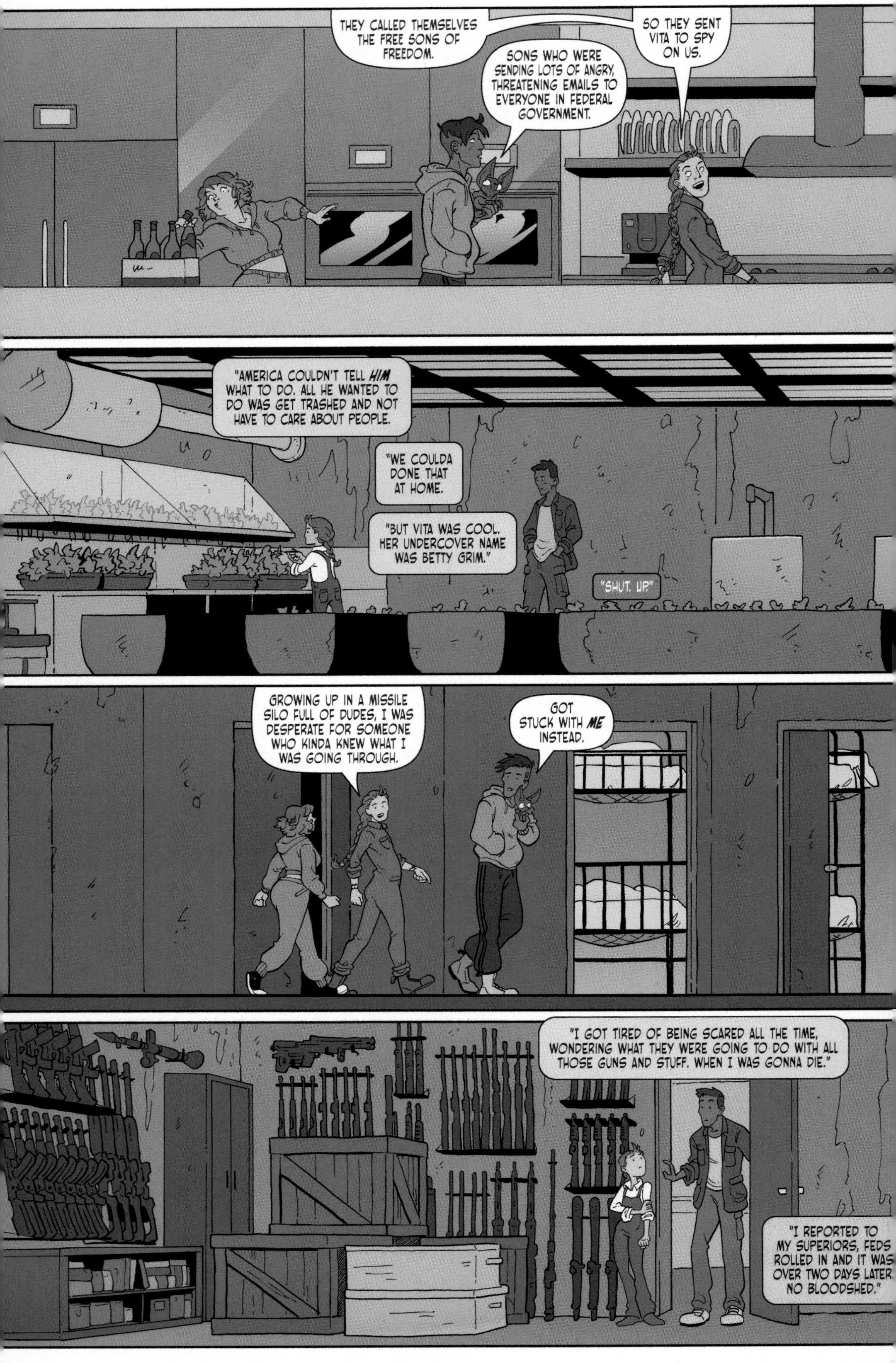
THEY CALLED THEMSELVES THE FREE SONS OF FREEDOM.
SONS WHO WERE SENDING LOTS OF ANGRY, THREATENING EMAILS TO EVERYONE IN FEDERAL GOVERNMENT.
SO THEY SENT VITA TO SPY ON US.
"AMERICA COULDN'T TELL *HIM* WHAT TO DO. ALL HE WANTED TO DO WAS GET TRASHED AND NOT HAVE TO CARE ABOUT PEOPLE.
"WE COULDA DONE THAT AT HOME.
"BUT VITA WAS COOL. HER UNDERCOVER NAME WAS BETTY GRIM."
"SHUT. UP."
GROWING UP IN A MISSILE SILO FULL OF DUDES, I WAS DESPERATE FOR SOMEONE WHO KINDA KNEW WHAT I WAS GOING THROUGH.
GOT STUCK WITH *ME* INSTEAD.
"I GOT TIRED OF BEING SCARED ALL THE TIME, WONDERING WHAT THEY WERE GOING TO DO WITH ALL THOSE GUNS AND STUFF. WHEN I WAS GONNA DIE."
"I REPORTED TO MY SUPERIORS, FEDS ROLLED IN AND IT WAS OVER TWO DAYS LATER. NO BLOODSHED."

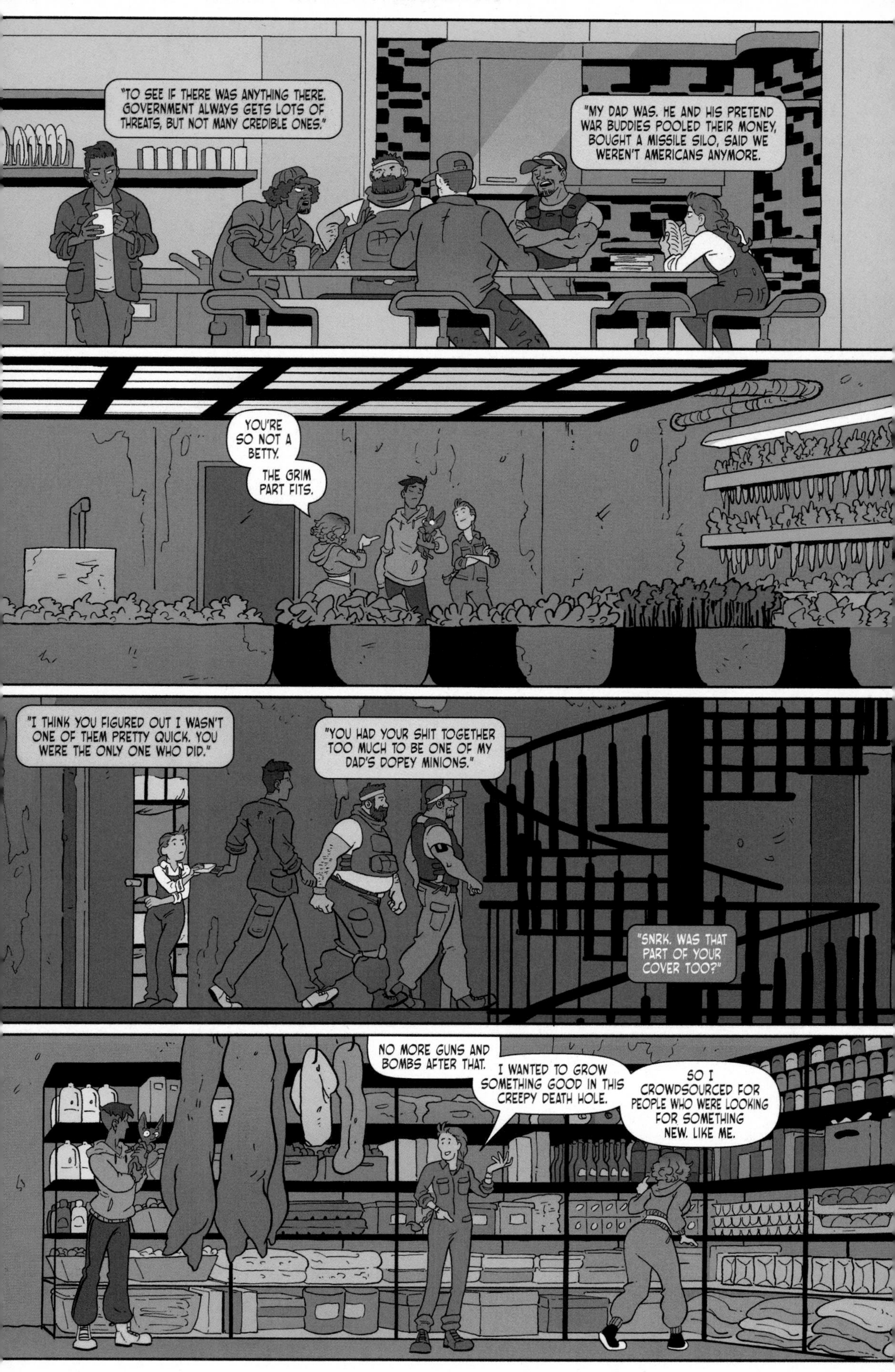
"TO SEE IF THERE WAS ANYTHING THERE. GOVERNMENT ALWAYS GETS LOTS OF THREATS, BUT NOT MANY CREDIBLE ONES."
"MY DAD WAS. HE AND HIS PRETEND WAR BUDDIES POOLED THEIR MONEY, BOUGHT A MISSILE SILO, SAID WE WEREN'T AMERICANS ANYMORE.
YOU'RE SO NOT A BETTY.
THE GRIM PART FITS.
"I THINK YOU FIGURED OUT I WASN'T ONE OF THEM PRETTY QUICK. YOU WERE THE ONLY ONE WHO DID."
"YOU HAD YOUR SHIT TOGETHER TOO MUCH TO BE ONE OF MY DAD'S DOPEY MINIONS."
"SNRK. WAS THAT PART OF YOUR COVER TOO?"
NO MORE GUNS AND BOMBS AFTER THAT.
I WANTED TO GROW SOMETHING GOOD IN THIS CREEPY DEATH HOLE.
SO I CROWDSOURCED FOR PEOPLE WHO WERE LOOKING FOR SOMETHING NEW. LIKE ME.

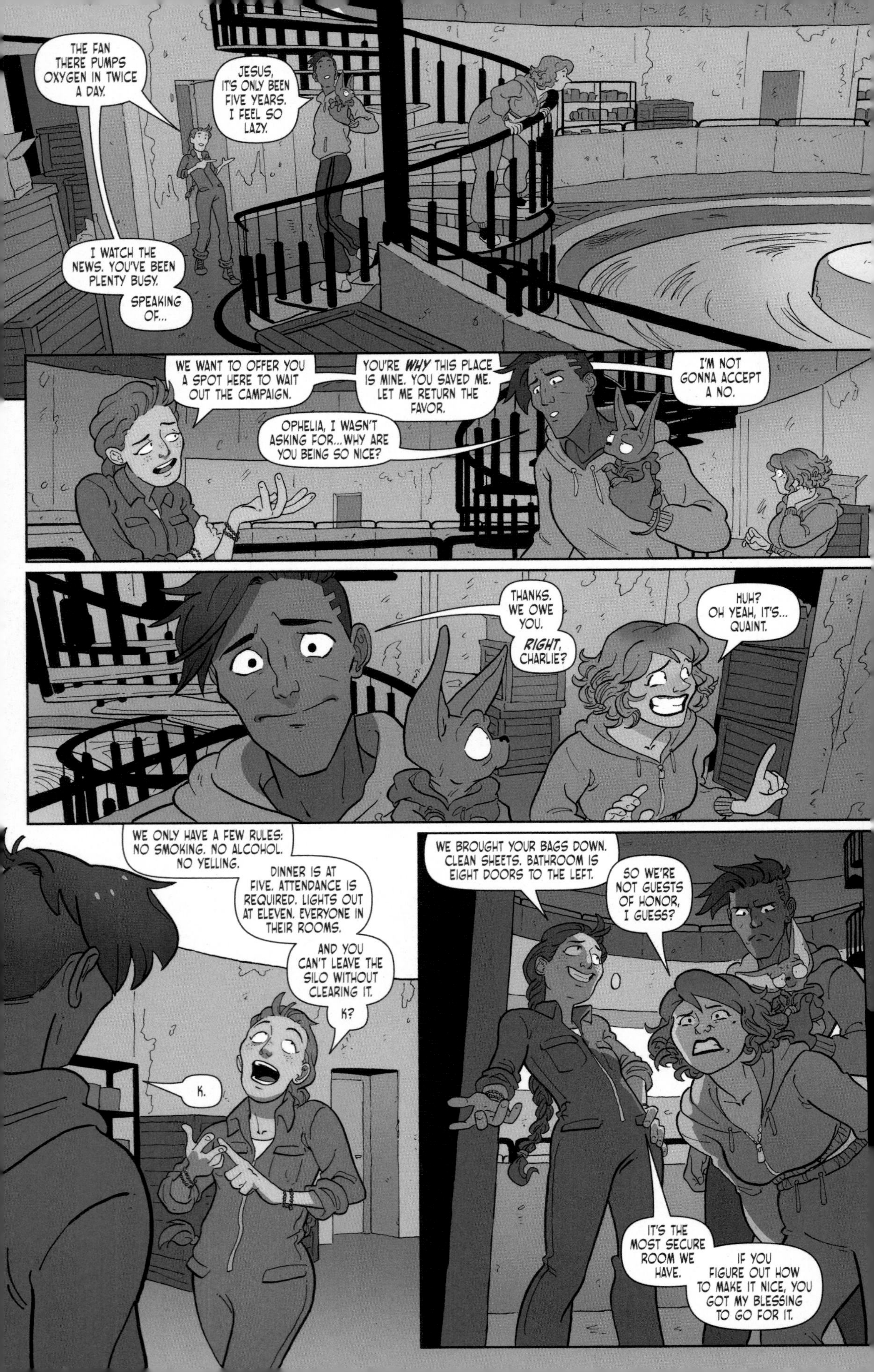
THE FAN THERE PUMPS OXYGEN IN TWICE A DAY.
JESUS, IT'S ONLY BEEN FIVE YEARS. I FEEL SO LAZY.
I WATCH THE NEWS. YOU'VE BEEN PLENTY BUSY.
SPEAKING OF...
WE WANT TO OFFER YOU A SPOT HERE TO WAIT OUT THE CAMPAIGN.
YOU'RE WHY THIS PLACE IS MINE. YOU SAVED ME. LET ME RETURN THE FAVOR.
I'M NOT GONNA ACCEPT A NO.
OPHELIA, I WASN'T ASKING FOR...WHY ARE YOU BEING SO NICE?
THANKS. WE OWE YOU. RIGHT, CHARLIE?
HUH? OH YEAH, IT'S... QUAINT.
WE ONLY HAVE A FEW RULES: NO SMOKING. NO ALCOHOL. NO YELLING.
DINNER IS AT FIVE. ATTENDANCE IS REQUIRED. LIGHTS OUT AT ELEVEN. EVERYONE IN THEIR ROOMS.
AND YOU CAN'T LEAVE THE SILO WITHOUT CLEARING IT.
K?
K.
WE BROUGHT YOUR BAGS DOWN. CLEAN SHEETS. BATHROOM IS EIGHT DOORS TO THE LEFT.
SO WE'RE NOT GUESTS OF HONOR, I GUESS?
IT'S THE MOST SECURE ROOM WE HAVE.
IF YOU FIGURE OUT HOW TO MAKE IT NICE, YOU GOT MY BLESSING TO GO FOR IT.

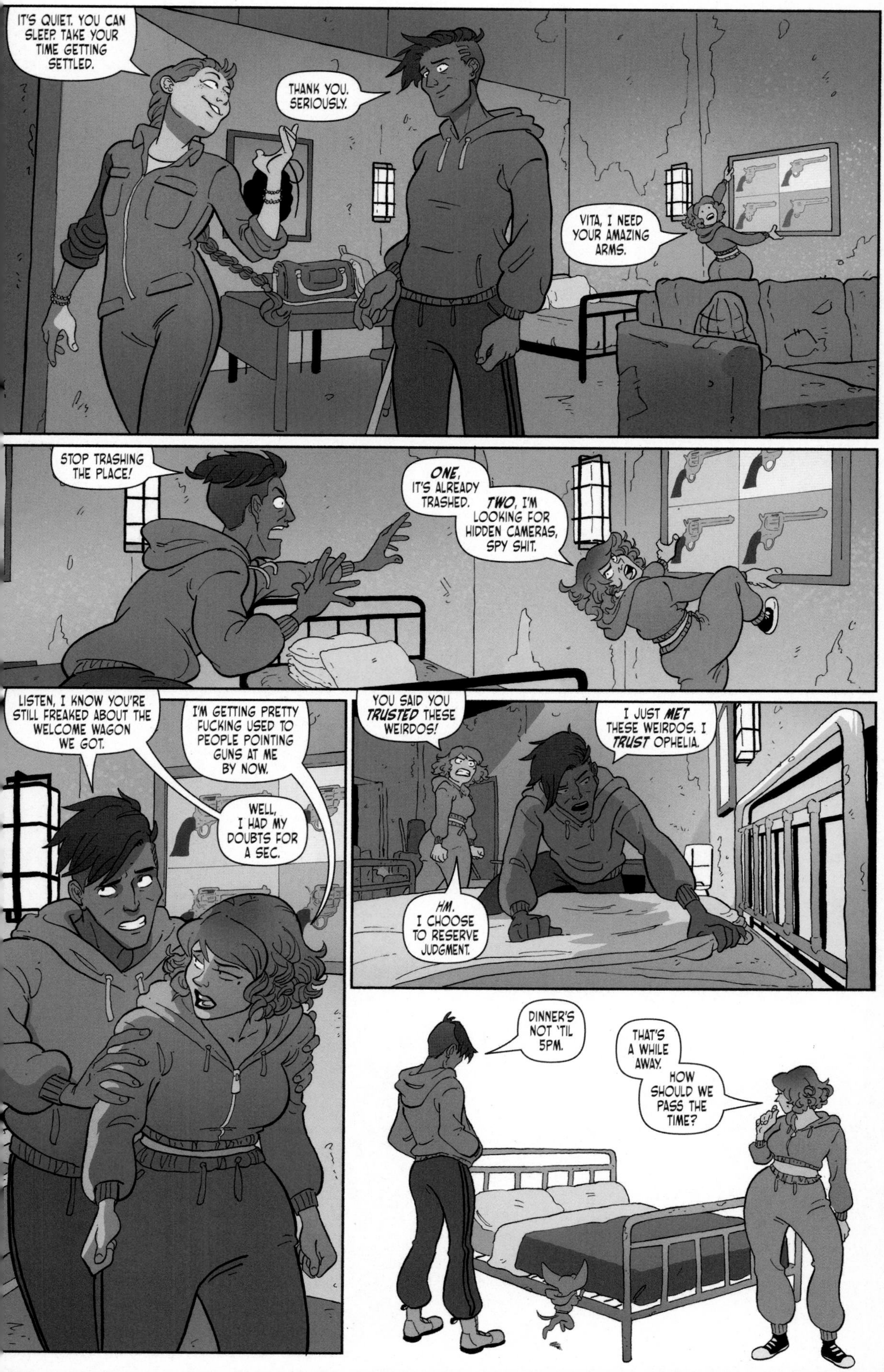
IT'S QUIET. YOU CAN SLEEP. TAKE YOUR TIME GETTING SETTLED.
THANK YOU. SERIOUSLY.
VITA, I NEED YOUR AMAZING ARMS.
STOP TRASHING THE PLACE!
ONE, IT'S ALREADY TRASHED. TWO, I'M LOOKING FOR HIDDEN CAMERAS, SPY SHIT.
LISTEN, I KNOW YOU'RE STILL FREAKED ABOUT THE WELCOME WAGON WE GOT.
I'M GETTING PRETTY FUCKING USED TO PEOPLE POINTING GUNS AT ME BY NOW.
WELL, I HAD MY DOUBTS FOR A SEC.
YOU SAID YOU TRUSTED THESE WEIRDOS!
I JUST MET THESE WEIRDOS. I TRUST OPHELIA.
HM. I CHOOSE TO RESERVE JUDGMENT.
DINNER'S NOT 'TIL 5PM.
THAT'S A WHILE AWAY.
HOW SHOULD WE PASS THE TIME?

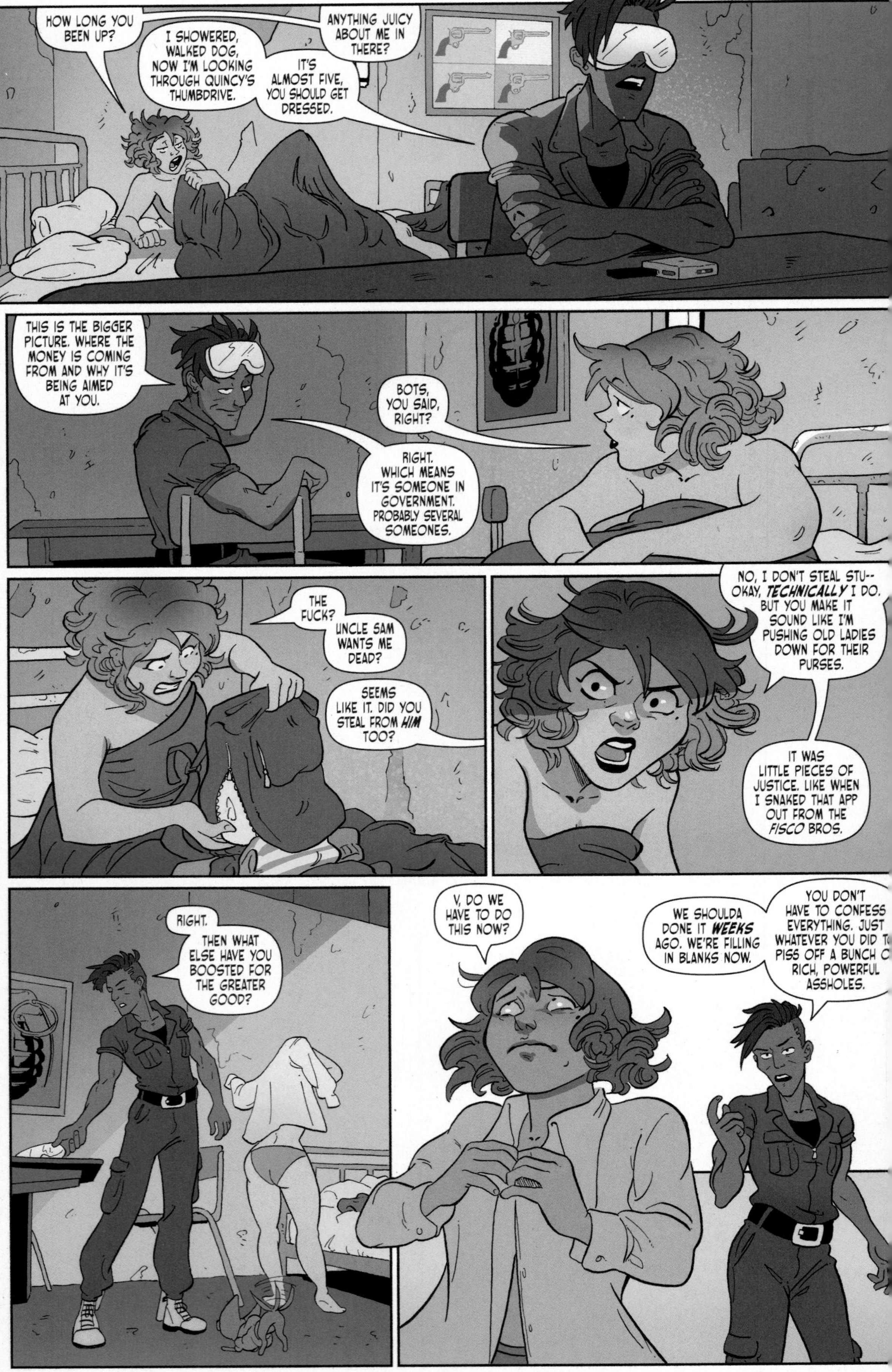
HOW LONG YOU BEEN UP?
I SHOWERED, WALKED DOG, NOW I'M LOOKING THROUGH QUINCY'S THUMBDRIVE.
ANYTHING JUICY ABOUT ME IN THERE?
IT'S ALMOST FIVE, YOU SHOULD GET DRESSED.
THIS IS THE BIGGER PICTURE. WHERE THE MONEY IS COMING FROM AND WHY IT'S BEING AIMED AT YOU.
BOTS, YOU SAID, RIGHT?
RIGHT. WHICH MEANS IT'S SOMEONE IN GOVERNMENT. PROBABLY SEVERAL SOMEONES.
THE FUCK?
UNCLE SAM WANTS ME DEAD?
SEEMS LIKE IT. DID YOU STEAL FROM *HIM* TOO?
NO, I DON'T STEAL STU-- OKAY, *TECHNICALLY* I DO. BUT YOU MAKE IT SOUND LIKE I'M PUSHING OLD LADIES DOWN FOR THEIR PURSES.
IT WAS LITTLE PIECES OF JUSTICE. LIKE WHEN I SNAKED THAT APP OUT FROM THE *FISCO* BROS.
RIGHT.
THEN WHAT ELSE HAVE YOU BOOSTED FOR THE GREATER GOOD?
V, DO WE HAVE TO DO THIS NOW?
WE SHOULDA DONE IT *WEEKS* AGO. WE'RE FILLING IN BLANKS NOW.
YOU DON'T HAVE TO CONFESS EVERYTHING. JUST WHATEVER YOU DID TO PISS OFF A BUNCH OF RICH, POWERFUL ASSHOLES.

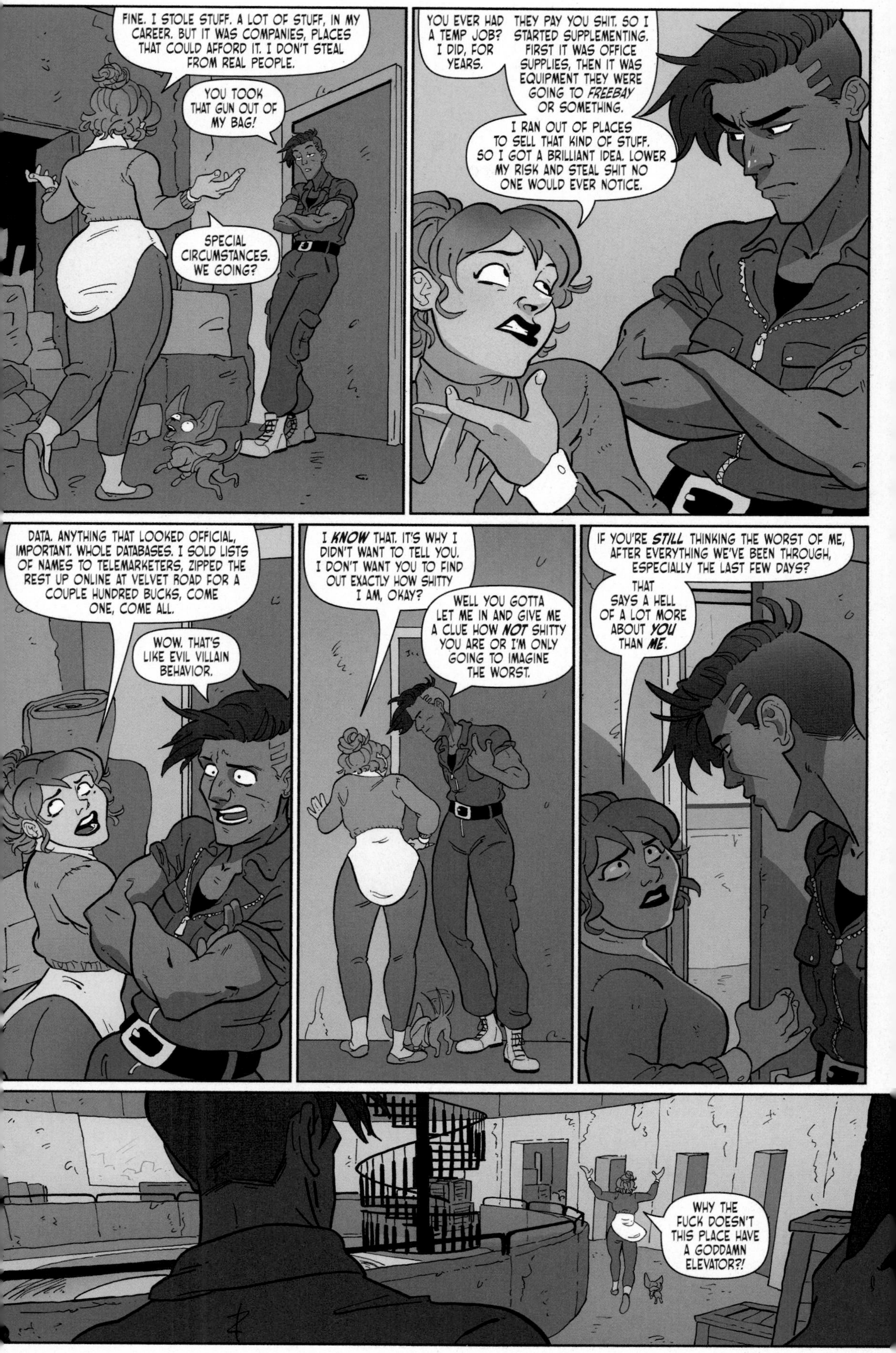
FINE. I STOLE STUFF. A LOT OF STUFF, IN MY CAREER. BUT IT WAS COMPANIES, PLACES THAT COULD AFFORD IT. I DON'T STEAL FROM REAL PEOPLE.
YOU TOOK THAT GUN OUT OF MY BAG!
SPECIAL CIRCUMSTANCES. WE GOING?
YOU EVER HAD A TEMP JOB? I DID, FOR YEARS.
THEY PAY YOU SHIT. SO I STARTED SUPPLEMENTING. FIRST IT WAS OFFICE SUPPLIES, THEN IT WAS EQUIPMENT THEY WERE GOING TO FREEBAY OR SOMETHING.
I RAN OUT OF PLACES TO SELL THAT KIND OF STUFF. SO I GOT A BRILLIANT IDEA. LOWER MY RISK AND STEAL SHIT NO ONE WOULD EVER NOTICE.
DATA. ANYTHING THAT LOOKED OFFICIAL, IMPORTANT. WHOLE DATABASES. I SOLD LISTS OF NAMES TO TELEMARKETERS, ZIPPED THE REST UP ONLINE AT VELVET ROAD FOR A COUPLE HUNDRED BUCKS, COME ONE, COME ALL.
WOW. THAT'S LIKE EVIL VILLAIN BEHAVIOR.
I KNOW THAT. IT'S WHY I DIDN'T WANT TO TELL YOU. I DON'T WANT YOU TO FIND OUT EXACTLY HOW SHITTY I AM, OKAY?
WELL YOU GOTTA LET ME IN AND GIVE ME A CLUE HOW NOT SHITTY YOU ARE OR I'M ONLY GOING TO IMAGINE THE WORST.
IF YOU'RE STILL THINKING THE WORST OF ME, AFTER EVERYTHING WE'VE BEEN THROUGH, ESPECIALLY THE LAST FEW DAYS?
THAT SAYS A HELL OF A LOT MORE ABOUT YOU THAN ME.
WHY THE FUCK DOESN'T THIS PLACE HAVE A GODDAMN ELEVATOR?!

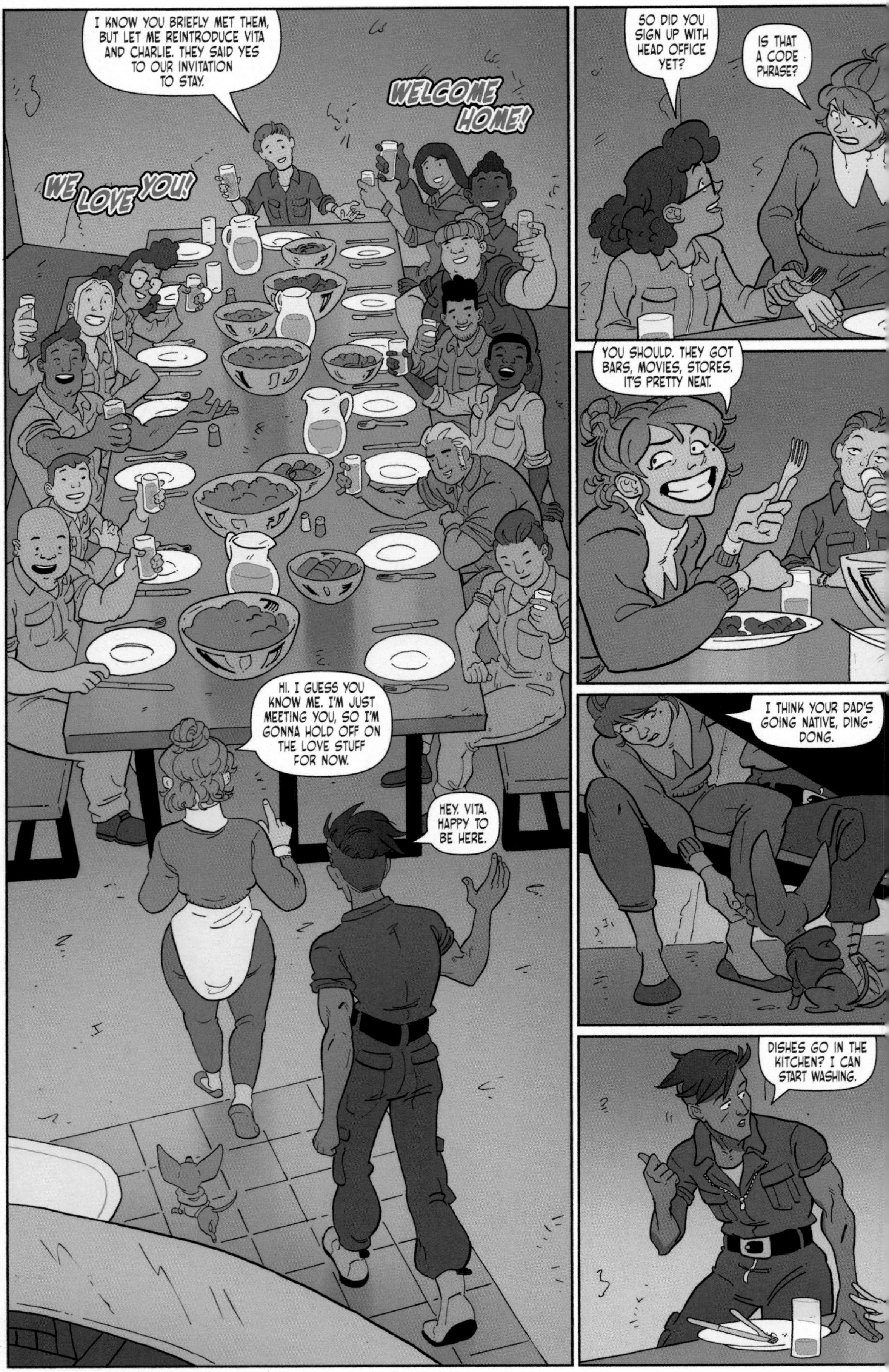

I KNOW YOU BRIEFLY MET THEM, BUT LET ME REINTRODUCE VITA AND CHARLIE. THEY SAID YES TO OUR INVITATION TO STAY.
WELCOME HOME!
WE LOVE YOU!
HI. I GUESS YOU KNOW ME. I'M JUST MEETING YOU, SO I'M GONNA HOLD OFF ON THE LOVE STUFF FOR NOW.
HEY. VITA. HAPPY TO BE HERE.
SO DID YOU SIGN UP WITH HEAD OFFICE YET?
IS THAT A CODE PHRASE?
YOU SHOULD. THEY GOT BARS, MOVIES, STORES. IT'S PRETTY NEAT.
I THINK YOUR DAD'S GOING NATIVE, DING-DONG.
DISHES GO IN THE KITCHEN? I CAN START WASHING.

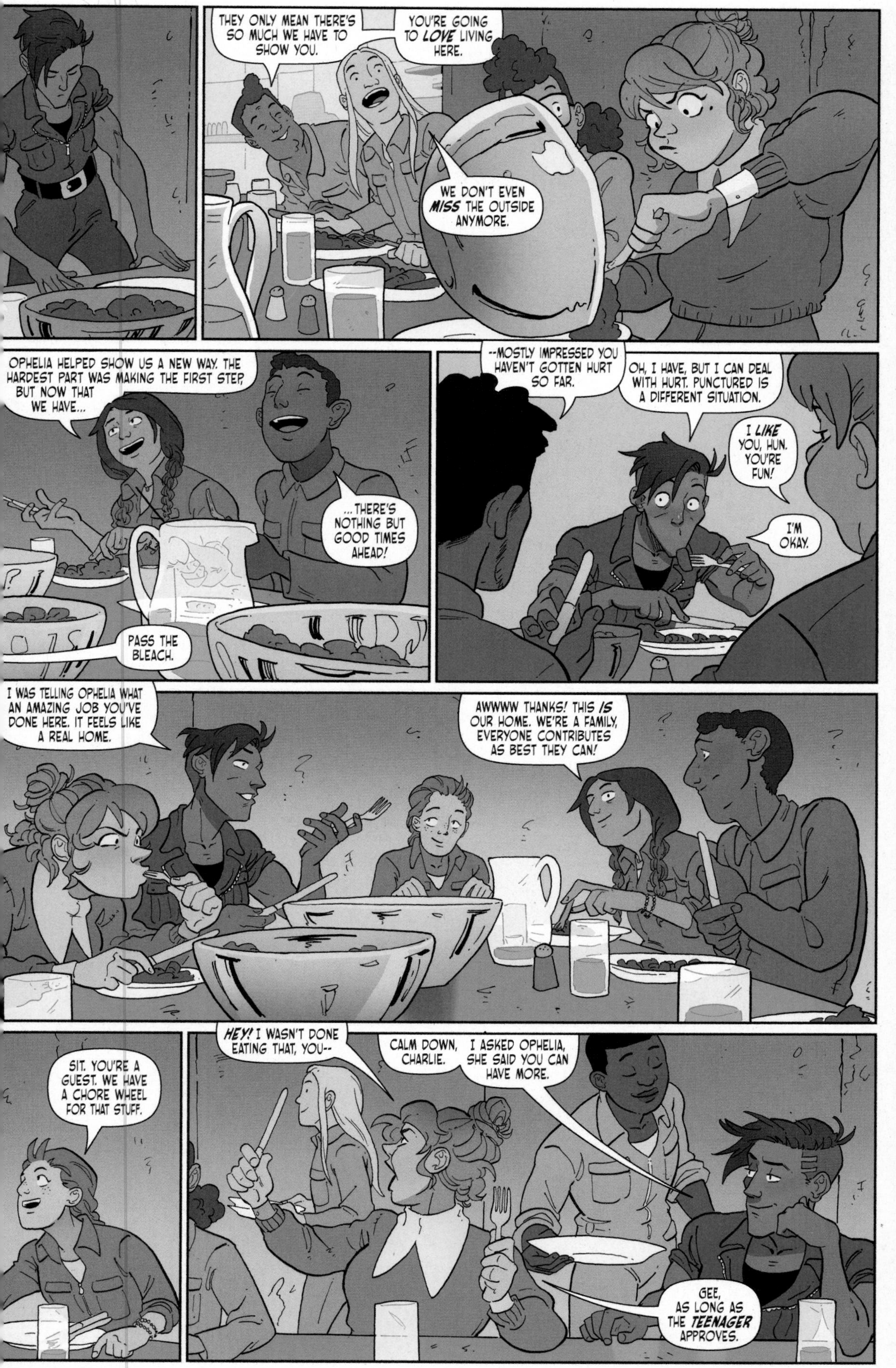
THEY ONLY MEAN THERE'S SO MUCH WE HAVE TO SHOW YOU.
YOU'RE GOING TO LOVE LIVING HERE.
WE DON'T EVEN MISS THE OUTSIDE ANYMORE.
OPHELIA HELPED SHOW US A NEW WAY. THE HARDEST PART WAS MAKING THE FIRST STEP, BUT NOW THAT WE HAVE...
...THERE'S NOTHING BUT GOOD TIMES AHEAD!
PASS THE BLEACH.
--MOSTLY IMPRESSED YOU HAVEN'T GOTTEN HURT SO FAR.
OH, I HAVE, BUT I CAN DEAL WITH HURT. PUNCTURED IS A DIFFERENT SITUATION.
I LIKE YOU, HUN. YOU'RE FUN!
I'M OKAY.
I WAS TELLING OPHELIA WHAT AN AMAZING JOB YOU'VE DONE HERE. IT FEELS LIKE A REAL HOME.
AWWWW THANKS! THIS IS OUR HOME. WE'RE A FAMILY, EVERYONE CONTRIBUTES AS BEST THEY CAN!
SIT. YOU'RE A GUEST. WE HAVE A CHORE WHEEL FOR THAT STUFF.
HEY! I WASN'T DONE EATING THAT, YOU--
CALM DOWN, CHARLIE.
I ASKED OPHELIA, SHE SAID YOU CAN HAVE MORE.
GEE, AS LONG AS THE TEENAGER APPROVES.

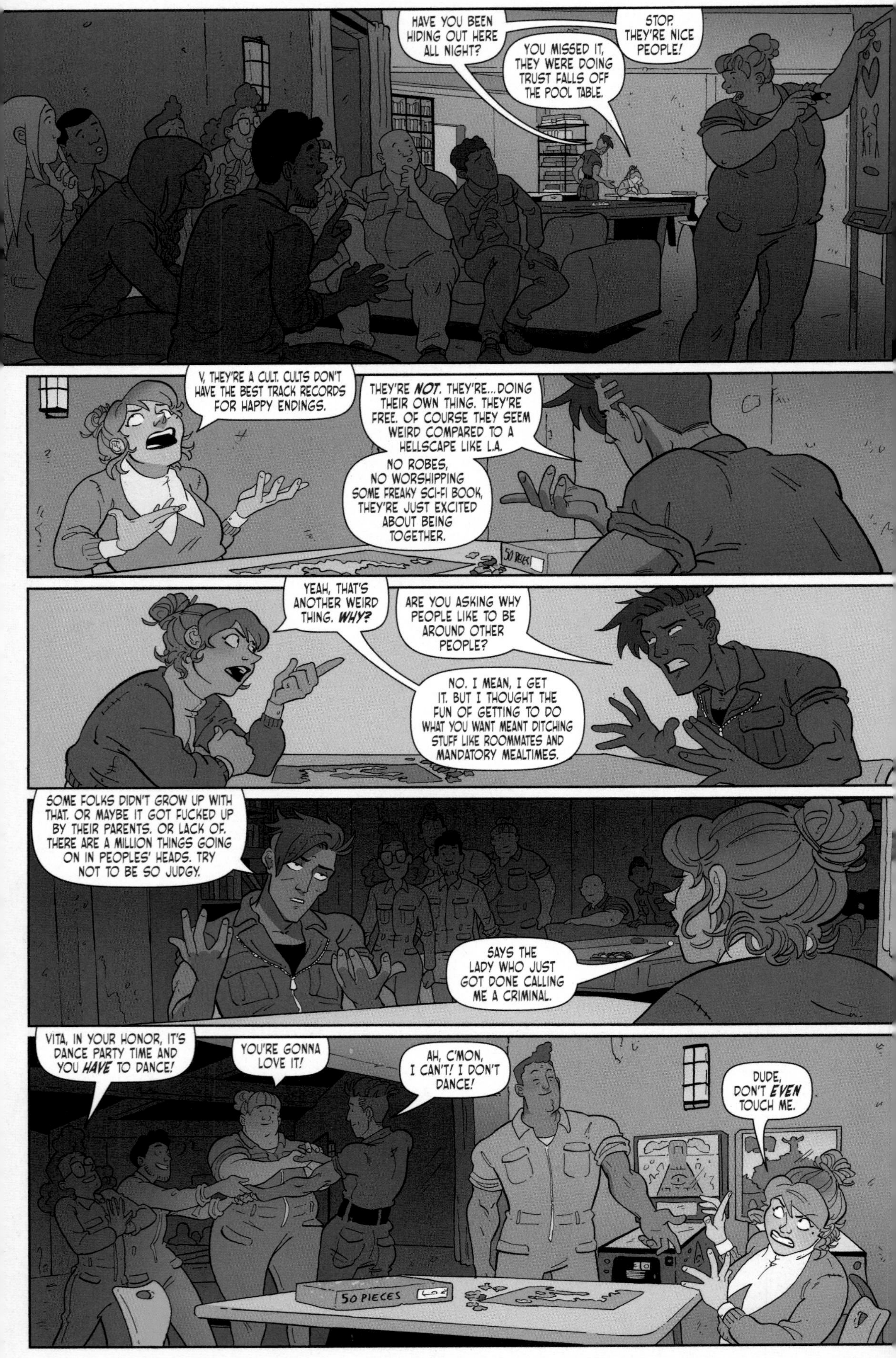

HAVE YOU BEEN HIDING OUT HERE ALL NIGHT?
STOP. THEY'RE NICE PEOPLE!
YOU MISSED IT, THEY WERE DOING TRUST FALLS OFF THE POOL TABLE.
V, THEY'RE A CULT. CULTS DON'T HAVE THE BEST TRACK RECORDS FOR HAPPY ENDINGS.
THEY'RE NOT. THEY'RE...DOING THEIR OWN THING. THEY'RE FREE. OF COURSE THEY SEEM WEIRD COMPARED TO A HELLSCAPE LIKE L.A.
NO ROBES, NO WORSHIPPING SOME FREAKY SCI-FI BOOK, THEY'RE JUST EXCITED ABOUT BEING TOGETHER.
50 PIECES
YEAH, THAT'S ANOTHER WEIRD THING. WHY?
ARE YOU ASKING WHY PEOPLE LIKE TO BE AROUND OTHER PEOPLE?
NO. I MEAN, I GET IT. BUT I THOUGHT THE FUN OF GETTING TO DO WHAT YOU WANT MEANT DITCHING STUFF LIKE ROOMMATES AND MANDATORY MEALTIMES.
SOME FOLKS DIDN'T GROW UP WITH THAT. OR MAYBE IT GOT FUCKED UP BY THEIR PARENTS. OR LACK OF. THERE ARE A MILLION THINGS GOING ON IN PEOPLES' HEADS. TRY NOT TO BE SO JUDGY.
SAYS THE LADY WHO JUST GOT DONE CALLING ME A CRIMINAL.
VITA, IN YOUR HONOR, IT'S DANCE PARTY TIME AND YOU HAVE TO DANCE!
YOU'RE GONNA LOVE IT!
AH, C'MON, I CAN'T! I DON'T DANCE!
DUDE, DON'T EVEN TOUCH ME.
50 PIECES

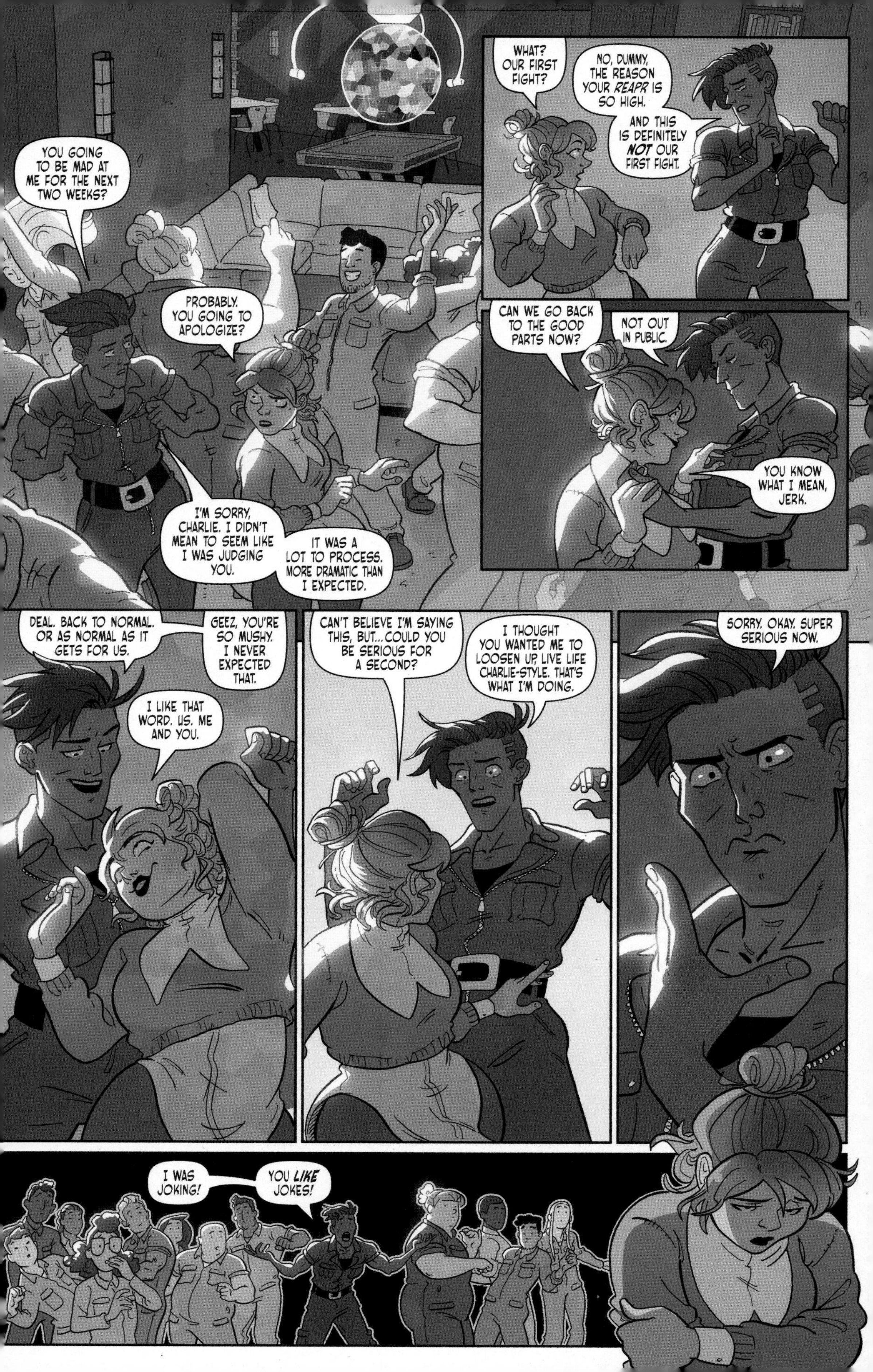
YOU GOING TO BE MAD AT ME FOR THE NEXT TWO WEEKS?
PROBABLY. YOU GOING TO APOLOGIZE?
I'M SORRY, CHARLIE. I DIDN'T MEAN TO SEEM LIKE I WAS JUDGING YOU.
IT WAS A LOT TO PROCESS. MORE DRAMATIC THAN I EXPECTED.
WHAT? OUR FIRST FIGHT?
NO, DUMMY, THE REASON YOUR REAPR IS SO HIGH.
AND THIS IS DEFINITELY NOT OUR FIRST FIGHT.
CAN WE GO BACK TO THE GOOD PARTS NOW?
NOT OUT IN PUBLIC.
YOU KNOW WHAT I MEAN, JERK.
DEAL. BACK TO NORMAL. OR AS NORMAL AS IT GETS FOR US.
GEEZ, YOU'RE SO MUSHY. I NEVER EXPECTED THAT.
I LIKE THAT WORD. US. ME AND YOU.
CAN'T BELIEVE I'M SAYING THIS, BUT...COULD YOU BE SERIOUS FOR A SECOND?
I THOUGHT YOU WANTED ME TO LOOSEN UP, LIVE LIFE CHARLIE-STYLE. THAT'S WHAT I'M DOING.
SORRY. OKAY. SUPER SERIOUS NOW.
I WAS JOKING!
YOU LIKE JOKES!

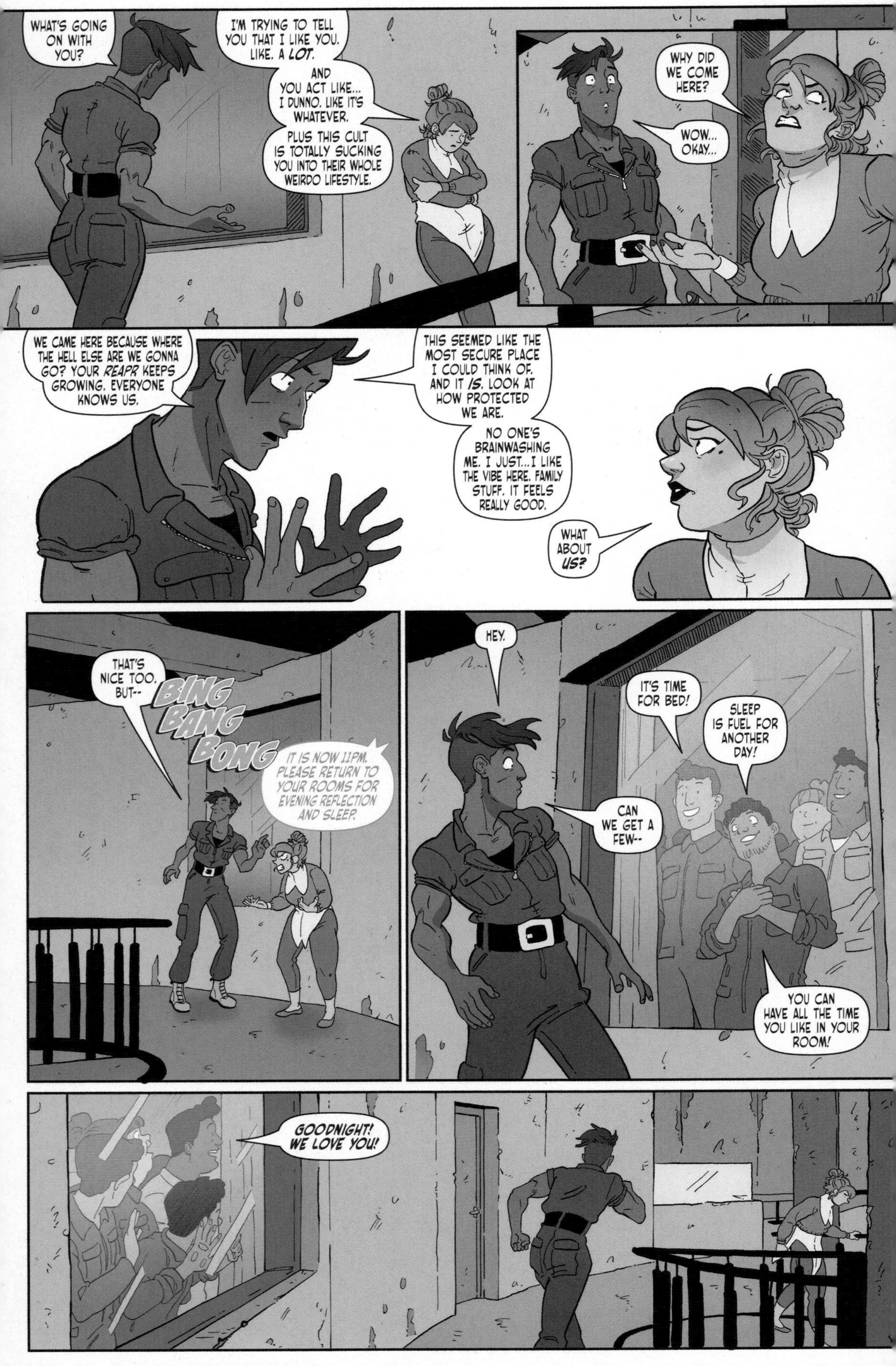

WHAT'S GOING ON WITH YOU?
I'M TRYING TO TELL YOU THAT I LIKE YOU. LIKE. A LOT.
AND YOU ACT LIKE... I DUNNO. LIKE IT'S WHATEVER.
PLUS THIS CULT IS TOTALLY SUCKING YOU INTO THEIR WHOLE WEIRDO LIFESTYLE.
WHY DID WE COME HERE?
WOW... OKAY...
WE CAME HERE BECAUSE WHERE THE HELL ELSE ARE WE GONNA GO? YOUR REAPR KEEPS GROWING. EVERYONE KNOWS US.
THIS SEEMED LIKE THE MOST SECURE PLACE I COULD THINK OF. AND IT IS. LOOK AT HOW PROTECTED WE ARE.
NO ONE'S BRAINWASHING ME. I JUST...I LIKE THE VIBE HERE. FAMILY STUFF. IT FEELS REALLY GOOD.
WHAT ABOUT US?
THAT'S NICE TOO, BUT--
BING BANG BONG
IT IS NOW 11PM. PLEASE RETURN TO YOUR ROOMS FOR EVENING REFLECTION AND SLEEP.
HEY.
IT'S TIME FOR BED!
SLEEP IS FUEL FOR ANOTHER DAY!
CAN WE GET A FEW--
YOU CAN HAVE ALL THE TIME YOU LIKE IN YOUR ROOM!
GOODNIGHT! WE LOVE YOU!

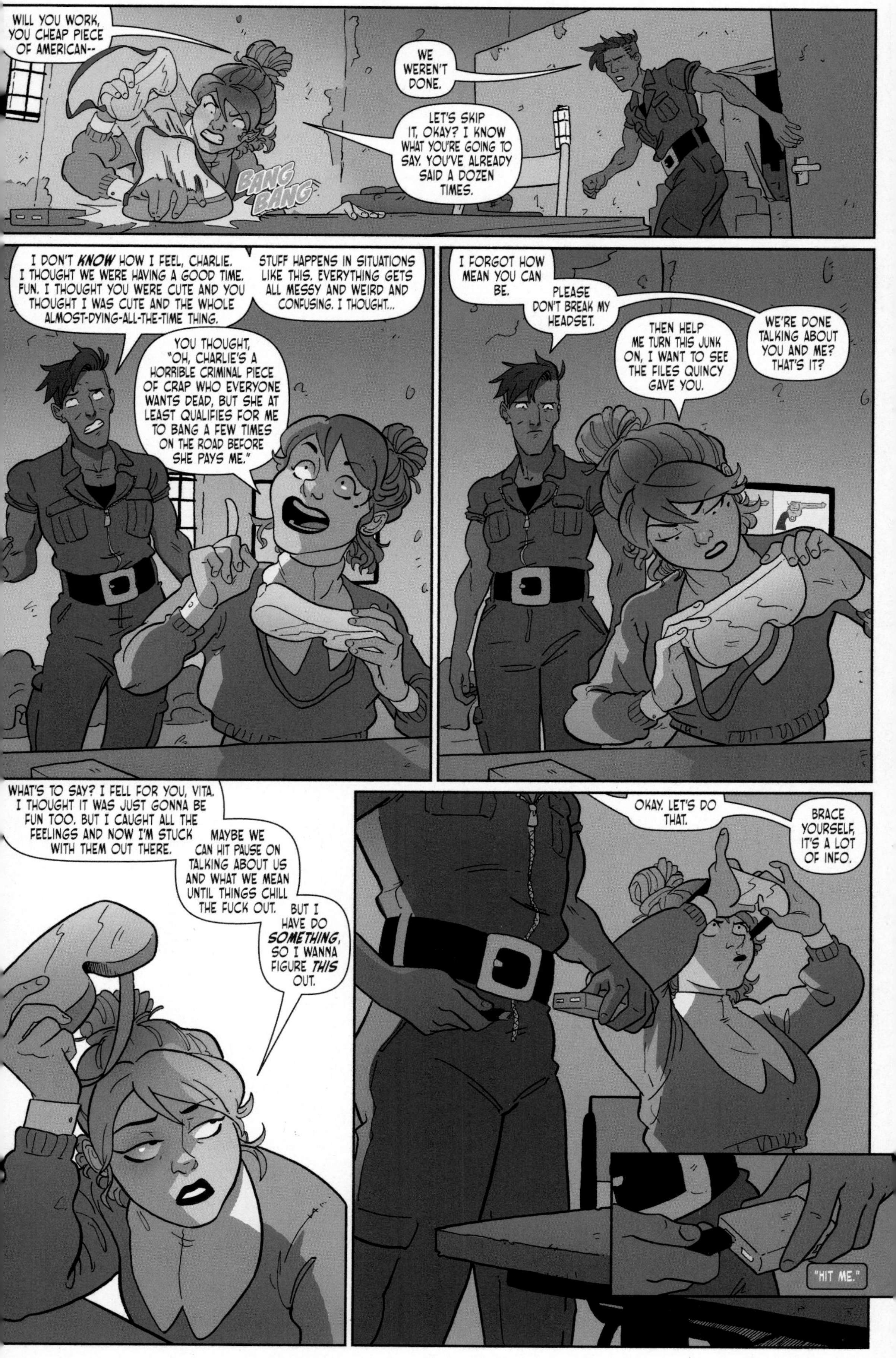

WILL YOU WORK, YOU CHEAP PIECE OF AMERICAN--
WE WEREN'T DONE.
LET'S SKIP IT, OKAY? I KNOW WHAT YOU'RE GOING TO SAY. YOU'VE ALREADY SAID A DOZEN TIMES.
BANG BANG
I DON'T KNOW HOW I FEEL, CHARLIE. I THOUGHT WE WERE HAVING A GOOD TIME. FUN. I THOUGHT YOU WERE CUTE AND YOU THOUGHT I WAS CUTE AND THE WHOLE ALMOST-DYING-ALL-THE-TIME THING.
STUFF HAPPENS IN SITUATIONS LIKE THIS. EVERYTHING GETS ALL MESSY AND WEIRD AND CONFUSING. I THOUGHT...
YOU THOUGHT, "OH, CHARLIE'S A HORRIBLE CRIMINAL PIECE OF CRAP WHO EVERYONE WANTS DEAD, BUT SHE AT LEAST QUALIFIES FOR ME TO BANG A FEW TIMES ON THE ROAD BEFORE SHE PAYS ME."
I FORGOT HOW MEAN YOU CAN BE.
PLEASE DON'T BREAK MY HEADSET.
THEN HELP ME TURN THIS JUNK ON, I WANT TO SEE THE FILES QUINCY GAVE YOU.
WE'RE DONE TALKING ABOUT YOU AND ME? THAT'S IT?
WHAT'S TO SAY? I FELL FOR YOU, VITA. I THOUGHT IT WAS JUST GONNA BE FUN TOO. BUT I CAUGHT ALL THE FEELINGS AND NOW I'M STUCK WITH THEM OUT THERE.
MAYBE WE CAN HIT PAUSE ON TALKING ABOUT US AND WHAT WE MEAN UNTIL THINGS CHILL THE FUCK OUT.
BUT I HAVE DO SOMETHING, SO I WANNA FIGURE THIS OUT.
OKAY. LET'S DO THAT.
BRACE YOURSELF, IT'S A LOT OF INFO.
"HIT ME."

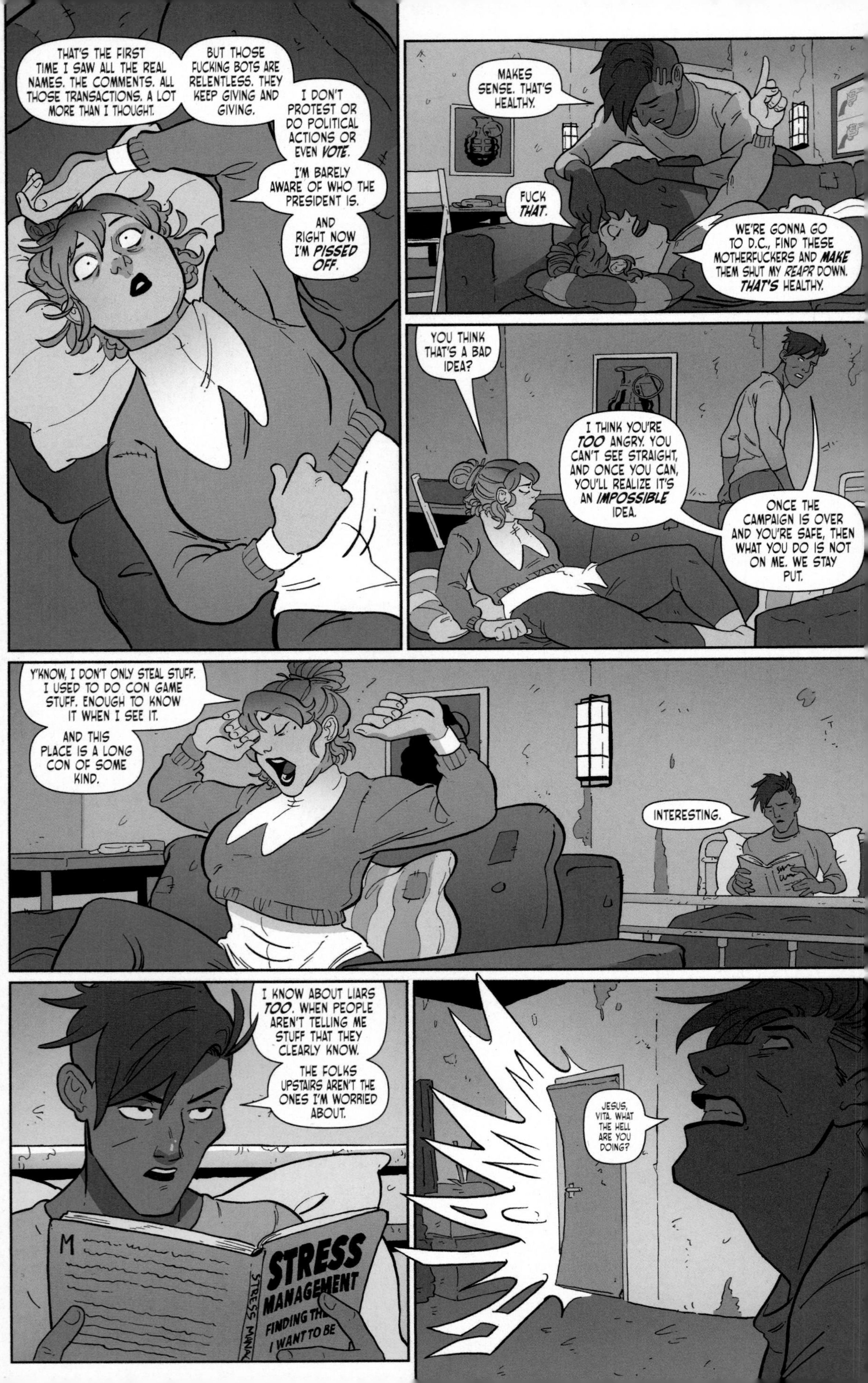

THAT'S THE FIRST TIME I SAW ALL THE REAL NAMES. THE COMMENTS. ALL THOSE TRANSACTIONS. A LOT MORE THAN I THOUGHT.
BUT THOSE FUCKING BOTS ARE RELENTLESS. THEY KEEP GIVING AND GIVING.
I DON'T PROTEST OR DO POLITICAL ACTIONS OR EVEN VOTE.
I'M BARELY AWARE OF WHO THE PRESIDENT IS.
AND RIGHT NOW I'M PISSED OFF.
MAKES SENSE. THAT'S HEALTHY.
FUCK THAT.
WE'RE GONNA GO TO D.C., FIND THESE MOTHERFUCKERS AND MAKE THEM SHUT MY REAPR DOWN. THAT'S HEALTHY.
YOU THINK THAT'S A BAD IDEA?
I THINK YOU'RE TOO ANGRY. YOU CAN'T SEE STRAIGHT, AND ONCE YOU CAN, YOU'LL REALIZE IT'S AN IMPOSSIBLE IDEA.
ONCE THE CAMPAIGN IS OVER AND YOU'RE SAFE, THEN WHAT YOU DO IS NOT ON ME. WE STAY PUT.
Y'KNOW, I DON'T ONLY STEAL STUFF. I USED TO DO CON GAME STUFF. ENOUGH TO KNOW IT WHEN I SEE IT.
AND THIS PLACE IS A LONG CON OF SOME KIND.
INTERESTING.
I KNOW ABOUT LIARS TOO. WHEN PEOPLE AREN'T TELLING ME STUFF THAT THEY CLEARLY KNOW.
THE FOLKS UPSTAIRS AREN'T THE ONES I'M WORRIED ABOUT.
STRESS MANAGEMENT
FINDING THE
I WANT TO BE
JESUS, VITA. WHAT THE HELL ARE YOU DOING?

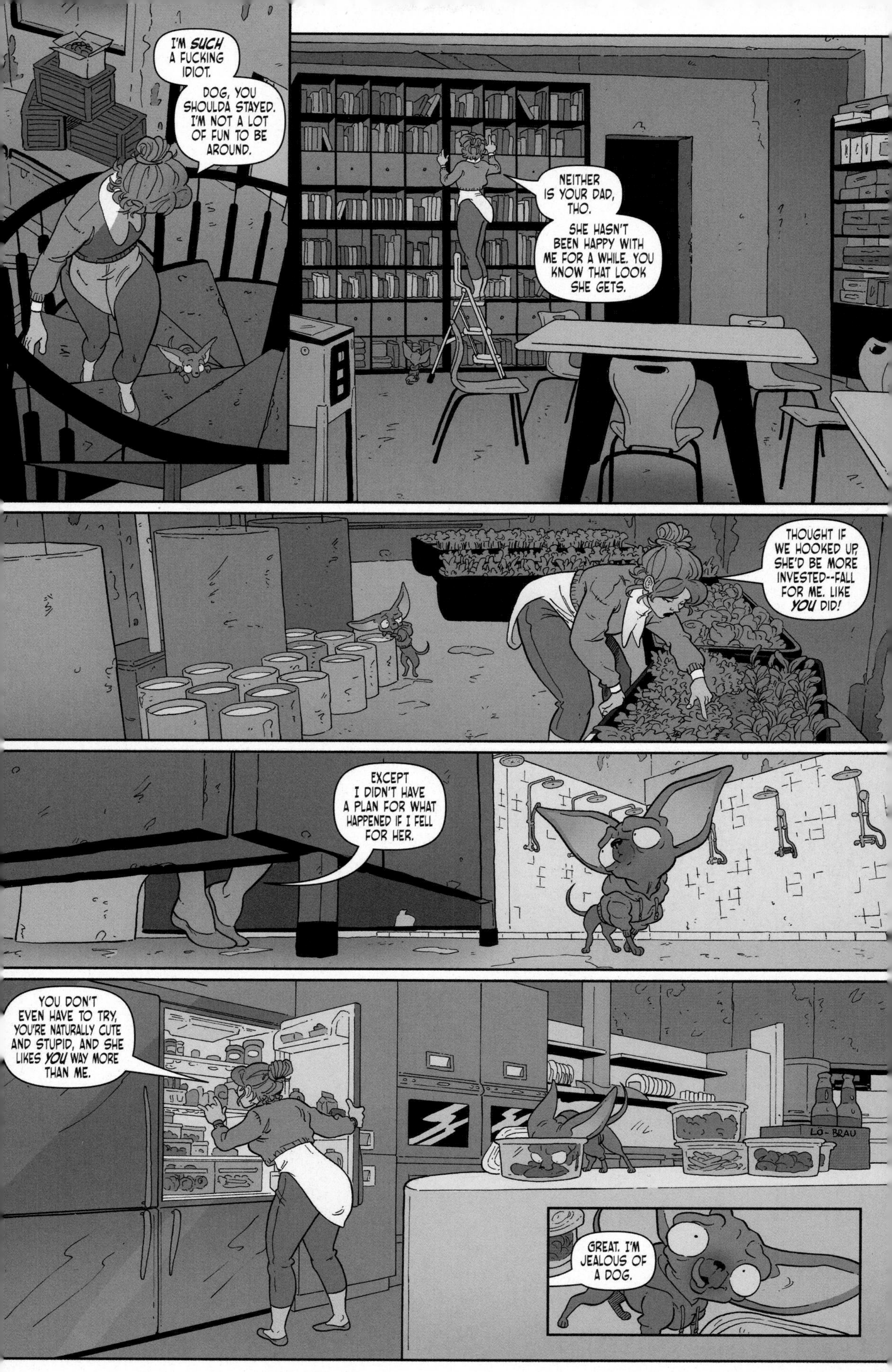
I'M SUCH A FUCKING IDIOT.
DOG, YOU SHOULDA STAYED. I'M NOT A LOT OF FUN TO BE AROUND.
NEITHER IS YOUR DAD, THO.
SHE HASN'T BEEN HAPPY WITH ME FOR A WHILE. YOU KNOW THAT LOOK SHE GETS.
THOUGHT IF WE HOOKED UP, SHE'D BE MORE INVESTED--FALL FOR ME. LIKE YOU DID!
EXCEPT I DIDN'T HAVE A PLAN FOR WHAT HAPPENED IF I FELL FOR HER.
YOU DON'T EVEN HAVE TO TRY, YOU'RE NATURALLY CUTE AND STUPID, AND SHE LIKES YOU WAY MORE THAN ME.
LÖ-BRAU
GREAT. I'M JEALOUS OF A DOG.

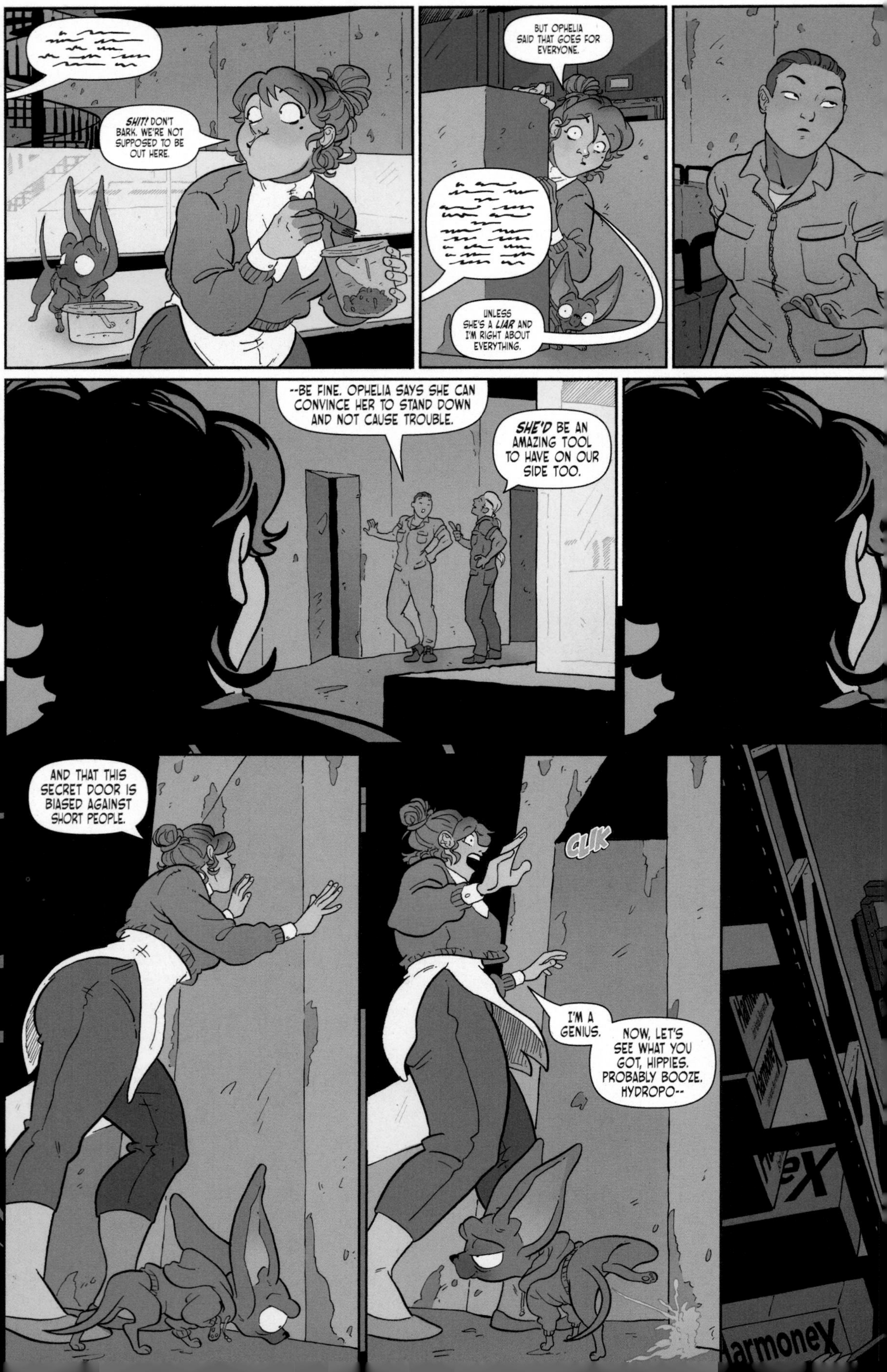

SHIT! DON'T BARK. WE'RE NOT SUPPOSED TO BE OUT HERE.
BUT OPHELIA SAID THAT GOES FOR EVERYONE.
UNLESS SHE'S A LIAR AND I'M RIGHT ABOUT EVERYTHING.
--BE FINE. OPHELIA SAYS SHE CAN CONVINCE HER TO STAND DOWN AND NOT CAUSE TROUBLE.
SHE'D BE AN AMAZING TOOL TO HAVE ON OUR SIDE TOO.
AND THAT THIS SECRET DOOR IS BIASED AGAINST SHORT PEOPLE.
CLIK
I'M A GENIUS.
NOW, LET'S SEE WHAT YOU GOT, HIPPIES. PROBABLY BOOZE. HYDROPO--
Harmonex

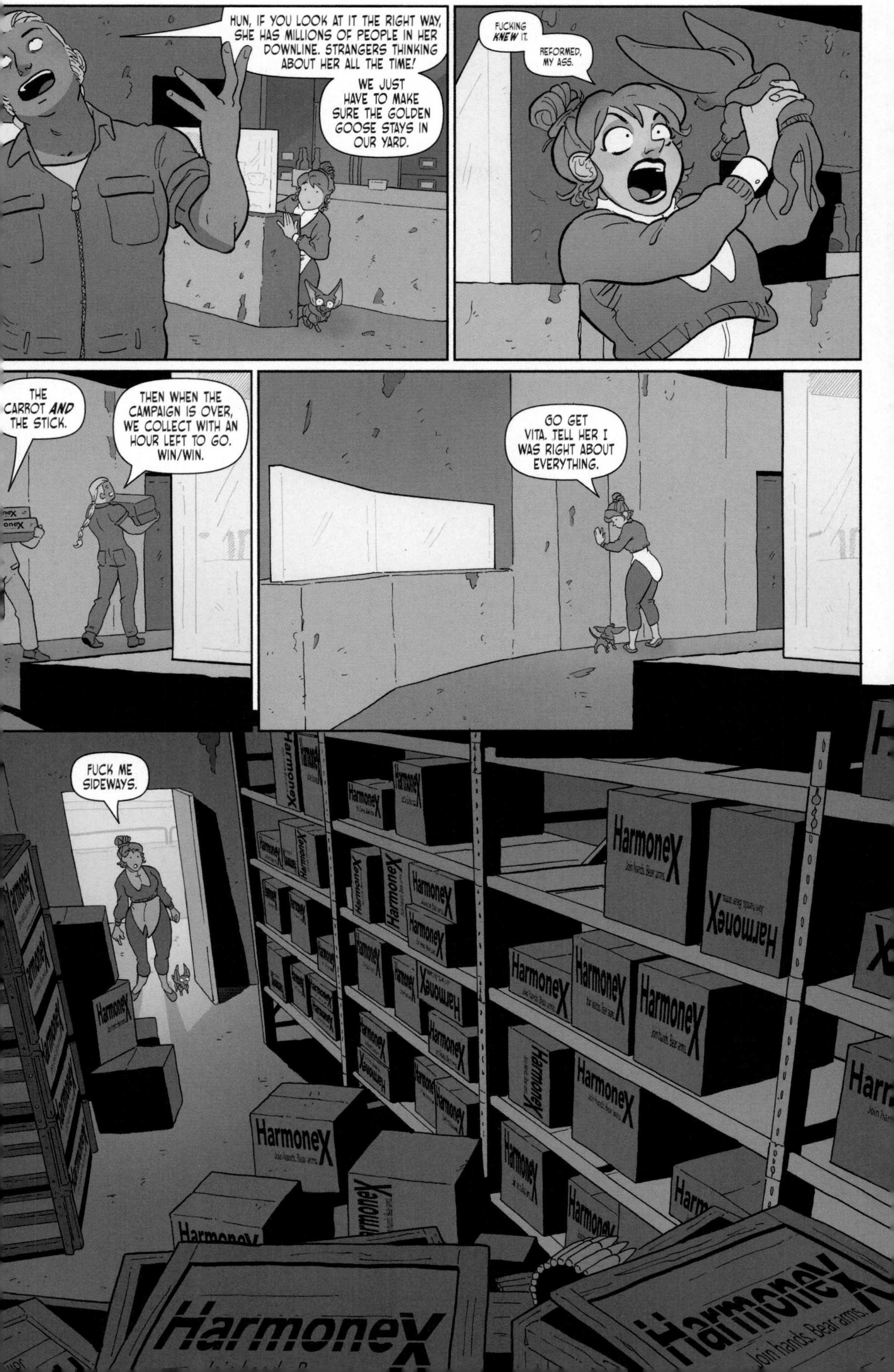
HUN, IF YOU LOOK AT IT THE RIGHT WAY, SHE HAS MILLIONS OF PEOPLE IN HER DOWNLINE. STRANGERS THINKING ABOUT HER ALL THE TIME!
WE JUST HAVE TO MAKE SURE THE GOLDEN GOOSE STAYS IN OUR YARD.
FUCKING KNEW IT.
REFORMED, MY ASS.
THE CARROT AND THE STICK.
THEN WHEN THE CAMPAIGN IS OVER, WE COLLECT WITH AN HOUR LEFT TO GO. WIN/WIN.
GO GET VITA. TELL HER I WAS RIGHT ABOUT EVERYTHING.
FUCK ME SIDEWAYS.
HarmoneX
Join hands. Bear arms.

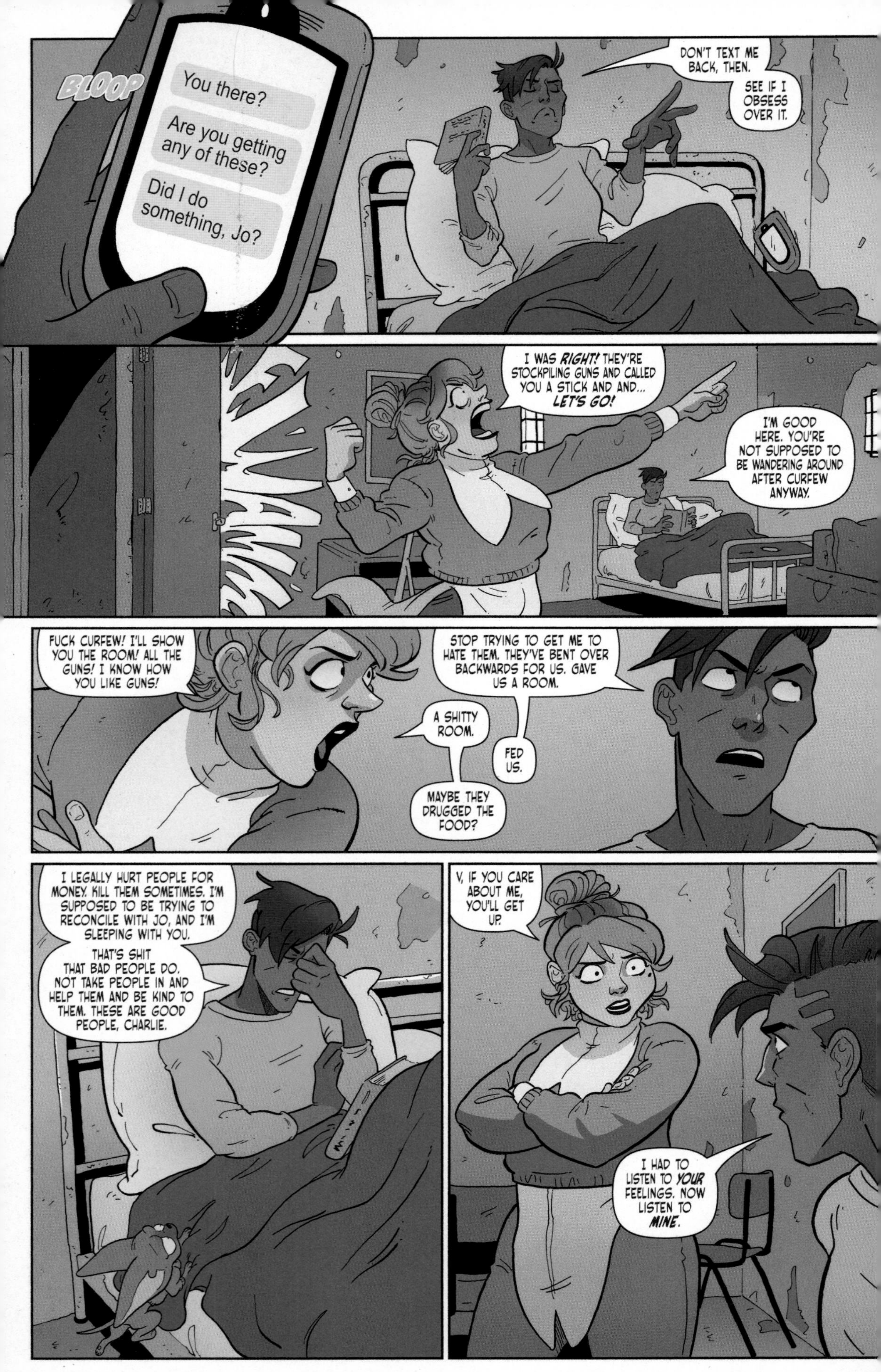
BLOOP
You there?
Are you getting any of these?
Did I do something, Jo?
DON'T TEXT ME BACK, THEN.
SEE IF I OBSESS OVER IT.
I WAS RIGHT! THEY'RE STOCKPILING GUNS AND CALLED YOU A STICK AND AND... LET'S GO!
I'M GOOD HERE. YOU'RE NOT SUPPOSED TO BE WANDERING AROUND AFTER CURFEW ANYWAY.
FUCK CURFEW! I'LL SHOW YOU THE ROOM! ALL THE GUNS! I KNOW HOW YOU LIKE GUNS!
STOP TRYING TO GET ME TO HATE THEM. THEY'VE BENT OVER BACKWARDS FOR US. GAVE US A ROOM.
A SHITTY ROOM.
FED US.
MAYBE THEY DRUGGED THE FOOD?
I LEGALLY HURT PEOPLE FOR MONEY. KILL THEM SOMETIMES. I'M SUPPOSED TO BE TRYING TO RECONCILE WITH JO, AND I'M SLEEPING WITH YOU.
THAT'S SHIT THAT BAD PEOPLE DO. NOT TAKE PEOPLE IN AND HELP THEM AND BE KIND TO THEM. THESE ARE GOOD PEOPLE, CHARLIE.
V, IF YOU CARE ABOUT ME, YOU'LL GET UP.
I HAD TO LISTEN TO YOUR FEELINGS. NOW LISTEN TO MINE.

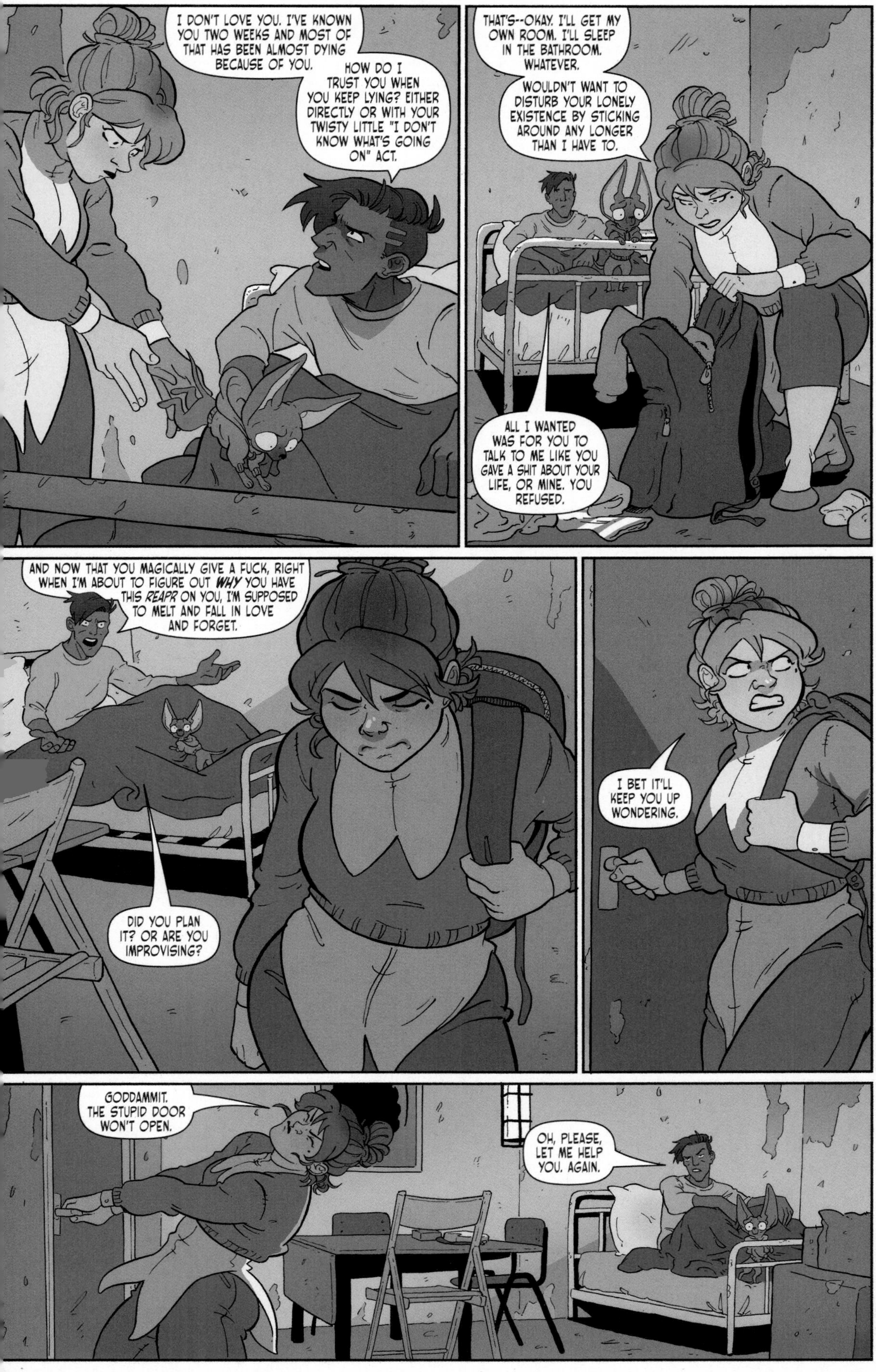
I DON'T LOVE YOU. I'VE KNOWN YOU TWO WEEKS AND MOST OF THAT HAS BEEN ALMOST DYING BECAUSE OF YOU.
HOW DO I TRUST YOU WHEN YOU KEEP LYING? EITHER DIRECTLY OR WITH YOUR TWISTY LITTLE "I DON'T KNOW WHAT'S GOING ON" ACT.
THAT'S--OKAY. I'LL GET MY OWN ROOM. I'LL SLEEP IN THE BATHROOM. WHATEVER.
WOULDN'T WANT TO DISTURB YOUR LONELY EXISTENCE BY STICKING AROUND ANY LONGER THAN I HAVE TO.
ALL I WANTED WAS FOR YOU TO TALK TO ME LIKE YOU GAVE A SHIT ABOUT YOUR LIFE, OR MINE. YOU REFUSED.
AND NOW THAT YOU MAGICALLY GIVE A FUCK, RIGHT WHEN I'M ABOUT TO FIGURE OUT *WHY* YOU HAVE THIS *REAPR* ON YOU, I'M SUPPOSED TO MELT AND FALL IN LOVE AND FORGET.
DID YOU PLAN IT? OR ARE YOU IMPROVISING?
I BET IT'LL KEEP YOU UP WONDERING.
GODDAMMIT. THE STUPID DOOR WON'T OPEN.
OH, PLEASE, LET ME HELP YOU. AGAIN.

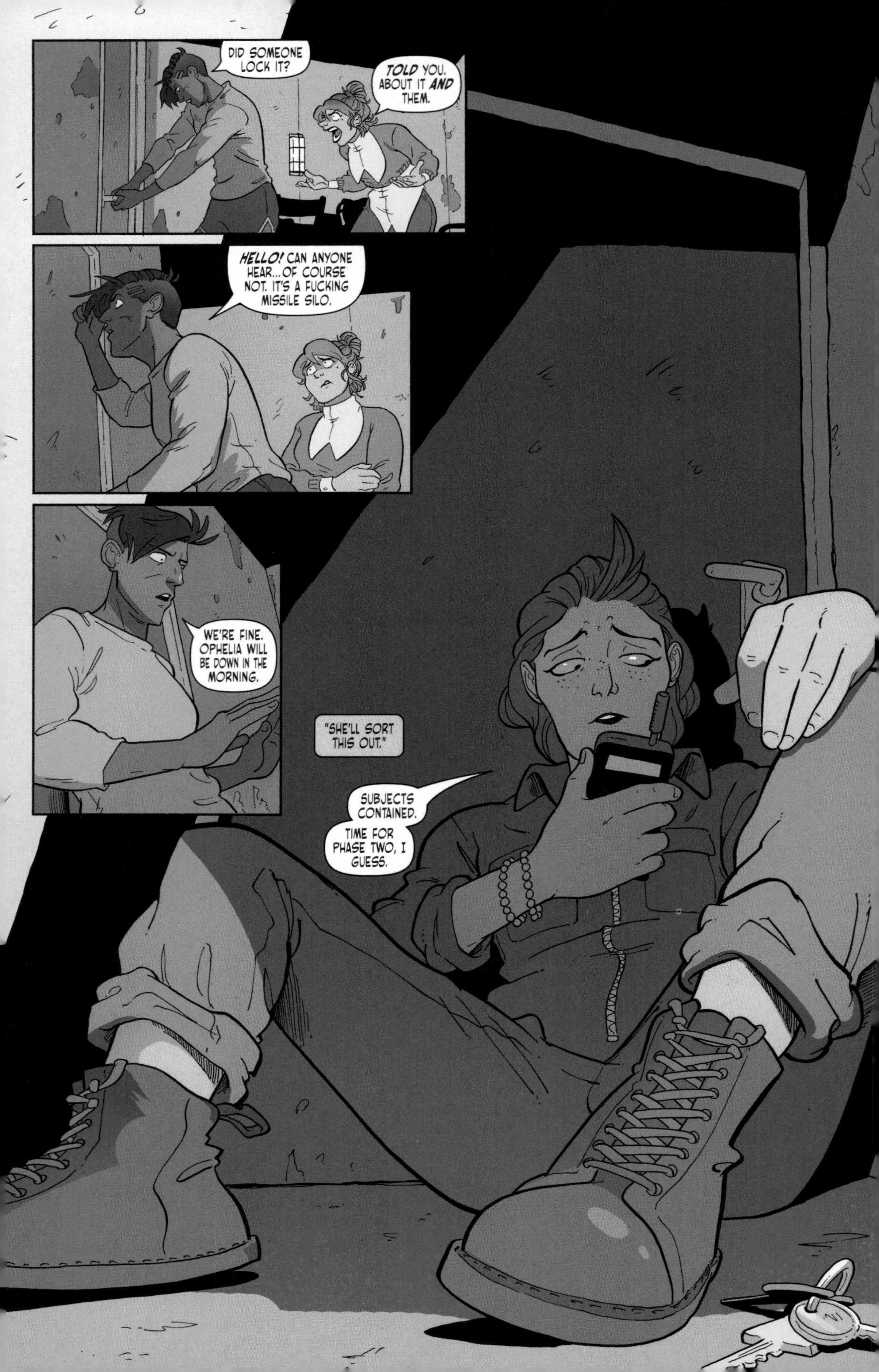
DID SOMEONE LOCK IT?
TOLD YOU. ABOUT IT AND THEM.
HELLO! CAN ANYONE HEAR...OF COURSE NOT. IT'S A FUCKING MISSILE SILO.
WE'RE FINE. OPHELIA WILL BE DOWN IN THE MORNING.
"SHE'LL SORT THIS OUT."
SUBJECTS CONTAINED.
TIME FOR PHASE TWO, I GUESS.

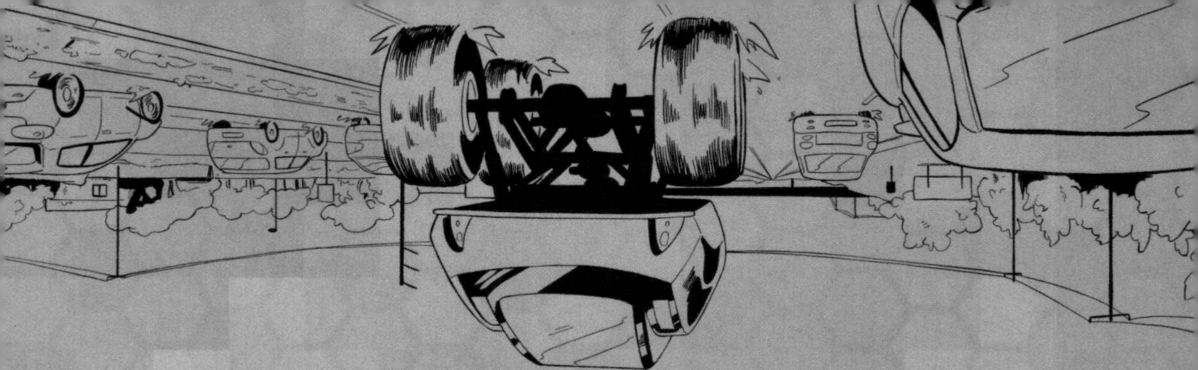

CHAPTER TWELVE

GLAD GIRLS

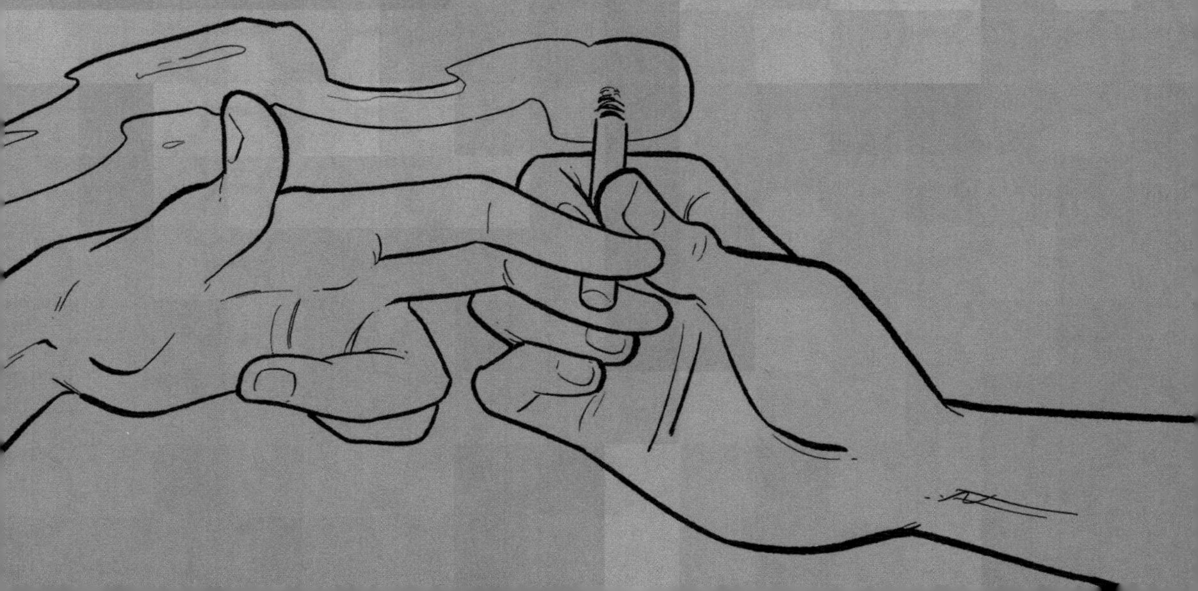

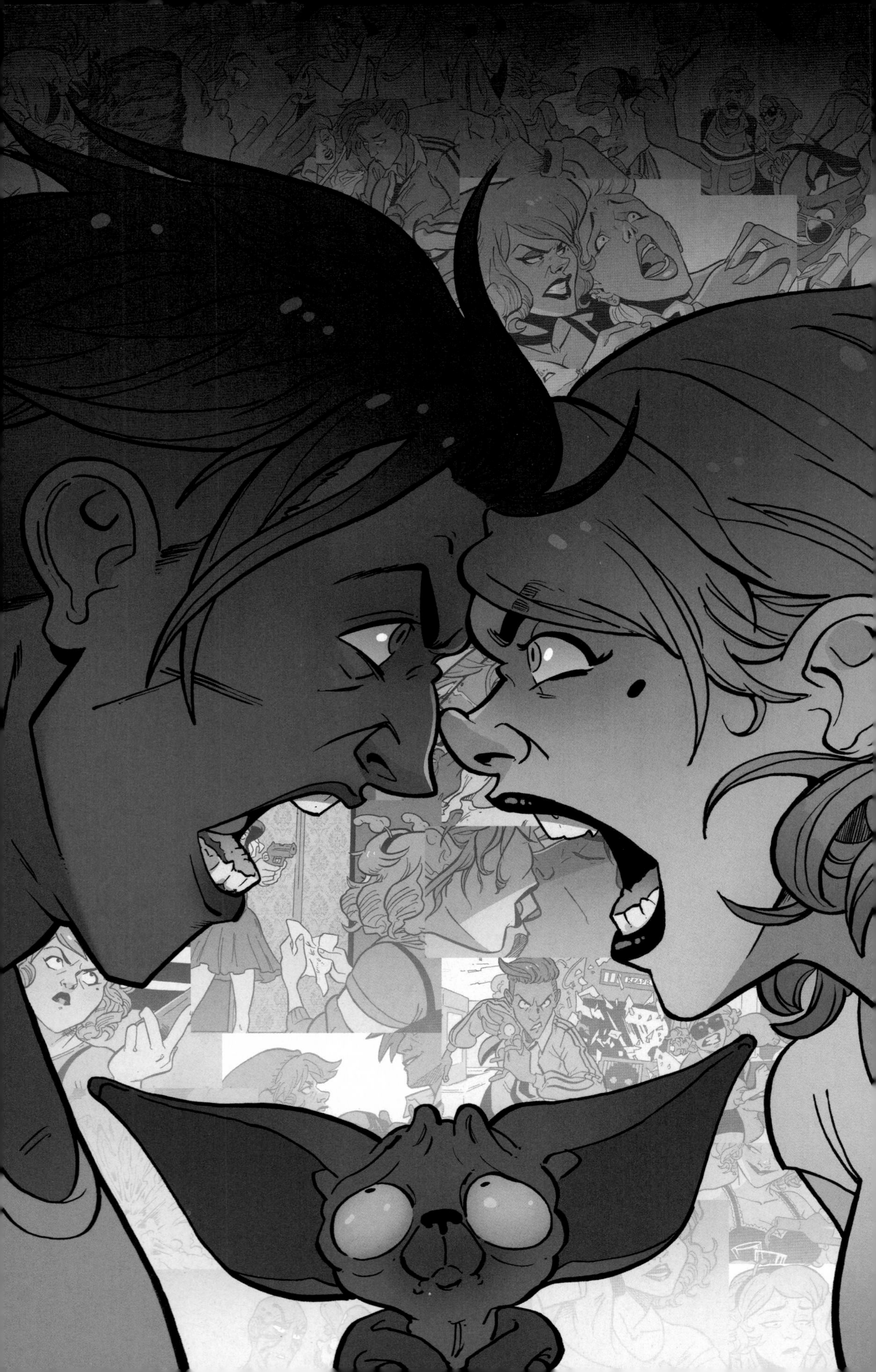

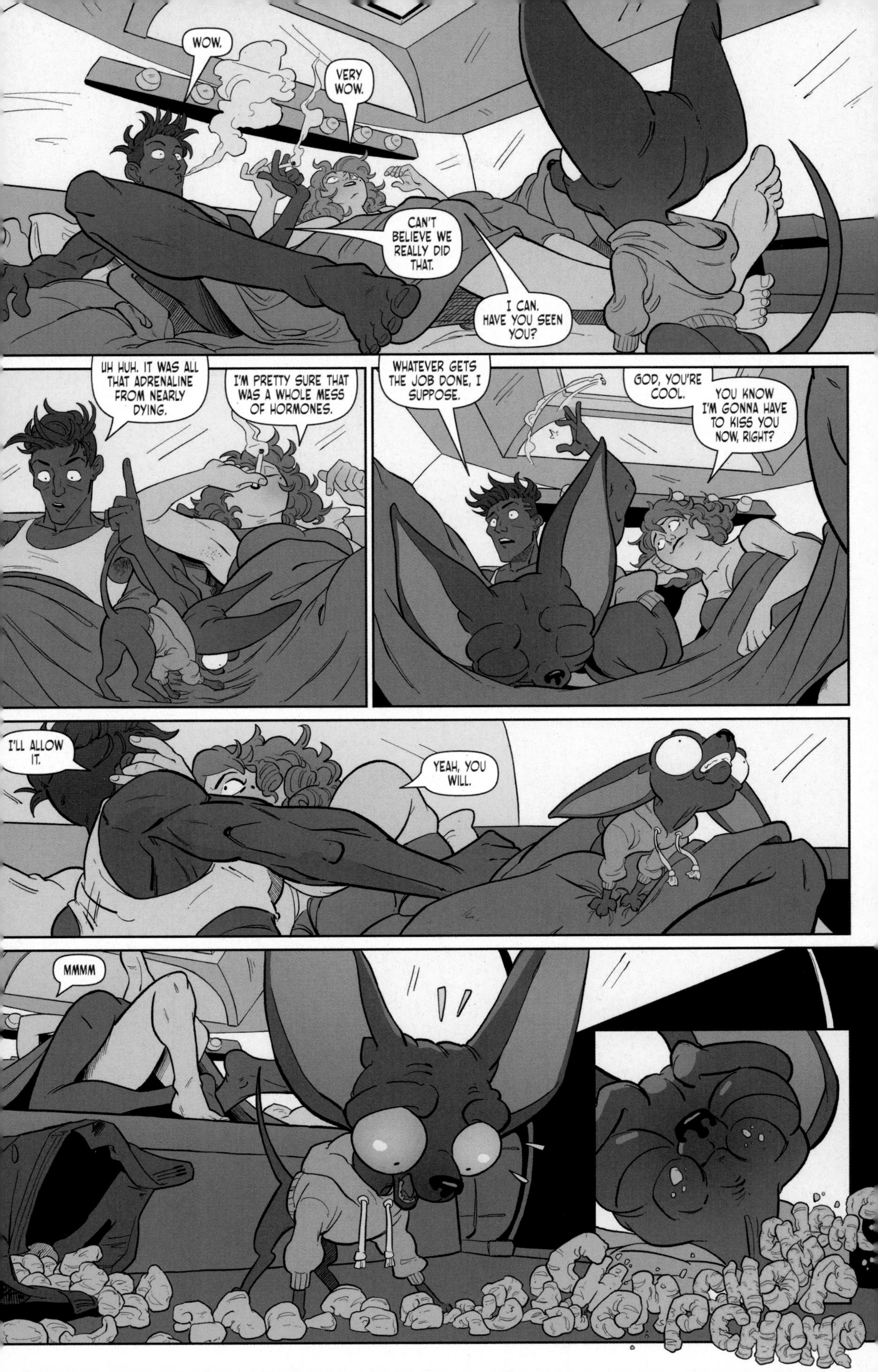
WOW.
VERY WOW.
CAN'T BELIEVE WE REALLY DID THAT.
I CAN. HAVE YOU SEEN YOU?
UH HUH. IT WAS ALL THAT ADRENALINE FROM NEARLY DYING.
I'M PRETTY SURE THAT WAS A WHOLE MESS OF HORMONES.
WHATEVER GETS THE JOB DONE, I SUPPOSE.
GOD, YOU'RE COOL.
YOU KNOW I'M GONNA HAVE TO KISS YOU NOW, RIGHT?
I'LL ALLOW IT.
YEAH, YOU WILL.
MMMM
CHOMP CHOMP

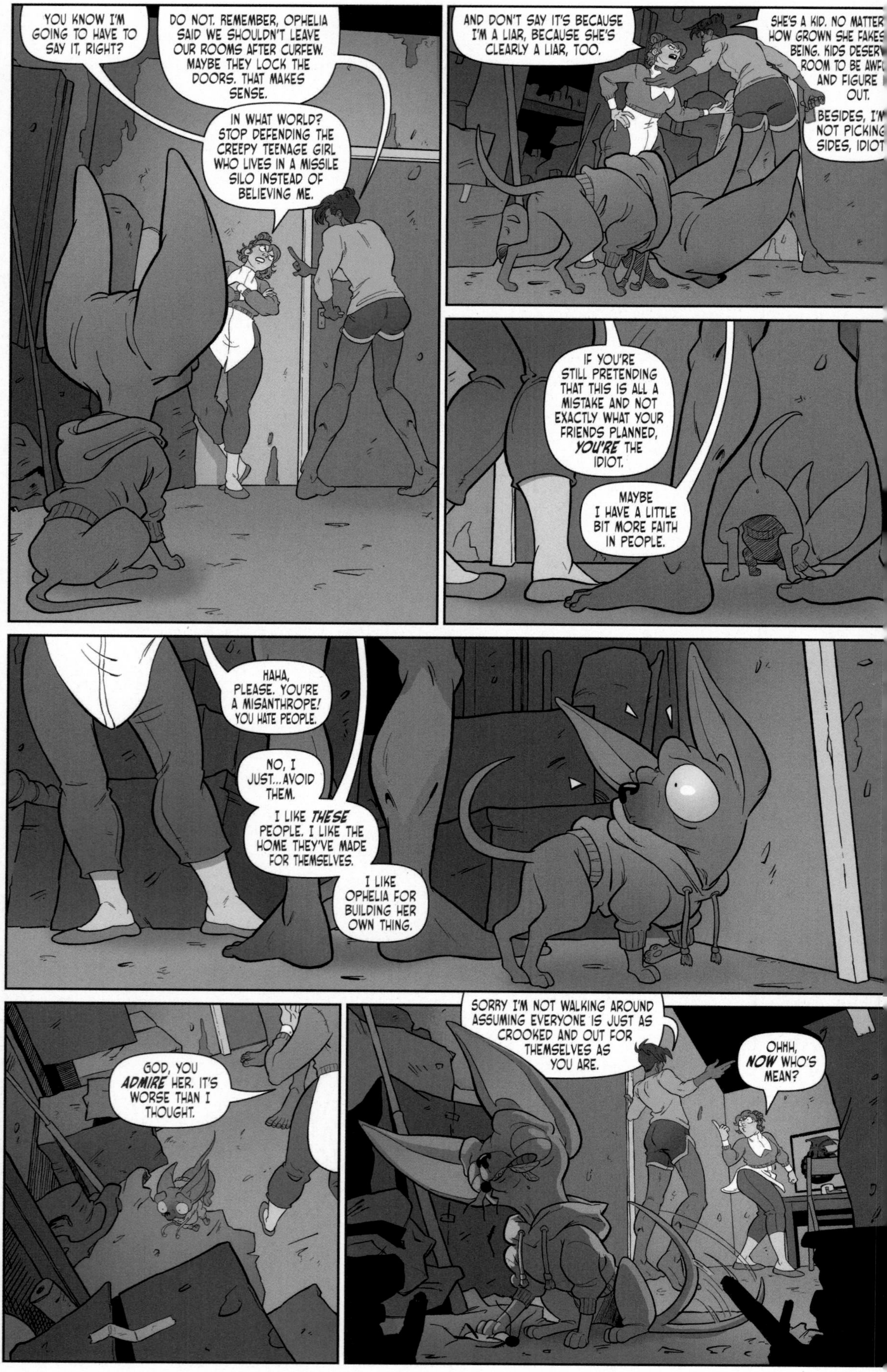
YOU KNOW I'M GOING TO HAVE TO SAY IT, RIGHT?
DO NOT. REMEMBER, OPHELIA SAID WE SHOULDN'T LEAVE OUR ROOMS AFTER CURFEW. MAYBE THEY LOCK THE DOORS. THAT MAKES SENSE.
IN WHAT WORLD? STOP DEFENDING THE CREEPY TEENAGE GIRL WHO LIVES IN A MISSILE SILO INSTEAD OF BELIEVING ME.
AND DON'T SAY IT'S BECAUSE I'M A LIAR, BECAUSE SHE'S CLEARLY A LIAR, TOO.
SHE'S A KID. NO MATTER HOW GROWN SHE FAKES BEING. KIDS DESERV ROOM TO BE AWF AND FIGURE OUT.
BESIDES, I'M NOT PICKING SIDES, IDIOT
IF YOU'RE STILL PRETENDING THAT THIS IS ALL A MISTAKE AND NOT EXACTLY WHAT YOUR FRIENDS PLANNED, *YOU'RE* THE IDIOT.
MAYBE I HAVE A LITTLE BIT MORE FAITH IN PEOPLE.
HAHA, PLEASE. YOU'RE A MISANTHROPE! YOU HATE PEOPLE.
NO, I JUST...AVOID THEM.
I LIKE *THESE* PEOPLE. I LIKE THE HOME THEY'VE MADE FOR THEMSELVES.
I LIKE OPHELIA FOR BUILDING HER OWN THING.
GOD, YOU *ADMIRE* HER. IT'S WORSE THAN I THOUGHT.
SORRY I'M NOT WALKING AROUND ASSUMING EVERYONE IS JUST AS CROOKED AND OUT FOR THEMSELVES AS YOU ARE.
OHHH, *NOW* WHO'S MEAN?

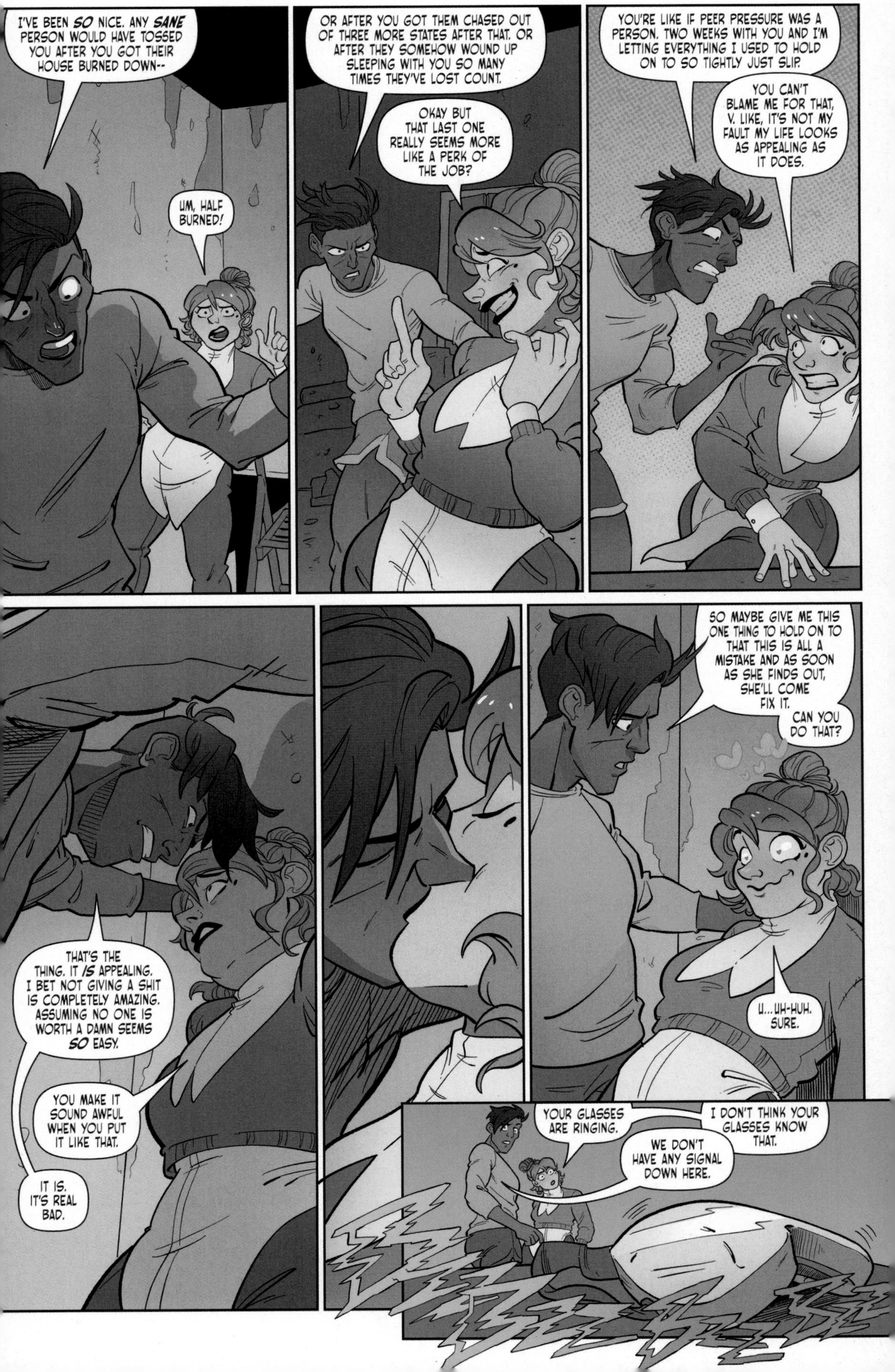

I'VE BEEN SO NICE. ANY SANE PERSON WOULD HAVE TOSSED YOU AFTER YOU GOT THEIR HOUSE BURNED DOWN--
UM, HALF BURNED!
OR AFTER YOU GOT THEM CHASED OUT OF THREE MORE STATES AFTER THAT. OR AFTER THEY SOMEHOW WOUND UP SLEEPING WITH YOU SO MANY TIMES THEY'VE LOST COUNT.
OKAY BUT THAT LAST ONE REALLY SEEMS MORE LIKE A PERK OF THE JOB?
YOU'RE LIKE IF PEER PRESSURE WAS A PERSON. TWO WEEKS WITH YOU AND I'M LETTING EVERYTHING I USED TO HOLD ON TO SO TIGHTLY JUST SLIP.
YOU CAN'T BLAME ME FOR THAT, V. LIKE, IT'S NOT MY FAULT MY LIFE LOOKS AS APPEALING AS IT DOES.
THAT'S THE THING. IT IS APPEALING. I BET NOT GIVING A SHIT IS COMPLETELY AMAZING. ASSUMING NO ONE IS WORTH A DAMN SEEMS SO EASY.
YOU MAKE IT SOUND AWFUL WHEN YOU PUT IT LIKE THAT.
IT IS. IT'S REAL BAD.
SO MAYBE GIVE ME THIS ONE THING TO HOLD ON TO THAT THIS IS ALL A MISTAKE AND AS SOON AS SHE FINDS OUT, SHE'LL COME FIX IT.
CAN YOU DO THAT?
U...UH-HUH. SURE.
YOUR GLASSES ARE RINGING.
WE DON'T HAVE ANY SIGNAL DOWN HERE.
I DON'T THINK YOUR GLASSES KNOW THAT.

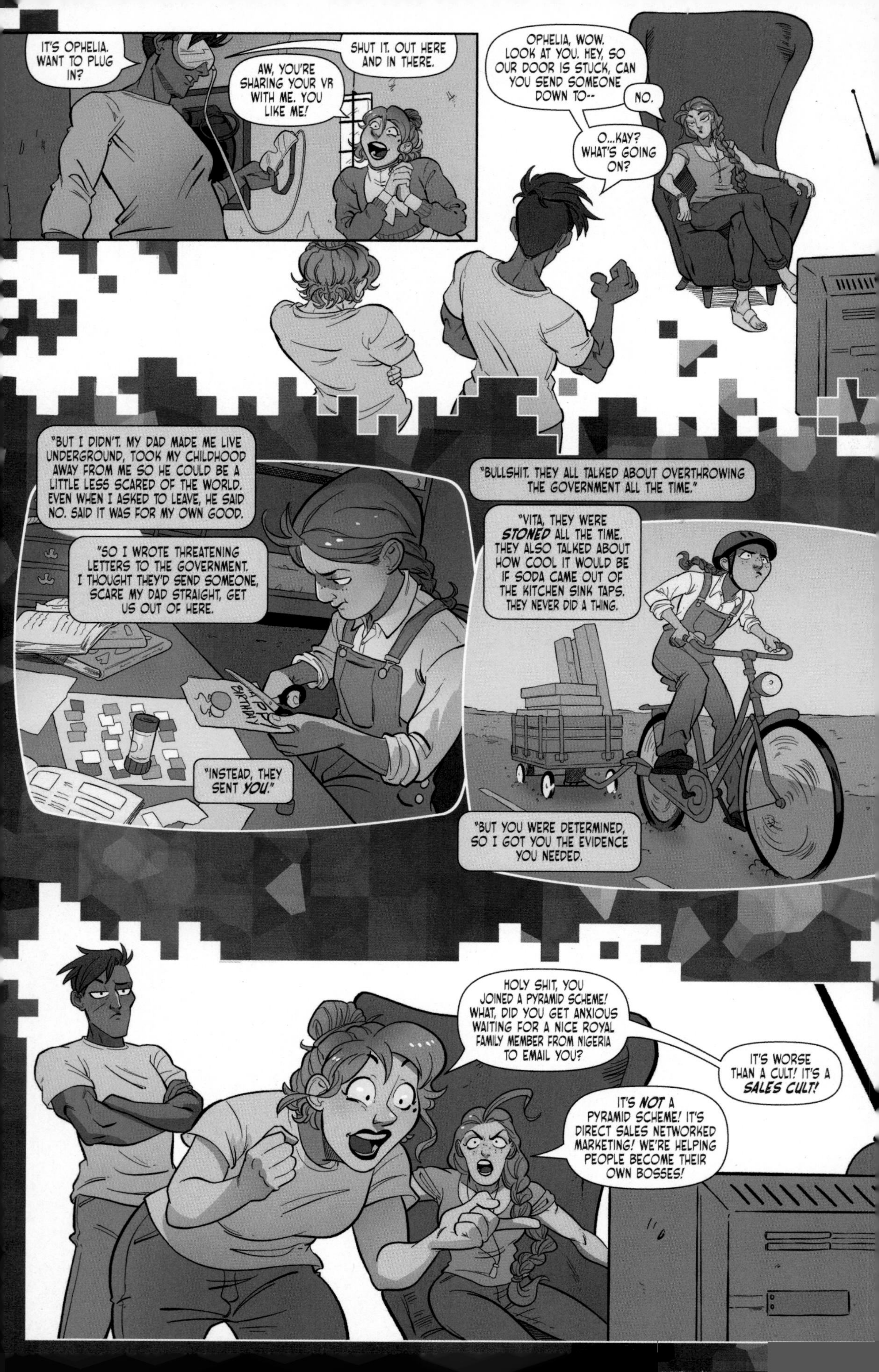

IT'S OPHELIA. WANT TO PLUG IN?
SHUT IT. OUT HERE AND IN THERE.
AW, YOU'RE SHARING YOUR VR WITH ME. YOU LIKE ME!
OPHELIA, WOW. LOOK AT YOU. HEY, SO OUR DOOR IS STUCK, CAN YOU SEND SOMEONE DOWN TO--
NO.
O...KAY? WHAT'S GOING ON?
"BUT I DIDN'T. MY DAD MADE ME LIVE UNDERGROUND, TOOK MY CHILDHOOD AWAY FROM ME SO HE COULD BE A LITTLE LESS SCARED OF THE WORLD. EVEN WHEN I ASKED TO LEAVE, HE SAID NO. SAID IT WAS FOR MY OWN GOOD.
"SO I WROTE THREATENING LETTERS TO THE GOVERNMENT. I THOUGHT THEY'D SEND SOMEONE, SCARE MY DAD STRAIGHT, GET US OUT OF HERE.
"INSTEAD, THEY SENT YOU."
"BULLSHIT. THEY ALL TALKED ABOUT OVERTHROWING THE GOVERNMENT ALL THE TIME."
"VITA, THEY WERE STONED ALL THE TIME. THEY ALSO TALKED ABOUT HOW COOL IT WOULD BE IF SODA CAME OUT OF THE KITCHEN SINK TAPS. THEY NEVER DID A THING.
"BUT YOU WERE DETERMINED, SO I GOT YOU THE EVIDENCE YOU NEEDED.
HOLY SHIT, YOU JOINED A PYRAMID SCHEME! WHAT, DID YOU GET ANXIOUS WAITING FOR A NICE ROYAL FAMILY MEMBER FROM NIGERIA TO EMAIL YOU?
IT'S WORSE THAN A CULT! IT'S A SALES CULT!
IT'S NOT A PYRAMID SCHEME! IT'S DIRECT SALES NETWORKED MARKETING! WE'RE HELPING PEOPLE BECOME THEIR OWN BOSSES!

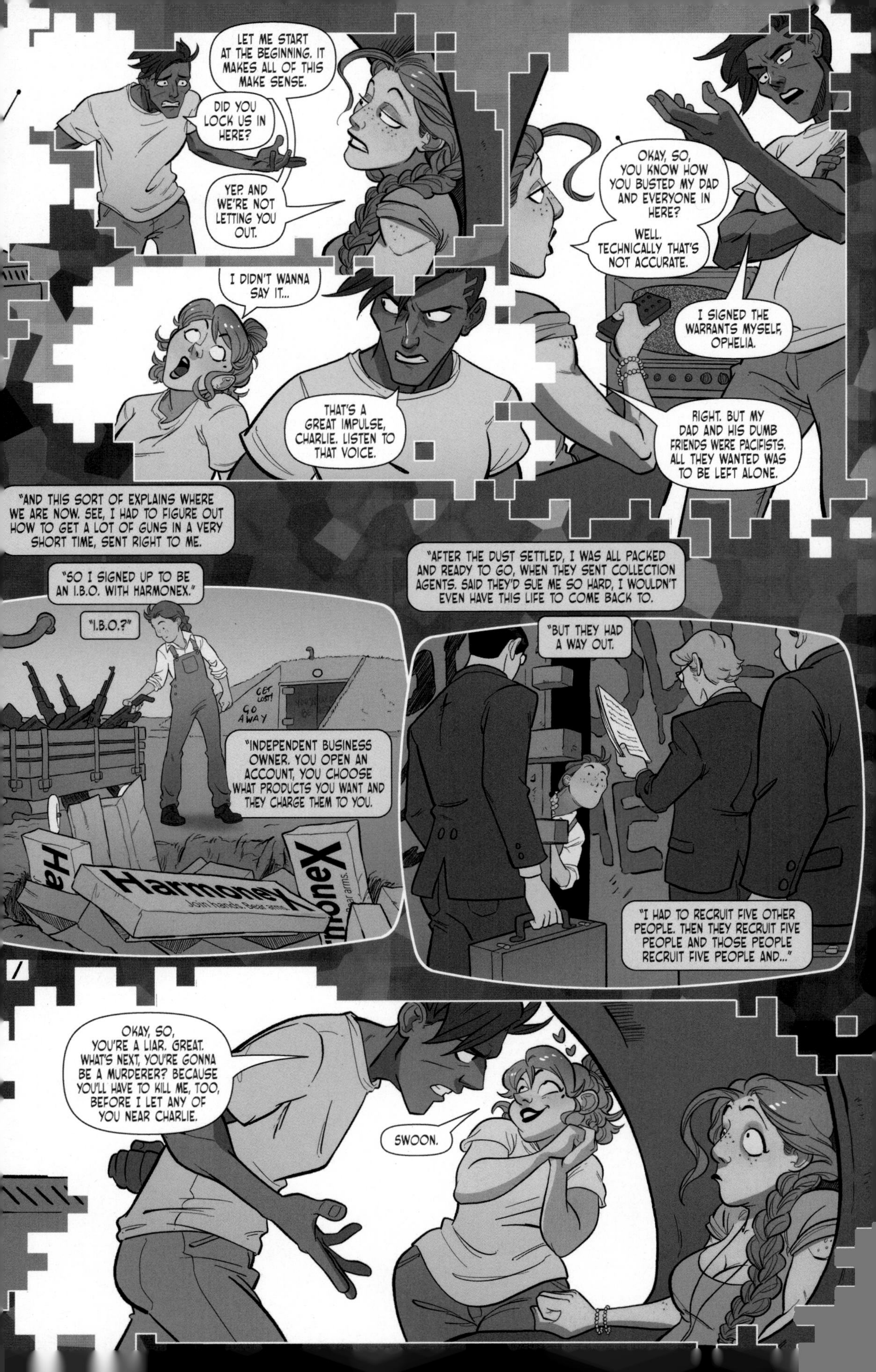

LET ME START AT THE BEGINNING. IT MAKES ALL OF THIS MAKE SENSE.
DID YOU LOCK US IN HERE?
YEP. AND WE'RE NOT LETTING YOU OUT.
OKAY, SO, YOU KNOW HOW YOU BUSTED MY DAD AND EVERYONE IN HERE?
WELL. TECHNICALLY THAT'S NOT ACCURATE.
I DIDN'T WANNA SAY IT...
THAT'S A GREAT IMPULSE, CHARLIE. LISTEN TO THAT VOICE.
I SIGNED THE WARRANTS MYSELF, OPHELIA.
RIGHT. BUT MY DAD AND HIS DUMB FRIENDS WERE PACIFISTS. ALL THEY WANTED WAS TO BE LEFT ALONE.
"AND THIS SORT OF EXPLAINS WHERE WE ARE NOW. SEE, I HAD TO FIGURE OUT HOW TO GET A LOT OF GUNS IN A VERY SHORT TIME, SENT RIGHT TO ME.
"SO I SIGNED UP TO BE AN I.B.O. WITH HARMONEX."
"I.B.O.?"
GET LOST!
GO AWAY
"INDEPENDENT BUSINESS OWNER. YOU OPEN AN ACCOUNT, YOU CHOOSE WHAT PRODUCTS YOU WANT AND THEY CHARGE THEM TO YOU.
HarmoneX
Join hands. Bear arms.
"AFTER THE DUST SETTLED, I WAS ALL PACKED AND READY TO GO, WHEN THEY SENT COLLECTION AGENTS. SAID THEY'D SUE ME SO HARD, I WOULDN'T EVEN HAVE THIS LIFE TO COME BACK TO.
"BUT THEY HAD A WAY OUT.
"I HAD TO RECRUIT FIVE OTHER PEOPLE. THEN THEY RECRUIT FIVE PEOPLE AND THOSE PEOPLE RECRUIT FIVE PEOPLE AND..."
OKAY, SO, YOU'RE A LIAR. GREAT. WHAT'S NEXT, YOU'RE GONNA BE A MURDERER? BECAUSE YOU'LL HAVE TO KILL ME, TOO, BEFORE I LET ANY OF YOU NEAR CHARLIE.
SWOON.

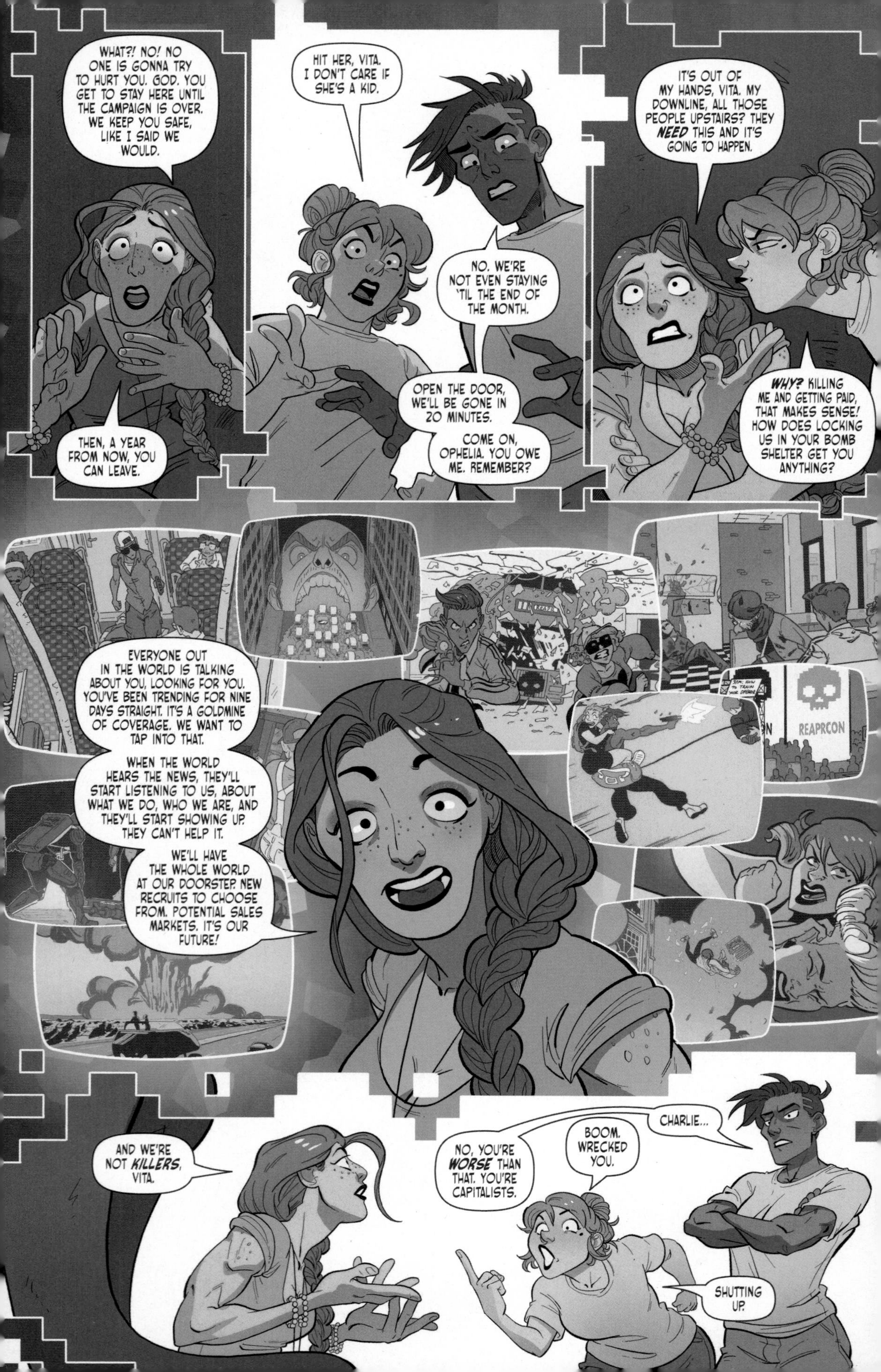
WHAT?! NO! NO ONE IS GONNA TRY TO HURT YOU. GOD. YOU GET TO STAY HERE UNTIL THE CAMPAIGN IS OVER. WE KEEP YOU SAFE, LIKE I SAID WE WOULD.
THEN, A YEAR FROM NOW, YOU CAN LEAVE.
HIT HER, VITA. I DON'T CARE IF SHE'S A KID.
NO. WE'RE NOT EVEN STAYING 'TIL THE END OF THE MONTH.
OPEN THE DOOR, WE'LL BE GONE IN 20 MINUTES.
COME ON, OPHELIA. YOU OWE ME. REMEMBER?
IT'S OUT OF MY HANDS, VITA. MY DOWNLINE, ALL THOSE PEOPLE UPSTAIRS? THEY NEED THIS AND IT'S GOING TO HAPPEN.
WHY? KILLING ME AND GETTING PAID, THAT MAKES SENSE! HOW DOES LOCKING US IN YOUR BOMB SHELTER GET YOU ANYTHING?
EVERYONE OUT IN THE WORLD IS TALKING ABOUT YOU, LOOKING FOR YOU. YOU'VE BEEN TRENDING FOR NINE DAYS STRAIGHT. IT'S A GOLDMINE OF COVERAGE. WE WANT TO TAP INTO THAT.
WHEN THE WORLD HEARS THE NEWS, THEY'LL START LISTENING TO US, ABOUT WHAT WE DO, WHO WE ARE, AND THEY'LL START SHOWING UP. THEY CAN'T HELP IT.
WE'LL HAVE THE WHOLE WORLD AT OUR DOORSTEP. NEW RECRUITS TO CHOOSE FROM. POTENTIAL SALES MARKETS. IT'S OUR FUTURE!
REAPRCON
AND WE'RE NOT KILLERS, VITA.
NO, YOU'RE WORSE THAN THAT. YOU'RE CAPITALISTS.
BOOM. WRECKED YOU.
CHARLIE...
SHUTTING UP.

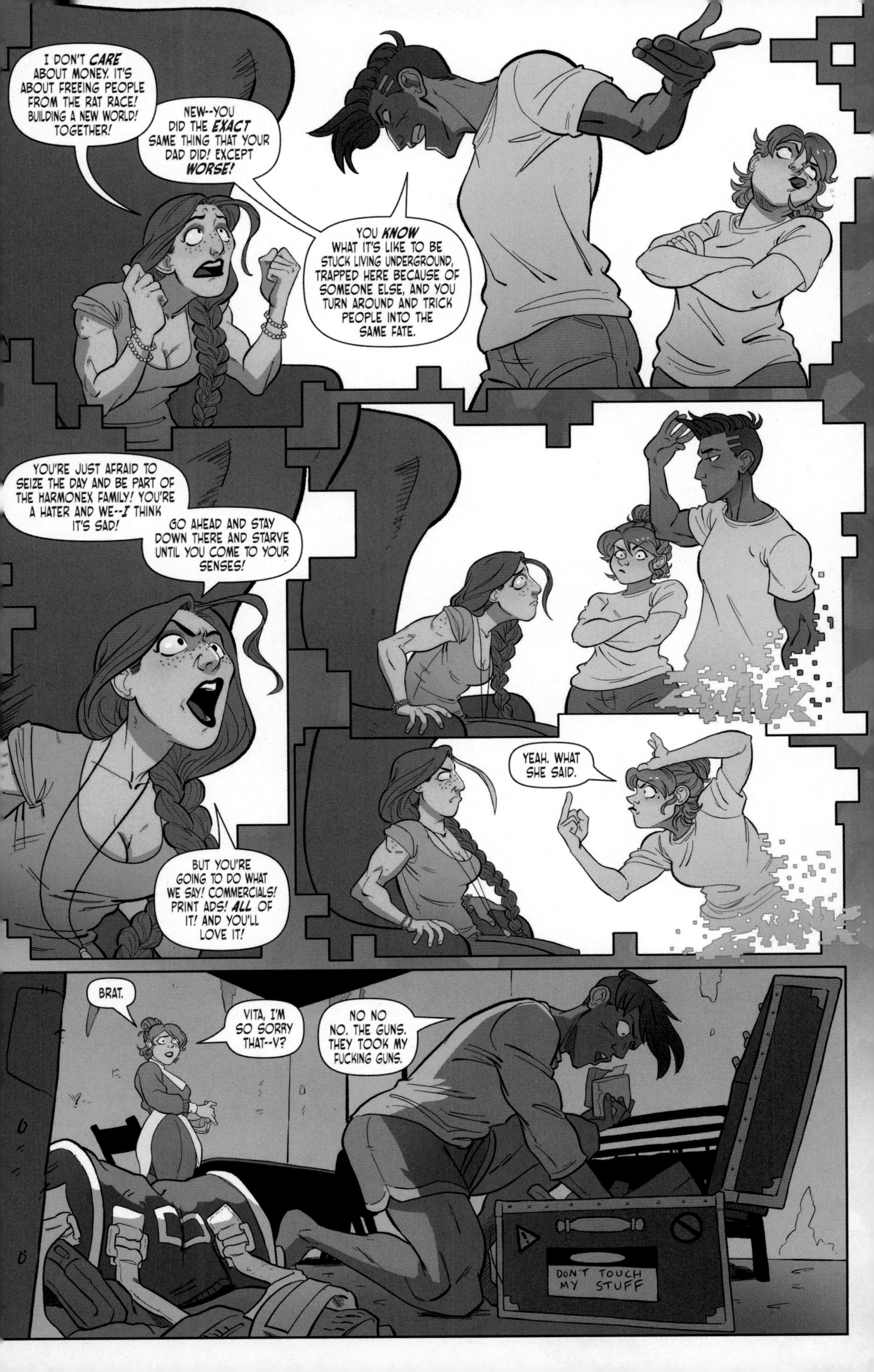
I DON'T CARE ABOUT MONEY. IT'S ABOUT FREEING PEOPLE FROM THE RAT RACE! BUILDING A NEW WORLD! TOGETHER!
NEW--YOU DID THE EXACT SAME THING THAT YOUR DAD DID! EXCEPT WORSE!
YOU KNOW WHAT IT'S LIKE TO BE STUCK LIVING UNDERGROUND, TRAPPED HERE BECAUSE OF SOMEONE ELSE, AND YOU TURN AROUND AND TRICK PEOPLE INTO THE SAME FATE.
YOU'RE JUST AFRAID TO SEIZE THE DAY AND BE PART OF THE HARMONEX FAMILY! YOU'RE A HATER AND WE--I THINK IT'S SAD!
GO AHEAD AND STAY DOWN THERE AND STARVE UNTIL YOU COME TO YOUR SENSES!
BUT YOU'RE GOING TO DO WHAT WE SAY! COMMERCIALS! PRINT ADS! ALL OF IT! AND YOU'LL LOVE IT!
ZWNK
YEAH. WHAT SHE SAID.
BRAT.
VITA, I'M SO SORRY THAT--V?
NO NO NO. THE GUNS. THEY TOOK MY FUCKING GUNS.
DON'T TOUCH MY STUFF

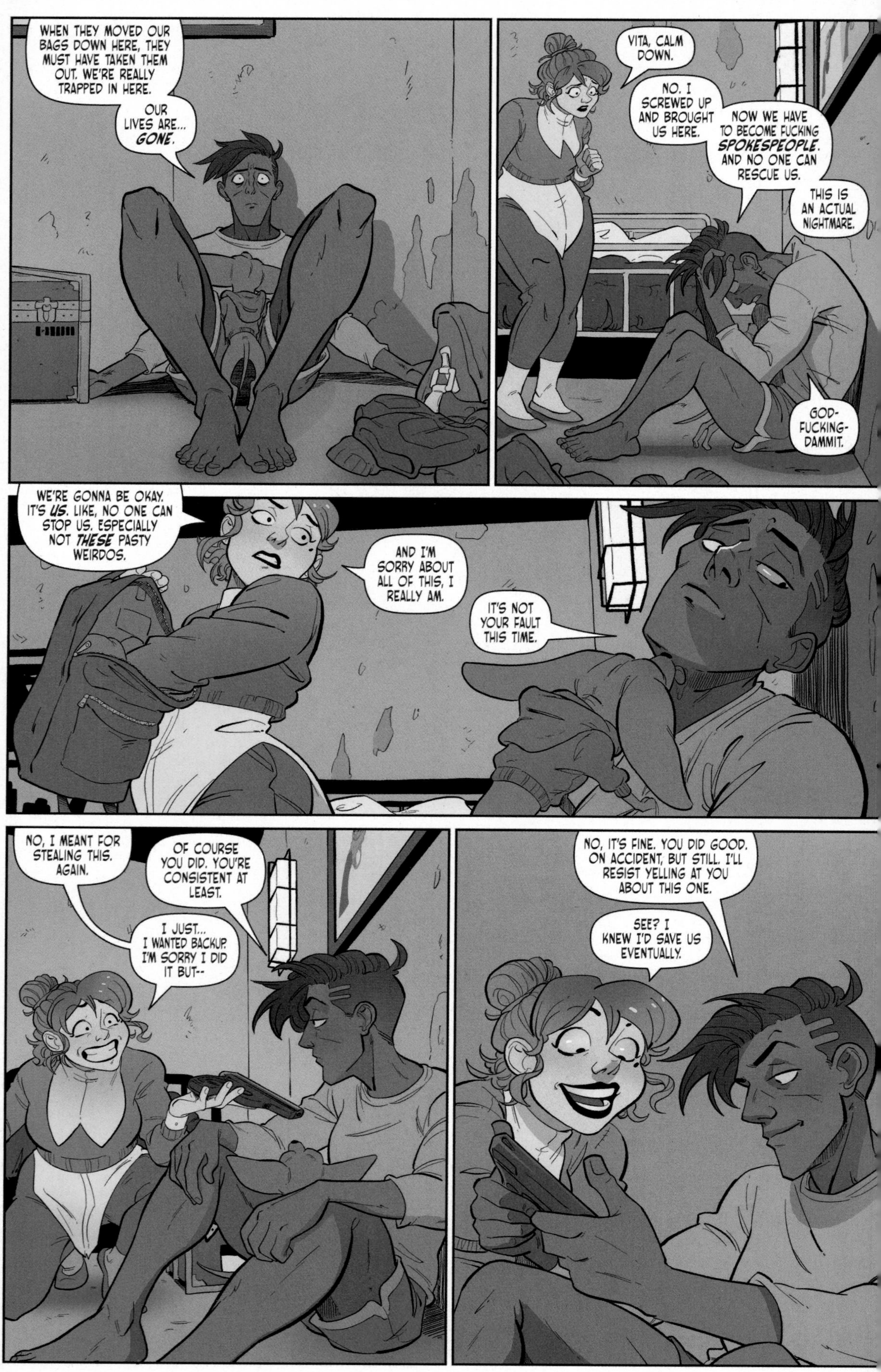

WHEN THEY MOVED OUR BAGS DOWN HERE, THEY MUST HAVE TAKEN THEM OUT. WE'RE REALLY TRAPPED IN HERE.
OUR LIVES ARE... *GONE*.
VITA, CALM DOWN.
NO. I SCREWED UP AND BROUGHT US HERE.
NOW WE HAVE TO BECOME FUCKING *SPOKESPEOPLE*. AND NO ONE CAN RESCUE US.
THIS IS AN ACTUAL NIGHTMARE.
GOD-FUCKING-DAMMIT.
WE'RE GONNA BE OKAY. IT'S *US*. LIKE, NO ONE CAN STOP US. ESPECIALLY NOT *THESE* PASTY WEIRDOS.
AND I'M SORRY ABOUT ALL OF THIS, I REALLY AM.
IT'S NOT YOUR FAULT THIS TIME.
NO, I MEANT FOR STEALING THIS. AGAIN.
OF COURSE YOU DID. YOU'RE CONSISTENT AT LEAST.
I JUST... I WANTED BACKUP. I'M SORRY I DID IT BUT--
NO, IT'S FINE. YOU DID GOOD. ON ACCIDENT, BUT STILL. I'LL RESIST YELLING AT YOU ABOUT THIS ONE.
SEE? I KNEW I'D SAVE US EVENTUALLY.

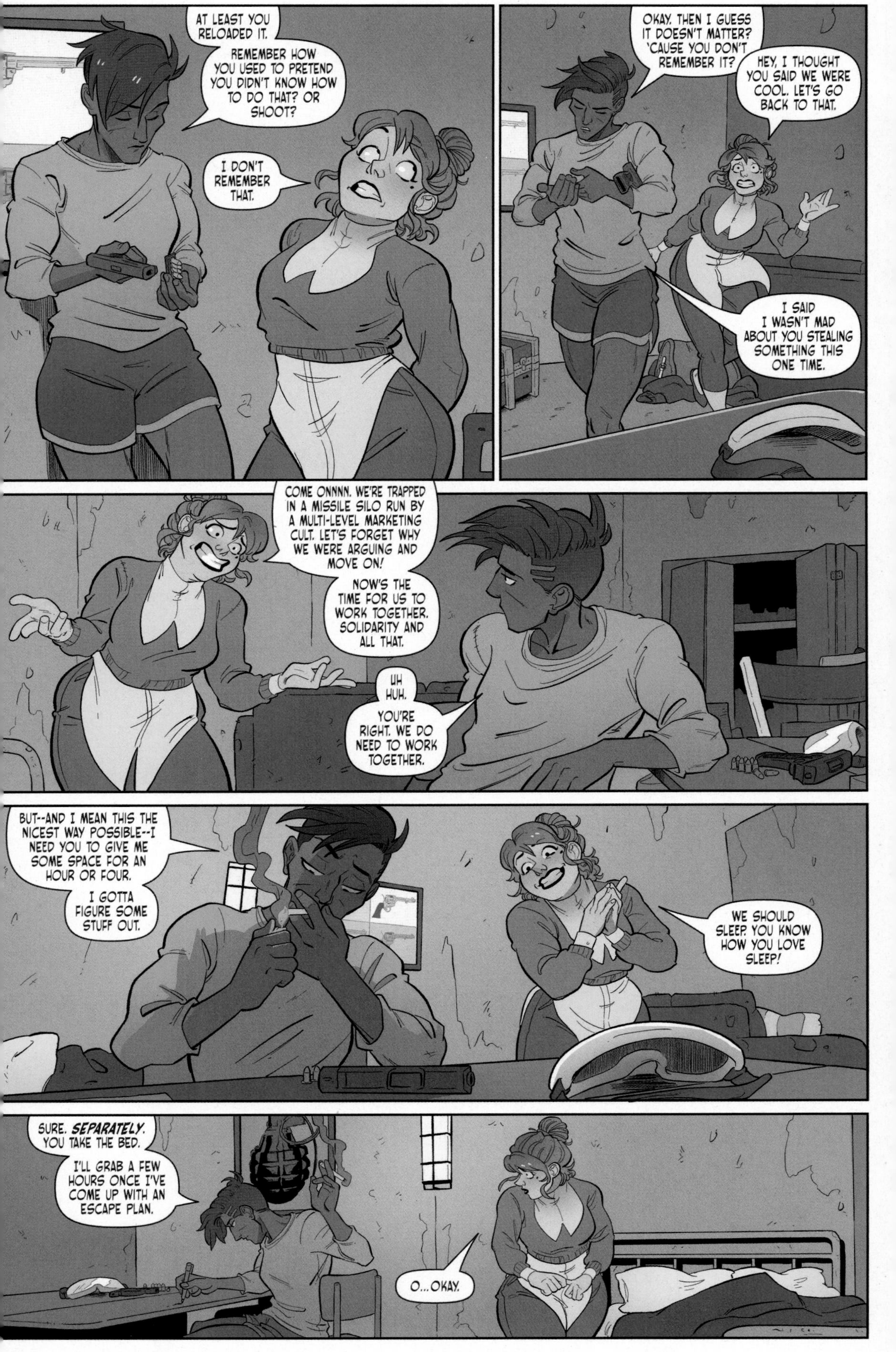
AT LEAST YOU RELOADED IT.
REMEMBER HOW YOU USED TO PRETEND YOU DIDN'T KNOW HOW TO DO THAT? OR SHOOT?
I DON'T REMEMBER THAT.
OKAY. THEN I GUESS IT DOESN'T MATTER? 'CAUSE YOU DON'T REMEMBER IT?
HEY, I THOUGHT YOU SAID WE WERE COOL. LET'S GO BACK TO THAT.
I SAID I WASN'T MAD ABOUT YOU STEALING SOMETHING THIS ONE TIME.
COME ONNNN. WE'RE TRAPPED IN A MISSILE SILO RUN BY A MULTI-LEVEL MARKETING CULT. LET'S FORGET WHY WE WERE ARGUING AND MOVE ON!
NOW'S THE TIME FOR US TO WORK TOGETHER. SOLIDARITY AND ALL THAT.
UH HUH.
YOU'RE RIGHT. WE DO NEED TO WORK TOGETHER.
BUT--AND I MEAN THIS THE NICEST WAY POSSIBLE--I NEED YOU TO GIVE ME SOME SPACE FOR AN HOUR OR FOUR.
I GOTTA FIGURE SOME STUFF OUT.
WE SHOULD SLEEP. YOU KNOW HOW YOU LOVE SLEEP!
SURE. SEPARATELY. YOU TAKE THE BED.
I'LL GRAB A FEW HOURS ONCE I'VE COME UP WITH AN ESCAPE PLAN.
O...OKAY.

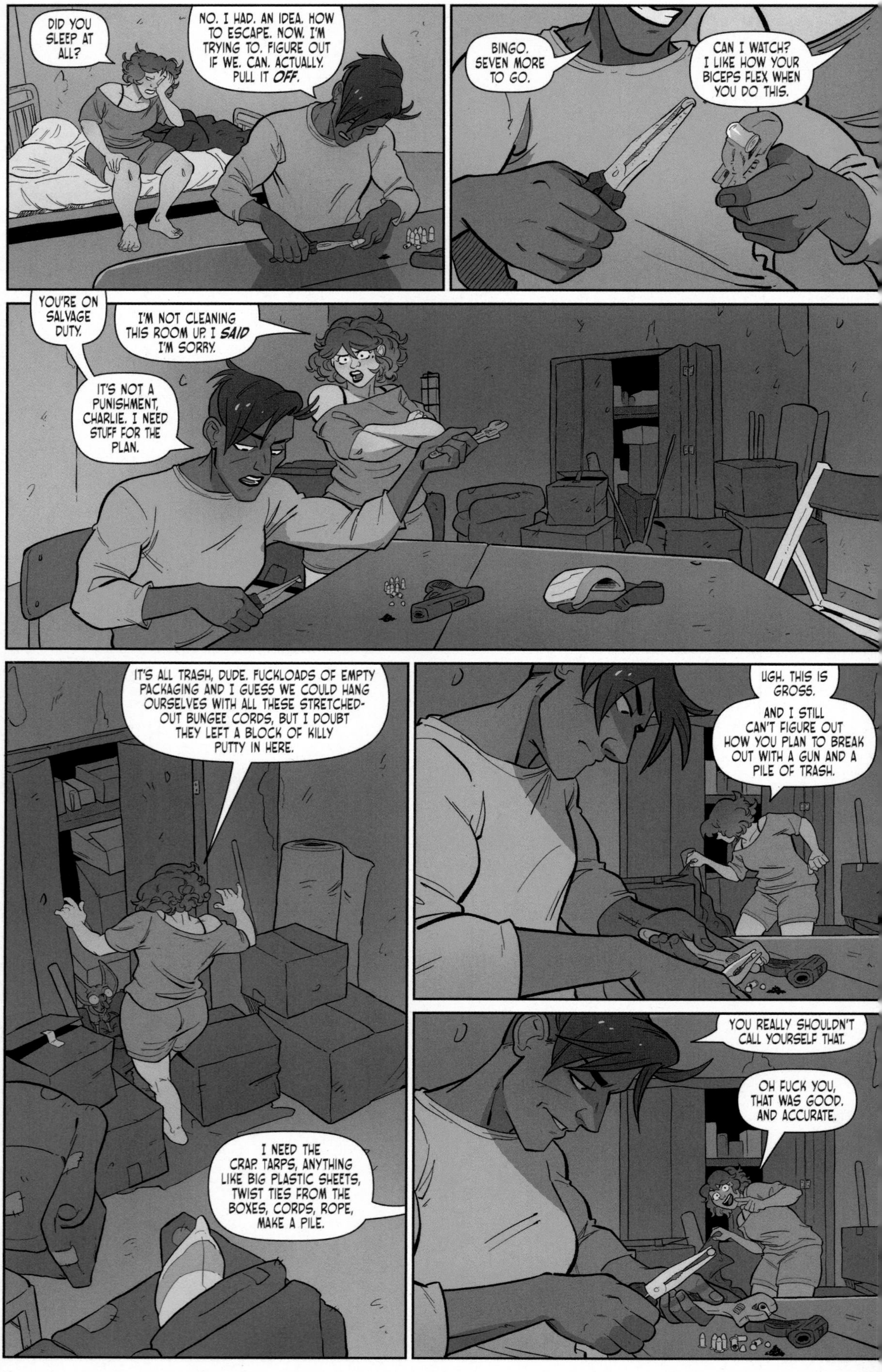
DID YOU SLEEP AT ALL?
NO. I HAD. AN IDEA. HOW TO ESCAPE. NOW. I'M TRYING TO. FIGURE OUT IF WE. CAN. ACTUALLY. PULL IT OFF.
BINGO. SEVEN MORE TO GO.
CAN I WATCH? I LIKE HOW YOUR BICEPS FLEX WHEN YOU DO THIS.
YOU'RE ON SALVAGE DUTY.
I'M NOT CLEANING THIS ROOM UP. I SAID I'M SORRY.
IT'S NOT A PUNISHMENT, CHARLIE. I NEED STUFF FOR THE PLAN.
IT'S ALL TRASH, DUDE. FUCKLOADS OF EMPTY PACKAGING AND I GUESS WE COULD HANG OURSELVES WITH ALL THESE STRETCHED-OUT BUNGEE CORDS, BUT I DOUBT THEY LEFT A BLOCK OF KILLY PUTTY IN HERE.
I NEED THE CRAP. TARPS, ANYTHING LIKE BIG PLASTIC SHEETS, TWIST TIES FROM THE BOXES, CORDS, ROPE, MAKE A PILE.
UGH. THIS IS GROSS.
AND I STILL CAN'T FIGURE OUT HOW YOU PLAN TO BREAK OUT WITH A GUN AND A PILE OF TRASH.
YOU REALLY SHOULDN'T CALL YOURSELF THAT.
OH FUCK YOU, THAT WAS GOOD. AND ACCURATE.

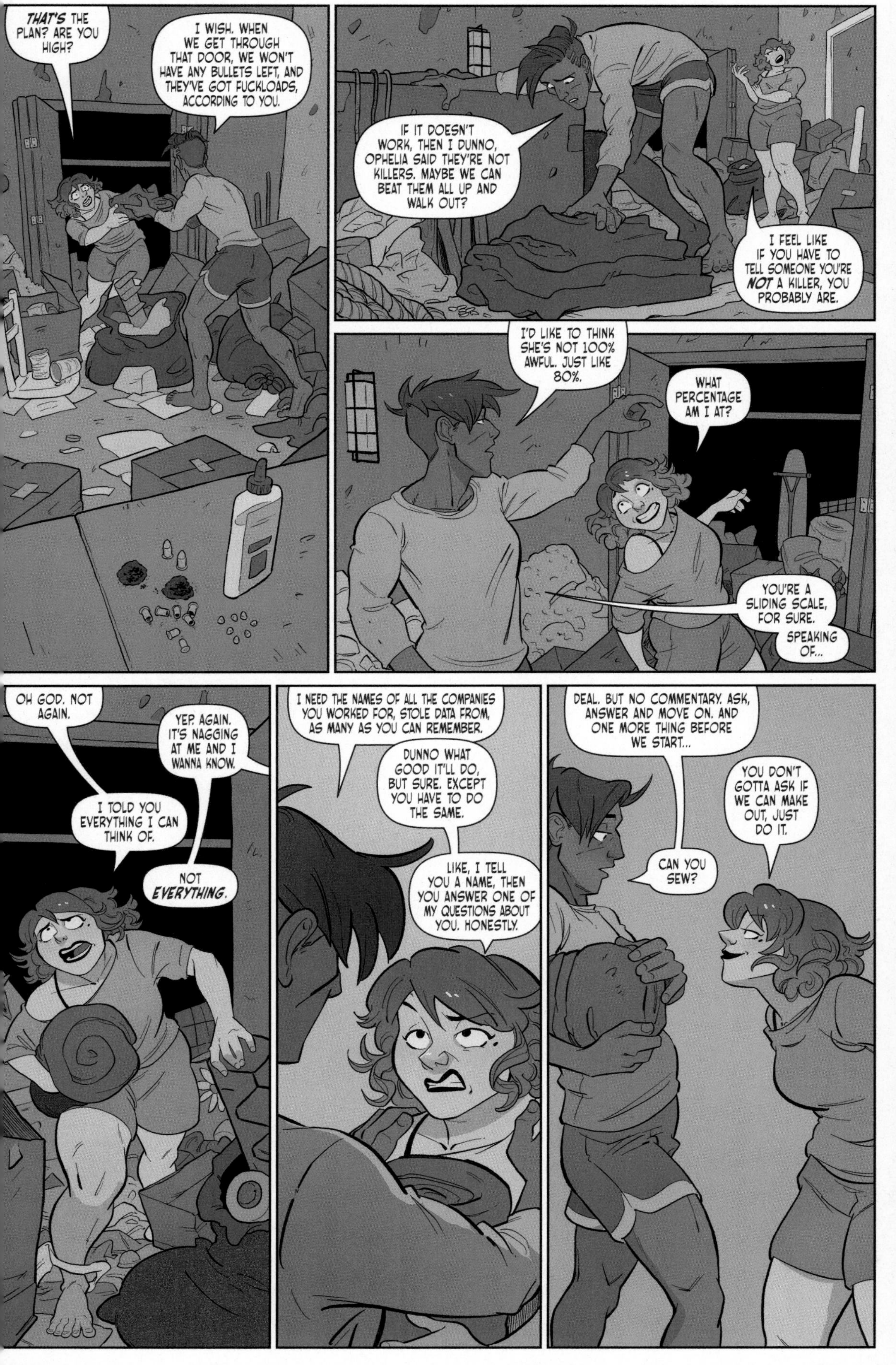

THAT'S THE PLAN? ARE YOU HIGH?
I WISH. WHEN WE GET THROUGH THAT DOOR, WE WON'T HAVE ANY BULLETS LEFT, AND THEY'VE GOT FUCKLOADS, ACCORDING TO YOU.
IF IT DOESN'T WORK, THEN I DUNNO, OPHELIA SAID THEY'RE NOT KILLERS. MAYBE WE CAN BEAT THEM ALL UP AND WALK OUT?
I FEEL LIKE IF YOU HAVE TO TELL SOMEONE YOU'RE *NOT* A KILLER, YOU PROBABLY ARE.
I'D LIKE TO THINK SHE'S NOT 100% AWFUL. JUST LIKE 80%.
WHAT PERCENTAGE AM I AT?
YOU'RE A SLIDING SCALE, FOR SURE.
SPEAKING OF...
OH GOD. NOT AGAIN.
YEP. AGAIN. IT'S NAGGING AT ME AND I WANNA KNOW.
I TOLD YOU EVERYTHING I CAN THINK OF.
NOT *EVERYTHING*.
I NEED THE NAMES OF ALL THE COMPANIES YOU WORKED FOR, STOLE DATA FROM, AS MANY AS YOU CAN REMEMBER.
DUNNO WHAT GOOD IT'LL DO, BUT SURE. EXCEPT YOU HAVE TO DO THE SAME.
LIKE, I TELL YOU A NAME, THEN YOU ANSWER ONE OF MY QUESTIONS ABOUT YOU. HONESTLY.
DEAL. BUT NO COMMENTARY. ASK, ANSWER AND MOVE ON. AND ONE MORE THING BEFORE WE START...
CAN YOU SEW?
YOU DON'T GOTTA ASK IF WE CAN MAKE OUT, JUST DO IT.

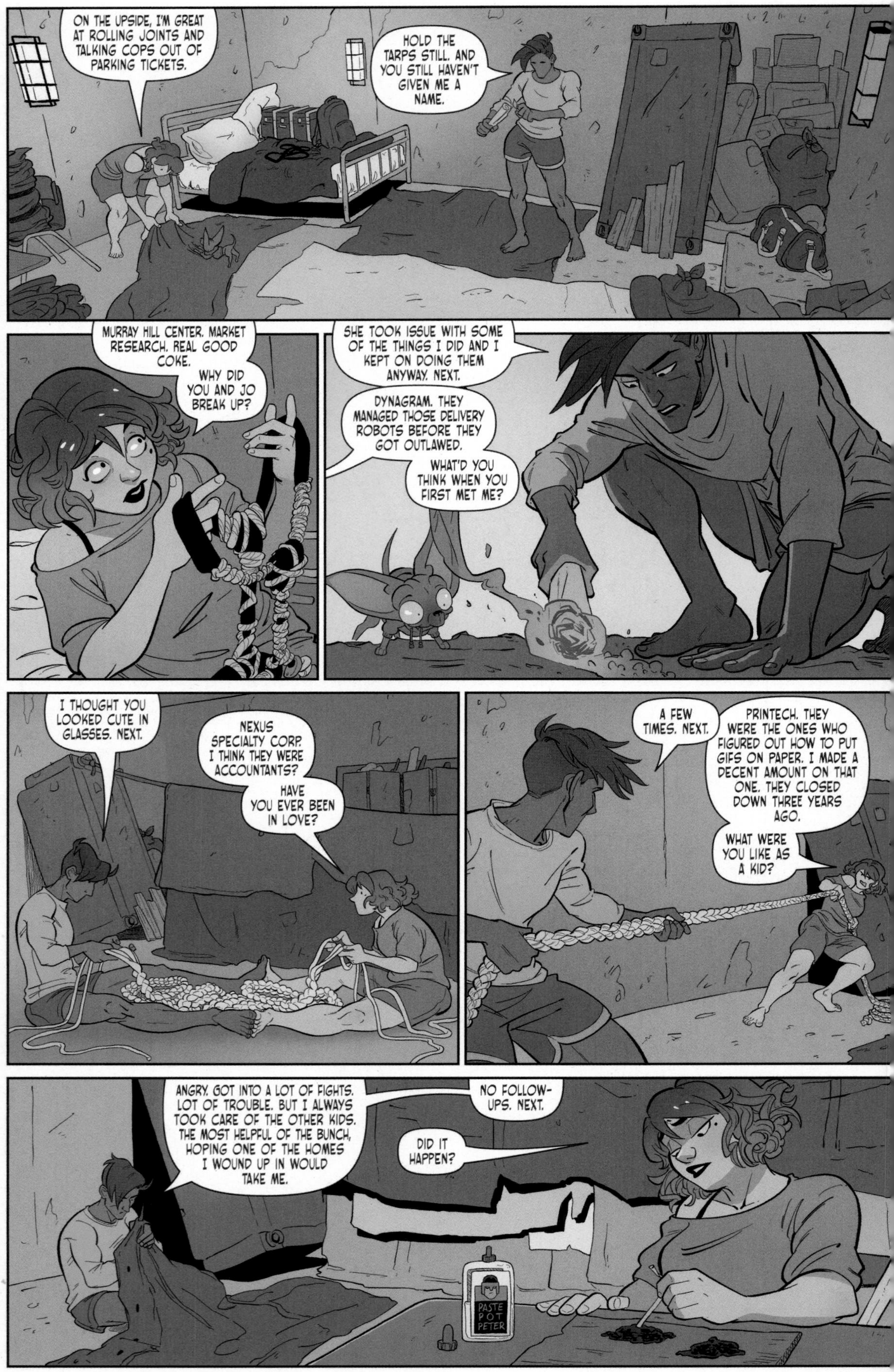
ON THE UPSIDE, I'M GREAT AT ROLLING JOINTS AND TALKING COPS OUT OF PARKING TICKETS.
HOLD THE TARPS STILL. AND YOU STILL HAVEN'T GIVEN ME A NAME.
MURRAY HILL CENTER. MARKET RESEARCH. REAL GOOD COKE.
WHY DID YOU AND JO BREAK UP?
SHE TOOK ISSUE WITH SOME OF THE THINGS I DID AND I KEPT ON DOING THEM ANYWAY. NEXT.
DYNAGRAM. THEY MANAGED THOSE DELIVERY ROBOTS BEFORE THEY GOT OUTLAWED.
WHAT'D YOU THINK WHEN YOU FIRST MET ME?
I THOUGHT YOU LOOKED CUTE IN GLASSES. NEXT.
NEXUS SPECIALTY CORP. I THINK THEY WERE ACCOUNTANTS?
HAVE YOU EVER BEEN IN LOVE?
A FEW TIMES. NEXT.
PRINTECH. THEY WERE THE ONES WHO FIGURED OUT HOW TO PUT GIFS ON PAPER. I MADE A DECENT AMOUNT ON THAT ONE. THEY CLOSED DOWN THREE YEARS AGO.
WHAT WERE YOU LIKE AS A KID?
ANGRY. GOT INTO A LOT OF FIGHTS. LOT OF TROUBLE. BUT I ALWAYS TOOK CARE OF THE OTHER KIDS. THE MOST HELPFUL OF THE BUNCH, HOPING ONE OF THE HOMES I WOUND UP IN WOULD TAKE ME.
DID IT HAPPEN?
NO FOLLOW-UPS. NEXT.
PASTE POT PETER

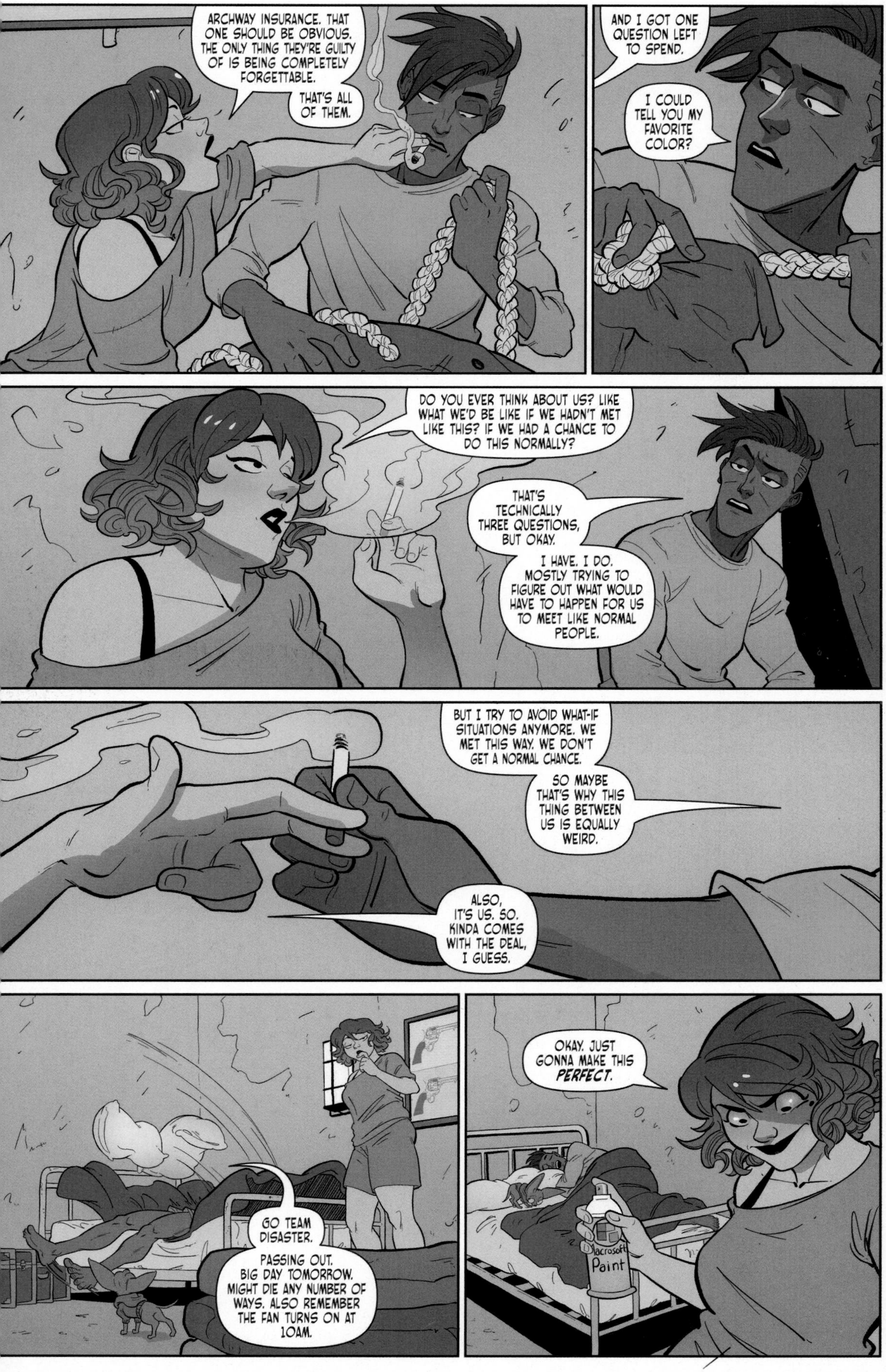
ARCHWAY INSURANCE. THAT ONE SHOULD BE OBVIOUS. THE ONLY THING THEY'RE GUILTY OF IS BEING COMPLETELY FORGETTABLE.
THAT'S ALL OF THEM.
AND I GOT ONE QUESTION LEFT TO SPEND.
I COULD TELL YOU MY FAVORITE COLOR?
DO YOU EVER THINK ABOUT US? LIKE WHAT WE'D BE LIKE IF WE HADN'T MET LIKE THIS? IF WE HAD A CHANCE TO DO THIS NORMALLY?
THAT'S TECHNICALLY THREE QUESTIONS, BUT OKAY.
I HAVE. I DO. MOSTLY TRYING TO FIGURE OUT WHAT WOULD HAVE TO HAPPEN FOR US TO MEET LIKE NORMAL PEOPLE.
BUT I TRY TO AVOID WHAT-IF SITUATIONS ANYMORE. WE MET THIS WAY. WE DON'T GET A NORMAL CHANCE.
SO MAYBE THAT'S WHY THIS THING BETWEEN US IS EQUALLY WEIRD.
ALSO, IT'S US. SO. KINDA COMES WITH THE DEAL, I GUESS.
GO TEAM DISASTER.
PASSING OUT. BIG DAY TOMORROW. MIGHT DIE ANY NUMBER OF WAYS. ALSO REMEMBER THE FAN TURNS ON AT 10AM.
OKAY. JUST GONNA MAKE THIS *PERFECT*.
Macrosoft Paint

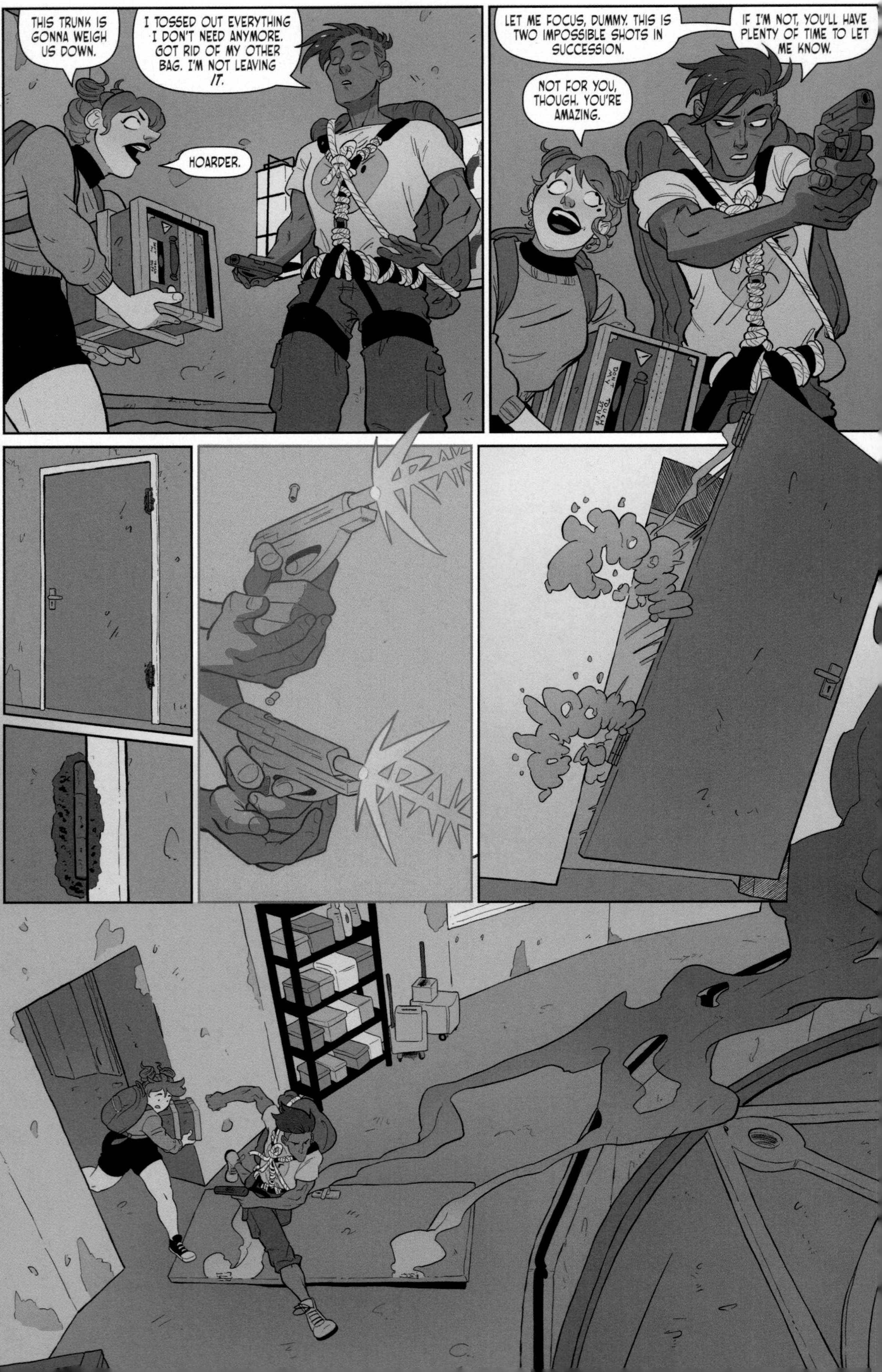
THIS TRUNK IS GONNA WEIGH US DOWN.
I TOSSED OUT EVERYTHING I DON'T NEED ANYMORE. GOT RID OF MY OTHER BAG. I'M NOT LEAVING *IT*.
HOARDER.
LET ME FOCUS, DUMMY. THIS IS TWO IMPOSSIBLE SHOTS IN SUCCESSION.
NOT FOR YOU, THOUGH. YOU'RE AMAZING.
IF I'M NOT, YOU'LL HAVE PLENTY OF TIME TO LET ME KNOW.
DON'T MY TRUNK STUFF
BRAK
BRAK

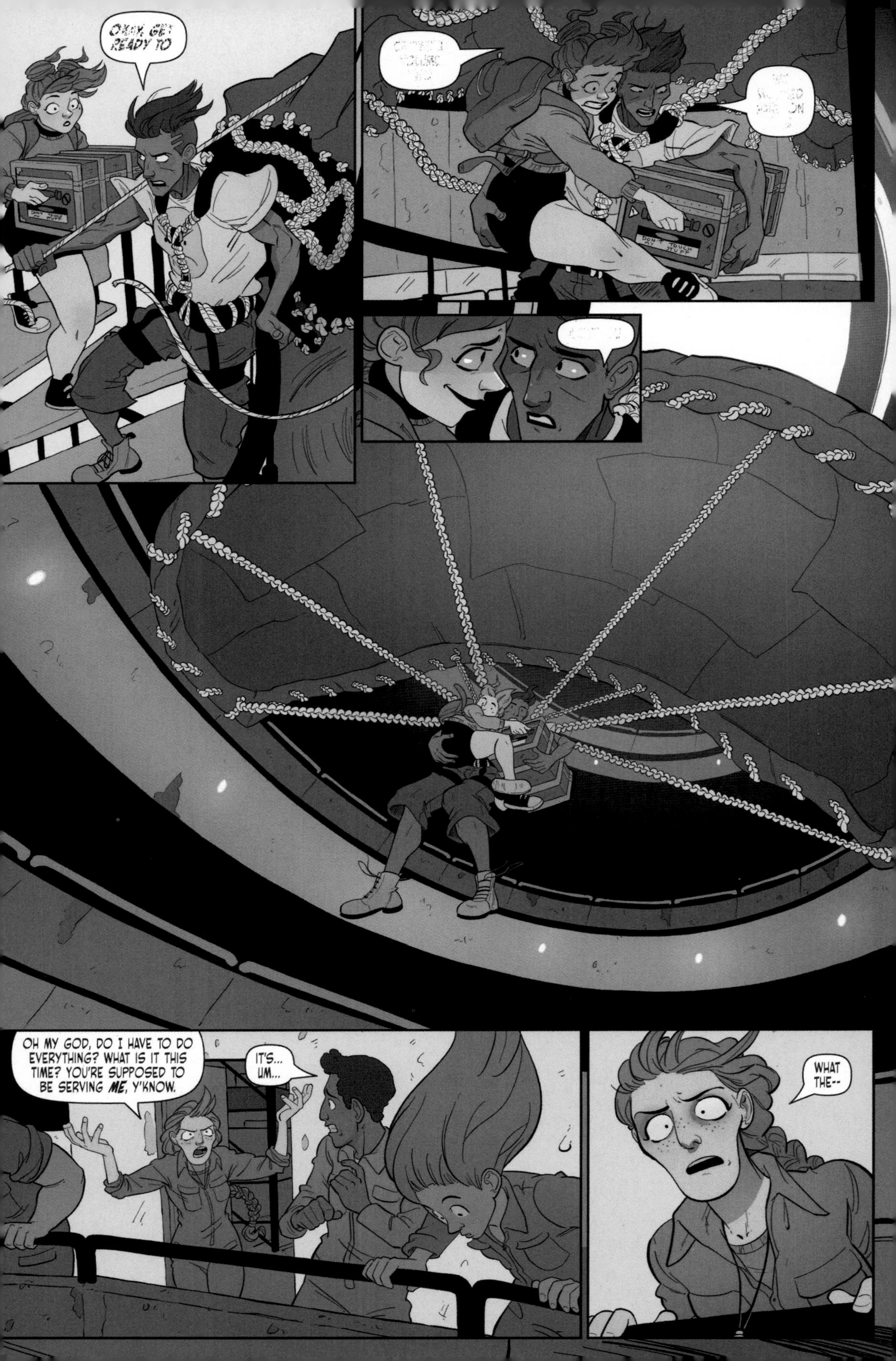
OKAY, GET READY TO
DON'T TOUCH MY STUFF
DON'T TOUCH MY STUFF
OH MY GOD, DO I HAVE TO DO EVERYTHING? WHAT IS IT THIS TIME? YOU'RE SUPPOSED TO BE SERVING *ME*, Y'KNOW.
IT'S... UM...
WHAT THE--

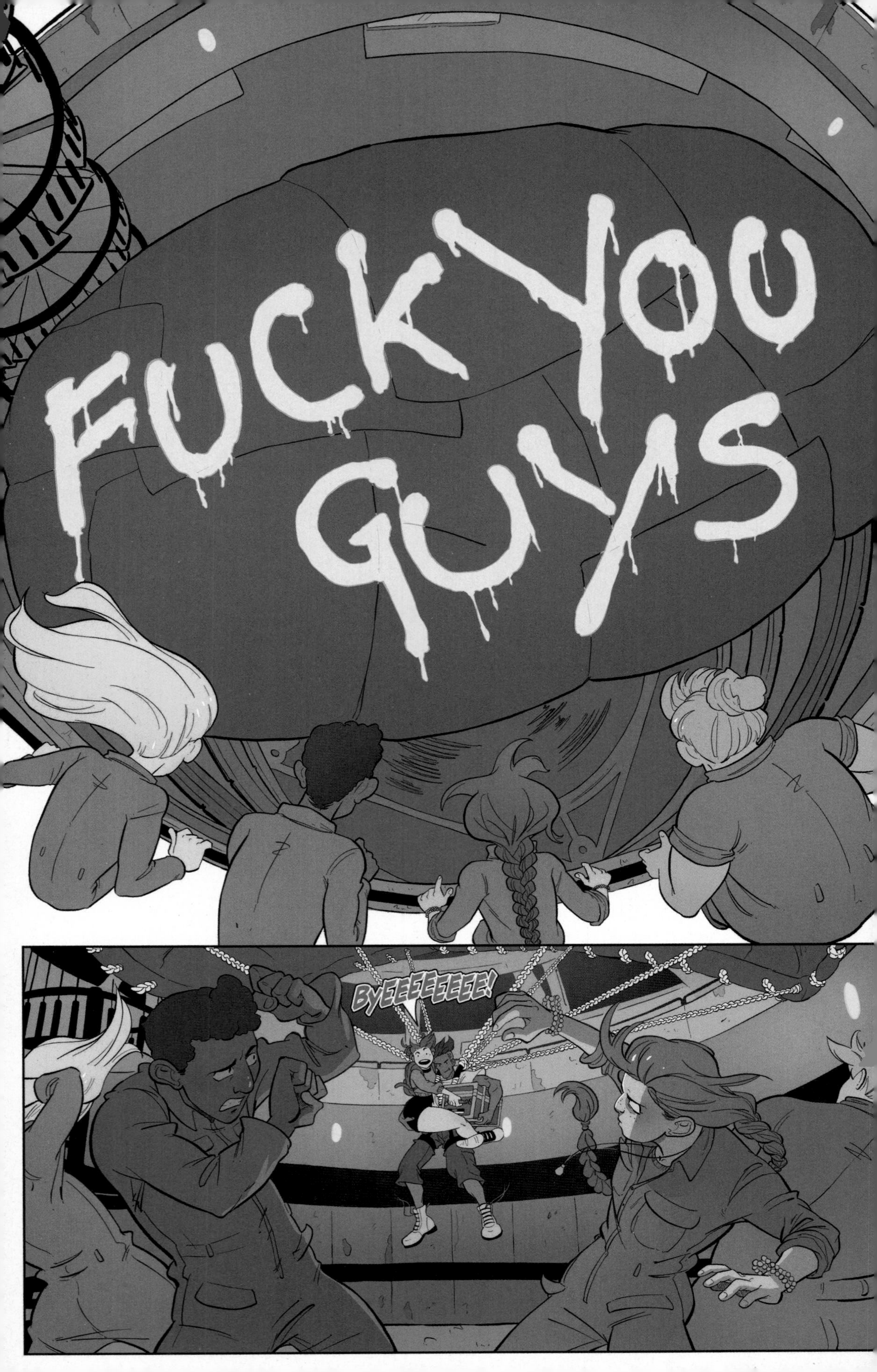
FUCK YOU GUYS
BYEEEEEEEE!

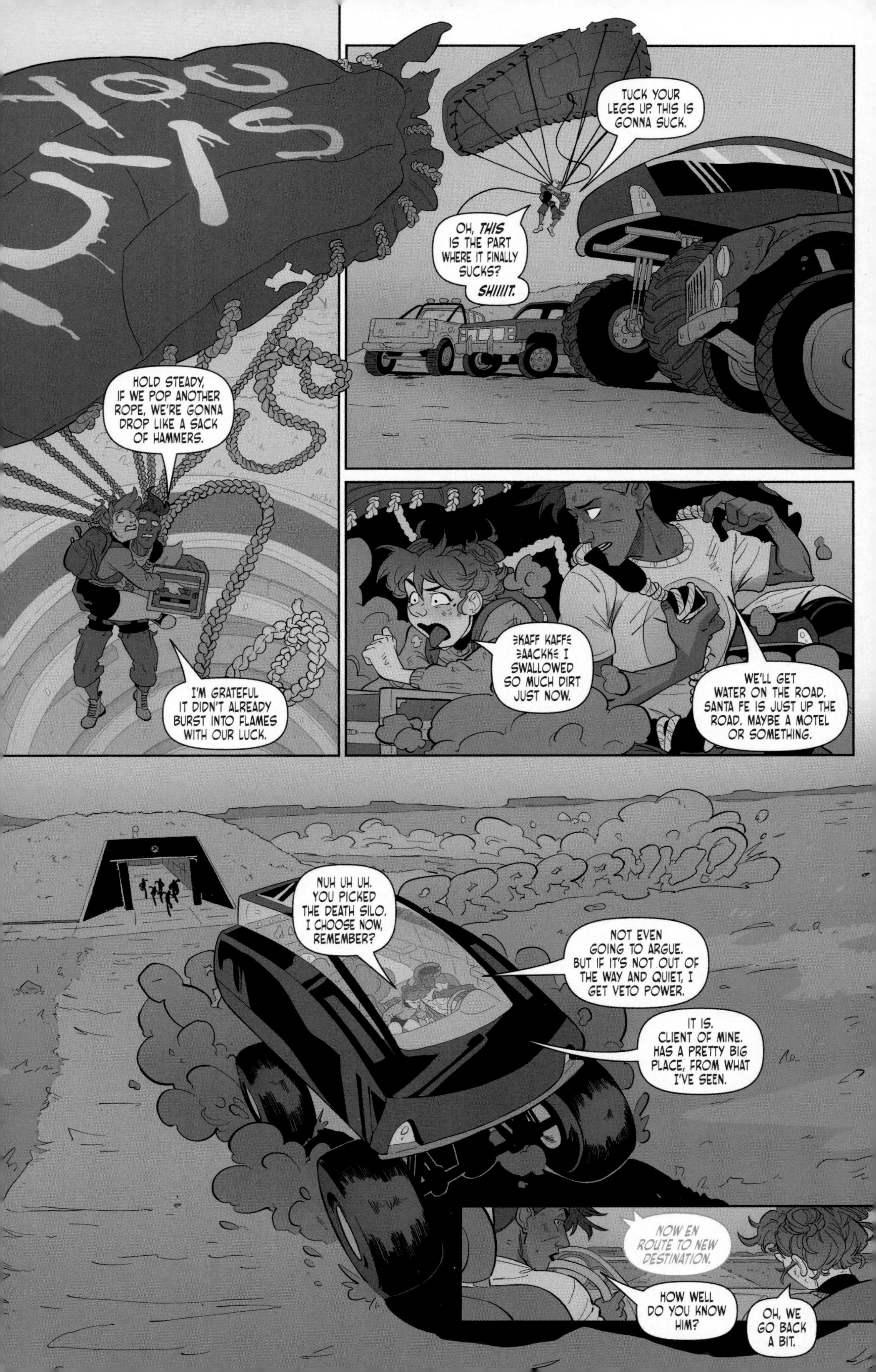
YOU GOT THIS
HOLD STEADY, IF WE POP ANOTHER ROPE, WE'RE GONNA DROP LIKE A SACK OF HAMMERS.
I'M GRATEFUL IT DIDN'T ALREADY BURST INTO FLAMES WITH OUR LUCK.
TUCK YOUR LEGS UP. THIS IS GONNA SUCK.
OH, THIS IS THE PART WHERE IT FINALLY SUCKS?
SHIIIIT.
KAFF KAFF AACKK I SWALLOWED SO MUCH DIRT JUST NOW.
WE'LL GET WATER ON THE ROAD. SANTA FE IS JUST UP THE ROAD. MAYBE A MOTEL OR SOMETHING.
VRRRRAWWM!
NUH UH UH. YOU PICKED THE DEATH SILO. I CHOOSE NOW, REMEMBER?
NOT EVEN GOING TO ARGUE. BUT IF IT'S NOT OUT OF THE WAY AND QUIET, I GET VETO POWER.
IT IS. CLIENT OF MINE. HAS A PRETTY BIG PLACE, FROM WHAT I'VE SEEN.
NOW EN ROUTE TO NEW DESTINATION.
HOW WELL DO YOU KNOW HIM?
OH, WE GO BACK A BIT.

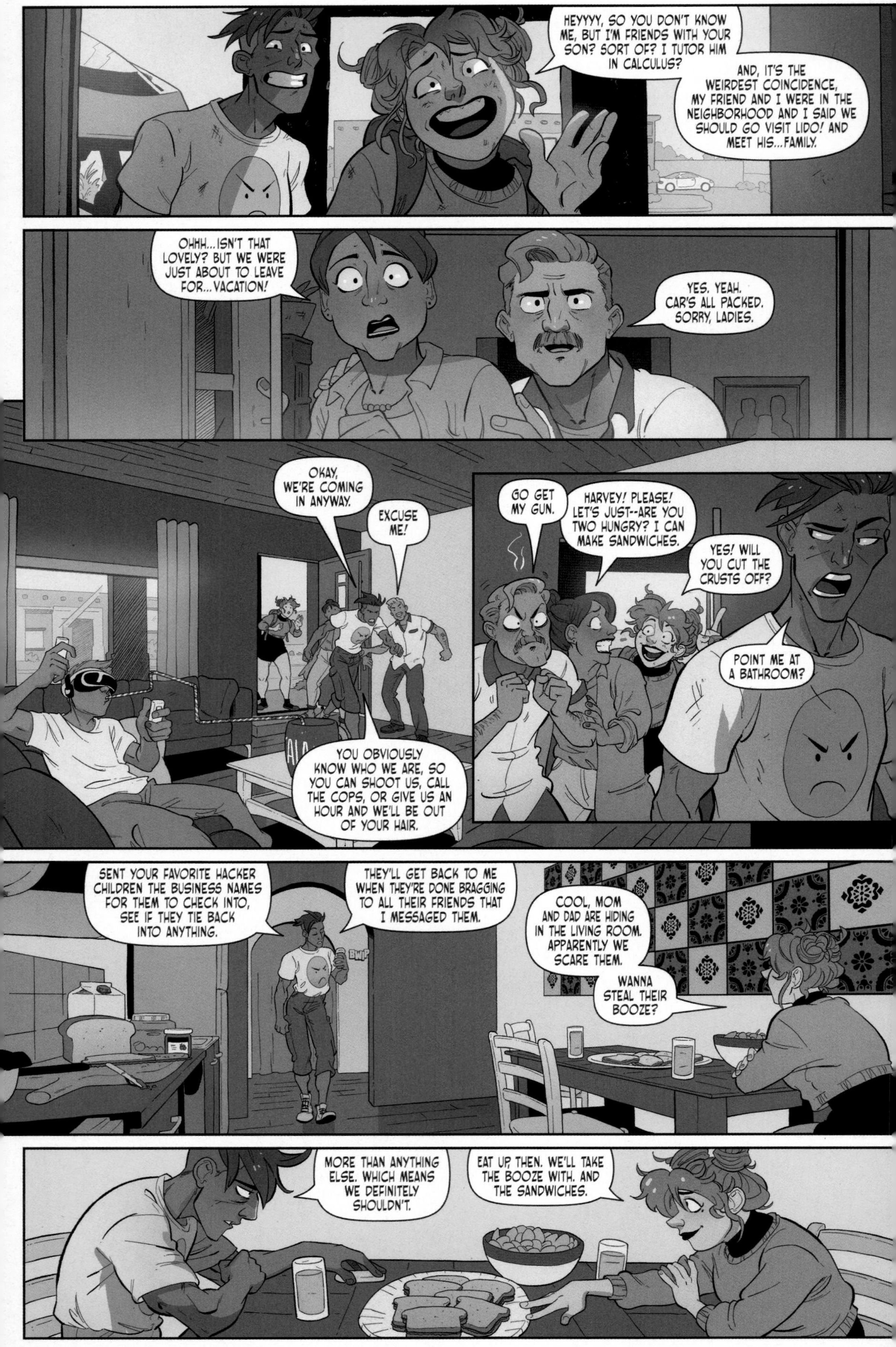
HEYYYY, SO YOU DON'T KNOW ME, BUT I'M FRIENDS WITH YOUR SON? SORT OF? I TUTOR HIM IN CALCULUS?
AND, IT'S THE WEIRDEST COINCIDENCE, MY FRIEND AND I WERE IN THE NEIGHBORHOOD AND I SAID WE SHOULD GO VISIT LIDO! AND MEET HIS...FAMILY.
OHHH...ISN'T THAT LOVELY? BUT WE WERE JUST ABOUT TO LEAVE FOR...VACATION!
YES. YEAH. CAR'S ALL PACKED. SORRY, LADIES.
OKAY, WE'RE COMING IN ANYWAY.
EXCUSE ME!
YOU OBVIOUSLY KNOW WHO WE ARE, SO YOU CAN SHOOT US, CALL THE COPS, OR GIVE US AN HOUR AND WE'LL BE OUT OF YOUR HAIR.
GO GET MY GUN.
HARVEY! PLEASE! LET'S JUST--ARE YOU TWO HUNGRY? I CAN MAKE SANDWICHES.
YES! WILL YOU CUT THE CRUSTS OFF?
POINT ME AT A BATHROOM?
SENT YOUR FAVORITE HACKER CHILDREN THE BUSINESS NAMES FOR THEM TO CHECK INTO, SEE IF THEY TIE BACK INTO ANYTHING.
THEY'LL GET BACK TO ME WHEN THEY'RE DONE BRAGGING TO ALL THEIR FRIENDS THAT I MESSAGED THEM.
BWIP
COOL, MOM AND DAD ARE HIDING IN THE LIVING ROOM. APPARENTLY WE SCARE THEM.
WANNA STEAL THEIR BOOZE?
MORE THAN ANYTHING ELSE. WHICH MEANS WE DEFINITELY SHOULDN'T.
EAT UP, THEN. WE'LL TAKE THE BOOZE WITH. AND THE SANDWICHES.

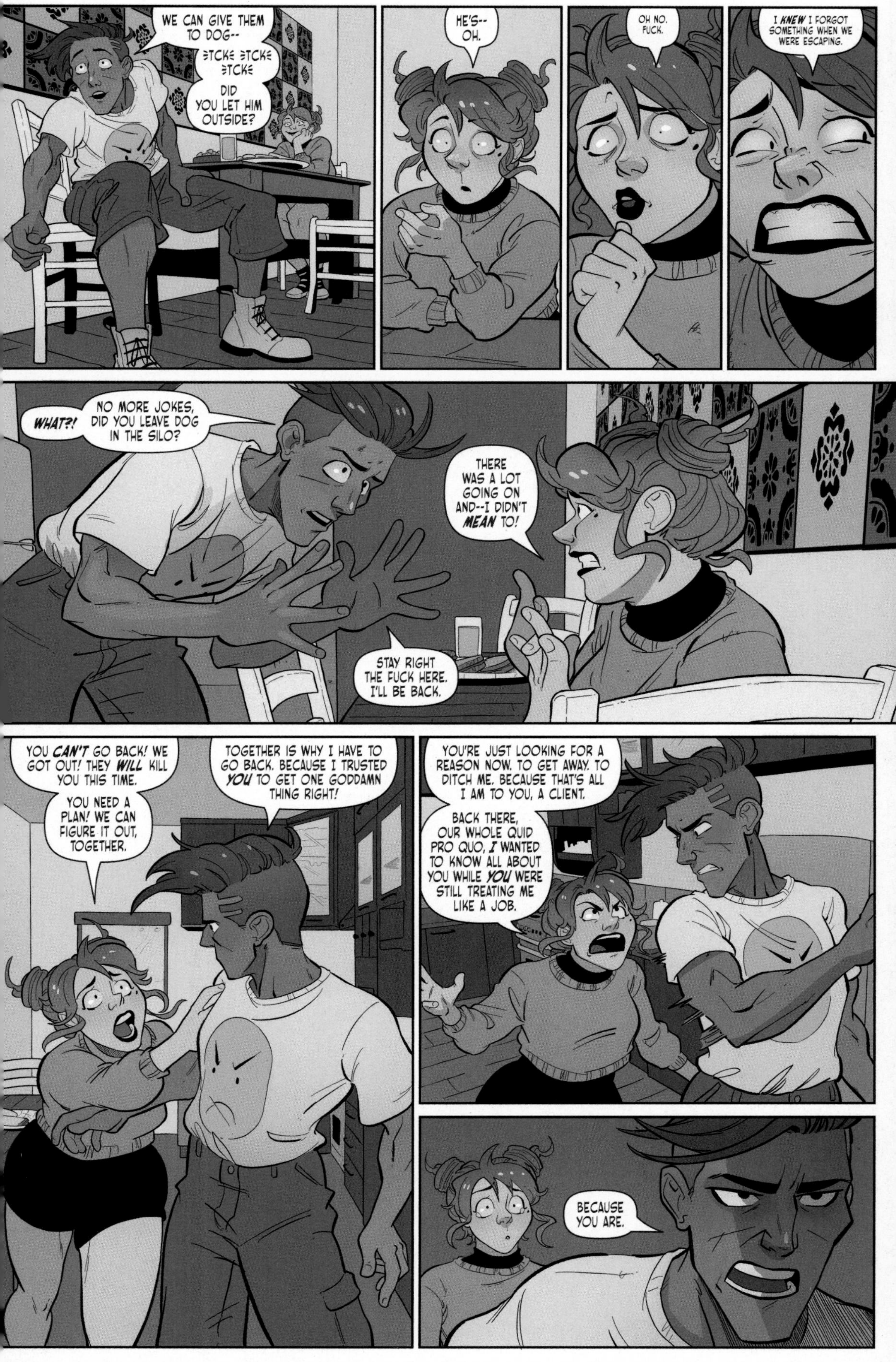
WE CAN GIVE THEM TO DOG--
ƎTCKƐ ƎTCKƐ ƎTCKƐ
DID YOU LET HIM OUTSIDE?
HE'S-- OH.
OH NO. FUCK.
I KNEW I FORGOT SOMETHING WHEN WE WERE ESCAPING.
WHAT?!
NO MORE JOKES, DID YOU LEAVE DOG IN THE SILO?
THERE WAS A LOT GOING ON AND--I DIDN'T MEAN TO!
STAY RIGHT THE FUCK HERE. I'LL BE BACK.
YOU CAN'T GO BACK! WE GOT OUT! THEY WILL KILL YOU THIS TIME.
YOU NEED A PLAN! WE CAN FIGURE IT OUT, TOGETHER.
TOGETHER IS WHY I HAVE TO GO BACK. BECAUSE I TRUSTED YOU TO GET ONE GODDAMN THING RIGHT!
YOU'RE JUST LOOKING FOR A REASON NOW. TO GET AWAY. TO DITCH ME. BECAUSE THAT'S ALL I AM TO YOU, A CLIENT.
BACK THERE, OUR WHOLE QUID PRO QUO, I WANTED TO KNOW ALL ABOUT YOU WHILE YOU WERE STILL TREATING ME LIKE A JOB.
BECAUSE YOU ARE.

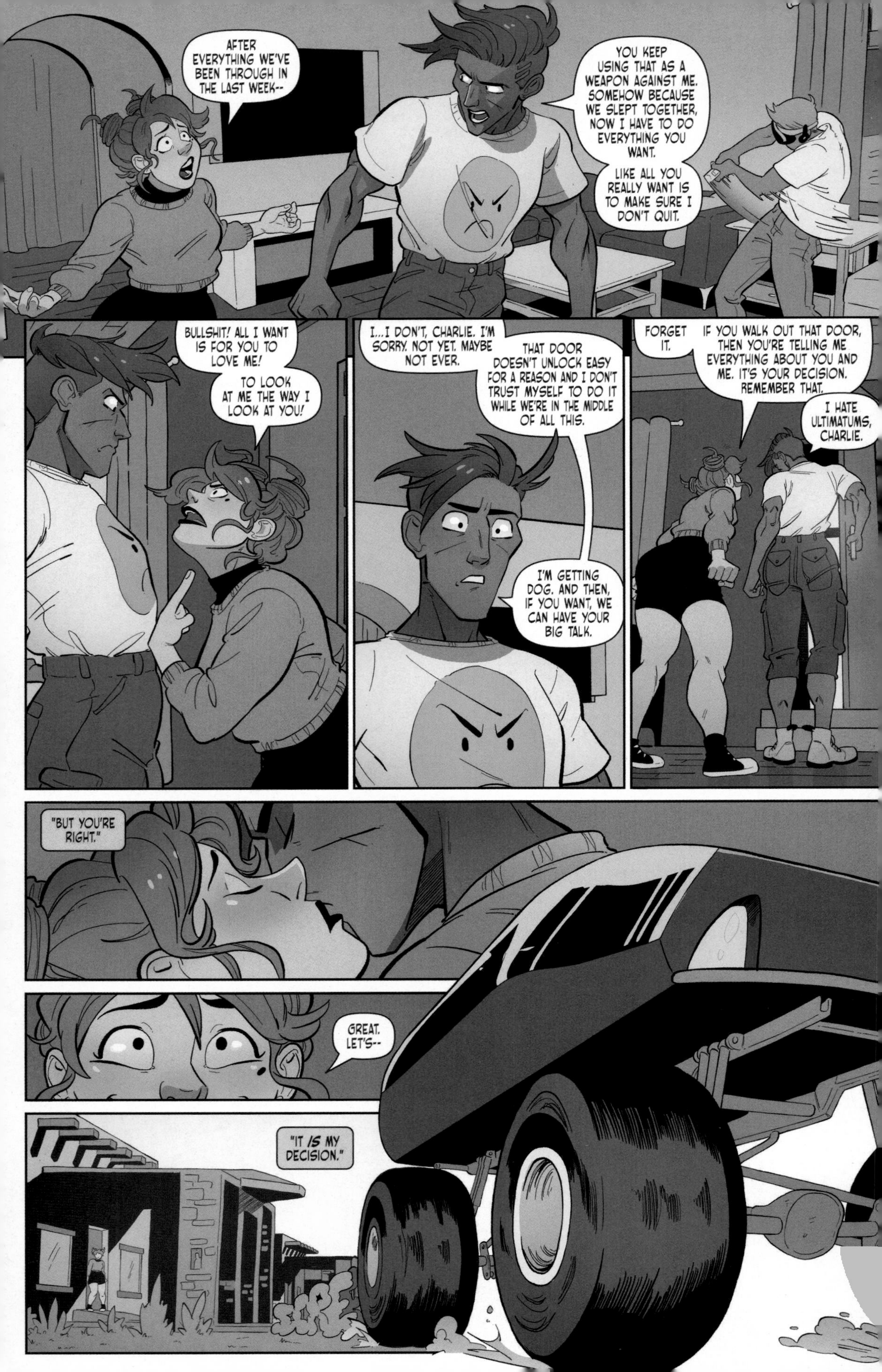
AFTER EVERYTHING WE'VE BEEN THROUGH IN THE LAST WEEK--
YOU KEEP USING THAT AS A WEAPON AGAINST ME. SOMEHOW BECAUSE WE SLEPT TOGETHER, NOW I HAVE TO DO EVERYTHING YOU WANT.
LIKE ALL YOU REALLY WANT IS TO MAKE SURE I DON'T QUIT.
BULLSHIT! ALL I WANT IS FOR YOU TO LOVE ME!
TO LOOK AT ME THE WAY I LOOK AT YOU!
I...I DON'T, CHARLIE. I'M SORRY. NOT YET. MAYBE NOT EVER.
THAT DOOR DOESN'T UNLOCK EASY FOR A REASON AND I DON'T TRUST MYSELF TO DO IT WHILE WE'RE IN THE MIDDLE OF ALL THIS.
I'M GETTING DOG. AND THEN, IF YOU WANT, WE CAN HAVE YOUR BIG TALK.
FORGET IT.
IF YOU WALK OUT THAT DOOR, THEN YOU'RE TELLING ME EVERYTHING ABOUT YOU AND ME. IT'S YOUR DECISION. REMEMBER THAT.
I HATE ULTIMATUMS, CHARLIE.
"BUT YOU'RE RIGHT."
GREAT. LET'S--
"IT IS MY DECISION."

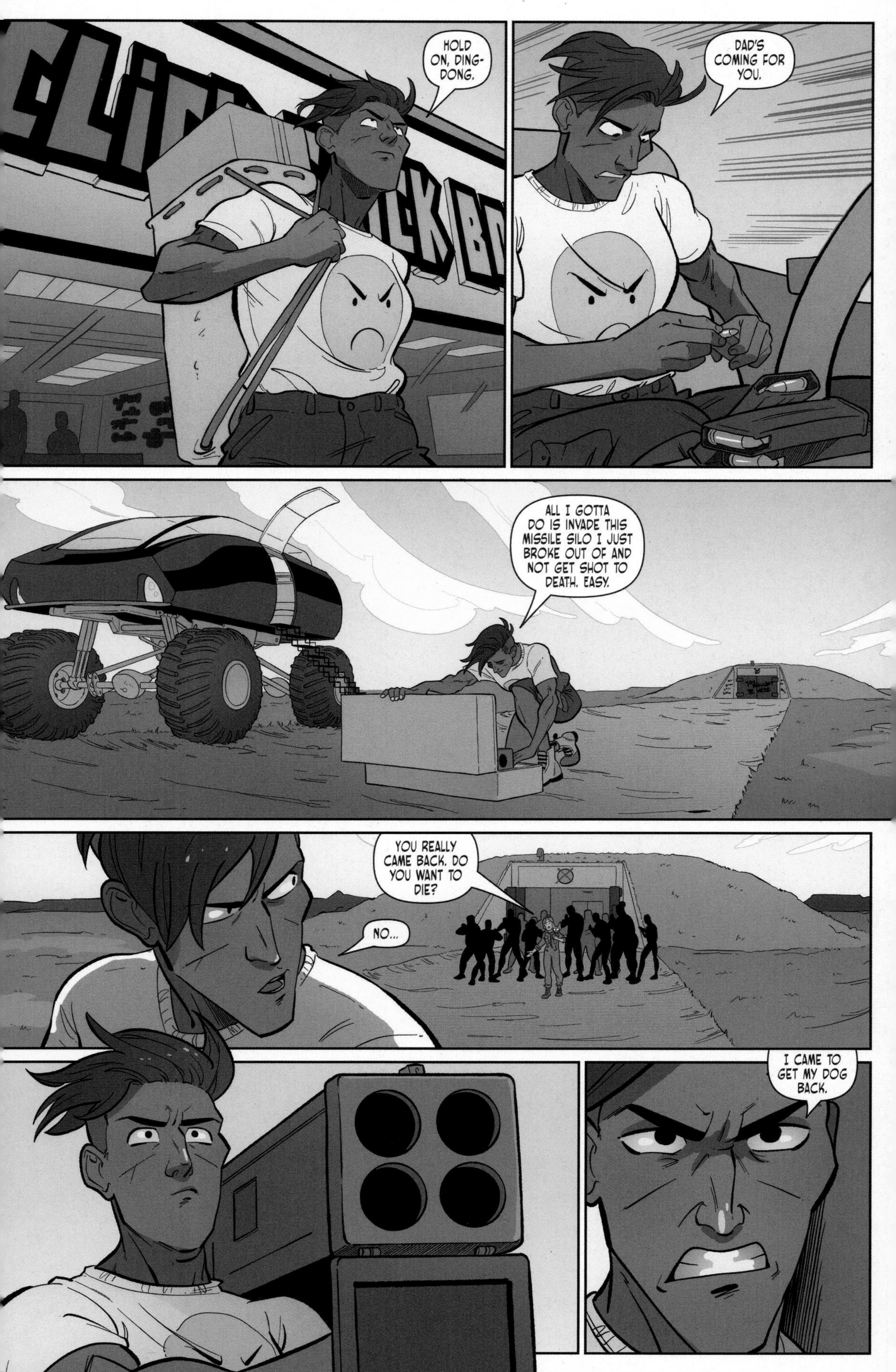

HOLD ON, DING-DONG.
DAD'S COMING FOR YOU.
ALL I GOTTA DO IS INVADE THIS MISSILE SILO I JUST BROKE OUT OF AND NOT GET SHOT TO DEATH. EASY.
YOU REALLY CAME BACK. DO YOU WANT TO DIE?
NO...
I CAME TO GET MY DOG BACK.

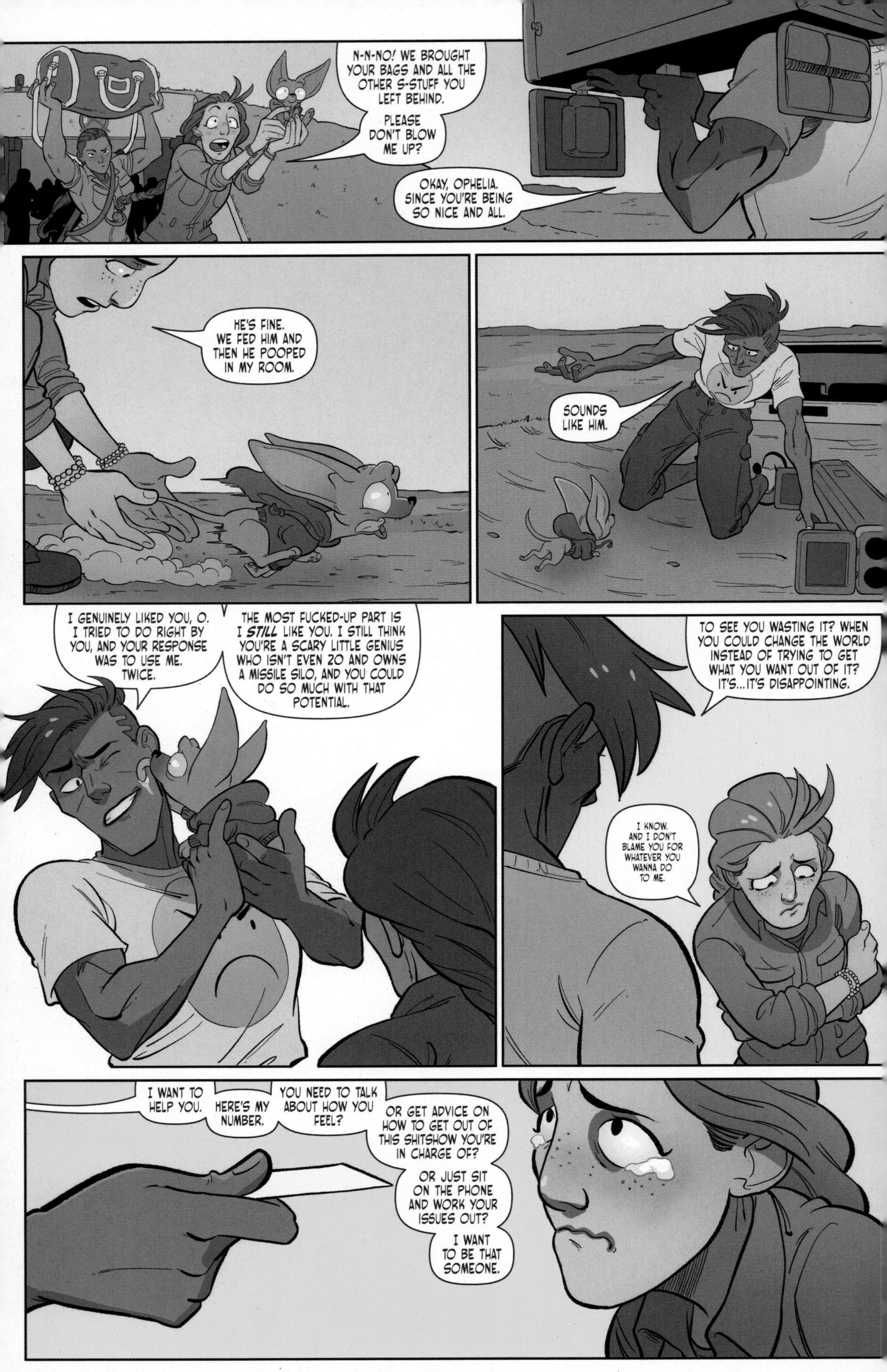
N-N-NO! WE BROUGHT YOUR BAGS AND ALL THE OTHER S-STUFF YOU LEFT BEHIND.
PLEASE DON'T BLOW ME UP?
OKAY, OPHELIA. SINCE YOU'RE BEING SO NICE AND ALL.
HE'S FINE. WE FED HIM AND THEN HE POOPED IN MY ROOM.
SOUNDS LIKE HIM.
I GENUINELY LIKED YOU, O. I TRIED TO DO RIGHT BY YOU, AND YOUR RESPONSE WAS TO USE ME. TWICE.
THE MOST FUCKED-UP PART IS I *STILL* LIKE YOU. I STILL THINK YOU'RE A SCARY LITTLE GENIUS WHO ISN'T EVEN 20 AND OWNS A MISSILE SILO, AND YOU COULD DO SO MUCH WITH THAT POTENTIAL.
TO SEE YOU WASTING IT? WHEN YOU COULD CHANGE THE WORLD INSTEAD OF TRYING TO GET WHAT YOU WANT OUT OF IT? IT'S...IT'S DISAPPOINTING.
I KNOW. AND I DON'T BLAME YOU FOR WHATEVER YOU WANNA DO TO ME.
I WANT TO HELP YOU.
HERE'S MY NUMBER.
YOU NEED TO TALK ABOUT HOW YOU FEEL?
OR GET ADVICE ON HOW TO GET OUT OF THIS SHITSHOW YOU'RE IN CHARGE OF?
OR JUST SIT ON THE PHONE AND WORK YOUR ISSUES OUT?
I WANT TO BE THAT SOMEONE.

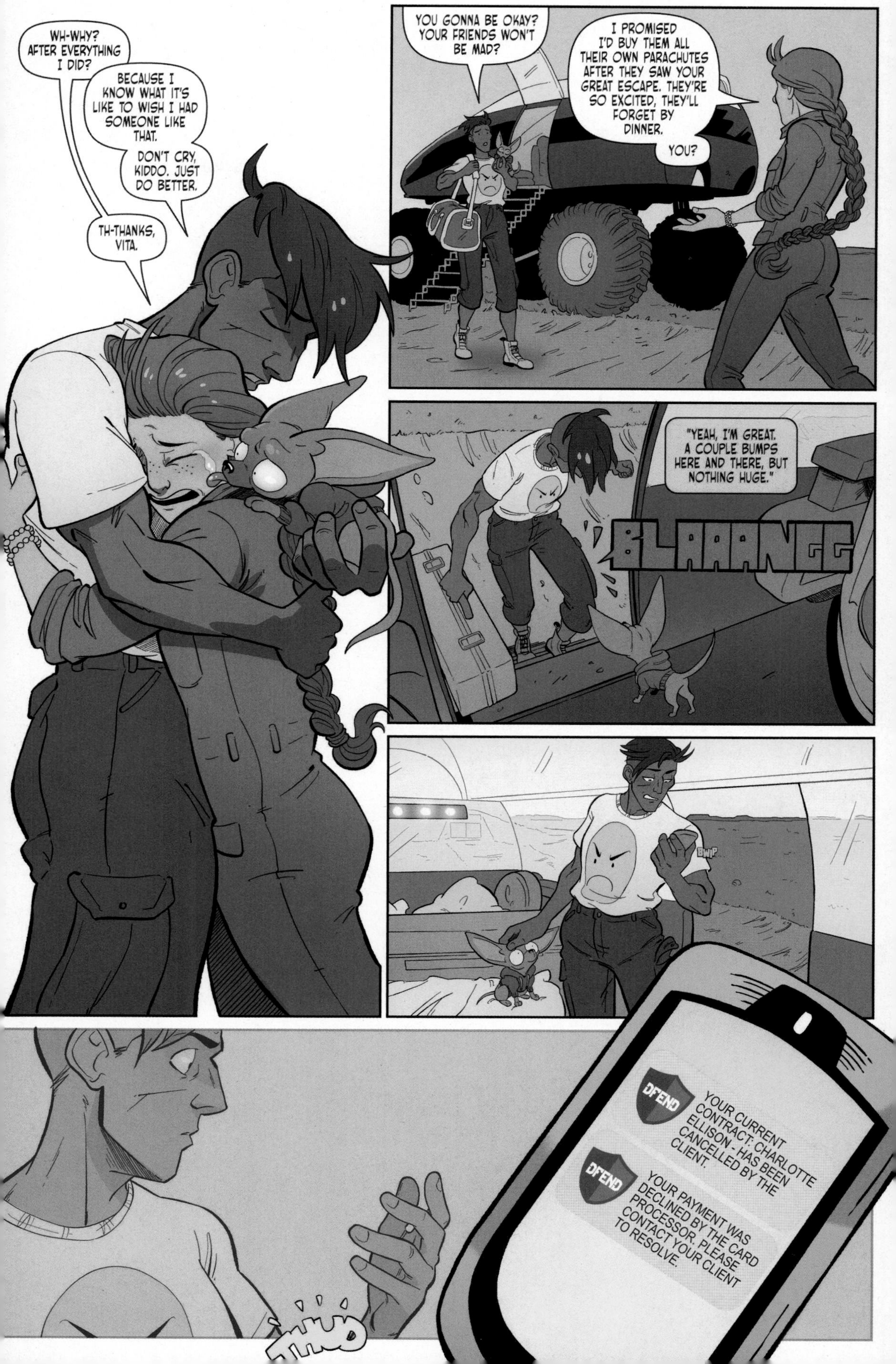
WH-WHY? AFTER EVERYTHING I DID?
BECAUSE I KNOW WHAT IT'S LIKE TO WISH I HAD SOMEONE LIKE THAT.
DON'T CRY, KIDDO. JUST DO BETTER.
TH-THANKS, VITA.
YOU GONNA BE OKAY? YOUR FRIENDS WON'T BE MAD?
I PROMISED I'D BUY THEM ALL THEIR OWN PARACHUTES AFTER THEY SAW YOUR GREAT ESCAPE. THEY'RE SO EXCITED, THEY'LL FORGET BY DINNER.
YOU?
"YEAH, I'M GREAT. A COUPLE BUMPS HERE AND THERE, BUT NOTHING HUGE."
BLAAANGG
BWIP
DFEND
YOUR CURRENT CONTRACT: CHARLOTTE ELLISON - HAS BEEN CANCELLED BY THE CLIENT.
DFEND
YOUR PAYMENT WAS DECLINED BY THE CARD PROCESSOR. PLEASE CONTACT YOUR CLIENT TO RESOLVE.
THUD

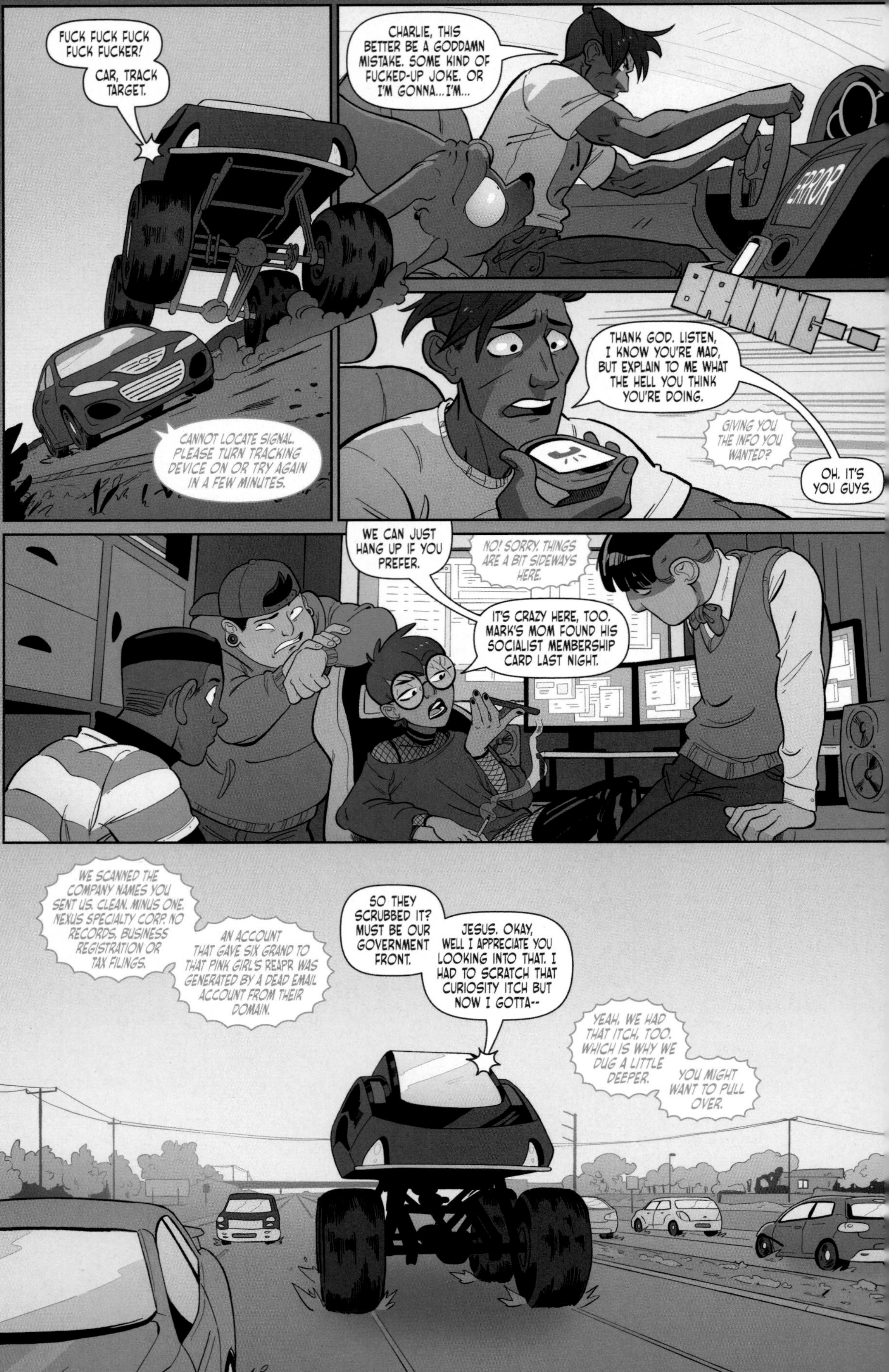
FUCK FUCK FUCK FUCK FUCKER!
CAR, TRACK TARGET.
CANNOT LOCATE SIGNAL. PLEASE TURN TRACKING DEVICE ON OR TRY AGAIN IN A FEW MINUTES.
CHARLIE, THIS BETTER BE A GODDAMN MISTAKE. SOME KIND OF FUCKED-UP JOKE. OR I'M GONNA...I'M...
ERROR
BRNNNG--
THANK GOD. LISTEN, I KNOW YOU'RE MAD, BUT EXPLAIN TO ME WHAT THE HELL YOU THINK YOU'RE DOING.
GIVING YOU THE INFO YOU WANTED?
OH. IT'S YOU GUYS.
WE CAN JUST HANG UP IF YOU PREFER.
NO! SORRY. THINGS ARE A BIT SIDEWAYS HERE.
IT'S CRAZY HERE, TOO. MARK'S MOM FOUND HIS SOCIALIST MEMBERSHIP CARD LAST NIGHT.
WE SCANNED THE COMPANY NAMES YOU SENT US. CLEAN. MINUS ONE. NEXUS SPECIALTY CORP. NO RECORDS, BUSINESS REGISTRATION OR TAX FILINGS.
AN ACCOUNT THAT GAVE SIX GRAND TO THAT PINK GIRL'S REAPR WAS GENERATED BY A DEAD EMAIL ACCOUNT FROM THEIR DOMAIN.
SO THEY SCRUBBED IT? MUST BE OUR GOVERNMENT FRONT.
JESUS. OKAY, WELL I APPRECIATE YOU LOOKING INTO THAT. I HAD TO SCRATCH THAT CURIOSITY ITCH BUT NOW I GOTTA--
YEAH. WE HAD THAT ITCH, TOO. WHICH IS WHY WE DUG A LITTLE DEEPER.
YOU MIGHT WANT TO PULL OVER.

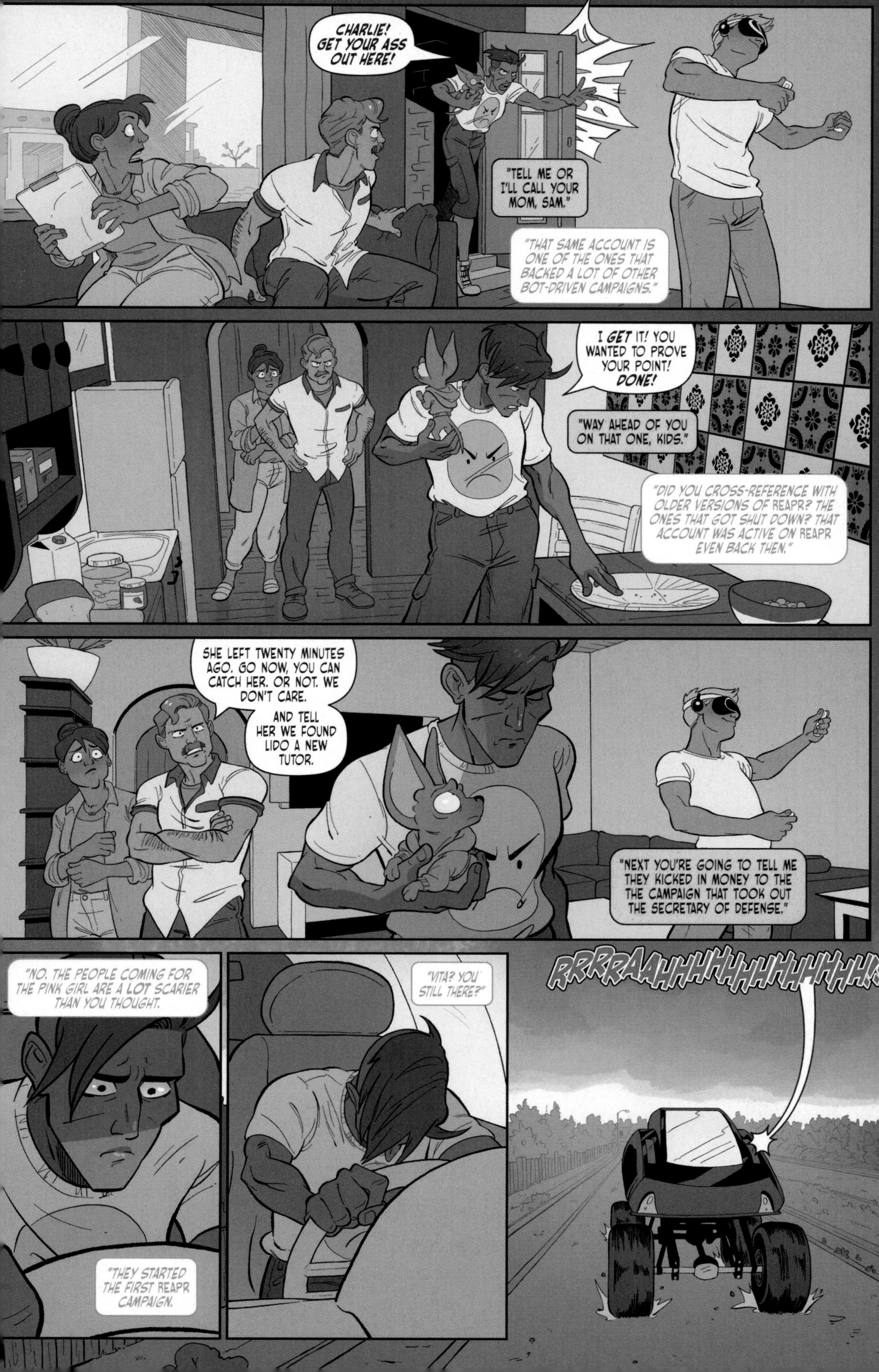
CHARLIE! GET YOUR ASS OUT HERE!
"TELL ME OR I'LL CALL YOUR MOM, SAM."
"THAT SAME ACCOUNT IS ONE OF THE ONES THAT BACKED A LOT OF OTHER BOT-DRIVEN CAMPAIGNS."
I GET IT! YOU WANTED TO PROVE YOUR POINT! DONE!
"WAY AHEAD OF YOU ON THAT ONE, KIDS."
"DID YOU CROSS-REFERENCE WITH OLDER VERSIONS OF REAPR? THE ONES THAT GOT SHUT DOWN? THAT ACCOUNT WAS ACTIVE ON REAPR EVEN BACK THEN."
SHE LEFT TWENTY MINUTES AGO. GO NOW, YOU CAN CATCH HER. OR NOT. WE DON'T CARE.
AND TELL HER WE FOUND LIDO A NEW TUTOR.
"NEXT YOU'RE GOING TO TELL ME THEY KICKED IN MONEY TO THE THE CAMPAIGN THAT TOOK OUT THE SECRETARY OF DEFENSE."
"NO. THE PEOPLE COMING FOR THE PINK GIRL ARE A LOT SCARIER THAN YOU THOUGHT.
"THEY STARTED THE FIRST REAPR CAMPAIGN.
"VITA? YOU STILL THERE?"
RRRRAAHHHHHHHHHHHH!!

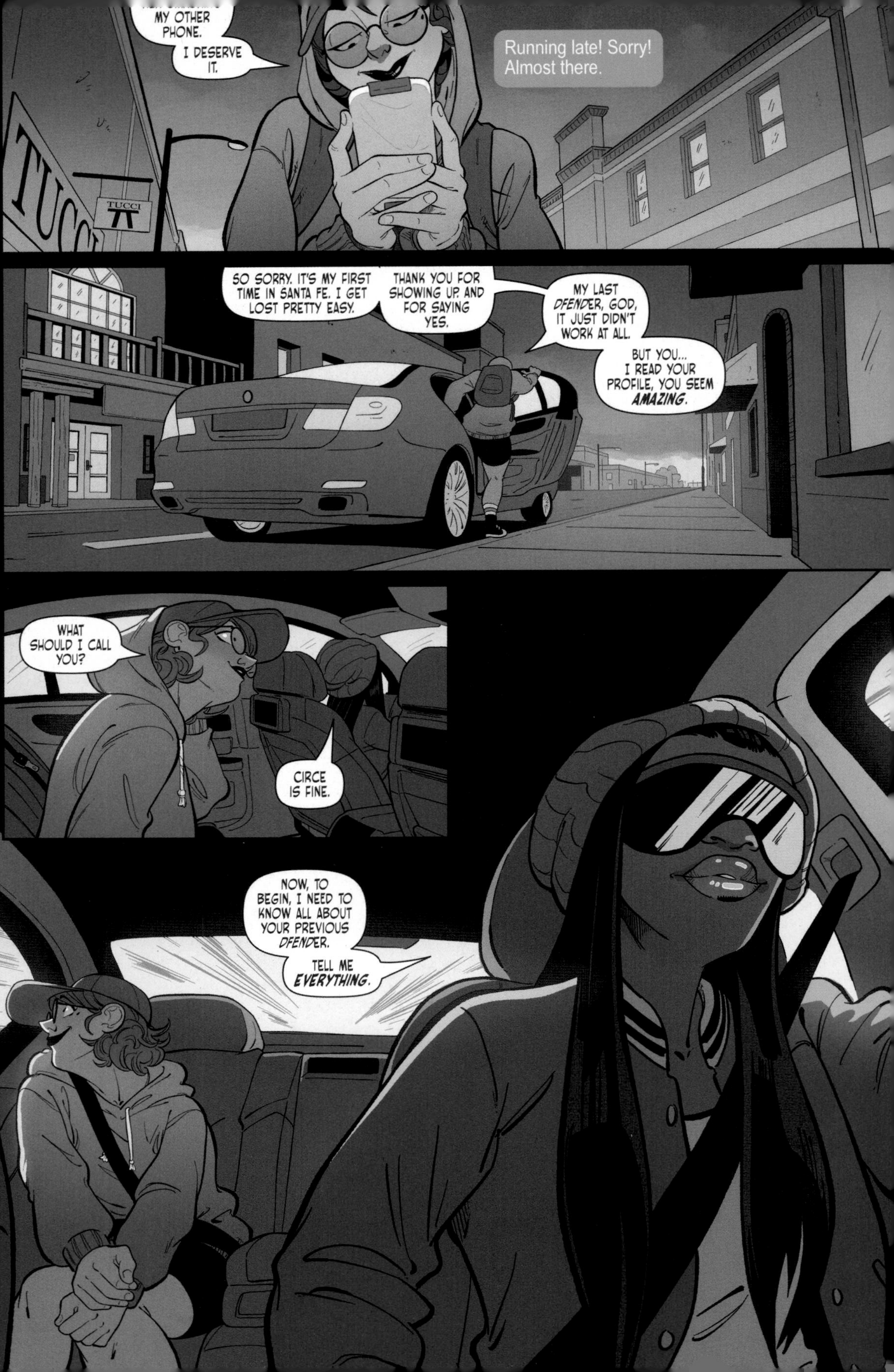

MY OTHER PHONE.
I DESERVE IT.
Running late! Sorry! Almost there.
TUCCI
TUCCI
SO SORRY. IT'S MY FIRST TIME IN SANTA FE. I GET LOST PRETTY EASY.
THANK YOU FOR SHOWING UP. AND FOR SAYING YES.
MY LAST DFENDER, GOD, IT JUST DIDN'T WORK AT ALL.
BUT YOU... I READ YOUR PROFILE, YOU SEEM AMAZING.
WHAT SHOULD I CALL YOU?
CIRCE IS FINE.
NOW, TO BEGIN, I NEED TO KNOW ALL ABOUT YOUR PREVIOUS DFENDER.
TELL ME EVERYTHING.

GABY EPSTEIN #7 VARIANT COVER

MJ ERICKSON #8 VARIANT COVER

SLOANE LEONG #9 VARIANT COVER —

— **LISA STERLE #10 VARIANT COVER**

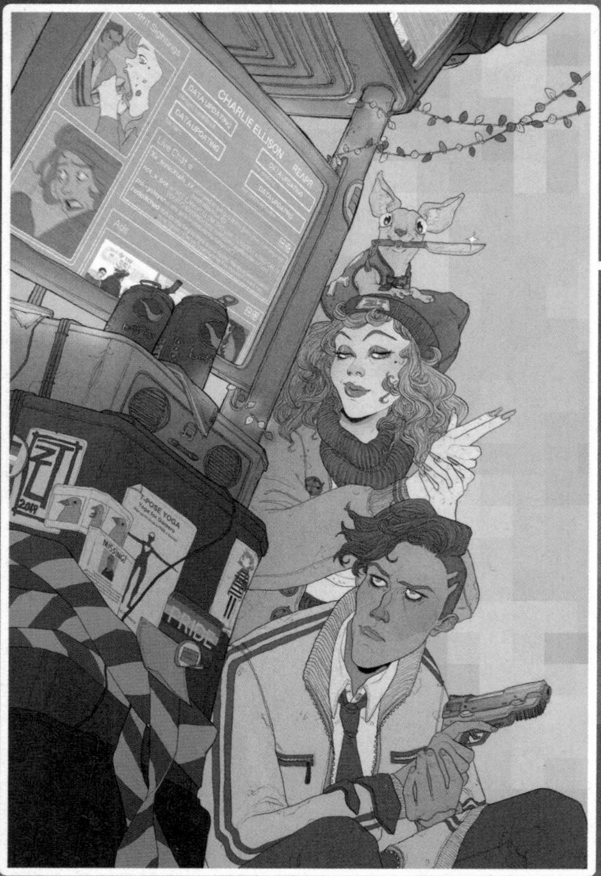
CHARLIE ELLISON
DATA UPDATING
T-POSE YOGA
PRIDE

ZOE THOROGOOD
#11 VARIANT
COVER

LINDSAY ISHIHIRO
#12 VARIANT
COVER

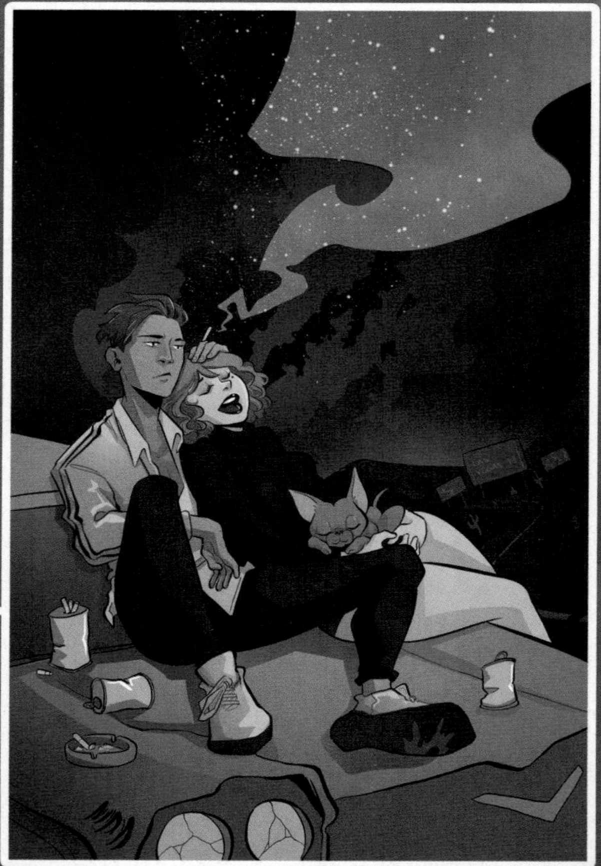

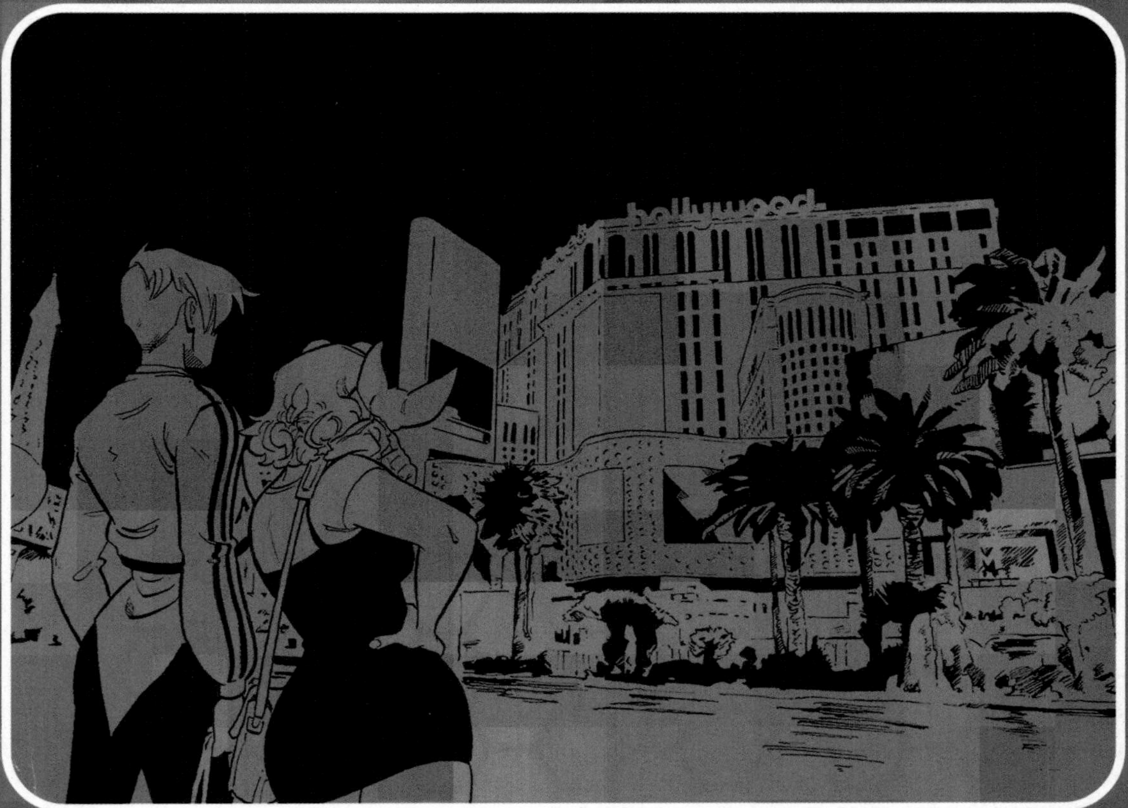
hollywood

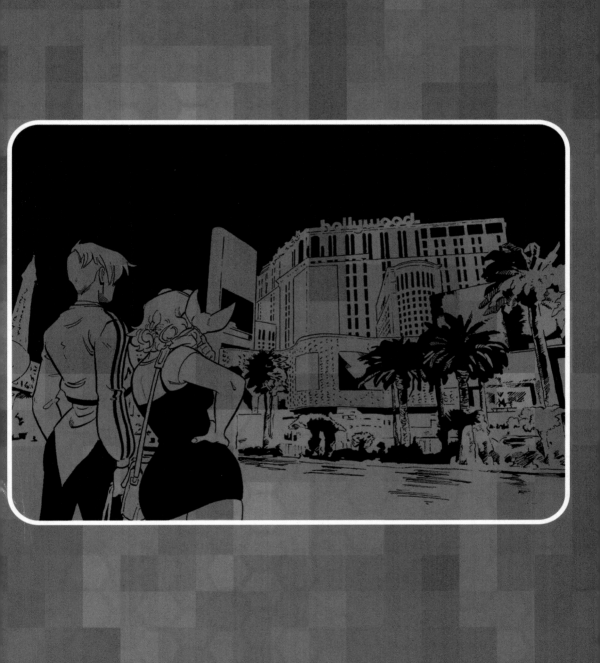

GRAPHIC NOVEL
Sebela, Christopher
Crowded. Volume 2,
Glitter dystopia

08/28/20